Here's what critic Kathleen Bacus's Cal

"Fans of Janet Evanovich will be glad to see always have to go to the burgh for mirthful murder and mayhem."
—*Booklist*

"Filled with dumb-blonde jokes, nonstop action and rapid-fire banter, this is a perfect read for chick-lit fans who enjoy a dash of mystery."
—*Publishers Weekly*

"Fun and lighthearted with an interesting mystery, a light touch of romance and some fascinating characters."
—*RT Book Reviews*

"Throw in two parts Nancy Drew, one part Lucille Ball, add a dash of Stephanie Plum, shake it all up and you've got a one-of-a-kind amateur sleuth with a penchant for junk food and hot-pink snakeskin cowgirl boots. A word to the wise: if you're prone to laughing out loud when reading funny books, try not to read Calamity Jayne when you're sandwiched between two sleeping passengers on an airplane…sometimes we learn these things the hard way."
—*Chick Lit Cafe*

"Bacus provides lots of small-town fun with this lovable, fair-haired klutz and lively story, liberally salted with dumb-blonde jokes."
—*Booklist* *starred review*

BOOKS BY KATHLEEN BACUS

Calamity Jayne Mysteries:
Calamity Jayne
Calamity Jayne and Fowl Play at the Fair
Calamity Jayne and the Haunted Homecoming
Calamity Jayne and the Campus Caper
Calamity Jayne in the Wild, Wild West
Calamity Jayne and the Hijinks on the High Seas
Calamity Jayne and the Trouble with Tandems
Calamity Jayne and the Sisterhood of the Traveling Lawn Gnome
Six Geese A 'Slaying (a holiday short story)

Graves Occurences young adult horror novels:
Vessel
Visions
Visitation

Other Works:
Fiancé at Her Fingertips
Trading Spaces

CALAMITY JAYNE AND THE SISTERHOOD OF THE TRAVELING LAWN GNOME

a Calamity Jayne mystery

Kathleen Bacus

CALAMITY JAYNE AND THE SISTERHOOD OF THE
TRAVELING LAWN GNOME
Copyright © 2015 by Kathleen Bacus

Published by Gemma Halliday Publishing
All Rights Reserved. Except for use in any review, the reproduction or utilization of this work in whole or in part in any form by any electronic, mechanical, or other means, now known or hereafter invented, including xerography, photocopying and recording, or in any information storage and retrieval system is forbidden without the written permission of the publisher, Gemma Halliday.

This is a work of fiction. Names, characters, places, and incidents are either the product of the author's imagination or are used fictitiously, and any resemblance to actual persons, living or dead, business establishments, or events or locales is entirely coincidental.

To my soon-to-be English lit grad student son, Erick, the best first reader/proofreader money doesn't buy. :) I'll miss you, Bub—especially our I Love Lucy *marathons. I know you're gonna be awesome! And, no. I won't be addressing you as "Professor."*

CHAPTER ONE

Blonde triplets were witnesses to a crime, so they went to the police station to identify the suspect. The police chief said he would show them a mug shot of someone for thirty seconds then ask each one for a description. After showing the photo to the first blonde sister, he covered it and asked her how she would recognize the suspect.

"Easy," she replied. "He only has one eye."

The chief was stunned. "He only has one eye because it is a profile shot! Think about it!"

He repeated the procedure for the second blonde and again asked how she would recognize him.

"He only has one ear," was her answer.

"What is the matter with you people? You're looking at a profile shot! You're seeing him from the side!"

He repeated the procedure for the third blonde, then said, "How would you recognize the suspect? Now think before you give me a stupid answer."

After viewing the photo, the third blonde thought for a minute.

"He's wearing contact lenses," she said.

This took the chief by surprise. He studied the picture closely and couldn't tell if the suspect had contacts or not, so he went into the database and looked at the report. Sure enough, when the mug shot was taken, the suspect *was* wearing contact lenses!

The officer went back to the third blonde. "How could you tell he was wearing contact lenses?" he asked. "Nobody else in the precinct saw that!"

"Well," the blonde said, "With only one eye and one ear, he can't wear regular glasses, can he?"

I touched the tip of the pencil to my lip and began to brainstorm.

"What do you do for a living?"

"Where were you born?"

"How did you really score that TribRide bodyguard gig?"

I made a face. "Brainstorm" might have been a reach. I could just about predict the way Manny DeMarco would respond to these "probing" questions.

"Facilitator."

"Hospital."

"Manny knew a guy who knew a guy."

I crossed out each lame-oh interrogative one-by-one.

"Nope."

"Nooo."

"Negatory, good buddy."

"Okay, okay. I hear you. No refill."

I looked up. Hazel's Hometown Café proprietress, Donita, hovered over me, coffee pot in hand.

"What? Oh. No. Fill 'er up," I said.

Donnie raised a brow and obliged.

"Working on a story?" she asked.

Yeah. A super secret story—the story of Manny DeMarco's life.

"It's a special assignment," I hedged. "Very hush-hush."

Just like the subject of the story.

"What's it about?" She asked.

"Secrets," I said.

She frowned.

"Secrets? In Grandville? Where gossip reigns and busybodies rule?" Donnie made a raspberry sound. "Right." She moved on to the next booth.

I sighed. Donita had a point. In small-town Iowa the latest dirt traveled faster than cornhusks down a farm lane after fall harvest.

I sipped my coffee, muddling over the question mark that was Manny DeMarco and the circumstances that had brought us together. Manny and I did not have a conventional first meeting. Far from it. I guess you could say Manny—a guy I'd first met during my ace cub reporter debut when I was out to convince authorities (and everyone else) that somebody stashed a dead body in the trunk of a car I'd mistaken for my own—was my first confidential informant. A confidential informant I'd bailed out of jail in exchange for information.

That...happenstance had turned out to be life changing—and lifesaving.

Literally.

In the last year our relationship had morphed from the Midwest's answer to Woodward's and Bernstein's *Deep Throat* to our own cockeyed version of *Guess Who's Coming to Dinner?* where my role was one of faux fiancée to my former CI. I'd recently broken off the bogus betrothal, but not before I'd come to realize Manny had developed feelings of an...er...tender nature for his dream date who—as it turned out—just couldn't resist a certain ranger's charms.

You're following, right? Let me know if you need me to clarify anything.

I'd known Manny for more than a year now. I'd worn his ring. I'd shared my feelings, my family (gladly), and my fears. I'd faced down his marriage-minded Aunt Mo without flinching. Okay, okay. So I flinched. Big whoop.

Manny had seen me at my best and at my worst. Up and down. Hot and cold. Happy and sad. Terrified and freaked out. (I'm pretty much a what-you-see-is-what-you-get cowgal.) But Manny DeMarco? He kept his cards so close to his vest he had an Ace of Spades imprint on his chest.

And oh, what a chest!

I put a hand to my face and waved it back and forth. Is it getting hot in here or is it just me?

Manny DeMarco represented a riddle protected by rippling muscles, bulging biceps, and a quiet, unassuming intellect. Talk about your hubba-hubba Houdini.

Several weeks ago, I'd successfully bartered a promise from Manny to answer five questions put to him that might assist me in figuring out who the guy was and what made him tick. I had one shot with Manny. Well, actually *five* shots. Five opportunities to unravel the enigma that was Manny Dishman DeMarco—Grandville, Iowa's man of mystery.

It wasn't every day you had the opportunity to get straight answers from a man who could make a mime look like a Chatty Cathy doll. I had to make each question count. Proceed carefully. Be contemplative and clever.

I tapped my pencil on the notepad.

I'd have to be diabolical and devious. Be prepared to get down and dirty.

I bit my lip. So not my strengths.

Fortunately I knew someone who did fit the bill.

"What? No cinnamon rolls!" Joltin' Joe Townsend, my newbie step-grandpappy by virtue of his recent marriage to my "gammy" aka my grandma, slid into the booth across from me. "I assume my breakfast order is coming."

I raised a brow. "Assume away."

"When someone invites a person to breakfast, the invitee expects to be fed," Joe said.

"Is that right?"

Joe nodded. "It's the only decent thing to do. Especially considering you've dragged me away from my blushing bride."

"Blushing bride" being a relative term here, I supposed, considering my gammy had probably inspired more blushes than she experienced.

"Donnie!" I raised a hand. "My breakfast guest here would like an order of steel cut oats with blueberries on the side and a glass of skim milk."

"Make that the Hazel's Deluxe Breakfast Platter with an extra side of bacon and a large orange juice," Joe said, sending me an irked look.

"Ah. You didn't have to order extra bacon for me," I told him.

"It's the only way to keep your bacon-burgling hands off mine," he said.

I grimaced.

Guilty as charged.

Joe sat back in the booth and crossed his arms across his chest.

"So what gives? What's behind this little breakfast tête-à-tête?" Joe asked. "You got something you want to tell me? Something about my grandson, perhaps?"

I made a face.

Ranger Rick Townsend, Division of Natural Resources officer and hometown hottie, and I share a yo-yo past. We were presently on the upswing, having uh, er, taken the relationship to the next level with a night of swashbuckling romance on the high seas on the final night of the wedding cruise from hell. Not my wedding, you understand. My gammy's and Joe's. I was strictly along for the ride.

And boy howdy, what a ride!

I reached for my water glass and gulped it down.

Anyway, since we'd returned from the cruise a month ago, Townsend (the younger) and I had decided to take things one day at a time, or rather, one "date" at a time. You see, I feel like it's important for a couple to *be* a couple before...er, "coupling." Do things regular couples do. Go to movies. Take in ball games. Hang out. You know. Relationship 101.

A "cockamamie cowgirl courtship" is what Townsend calls it.

Gotta love a silver-tongued man in uniform.

We were feeling our way (hey now, I know what you're thinking) and taking it slow and easy—the ideal speed for a good ol' girl who didn't want to fall too hard too soon and run the risk of never getting back in the saddle again.

"Joe. Joe. Joe," I adopted my best hangdog look—similar to the ones my pooches wear when I get home and find they've used a favorite pair of boots as a chew toy. "I don't always have to have a secret agenda in order to sup with my stepper, now do I?" I said, certain he would hate the moniker. "Can't I just ask you here simply for the pleasure of your company?"

Joe shook his head. "You can't hustle a hustler, Blondie," he said. "Spill it."

Joe Townsend, legend in his own mind. I shifted in my seat—uncertain now that this was such a good idea after all.

Joe frowned. He leaned forward. "Wait a minute. Did your grandmother put you up to this?"

It was my turn to frown.

"Come again?"

"Does she want you to put your 'investigative skills' to work on her behalf? Solve her little mystery? Save the day?"

"What? What mystery?" The dots still didn't connect. "What are you talking about?"

"That ridiculous lawn gnome, of course!" Joe said.

The picture wasn't getting any clearer.

"Lawn gnome? What lawn gnome?"

"Not what gnome! *Whose* gnome!"

What in Sam Hill? Rarely had I seen Joe this upset—and let me tell you, I've seen the old guy in some pretty tricky situations. Okay. So I'd put him in some of those tricky situations, but let's not get off topic here.

"*Oo*kay. Whose gnome then?"

"Abigail Winegardner's," Joe muttered.

"Who? Who did you say?"

Joe looked left and then right. "Abigail Winegardner," he responded, his voice hushed and low.

I gasped.

"She whose name is not to be spoken?" I whispered.

Joe nodded.

"And?"

"And her friggin' lawn gnome disappeared."

"The ugly one that sits in her front yard near your driveway?"

He nodded.

"The one your wife dubbed *Chucky*? The same gnome she tried to bribe the public works guys to toss into a pit and cover with gravel, dirt, and sod when they were working on the storm sewers? That gnome?"

He nodded. "Abigail somehow has the idea that, well, that Hannah...your grandmother has well—"

"Absconded with the little troll?"

"Gnome—not troll! And yes, that's about the size of it, Blondie. Now your grandmother is obsessed with the need to discover who pilfered the damned troll, er, gnome and prove her innocence. I've tried to help. I've looked everywhere for a replacement for the god-awful gremlin, but apparently the freaking little gnome is an antique and one-of-a-kind."

"Gee, Joe. I'm sorry," I said. "That's rough. Real rough."

Joe must've caught the amusement in my voice. He sat back.

"You're sorry, my skinny rear," Joe said. "You can't even keep a straight face."

"Honest, Joe—"

"Listen, missy. You're on the hook, too, you know. She's going to enlist your assistance with this little gnome hunt next. It's just a matter of time." He scratched his chin. "In fact, that's not such a bad idea. You do have a certain knack. And it'll get me off the hook."

"You wouldn't!"

"Oh, wouldn't I?"

We eyeballed each other across the table—at an impasse—until I realized Joe was right. My gammy *was* almost certainly going to drag me into the great gnome caper. It *was* just a matter of time. I might as well negotiate for the best terms possible.

I took a deep breath.

"You've heard the term quid pro quo, right?"

Joe nodded. "I'm listening."

"You do me a solid, and I do you one."

"Still listening," he said.

I cracked my knuckles.

"I'm working on a project that requires...finesse, and I could use your expertise," I said, aiming straight for his big ol' bull's-eye of a male ego.

Joe sat a little straighter in his chair and puffed his chest out. He reminded me of the banty roosters that used to strut around my great-grandmother Blackford's backyard.

"When you say 'project'—"

"Manny DeMarco," I blurted.

Joe sat back in his chair and pursed his lips.

"Go on."

"Here's the deal. I did a favor for Manny. In return I get to ask him five probing questions, and he's promised to answer them truthfully."

"And?"

"I don't want to squander them."

"Huh?"

"I want to come up with the five most brilliant, airtight, can't wiggle out of 'em questions Manny DeMarco has ever been asked. By the time that man-o-mystery has answered question five, I want to have unmasked the real Manny DeMarco-Dishman-whatever his legal name is."

Joe's eyelids lowered, and he rubbed his chin.

"So you want to pull a Perry Mason on Manny."

I frowned. Perry who?

Joe shook his head.

"Your generation's ignorance of truly groundbreaking television is so sad. Perry Mason is an iconic defense attorney created by author Earle Stanley Gardner who was known for his 'gotcha' moments on cross-examination."

"Good to know. Now, can we get back to the issue at hand? Creating our own 'gotcha' moment for Manny DeMarco."

"It won't be easy to pin him down," Joe said. "We'll need do our homework, do some legwork before we dive in."

"Legwork?" I already didn't like the way this collaboration was going.

"Of course. You want to get the best bang for your Five Questions buck, don't you?"

I did. But...homework?

"Your big ol' breakfast," Donnie said, placing a heaping helping of Hazel's hometown cooking in front of Joe.

I closed my eyes and savored the aroma of bacon like a *Survivor* contestant who's won a steak fry in an award challenge.

Donnie turned to me. "I'm surprised you're still here, what with all the activity on the police scanner."

I frowned.

"Activity?"

"Police got a call about the taggings over on the east side of town by the alternative high school," Donnie said.

"Taggings?"

Joe's snort of derision was only marginally muffled by the mouthful of biscuit and gravy he'd shoveled in his mouth.

"Some investigative reporter. Maybe I better reconsider this tit-for-tat quid pro quo."

"Huh?"

He shook his head. "Tagging is when somebody vandalizes homes, automobiles, buildings, and what have you using spray paint. They 'tag' that property," Joe explained. "It's often gang-related."

"And there are reports of tagging on the east side of town?"

"Apparently so, Ace Cub Reporter," Joe said.

"And you heard this on the police scanner?" I asked Donnie.

"Yep. Nothing gets past Hazel's."

Apparently not.

I tore off a sheet from my notepad and slid it across the table to Joe.

"Your assignment, Joe Townsend, should you decide to accept it, is to brainstorm questions for Mission—Manny DeMarco," I said. "Email me, oh, twenty questions for a start. I'll review them and get back to you."

"Now who thinks they're Agent 99?"

"Who?"

"Never mind, Blondie."

I grabbed my bag and got to my feet.

"Oh, look! It's my gammy!"

Joe's head did an *Exorcist* head-spin number in the direction of the door. I took advantage of his gullibility and poached the bacon from his plate before boogying out Hazel's back door.

Now that's what you call beating a "tasty" retreat!

CHAPTER TWO

"How many vehicles does that make?"
"An even dozen."
"And they all have the same tag?"
"Affirmative, Chief."
I crept alongside the uniforms surveying the colorful collection of graffiti and pulled out my cell phone and started clicking away.
"Hey! Hold on there! What do you think you're doing?"
I snapped a couple more pictures before fumbling around for my press credentials.
"Tressa Turner, *Grandville Gazette*," I said, waving my card in front of the officers.
"Uh, newsflash. That's a sub sandwich punch card," the officer nearest me pointed out. "Congratulations. Looks like you're one punch away from a free sub."
I snatched the freebie card back, confirmed his observation (sweet!), and shoved it into a pocket.
"We know who you are, Miss Turner," longtime chief of police, Dan Scott, said, stepping forward.
Sad…but true.
It was Chief Scott who'd responded the time I got buried beneath an avalanche of pumpkins searching for the most sincere one. It was also Chief Scott who took the call from the car wash owner complaining about the mess I made when I hosed the horse trailer out in one of the bays. Chief Scott had also regularly pulled me over for one equipment violation or the other, the occasional lead foot, and one time for littering when my horse, Joker, left a pile of fresh poo outside City Hall on parade day, and the chief stepped in it on his way to his patrol vehicle.

That incident didn't represent some kind of governmental protest, you understand. Droppings…happen.

"Good to see you, Chief," I said, noticing he did not return the sentiment. "So a total of twelve cars, huh?" I pulled out my notepad.

Neither officer jumped to issue a confirmation or denial.

"What time did it happen? How many vehicles had windows broken out? Did anybody see anything? When you say 'tag'—"

"It's too soon to comment. The investigation is ongoing." Chief Scott snapped.

"When you say 'ongoing'—"

His portable radio crackled. "Excuse me," he said, moving away.

Left alone, I walked down the street, examining the damage and taking more pictures. Besides broken windows and cracked windshields and flattened tires, each car had been targeted with spray paint graffiti. I walked around what used to be a red Ford Focus, shaking my head.

"Holy *Fantasia*!" I whispered. The car looked like it had been driven through a psychedelic carwash—kaleidoscopic streaks of color turning the family sedan into perfect clown parade transportation.

I moved to the hood of the car and blinked. A ginormous pink whirligig that resembled a tornado covered the hood. The hot pink cyclone stood out like my gammy's pink polyester Easter ensemble two years back.

"What messages do you suppose *that* is supposed to be sending?"

I looked to my right. Shelby Lynn Sawyer, freshman college student and part-time *Grandville Gazette* gopher and apprentice, peered down at me.

At six-foot-two, Shelby's a big girl. Shelby and I had done a bit of female bonding last fall when we teamed up to score a coveted interview with hometown girl turned big-name reclusive author Elizabeth Courtney Howard. Our…er…collaboration had its ups and downs, and despite a wee bit of um, career insecurity (encouraged by Drew Van Vleet, my counterpart at the rival *New Holland News*) that had me keeping an eagle eye on my coworker and our boss for signs of employment shenanigans, Shelby and I had formed a friendship of sorts—professional paranoia notwithstanding.

"What do you mean 'message'? You mean the *foo foo* artwork?" I motioned at the canvas in question.

"You call that art? It looks like something my nephew makes in preschool and my sister hangs on her fridge," Shelby pointed out. "No, I'm talking about the commonalities among the vehicles."

I gave her a sideways look.

"Commonalities, Profiler Sawyer?" I asked.

Shelby shook her head.

"The pink tornadoes, Ace Reporter," she responded. "Didn't you take a good look at all the vehicles? They all have the hot pink cyclone symbols."

I shrugged. "So, they're rabid Iowa State fans gone loco."

"Why here? Why now? The college kids are back on campus. Football season is still weeks away." She scratched her chin. "No. This is something else."

"Do you want my job?" I heard somebody blurt and discovered the blurter was me.

"Wait. What?"

I bit my lip. Yeah. I know. Too late, Miss Blabbermouth.

"Do you have designs on my job?" I followed up. You know. In for a penny and all that.

"Designs? On your high-paying, high-profile, highly sought-after small-town reporter gig that barely pays enough to cover the costs of keeping your herd of horseflesh in grain and hay and your hounds in kibbles and bits? That job?"

I hung my head.

"You are aware that I'm starting college," Shelby said.

"*Community* college," I countered. "And you're commuting."

"Yes. So?"

"So, you could conceivably work and go take classes. You know. Like I did last year."

"God. Let's hope not."

I winced. Nice.

Shelby reached over and put the back of her hand against my forehead.

"How long have you been suffering from these…delusions?" she asked.

"Excuse me. Am I interrupting a private moment?"

I looked up. Chief Scott surveyed us from his position near the trunk of the vehicle.

"Apparently delusions are contagious," Shelby mumbled.

"Chief Scott!" I hurried to the rear of the vehicle where a tow truck was just pulling up. "I just have a few questions. Were there any witnesses? Do you have any leads or suspects yet? Have you seen signs of gang activity in the community? If so, could this be gang-related? What are your thoughts regarding the spray-painting itself? I'm sure it hasn't escaped you that one particular symbol appears on all the vehicles." I ignored Shelby's "Oh, brother" and plowed ahead. "Any idea what the weird tag thingies mean?"

The chief shook his head and put a hand up.

"I told you before, it's too early in our investigation for me to comment," he said.

"Have you seen this particular tornado symbol before?" I asked.

He hesitated, his gaze sliding away.

"You have!" I said. "You've seen the pink tornado before! When? Where?"

A deep flush began to spread from the chief's neck upward.

"I said no comment," Chief Scott said. "Now, if you ladies would kindly move so the tow truck can hook up, we'd appreciate it."

I rejoined Shelby Lynn and we crossed the street, looking on as the tow truck operator did his thing.

"Did you pick up on the chief's reaction when I asked about the pink tornado symbol? He's definitely hiding something." I asked. "He's seen it before."

Shelby nodded. "Looks that way."

"Were there any reports of similar acts of vandalism while I was on TribRide?"

"Now that you mention it, yes. There was a flurry of incidents of malicious mischief, but most of those were out in the county—not in town."

"Oh? What kind of mischief?" I asked.

Shelby shrugged. "Random stuff. Minor property damage. Break-ins at a couple of rural residences. A detached garden shed was targeted. Miscellaneous lawn items damaged or taken. The other incident that stands out was at Country Acres Greenhouse. Planters got overturned and plants were yanked out of pots."

"Any graffiti?"

"I'm not sure."

"Not sure?"

Now it was Shelby Lynn's turn to hang her head. She shifted her weight from one size 11½-wide to the other.

"I didn't actually go and check out the scenes," Shelby acknowledged.

"So you got the information from police reports."

She shook her head.

"Not really."

"What do you mean? How did you file a story?"

That hangdog look again.

"I spoke to someone with the county. It all seemed pretty cut and dried. High school shenanigans. Kids letting loose before the new school year started. That kind of thing."

"Oh? Who was it you spoke with at County?" I asked, wondering if Shelby Lynn had somehow managed to finagle a solid source within the sheriff's department—at odds with my own somewhat shaky history with the law enforcement agency.

More Bigfoot shuffling.

"Just someone I've been cultivating," she said.

Cultivating? Who'd she think she was, Mrs. Green Jeans?

"You have a source within the sheriff's office?" I asked, suspicion beginning to rear its ugly head again.

"Maybe."

"Maybe?" I raised an eyebrow. "I detect…subterfuge."

"Subterfuge? Seriously?"

"Just answer the question. Do you have a source or not?"

Shelby crossed her arms, looking uncomfortable.

"I don't have to take this third degree."

"Ooh. Now we're becoming defensive," I said.

"Would you just stop?" Shelby Lynn said. "I admit it. I goofed up. I didn't personally check out either scene. Can we leave it at that?"

I frowned. So, Shelby Lynn Sawyer had a secret source in the SO.

And me? I had an interim sheriff who held a grudge.

"Sure. No problem. The good news is it's not too late to get a firsthand account of the vandalism," I told Shelby.

"What do you suggest?"

"The personal touch. We visit every scene. Interview property owners. Find out what happened and if they took pictures."

Shelby nodded. "If there was substantial damage, they'd take photos for insurance purposes. I'll text you the entire list."

"You take the garden shed. I'll take the greenhouse. And I'll be in Scotland afore ye," I warbled.

Shelby shook her head.

"You are so weird."

Okay. Yeah. Fair enough. I'll own it.

I was also a bit of a bull you-know-what detector, and I knew when something was in the air.

And it drove me crazy until I figured out what that something was.

Tressa Turner. Human bloodhound.

Woof.

CHAPTER THREE

I coaxed my almost-antique Plymouth into a parking spot in the gravel lot at Country Acres Greenhouse. A decade earlier East Coast transplants Michael and Michele Colby had left their white-collar jobs behind and put down new roots (literally!) in the fertile soil of the upper Great Plains.

Middle-aged and childless, the Colbys had acquired the reputation for having four of the greenest thumbs in the county. You wanted a shrub that wouldn't shrivel, a flower guaranteed to flourish, and a tree that Paul Bunyan would lust over one day, Country Acres was your greenhouse.

This late in the season the bedding plants had been replaced by colorful mums, hardy perennials, and traditional fall offerings like gourds and pumpkins for decorating, and festive Indian corn of all colors and sizes.

Michele Colby, garden hose in hand, was giving a row of tall, decorative grasses a drink when I walked up. She saw me and looked beyond me, the stream of water doing a sudden dipsy-doodle.

I totally understood the reaction. The last time I'd been to Country Acres I'd brought my grandma along to purchase Memorial Day plants. Who knew dead people were so picky about plants they would never see? The term "grave" situation doesn't come close.

I put my hands up. "You can relax, Mrs. Colby," I said. "I'm all by my lonesome today."

She smiled and turned the water hose off.

"How *is* your grandmother?" Michele asked. "I hope she was satisfied with her Memorial Day plant purchases."

"Oh. Sure. She was satisfied."

"Satisfied" being a relative term when it comes to my gammy. After two-and-a-half hours selecting, rejecting, re-selecting, and re-rejecting flowers, ferns, and foliage, Gram had eventually ended up buying the very first plants I'd loaded into the cart. Sigh.

"So what can I do for you today, Tressa? In the market for the most sincere pumpkin already? You're a tad early you know."

I winced. My preoccupation with procuring the perfect carving pumpkin was a matter of public record.

"I'm good for now," I said, flashing her a sheepish grin. "I'm actually here about the malicious mischief you reported a week or so ago."

She pushed her hair away from her face.

"Malicious is right," she said, a pained expression creating furrows in her forehead. "We came home to utter devastation. All those lovely plants and flowers ruined. Pots overturned and broken. Paint everywhere. It was so sad. So senseless. You don't expect something like this to happen here. The coasts? Maybe. But not in America's Heartland."

"I'm sorry, Mrs. Colby. I can imagine how it must feel to come home to discover someone has trashed your business and property." I knew exactly how it felt. A year earlier I'd been victim to a home invader who'd left the place a shambles.

"We felt so…violated. We'd never had that kind of problem here before. It was so disheartening." She stopped. "Why is the *Gazette* interested now?"

I explained about the early morning vandalism.

"And you think it could be the same individuals?"

I shrugged. "It's possible. I was wondering if you took pictures of any of the damage. I'd like to compare them against this morning's incidents. You know. Check for *commonalities*."

Take that, Ms. Smartie Pants Shelby Lynn Sawyer. Take that.

"Isn't that something law enforcement should be doing?" Michele asked.

"Oh, I'm sure they'll get to it. You know. In time. But a little pressure from well-meaning media might help get the ball rolling."

"We do have some photos that we took for insurance purposes," Michele said. "And it would be nice if the sheriff's department would make some headway so we wouldn't have to worry about this happening again."

"My thoughts exactly. Perhaps a news article could generate some leads for the authorities to follow up on."

"The photographs are in the office." Michele stopped. "Darn it! Mike's out on a sod delivery. If you could keep an eye out for customers, I'll just run in and grab the photos."

"No problem," I said. "It'll give me a chance to peruse your fall fare."

Michele hurried off, and I made my way to the autumn merchandise section, checking out the teeny-tiny, mini pumpkins—some painted with scary-cute faces—rough, gnarly gourds, plastic bags of potpourri tied with orange ribbons, and assortments of various-sized pinecones.

I bent over to check out a colorful scarecrow decoration.

"I know you!" I heard behind me. I frowned, fairly certain the only part of me visible was a panoramic view of my patootie.

"I knew it! I'd know that Blackford booty anywhere!"

I turned.

"As I live and breathe, if it isn't Tressa Jayne Turner! Long time. No see. How's it shaking, T-ball?"

"Aunt Eunice?" I said, dumfounded to discover my great-aunt Eunice standing not three feet from me. "Is that you?"

"In the flesh, kiddo. In the flesh. Come and gimme some sugar." She grabbed me and threw her arms around my midsection in a massive bear hug, clutching me to an ample bosom that was nothing like the bosom I'd inherited, squeezing me so hard, I couldn't feel my legs. "How the hell are you, Tressa Jayne? Find any stiffs lately? I sure hope you're not searching for one here. Should I be afraid? Hahaha!"

"Aunt Eunice?" I croaked, feeling my air supply being compromised by breasts that could double as flotation devices. "I can't breathe!"

She gave me a final squeeze that almost made me see white, slapped me on the back twice, and released me.

I did the Weeble wobble and stared at her.

"What are you doing in Grandville?" I asked.

"I'm back for a surprise visit," she said and put her hands out in a "ta-da" gesture. "Surprise!" She grinned. "Are you surprised, Tressa? Did I surprise you?"

I nodded. "You sure did. You got me. You really got me." In fact, I couldn't be more surprised if Indian corn started pop-pop-popping off their cobs and the wooden scarecrow began to belt out "Jimmy Crack Corn."

"You're working at a greenhouse now?" she asked. "I thought you were a reporter with the *Gazette*."

"Oh, no. I'm just watching the counter for the owner. I'm actually here on a story. You said you were here for a visit?" I asked. "I thought you weren't going to make it back for the family reunion."

Eunice Esmeralda Blackford, my grandmother's "much older" sister—at least according to my gammy—currently lived in Scottsdale. She'd never married. Never had children. Her, uh, er, sexual orientation had been the subject of speculation. My gammy had always been mum on the issue.

And that, ladies and gentleman, is a first.

"Like I said, I wanted to surprise everyone by showing up for the reunion. Do you think they'll be surprised?"

The last time Eunice showed up at a family reunion fur flew. Actually it was deviled eggs that flew, but you get the point. So, yeah. I could safely assume they'd be surprised.

"There you are, Eunice. I was browsing through the lawn ornaments, looked up, and you were gone."

I stared. Abigail Winegardner, wearing a perturbed look and a straw hat that looked a lot like one I'd seen *Mr. Ed* wear on a cable TV rerun last week, gave me a curt nod. "Hello there, Tressa."

"Uh, er, hello Mrs. Winegardner," I stammered. "It's nice to see you."

"Likewise," Abigail said.

"You know Abigail?" I asked my great aunt.

"Of course, dear. We went to school together, didn't we, Abby?"

Abby? I looked at Abigail Winegardner. She sure didn't look like an Abby.

"Any luck, Abby?" Aunt Eunice asked.

"No. Nothing suitable. Nothing at all. I told you. The gnome is one of a kind. It's been in my family for ages."

I swallowed.

"Gnome?"

"Abby had a gnome go missing under some very suspicious circumstances," Aunt Eunice said.

"Oh?"

"I'm surprised you haven't heard," she went on. "Given your grandmother's proximity to the scene of the crime."

"Scene of the...*crime*?"

"It's obvious the gnome has been stolen. It was there one evening and gone the next morning."

"Oh?"

"I'm determined to find out who took it," Abby said. "It's a family heirloom. I want it back."

"Oh, I see." Boy did I ever. Abigail wasn't all that savvy in the subtlety department. Joe was right. She did suspect my gammy of nicking her gnome.

"Would you look at the time?" Aunt Eunice said. "We've got hair appointments."

"Oh, you're right. I so wanted to ask Mrs. Colby if she might know where to find a replacement gnome. But we do have to run. After we're done, we can check in at the police department and see if they've made any progress in the investigation."

Investigation?

"Then perhaps we could check out the antique and secondhand stores over in New Holland for a replacement lawn decoration," my great-aunt went on. "You know. Until we find yours, that is."

"I suppose we could always look," Abigail said.

"Now, remember Tressa Jayne!" Aunt Eunice warned. "Don't you go blabbing and spoil my little surprise!" She put her fingers to her lips as if turning a key. "Mum's the word."

I nodded.

"Mum's the word," I agreed. And totally meant it.

No way was I going to be the one to break the news to my gammy that the sister she'd had a running feud with for decades was sleeping with the enemy.

Er, you know what I mean.

"Sorry. It took me longer to find the pictures than I anticipated." Michele said, walking up to me. "Was that Mrs. Winegardner I saw leaving?"

I nodded.

"Oh, dear. I'm sorry I missed her. She's such a good customer. Was she looking for anything in particular?"

I shrugged, trying to look nonchalant.

"She said something about replacing a lawn gnome."

Michele frowned. "Lawn gnome? That's odd."

"Odd?"

"One day last week Michael and I were driving home, and we saw a strange little lawn gnome statue sitting out near the greenhouse driveway. At the time we were on a delivery and in a bit of a hurry, so we didn't think much about it at the time. We didn't get home until after dark, and it totally slipped our minds. Then, with the vandalism and all, we forgot all about it. The next time we thought to look for it, it was gone."

"That *is* weird," I said, wondering if my gammy was onto something with her Chucky the lawn gnome comparison.

"Here are those photos," Michele said and handed me a stack of pictures.

I flipped through them and stopped, frowning. I brought the photos closer.

"Is something wrong, Tressa?" Michele asked.

I stared at the garden shed in the picture, bright pink tornadoes painted on the side.

Hot pink cyclones, disappearing lawn gnomes, and reunion gotchas.

How do you say "spree"?

CHAPTER FOUR

"I know something you don't know. Nah nah nah nah nah nah."

The childhood taunt hounded me as I flew down the county road to my humble abode. I live in a double-wide mobile home next door to my parents. When my Paw-Paw Will died, my grandmother had a very nice three-bedroom manufactured home delivered to a building site on my folks' acreage. She lived there until health issues forced her to move in with my folks so that my mother, who works from home, could keep an eye on my grandma.

We traded spaces.

That is, until my grandmother decided she required more freedom than "Jailer Jean" (aka my mother) permitted, and Gammy and Hermione (her very own grumpy cat) moved back into the mobile home with me and my two lovable, but feline-loathing labs, Butch and Sundance.

In a year that felt like ten, my gammy had reignited an old flame, put this granddaughter to shame in the dating department, and managed to wrangle a proposal of marriage—followed by a Grand Canyon wedding and a Caribbean honeymoon cruise this landlubber wouldn't soon forget.

The happy couple aka Mr. and Mrs. Joseph Townsend, Esquire, now resided in the groom's home in a very nice subdivision in Grandville—right next door to none other than arch villainous Abigail Winegardner—giving, I realized, my gammy both motive and opportunity to pilfer the mysterious missing gnome.

Oy vey. The plot thickens.

I shut the car off. The sound of laughter reached me about the same time I picked up the scent of sizzling beef juices. I glanced over at my folks' patio. Smoke billowed from my dad's monster-sized grill. My mouth watered. I might've even drooled a bit.

Beef. It's what's for dinner.

Only when I'd succeeded in dragging my hungry gaze from the gas grill did I take in the cookout attendees gathered on the patio. Right away I recognized the beanpole frame of my brand new step-gampy, Joltin' Joe Townsend. My grandma, "Hellion Hannah" to those who knew her in her younger days, sat on a cushioned lawn chair, big ol' white sunglasses perched on her nose, and a floppy-brimmed straw hat on her head. The other side of seventy (even I don't know exactly how far on the other side) and that nickname continues to be appropriate. Sometimes I look at my grandma and wonder if that's what I'll be like in fifty years. I try to console myself with the possibility I won't live that long.

My brother, Craig, and his wife, Kimmie, also on hand, sat next to each other on a wicker love seat. Craig is a car salesman, and Kimmie works in the county treasurer's office. There's been a wee bit of tension between the two of late. Kimmie wants to start a family. Craig is still dragging his feet.

I'm always working on Craig. I can't wait to become "Auntie Tressa." Oh, the paybacks I've got planned when I have a niece or nephew. Hehehe.

I got out of the car. Before I'd even taken a step, the pooches were on me, sniffing around for signs that I'd been to the Dairee Freeze and brought home a doggie bag.

"Sorry, guys," I said and bent down to put an arm around each of the pups. "No bacon burgers today. But if you're good, I'll let you come to the cookout next door and sneak you some prime Iowa beef underneath the table."

I'd have to do it without my mother, the bean counter, catching on. She'd prefer leftovers go in the fridge rather than provide a four-star dining experience for two scrap-eaters with dog breath and bouts of inappropriate scratching.

I hurried inside, yanked off my work clothes, put on a pair of navy shorts, white tank top, and a pair of canvas

Skechers, and headed next door, my optimistic pups on my heels.

"All I want to know," my gammy was saying, "is how those girls on *Survivor* can parade around in skimpy bikinis without having pubic hair growth? Do they get regular waxes? And if they do, how can they call that roughing it? They don't shave or we'd see those unsightly bumps."

I intercepted one of my mother's "do something about your mother" looks in transit to my dad. He shook his head and raised one shoulder in his "what can I do?" response and went back to tending the grill.

"Hannah, I don't think that's an appropriate dinnertime subject," my mother said.

"Dinner? I don't see any dinner!"

"Just a few more minutes," my dad assured her.

"I like my steak medium well."

"I remember, Mom."

"I hope the roasting ears don't get cold."

"They'll be fine, Hannah," my mother said.

"And you're sure you got all the silks off? The last time we had roasting ears it felt like I was chewing on a hairbrush. Took me a week to get all those little strings out from between my teeth."

"We've got flossers, Hannah."

I paused long enough to give thanks that my gammy had found love the second time around before dropping into a seat next to her.

"Greetings, *familia*!" I said. "How is the Turner clan this fine evening?"

"Turner-Townsend," my grandma reminded me. "Don't forget, I'm a Townsend now too, dear."

Who could forget?

"That beater of yours is still running?" Craig said.

More along the lines of fits and starts, but at least it was paid for.

"It gets me from point A to point B," I said.

"Yeah. At the end of the hook on a truck at Dan's Towing. I hear you've got Dan on speed dial. Right after the Dairee Freeze and before Fong's Chinese Takeout."

"That's what you know," I said. "Fong's is no longer in my top ten. Wang's Garden offers two complimentary crab rangoon with a meal. Funny man, your husband," I told my sister-in-law.

"Oh, yes. He's a regular sidesplitter," Kimmie responded. "I'm a lucky, lucky woman." The look she gave Craig didn't exactly convey one of good fortune.

"Speaking of towing, the local tow companies sure were busy today," Craig said. "We had at least half-a-dozen cars brought to the body shop today for estimates on new paint jobs."

"How's come?" Gram asked.

"A rash of car vandalism on the east side of town overnight," Craig said. "Apparently, the vandals got spray-paint happy and trashed a bunch of cars."

"We got a rumble in the Bronx goin' on here in Grandville?" Gram asked.

"I see someone's rubbing off on my gammy," I said, looking over at Joe whose hand hovered above the relish tray. He nabbed an olive and popped it in his mouth. "Did you know over time couples who live together begin to take on the characteristics of each other?"

Joe lifted a brow.

"Oh? Then I suppose we can expect to see you developing additional canine teeth, growing a nice coat of fur, slobbering all over the place, and licking yourself in awkward places since you've been shacking up with two hairy males for years," he said, plucking a baby carrot from the tray before dunking it in dip and taking a bite.

"You got any inside info on the spray-paintin', Tressa?" Gram asked. "You know. One of them scoops?"

"The only scoop Tressa's likely to get is the one she uses to pick up pooch poop in the yard so Mom won't step in it and go ballistic," Craig said.

"For heaven's sake, give it a rest, would you, Craig?" Kimmie said. "You're always on her case."

"Tressa knows I'm just giving her a hard time for the heck of it," Craig said. "She doesn't mind. Do you, Tressa?"

I shrugged. "Well, actually I—"

"Well, of course she minds!" Kimmie cut me off like the raggedy split ends I crop after an unpleasant encounter with the flat iron. "Who wouldn't? The constant teasing. The incessant digs. The dumb blonde jokes."

I blinked. "Dumb blonde jokes?"

"Well excuse me for having a little fun," Craig said.

"Fun? Fun? You think it's fun to needle someone all the time? To denigrate them! Make them feel like losers and twits and airheads?"

Losers? Twits? Airheads?

"I don't think Craig really thinks—" I began.

"Why, I wouldn't blame Tressa if she gave you a dose of your own medicine!"

Craig snorted.

"What? You've got to be kidding. Have you been living in an alternate reality or something? Tressa never lets an opportunity to mess with me go by. She gives as good as she gets."

I felt my chest puff with a pride and warm fuzzies. Sweet! He noticed!

"Please," Kimmie went on. "You honestly don't realize how insensitive and glib you appear at times? How cavalier and dismissive? How often you seem to trivialize the feelings of others?"

"Are we still talking about Tressa now? 'Cause I'm getting the feeling we're not," Craig said.

"Oh, wow! If only you would direct such perceptiveness and discernment towards your own insecurities and commitment phobias, I'd really be impressed," Kimmie snarled.

Cookout attendees held collective breaths.

Craig shook his head and got to his feet.

"Seems like I can't do anything right where you're concerned, Kimberly," he said and walked away. "Dad? You got a cold one with my name on it?"

Craig popped the top of a light beer and swallowed.

Kimmie—trying to look like she wasn't about to burst into tears and failing epically—bit her quivering lower lip and stared at her hands.

Now normally this is when you experience one of those awkward silences. You know. Where nobody knows what to say. *Normally*. However, with my gammy and me around—both having inherited a gift for gab—that nasty, uncomfortable void is generally avoided.

This time my gammy beat me to the punch.

"What bee's got under Craig's bonnet this time?" Gram asked. "All this tension isn't good for my appetite."

I stifled a snicker. So far nothing known to mankind had an adverse effect on my grandma's appetite. Okay, or mine.

Gram turned to Kimmie.

"Is there somethin' going on with the two of you I should know about?" she asked. "You aren't preggers are you?"

Kimmie's stoic façade crumbled like packaged cinnamon streusel crumb cake. She made a strangled hiccough sound, put a hand to her mouth, jumped to her feet, and ran into the house.

Gram looked from Joe to me and back again.

"Was it something I said?" she asked.

I shook my head.

"No, Gram. Not really."

"So what's the deal? Craig!" Gram spoke up. "Craig! What's wrong with your wife? She isn't preggers, is she?"

"No, Gram. She's not pregnant."

"Well, why not?"

Craig ran a hand through his hair.

"Listen, Gram. This is between Kimmie and me."

"You don't have slow swimmers, do you?" Gram asked. "I told your mom she shouldn't put you in tight briefs. You're wearin' boxers now, right? Or do you go Comanche?"

"Comanche?" Craig got a what-in-God's-name look on his face and, despite the situation, I found myself trying not to smile.

"I think she means commando, dude," I translated.

"Ye gads," Craig said and followed in Kimmie's wake.

Gram got to her feet.

"Jean! How much longer 'til we eat? I've got pills to take you know," she said and wandered over to the table.

Joe dropped into the seat she vacated.

"So. Have you learned anything?" Joe asked.

"About the vandalism?"

"No! The gnome!" he hissed.

"As a matter of fact, I have made some progress in that regard," I said.

I know something you don't know.

"What kind of progress?"

"I can't say anything more right now," I hedged, my knees beginning to bob up and down in a funky jiggle.

I know something you don't know.

"More? You haven't said anything yet."

I know something you don't know.

"I'm ruminating," I said, using last Tuesday's word of the day.

"Ruminating? Stalling is more like it."

My toes started tip-tap-tapping a nervous beat due to the strain of safeguarding Aunt Eunice's surprise. Honestly, it's harder for me to keep a secret than it is to refrain from snitching cookie dough out of the bowl when my mother isn't looking.

I know something you don't know.

"What's up with the jitterbug feet?" Joe eyed my tapping tootsies. "Just what are you hiding?"

"Me? Hide something from Grandville's senior sleuth? Pfft!" I made a raspberry sound.

"Right." Joe raised an eyebrow. "You might fool other folks with that laissez-faire attitude, missy, but not me. I know when I'm being sold a bill of goods. And you know how much I like being left out of the loop."

"Sorry, Joe. But, really. I'm not hiding a thing. Girl Scout's honor."

He gave a disgusted harrumph.

"According to your grandma you couldn't even cut it as a Brownie."

I lifted an eyebrow. Let's see. A chocolate brown sash, high-waist shorts paired with a butt-ugly beanie? Need I say more?

"Joe! Come look at this potato chip! It looks just like George Washington!" Gram exclaimed.

"To be continued," Joe promised before he hurried over to ooh and ahh at his new wife's presidential discovery.

Whew. Dodged one bullet. Unfortunately the reunion surprise was still a few days off.

Tressa Turner, Secret Agent Woman.

Better make that *Mission Impossible*.

CHAPTER FIVE

"And this, ladies and gentlemen, is what investigative reporters call commonalities."

I ignored the dark look Shelby shot me over the top of Stan's shiny, balding head and surveyed my boss and our young apprentice as they bent over an array of photographs displayed on the table in the multipurpose conference room.

I handed Shelby a magnifying glass.

"If you will observe what I have marked as Exhibits A and B. Exhibit A is a photograph taken at Country Acres Greenhouse. Please note the large pink tornado spray-painted on the door of the shed." I paused for effect. "Now, if you would please take a look at what is marked as Exhibit B which is an investigative report written by our very own Shelby Lynn Sawyer generated from an investigative interview with one Bert Blakely who resides at 813 118th Avenue. I've noted the passages I'd like you to pay closest attention to. Shelby, would you please read the highlighted section out loud for us?"

Shelby did an eye roll number.

"Seriously?" she said.

"Well, you can read it any way you like, Shelby, but given the circumstances, a serious tone would probably be best," I said.

Shelby shook her head.

"Good grief." She took the paper from Stan. "'Mr. Bert Blakely indicated that included among the spray-painted graffiti defacing his outbuildings was a pink tornado-shaped figure.'" She handed me Exhibit B. "Satisfied?"

"Very nice. Thank you, Ms. Sawyer."

Shelby sighed.

"If you two could manage to quit law and ordering me to death and cut to the chase, I'd appreciate it," Stan said, his unlit cigar hanging out one side of his mouth. "So we've established that a number of the incidents are linked—"

"When you say 'we'—" I began, stopping when I saw Stan bite down on his stogie.

"—and presumably carried out by the same individual or group of individuals—"

"Given the amount of damage, we're probably looking at more than one person—" I interrupted again. "But, of course, you've no doubt figured that out already, Oh Clever and Knowledgeable Leader," I added seeing Stan's eyebrows lower. "So, we go to print, right?"

Stan's frowny face got frownier.

"There's still something missing here, Turner," Stan said.

Now I frowned.

"What do you mean? What's missing?"

"The part where you take this information to law enforcement and get their response."

My slam-dunk turned into an air ball.

"I was afraid you were going to say that."

"We need to present these facts to the authorities and see what they have to say before we put it out to the community. There may be good reasons law enforcement is keeping the link between these incidents under wraps."

"You think they've made the connection then?" Shelby asked.

"I don't know. It depends on how much interdepartmental give-and-take there is between the Grandville P.D. and Knox County," I said.

"Well, we'd better find out before we print something the cops don't want out there. I'd rather make friends in law enforcement than enemies," Stan pointed out.

I sighed. The big boss man was right. Like it or not—and I so didn't like it—before we ran our story, we had to give the local police and county officials a chance to weigh in.

"Okay, troops. We need to get on this. Turner, you take one agency. Shelby, you get the other," Stan instructed and walked to the door. "And we'll meet back here after lunch and see where we stand. *Capisce?*"

I *capisced* all right. I was going to have to choose between prying a statement from a police chief who still saw me as a blonde ditz or an acting sheriff with whom I had a complicated—and decidedly non-convivial past.

"I'll take the sheriff's office," Shelby Lynn said before I could suggest we flip a coin.

"Oh? What if I want the SO?" I asked, remembering Shelby's reaction when I'd asked if she had a contact with the sheriff's office.

"Do you?"

"Do I what?"

"Do you want to talk to the county?"

Did I? God, no!

"If you think your source can assist—" I hedged.

"Who says I have a source?"

"Did I say source? I meant if you feel you have more of an amicable, er, relationship—"

"Relationship?"

"What I'm saying is, if you think you can get more cooperation, then I say go for it. After all, it's what's best for the story that counts, right?"

Shelby grimaced.

"Yeah. Uh-huh. It's what's best for the story. You're obviously overlooking the fact that you exposed criminal activity in the sheriff's department and ended up putting the head honcho behind bars."

I grimaced.

Shelby was right. Alienating an entire police agency trumped horse poop in a car wash any day.

"I'll take local law enforcement. You take the county," I said.

"Good call, Ace Cub Reporter," Shelby said. "Good call."

* * *

"So, Chief Scott, what does the Grandville Police Department have to say about the apparent connection between recent incidents of vandalism in the city and similar incidents in the county?" I asked with my pen poised above my notepad to take down his response.

"No comment."

"What about the pink painted tornadoes that appear at the scenes?"

"No comment."

"What about leads? Do you have any credible leads?"

"No comment."

"Can I quote you on that?" I asked.

"Listen, Miss Turner. I can only tell you what I've told you ad nauseam before. Our—"

"—Investigation is continuing," I finished for him. "Honest Chief, I get it if there is some compelling reason you don't want certain facts made public. Just tell me, and I can take the information back to my boss. But surely the public has a right to information that might help them protect their properties and, perhaps, help them help you discover who is responsible for these acts of vandalism," I said, thinking I sounded pretty reasonable even to me.

"Miss Turner. I've told you before. I can't confirm or deny any connection between these incidents."

"I'm not looking for confirmation, Chief. I've shown you proof of the link between these incidents. This is more along the lines of a you-help-me-I-help-you call. The *Gazette* wishes to fully cooperate with local law enforcement, but we must balance that desire with our obligation to appropriately inform the citizens that depend on us for truthful reporting."

Chief Scott got a surprised look on his face. I was guessing he hadn't expected such eloquent defense of the First Amendment from the girl who got caught up straddling a barbed wire fence when she tried to cross it.

"Is that a threat, Miss Turner?"

Yikes! I'd apparently done a better job of reinventing myself than I'd thought. In record time, I'd graduated from bimbo to blackmailer.

Gulp.

"Threat? No way! Not at all!" I gushed. "It's just a heads-up, that's all. A courtesy call—you know—hey, Mr. Police Chief, I've got this story, and I'd like for you to comment. That kind of thing. You know. Just so I cover my bases."

Babble, babble.

"Stan Rodgers sent you here, didn't he?" Chief Scott said.

"Well, um, I er—"

"Well, you go back and tell Mr. Rodgers that he better remember, nothing stays a secret in a small town. Nothing." Chief Scott got to his feet.

I grimaced.

Another message I so didn't plan on forwarding.

"Oh, by the way, I was almost certain that was your Great Aunt Eunice I saw over in New Holland yesterday. I bet your grandma is tickled to death her big sister is back in town. Give them both my best wishes for a joyous reunion, won't you?" Chief Scott said and practically shoved me out of his office.

*Oo*kay. Make those three messages that would never leave my Inbox.

Delete. Delete. Delete.

CHAPTER SIX

The story ran the next day under the headline, "Area Vandalism Reported." I scanned the article online.

"You've got to be kidding me. You can't be serious. Un-freaking-believable!"

I sat at the kitchen table, seeing red—and not from the glamour girl red nail polish I'd spilled on the tablecloth.

Stan the spineless had gone through and deleted all references to pink tornadoes and the recent incidents being linked.

"I don't frigging believe it! The sell out! That First Amendment fraud! That…gigantic ass!"

"Knock, knock! You decent or am I interrupting something?"

I looked up.

I stared. An elderly, mustachioed man wearing a Chicago Cubs baseball hat and gray sweatshirt and sweatpants stood in the doorway.

"Excuse me?"

"I heard you ranting and raving and name-calling, and I didn't want to interrupt your diatribe."

I got to my feet.

"Can I help you?"

"Well, that's why I'm here."

I shook my head. "I don't understand. Do I know you?"

The old guy began to cackle. I gasped. There was something familiar about that wheeze.

"Close your mouth, girl. Or you'll swallow a fly."

"Aunt…Eunice?"

"In the flesh—or close approximation," the old man said before reaching up to pull off his hat—along with his hair—and then peeling off his mustache with a flourish and sticking it on the refrigerator door.

I took a step back.

"Aunt Eunice?"

I'd heard the rumors about my eccentric Aunt Eunice's er, unmarried status. Still, the subject of cross-dressing had never been part of that conversation.

"What are you doing here?"

And why are you dressed like a man?

"I'm safeguarding my surprise, that's what," she said, moving to take a seat at the table. "Staying with Abigail turned out to be a big mistake. I forgot how much of a nosy Nellie Hannah could be. Up at all hours of the night. Peeking out the windows. Watching the neighbors coming and going." She let out a long, disgusted breath. "And those binoculars of hers. I'd like to tell her where to put them. I have to wear a disguise every time I go out to keep her from recognizing me."

"That's why you're...dressed that way?" I asked, pointing at the wig and the mustache on the fridge.

"Of course, that's why. You don't think I get off dressing like this do you?" Her eyes narrowed to slits. "Did your grandmother tell you I liked to wear men's clothes?"

I shook my head so violently I got light-headed.

"No. Of course not. No way. Absolutely not!"

The Queen of Babel had officially made her entrance.

"Well, it's a good thing," Aunt Eunice grumbled.

"So, you're here because—?"

"I told you! Anonymity, Tressa Jayne! Anonymity! It'll only be for one night. The reunion is a couple days off, and I need to catch up on my beauty sleep so I'll be fresh as daisies come Sunday. Can't do that with your gramma peeking in the windows at all hours."

I winced.

"How did you get here?" I asked.

"Abigail dropped me off."

"That was nice of her," I said, thinking maybe my gammy had cause to dislike the woman after all.

"I wanted to hitchhike, but Abigail wouldn't hear of it."

"Hitchhike? Isn't that dangerous?"

"Please. Who wants to roll a homeless, old geezer? Still, I'd have given money to see Hannah's eyes bug out when I came out of Abigail's house dressed like a dude. I even gave her a big fat smooch before I helped her into the car. That ought to give your granny some sleepless nights of her own trying to figure out who ol' Abby was with. Hehehe!"

I shook my head. Poor Joe. If I knew my gammy, he'd be having some sleepless nights, too.

"So which room's mine?" Eunice asked. "I'm not picky, but the one closest to the loo would be best."

I showed her to the room my gammy used when she'd moved back in with me.

"Sorry about the mess," I said, hurrying ahead of her to clear a path. "I keep some of my boots in here."

"Just how many feet do you have?" Eunice asked.

I grimaced.

"The bathroom is right across the hall."

"Good to know. What time do we eat?"

"Eat?"

"Dinner! Supper! What time?"

I bit my lip.

"Well, actually, I have dinner plans," I said.

"With that Townsend chap?"

I nodded.

"Where you eating?"

"At Calhoun's."

"They still got those rarebits?" she asked.

I nodded.

"Order me one to go. With extra onions."

I sighed.

Only one day, I reminded myself. Just one day.

* * *

I swallowed the last of my beer and raised my hand to get the attention of the waitress. My date shot me a questioning look, and I managed a reassuring smile.

"Did we have a bad day?" Rick Townsend whispered in my ear. "Or do you require liquid courage to get through our second official date?"

"A little of both," I admitted, not quite comfortable with the role of girlfriend in Grandville's very own version of *The Bachelor* starring Ranger Rick Townsend in the leading role.

Townsend chuckled.

"I saw the article. It was a little light on the details."

"Tell me about it," I said, picking up my empty glass and raising it in the direction of the waitress. "Stan the hard-nosed newshound wussed out."

"What do you mean?"

"Stan decided to take out some rather important details."

"Ah. I see. Stan screwed with your article."

"Screwed with it? Screwed with it! Try going after it with a frigging scalpel and hacking it to pieces, the maniacal slasher!"

"Where is that waitress?" Townsend said, looking around. As if by magic, our recalcitrant server showed up. "She'll have another," he instructed, pointing to my empty glass.

"And you, sir? Would you care for a refill?" the buxom brunette with fangs, er, teeth so white they nearly blinded me, inquired of my date.

"I'm good, thanks," Rick said.

I snorted.

"Well, I am good, aren't I?" he asked, with a teasing lift of a brow. He looked at his watch. "I wonder what's keeping your bestie," he said. "You did say this was to be our first official double date, right? So where are the happy newlyweds?"

The tart arrived with my beer. I took a long sip.

"I'm sure I told them seven," I said. "Oh, there they are!" I waved to my best friend. "Kari! Brian! Over here!"

Several weeks earlier, Townsend and I had agreed that if our relationship stood any chance of thriving, we needed a history. A dating history. A history as a couple. You know. Going places. Doing things. Tonight's dating game episode featured our first foray into the double-dating scene. My best friend, Kari, taught middle school Language Arts. Her husband, Brian, was a physical education instructor who'd recently transferred from one of the elementary schools to teach at Grandville High School.

I'd been Kari's maid of honor at Kari's and Brian's wedding a year earlier, with rather…er…revealing results.

I looked up and saw them heading in our direction.

"Good evening, Mr. and Mrs. Davenport!" I greeted the newlyweds. "How nice of you to join us."

"I'm sorry we're late," Kari said, sending an annoyed look at her significant other as she slid into the bench across from us. "My husband couldn't seem to pull himself away from work."

"Oh? Coaching responsibilities?" Townsend asked.

Kari snorted.

"So-called mentoring responsibilities," she said, with a "can you believe it?" roll of her eyes.

"What kind of mentoring?" Rick asked.

"The pretty, new Life Skills teacher kind of mentoring," Kari responded. "It seems every time I turn around she's calling or texting her mentor. Isn't that right, *sweetie*?"

"Kari here seems to think Martina is making moves on me," Brian said.

"Martina?"

Kari made a face.

"Miss Banfield," she said. "And what am I supposed to think? She calls or texts at all hours of the day and night. A girl like that?" She shook her head. "It's not mentoring she's after."

"Would you give it a rest, Kari, and let us enjoy the evening?" Brian said.

"Fine by me. I'll enjoy the break from mentee mania," Kari said. "What do you have to do to get a waitress? I could use a glass of wine."

The waitress miraculously appeared and took our orders.

"So, Tressa," Kari said, when the drinks arrived. "What's this I read about a rash of vandalism? How many incidents are we talking about?"

"Unofficially? Up to a dozen in the last couple of weeks," I said.

"Wow. That many, huh? We don't see that kind of activity around here all that often. Is there a connection? The *Gazette* article didn't exactly say."

"Noticed that did you?" I said, tipping my glass to take a long swallow.

"Tressa seems to think the incidents were committed by the same individuals," Rick said.

"Oh?" Brian raised an eyebrow.

"I told Brian you'd have the inside scoop," Kari said.

"Actually, she said you'd have the inside 'poop,'" Brian said. "So, what makes you think the incidents are linked, Tressa?"

"Yes. Do tell, bestie," Kari urged.

I bit my lip. Should I, or shouldn't I? Just because Stan wimped out and gave in to pressure from popo, was no reason for me to do the same. And wasn't the press supposed to be the people's watchdog? Look out for them? Be their eyes and ears?

"There was physical evidence at each scene that suggested the malicious mischief was committed by the same perpetrators," I said, sounding very authoritative if I do say so myself.

"What kind of evidence?" Kari asked. "Footprints? Fingerprints? DNA?"

I shook my head. "Nothing like that."

"What then?" Brian asked.

"More along the lines of a signature, I guess you'd call it," I said, trying to be forthcoming and vague at the same time.

"Signature? What do you mean? They signed their spray-painted masterpieces?" Kari asked.

"Not exactly," I said, wishing I'd buttoned my lip.

A cell phone notification sounded and four of us checked their phones.

"It's mine," Brian said.

"Of course it is," Kari said.

Brian stared at the phone, smiled, and keystroked a text message.

"Well?" Kari said. "It's little Miss Mentee, isn't it?"

Brian shrugged and put the phone in his pocket.

"What does she want this time? More hand-holding? Or does she want you to proof her paper?"

"She has to fill out self-evaluation forms and wants me to look over the section on goals and tactics and strategies for success," Brian told his put out spouse.

"What is she trying to be successful at? Creating wedges between newlyweds? Manufacturing mentor marital strife?" Kari said, taking a long gulp of wine. "Cheers."

"For God's sake, Kari. It's my job."

"Teaching is your job. Not babysitting newbie teachers."

Brian's phone rang. He checked the display and frowned.

"Excuse me. I've got to take this," he said and left the table.

Kari's eyes may have fired invisible daggers at her husband's back, but I suspected the sudden sheen I noticed there had less to do with anger than with hurt feelings.

"Who is this Martina again?" Rick asked.

"She's a new teacher Brian's been assigned to mentor. I just met her once. She seemed very…intense."

"I'm sure she's just super anxious to do a good job," I assured my friend. "She probably doesn't want to make any mistakes."

"Too late for that," Kari said, taking another sip of wine. She shook her head. "I refuse to let my clueless husband ruin this evening. I've looked forward to the four of us getting together for ages. I'm so happy we finally made it happen. I'm thrilled the two of you are putting yourself out there as a couple. Now, what were we talking about when we were so rudely interrupted? Oh, yes. You were about to tell us about the signature that linked those property crimes."

I'd hoped Martina the mentee had distracted Kari long enough for her to forget follow-up questions about the local vandals. No such luck.

"I really shouldn't say anything—"

"Come on, Tressa. I won't say anything to anyone. Girl Scout promise."

I sighed. Kari really had been a Girl Scout. What choice did I have but to trust her?

"There were some rather unique drawings at each of the scenes," I said, lowering my voice to just above a whisper.

"Drawings? What kind of drawings?" Rick asked. "Like gang signs?"

I looked at him.

"You know about gang tags?" I asked.

He shrugged. "You pick this stuff up."

"Never mind that. What about the drawings?" Kari asked.

"Pink tornadoes," I said in a conspiratorial whisper.

"Huh?" Rick and Kari said.

"Pink spray-painted tornadoes," I repeated.

"Someone spray-painted pink tornadoes on cars and buildings?" Kari asked.

I nodded. "Big, fat, pink tornadoes."

Kari frowned. "Huh," she said. "You know. I seem to recall seeing pink tornadoes somewhere, but I can't recall where." She rubbed her forehead. "I wish I could remember where I'd seen them. Oh, don't look now, but here comes Mr. Mentor."

Brian returned to the table.

"Sorry about that," he said and picked up his beer.

"I'll just bet you are," Kari said. "What's the big emergency now? Martina can't figure out where she needs a comma, how to number pages, or how to refill a stapler?"

"Would you lay off, Kari? I'm sick and tired of your attitude," Brian said.

"So. Brian. How do you think the Hawkeyes will fare this season?" Townsend attempted an intervention.

Without success.

"Oh, really, Brian?" Kari said. "Well, I'm sick and tired of you kowtowing to some chippie with performance anxieties."

"Kowtowing? I'm doing my job, for God's sake."

"Has anyone seen a good movie lately?" I waded in, not about to let Townsend attempt this rescue mission alone.

"Your contract hours are 7:30 to 3:30, five days a week, Einstein. Not twenty-four seven."

"Oh. And I suppose you never go the extra mile—or extra hour—for your students. What about the plays? What about the writing contests? What about the endless events you've forced me to chaperone?" Brian countered.

"Forced? Forced? So all this time you only pretended to enjoy chaperoning."

"Hell yes, I pretended. What guy enjoys standing around a gym where nobody's dribbling a ball?"

I held my breath. I knew my bestie well enough to sense an impending eruption.

Stand back! She's fixin' to blow!

No sooner had that thought entered my head than I saw my bestie throw her napkin down, get to her feet, and dump what was left of her wine on her hubby of a year's head.

"Sorry, Tressa," she said and ran out of the restaurant.

Rick handed Brian his napkin.

"See ya, bud," Rick told his friend.

Brian wiped his face and head and got to his feet.

"See ya," he said and left.

We sat silent and speechless and stared at each other over wine-soiled linens and lukewarm beer. Townsend raised his glass.

"A toast. To our second date. May the third one be the charm," he said.

I clinked his glass and drained mine.

Date one had culminated in a hit and run and a missing celebrity.

Our second date had ended with newlyweds making a public scene.

Who knew the *Dating Game* could turn into *The Hunger Games*?

CHAPTER SEVEN

We'd finished our meals—changing our double dates' orders to carryouts—and were preparing to leave when I remembered Aunt Eunice's rarebit.

"Shoot!" I said. "I forgot I was supposed to place a rarebit order to go."

Rick frowned.

"You've already got baked cavatelli, teriyaki steak, and sides, T," he pointed out. "What do you need with a rarebit?"

I bit my lip, remembering the vow of secrecy Aunt Eunice had almost made me sign in blood. Mine.

"Oh. Well, I thought since you paid for the meals, you'd take them," I covered.

"Right. Like that was going to happen," my date said.

I shrugged, recognizing the validity of his statement. The clever ranger-type had a point—and a history of past conduct on his side.

Let her eat steak and pasta!

By the time we headed for the homestead, the sun had set and those last faint glimmers of light faded slowly into the horizon. Rick whistled a contented tune while the motion of the pickup and the heaviness of a full stomach lulled me into a satisfied glow. I thought about my friend's recent marriage—how insecure and unhappy she'd seemed, reflecting on Craig and Kimmie's baby battle, as well—and sighed.

Was that what marriage was these days? A constant battle to keep outside forces at bay—to prevent destructive influences from breaching the sanctity of the institution? I didn't think I could live that way—always looking for some breach—a growing gap in the relationship somebody waiting in the wings was only too happy to step in and fill.

I looked over at Townsend. Would it be that way with us, too? Was trust within a marriage a vanishing concept? Was marriage itself antiquated and old-fashioned? Faithfulness and fidelity old-style and cliché?

Maybe I was the old-fashioned one to want something solid and lasting. Maybe I was living in a fairy tale world that didn't exist any more. Maybe I was just a sappy, hopeless romantic.

I felt the sting of tears and turned my head to look out the passenger window as the pickup cruised down the county road. Townsend slowed to turn onto the gravel road by Harve Dawson's place.

Harve is a good ol' boy who is about the best horse trimmer and horse shoer in these parts. As long as we've had horses, Harry has performed their pedicures.

As we turned off, the glare of Townsend's headlamp bounced off an object next to Harry's mailbox. I frowned. It looked kind of like one of those lawn gnomes. Weird. I'd never noticed before that Harve had a gnome. I turned to look out the back of the truck as we drove away.

"Something wrong?" Townsend asked.

I shook my head.

"I guess not."

Minutes later we pulled into my driveway.

"Geez. You think you left enough lights on? I bet your folks are enjoying the view."

I turned to stare at the double-wide and groaned. Aunt Eunice had every light on—indoors and out. I could hear kilowatts clicking off.

"With all the vandalism going on, a person can't be too careful," I explained.

"Well, I don't think you'll have to worry about security tonight," Townsend said, snaking an arm across the back of the truck seat and around my shoulders. "I'd like to volunteer my services as your personal bodyguard." He held me close and kissed me softly.

I closed my eyes and, like a stick of taffy left in a car in midsummer, melted.

We kissed and kissed some more, squeezing, stroking, and caressing as things heated up.

"T?" Ranger Rick said, his lips on mine.

"Huh?"

"I think we better continue indoors."

"Uh-huh."

"Now T," Rick urged.

Rap! Rap! Rap!

The pounding on the passenger window next to me brought me up.

"Hey! You in the truck! Your windows are all fogged up. You okay in there? Helloo?"

Rick let go of me.

"What in God's name?" he said.

Bam! Bam!

The knocking came at the driver's side this time.

"Hello in there! Tressa Jayne? Is that you?"

Rick looked at me, a confused look on his face.

"Who the hell is that?"

I bit my lip. Honestly, it was anyone's guess. Behind door number one we might discover eccentric Great Aunt Eunice. On the other hand, behind door number two Eunice's male alter ego could be lurking.

Pick a door. Any door.

"Open up or I'm calling the police!"

Rick rolled down his window.

I held my breath.

"Can I help you, sir?" Rick said.

"Help me? You're the one parked out here with fogged up windows!"

I winced.

And behind door number two we have...*Mr. Bojangles.*

Rick opened his door and got out. I climbed across the seat after him.

Aunt Eunice, in old man regalia—my living room quilt thrown over his...er...her shoulders—peered at Ranger Rick over the top of a pair of reading glasses Gram had left behind when she moved.

"Are you lost, sir? Are you well? Do you need me to contact someone for you?" Rick asked, his concern for the elderly man touching, if a tad misplaced.

"No, I don't need nothing. I'm just chillin'. Know what I'm saying?" Great Aunt Eunice had obviously been practicing her old dude act. And apparently she'd been taking those lessons from *Cops Reloaded* because she sure as shoot had a bad boy thing going on.

"What are you doing out here, pardner?"

"Oh, just hangin' with my girlfriend here. Know what I'm sayin'?"

I winced.

"Girlfriend? And how do you know Tressa?" Rick asked.

"Oh, Tressa and I go way back, *pardner*. W*aay* back. Know what I'm sayin'?"

"Not really," Rick replied. "Tressa?" He looked at me.

"Well, um, you see—"

"Tressa Jayne is my great niece," Bojangles said. "I skidded into town short on funds, but full of love for my family, and my sweet little ol' niece gave me a place to hang before the family shindig. Know what I'm sayin'?"

"You're Tressa's great uncle?" Rick said, shaking his head.

"Well, I wouldn't actually say I was all that *great* of an uncle. Hey, hey, hey."

Now Aunt Eunice, clearly enjoying her role, sounded more like *Fat Albert*.

"Uncle, er, Bo has been, um, estranged from the family." The "strange" part was definitely on the money.

"I been what you call amiss about keeping in touch with kin. Know what I'm sayin'?"

"I think he means 'remiss,'" I inserted.

"I know what he meant, Tressa. Your grandmother's side of the family, I take it."

I shrugged. How the heck did I know what backstory Aunt Bo, er, Eunice had in mind?

"I'm kinda the black sheep of the family," Uncle Bo said. "The rebel. You know what I'm sayin'?"

Townsend frowned and looked at me. "I didn't know your grandmother had a brother. The only great I know about is the great aunt your grandmother refers to as the homely Blackford sister."

I gasped. Holy sibling rivals!

"Now, now, now," Bo said, wagging a finger at Townsend. "Don't you be talkin' smack about Eunice, boy," 'Bo' said. "'Cause them be fightin' words." Aunt Eunice brought her fists up in a pugilist's stance.

I cringed when I saw the mystic mauve nail polish. I hoped to God Rick didn't notice it.

"Now Uncle...um, er, Bo," I said, cupping my hands around Aunt Eunice's balled-up fists to rein her in. "Rick here didn't mean anything. Honest. He's a good guy."

"Rick? Rick Townsend? The Rick you used to call turd muffin? A guy whose ego is only eclipsed by 'the Donald's?' The feller who, when he bends over in his Levis, gives a gal dry mouth and heart palpitations."

Rick looked at me.

"I give you palpitations?"

I shook my head.

"That was my gammy."

He blinked.

"Bo here's a halfer," Aunt Eunice said.

"A heifer?" Townsend looked at me and shook his head.

"Half bro. See Bo struck out on his own when he was a lad and never looked back. Haven't seen family since I was a strapping younker. "

Holy Hemingway! The backstory thickened.

"So your Uncle Bo is staying here with you?" Townsend asked. "How come you didn't mention it before now?"

"It was one of them surprises, sonny," Uncle Bo said. "Know what I'm sayin', Rick?"

"A surprise."

I put my hands up and stuck my foot out in my own "ta-da" pose.

"Surprise!" I said, wishing I'd let Rick in on the charade sooner and vowing to clear things up with a phone call as soon as Rick drove away.

"You gonna keep our little secret until the reunion, ain't ya, Rick?" Aunt Bo, I mean Uncle Bo asked.

Rick looked at Uncle Bo and back at me.

"Uh, yeah. Sure. Your secret is safe with me," he said.

"That's what I'm talkin' 'bout!"

I watched in horror—okay and some morbid fascination—as Uncle Bo grabbed Townsend and planted a long, loud kiss on his unsuspecting lips.

Once the kiss ended, Townsend took a shaky step back and wiped his mouth.

"Now let me tell you, that is one mighty fine kisser," *Uncle Bo* exclaimed and gave Townsend a big wink. "Know what I'm sayin'?"

Townsend sent me a look I couldn't begin to read and scurried to the safety of his truck and drove off, leaving behind little white swirls of gravel dust.

I winced.

So not a case of "kiss and tell," right?

I thought about Townsend's horrified expression. Hmm. Maybe I'd let the macho ranger-type sweat it for a bit before I made that call.

I know. I know. I'm a little stinker.

CHAPTER EIGHT

"You actually drive this car?" Uncle Bo asked from the passenger seat.

"Only when I want to go somewhere," I responded.

"It sounds like a German tank. And rides like one."

I looked over at her.

"And you've ridden in a German tank when?"

Aunt Eunice shrugged.

"Could use a good wash, too."

"I live on a gravel road. It gets dusty."

She sniffed. Her mustache wriggled like a caterpillar who'd seen hard times and was in its final death throes.

"Smells funny, too."

I shrugged. Like I haven't heard that before.

"I've got dogs," I said.

"Dogs? It's horsey I smell. But you got those, too, don't you? A regular menagerie as I recall."

Well, maybe not a regular one.

"So, let me get this straight," I said. "You want me to park around the corner from Abigail's place and let you out so my grandma won't see my car."

"That's right."

"But you don't mind if she sees you."

"'Course not. In this disguise, she won't know it's me." She patted her wayward mustache.

"She'll think Abigail's got her a secret lover."

There went that twitching mustache again.

"Uh-oh. Watch out. Popo ahead," Eunice said, and she pointed at the windshield.

I frowned. Popo?

"Looks like the county popo," she clarified.

Eunice was right. A county sheriff's vehicle sat on the shoulder near the entrance to Harve Dawson's driveway, whirligig lights going. I slowed. As we passed the rural mailbox, I stared. If I wasn't seeing things, Harve's previously utilitarian gray mailbox was presently a girlie shade of pink.

I made a U-turn and pulled in front of the patrol car.

"What's going on? Why are you pulling over here?" Aunt Eunice asked.

I grabbed my phone and notepad.

"I just want to check out what's going on," I said. "You know. For the paper."

"Ooh. Gotcha. You're on the trail of one of your stories," she said. She unfastened her seat belt and started to open her door.

I reached over to grab her sleeve.

"Just where do you think you're going?" I asked.

"To check things out with you. Two pairs of peepers is always better than one, you know."

"Thank you, but I think you'd better stay in the car," I said.

"This smelly old clunker? The exhaust fumes are enough to make you pass out."

"Open the window."

"I tried. It won't roll down."

I winced. "Oh, yeah. I'll open mine then. That should give you some good cross ventilation."

"And have me inhale enough gravel dust to start one of my asthma attacks," she said and put her mouth to her armpit and began coughing into it.

"Okay, okay. I give up. Just watch your step on the shoulder and the driveway. And stick close to me. Oh, and don't talk to anybody. Or make eye contact."

"Anything else, General Patton?" She put a hand to her forehead in mock salute.

"That'll do for now, Private Bo," I said, not about to forget Aunt Eunice shared a gene pool with my gammy—okay, okay—and with me, too—where unpredictability was hardwired into our DNA.

I put my four-way flashers on—well two-way since two of them wouldn't work—and got out of the car and headed around to the other side to help Eunice out. By the time I got there, she was out of the car and had her forehead pressed against the passenger side window of the county car, looking inside.

"Would you get a load of all the equipment?" she said. "They even got computers and printers in their cars now. Fancy that. All those high-tech gadgets to help catch bad guys. Wowee!"

I'd been up close and personal with a cop car in the not-so-distant past. Unfortunately I'd been relegated to the seat facing the cage, so I couldn't resist the impulse to put my head against the glass and peek in as well.

"What's that thingamajigger?" Eunice asked.

"What thingamajigger?"

"That thing over there."

"That's the radio. Or maybe a scanner."

"Where do they keep the shotgun?"

"I don't know. The trunk maybe?"

"Uh hem. Do you mind? You're getting nose prints on my car window."

I turned.

Deputy Doug Samuels, aka "Deputy Dawg," "Deputy Doughboy"—along with several even more graphic monikers—made a blurry reflection on the windshield.

I groaned, pulling Eunice's face away from the glass as I straightened and turned.

"Oh, hey. Hello there, Deputy Samuels."

"*Acting Sheriff* Samuels," he reminded me. As if I needed reminding. "Tressa Turner. I could tell from fifty yards away that was you."

I didn't know whether to be flattered or offended.

"You got some super-duper spyglasses that magnifies us, Officer?" Eunice asked.

Lord, I hoped not.

"Nope. Just super-duper skills of detection," Samuels said. "And a certain... familiarity with the subject."

I snorted.

"Right. Right. So *Acting* Sheriff Samuels," I said, whipping out my pen and notepad, "can you tell us what your super-duper detection skills are being utilized for here at the Dawson residence? Would it have anything to do with the thoroughly modern look someone has given Harve's formerly drab mailbox?" I asked.

Samuel's expression went from sunny to sour in a heartbeat.

"How do you know Harve didn't decide to go retro?" he asked.

"I know Harve," I said. "So, what's the deal with the mailbox? Anything else tagged? Can I see the damage? This is tied to all the other incidents, isn't it? Country Acres Greenhouse, Keefer's shed, the East Side artwork? The other incidents. They're all connected, right?"

Samuel's eyes narrowed to slits. "Where did you get that idea?"

"Oh, come on. It's as plain as a pink tornado on a garden shed," I said.

"Where do you get this stuff, Turner? The *SyFy* channel?"

"Come on, Deputy. We both know this isn't made-for-TV-fiction," I said. "I've got proof the same individuals are responsible for these incidents. What I want to know before I go to press is if your department has any leads on the perpetrators?"

Samuels ran a hand through his hair.

"Know what, Turner? You're a real pain in the butt."

"Hey! You can't talk to my niece that way!"

I'd forgotten about Uncle Bo.

"Your niece?"

"That's right."

"You're Turner's uncle?"

"Great Uncle." Aunt Eunice smoothed her mustache and stuck her hand out. "Beauregard Blackford at your service," she said with a touch of southern twang. I cringed, letting my breath out when I saw Uncle Bo had put on a pair of my work gloves to cover the candy apple red nail polish.

The deputy shook Aunt Eunice's hand, a dazed look on his face. I could relate.

"You know, young man, as patriarch of the Blackford clan, I have a certain responsibility," Bo said.

"Responsibility?"

"To defend the honor of my family."

I shook my head at Aunt Eunice. I might as well have been invisible.

"Honor?" Samuels said. "I don't follow."

"It's up to me to make sure Tressa's reputation isn't sullied or tarnished."

I frowned. Aunt Eunice made me sound like my gammy's silver teapot that hadn't seen polish since Bush was pres. Bush one.

"It's okay, Au...er, Uncle Bo," I tried to assure my aunt it wasn't necessary for her to be my er, knight in ancient armor, but she forged ahead.

"Now don't get me wrong. I know Tressa Jayne here can get under your skin now and then—kinda like one of those annoyin' itches you can't scratch in public. Know what I'm sayin'? And she's got just enough of her grandmamma in her to be a bit of a, well, Magoo at times."

"No. Really. Uncle Bo. You don't have to—"

"Every family tree has a branch here and there that doesn't exactly hang like the other branches—ones that lose their leaves too soon or never lose 'em at all. Branches that lean this way when the others go that way. Every family's got 'em. But that doesn't excuse your disrespect. It's unbecoming of a man in uniform. Know what I'm sayin'? Why, when I was in Nam—"

"Really. It's okay, Uncle Bo," I took Eunice's elbow in an attempt to derail a line of inquiry into Uncle Bo's bogus military service. "Deputy Samuels was just teasing. He and I go way back. Right, Deputy?" I gave him a "work with me" wink.

"Uh, yeah. Sure. Whatever." Samuels shook his head.

"So, any leads on our little Grandville gang fest?" I asked.

Samuels' brow crinkled.

"Gang? Who said anything about a gang?"

"Well, obviously the spray-painting suggests—"

"It suggests someone has issues and wants to make a statement."

I frowned. "What statement does a pink tornado make?"

"Pink tornado?"

"Oh, come on Samuels. You can't have missed the recurring theme in these incidents. It doesn't take Holmes and Watson to figure out they are connected."

He shrugged. "Maybe someone really likes pink tornados. We're not prepared to make that leap yet."

I frowned. "Leap? Leap! What leap? We're talking facts, here, Deputy, facts the public has a right to know."

He crossed his arms. "The public's right to know. The media's mantra—and their convenient excuse for sticking their noses where they don't belong."

"We don't need an excuse. We've got the First Amendment," I said.

Samuels raised a brow, but didn't say anything.

"Listen, Deputy, er, Sheriff. I'd really like to include a comment from law enforcement confirming the connection and alerting the public on what to be looking for."

"Well, you're not gonna get that from me today, Turner. In fact, we'd prefer you hold off on putting that information out there. This investigation is ongoing, and the appropriate authorities will disseminate appropriate information at the appropriate time through the appropriate channels." He unfolded his arms. "And you can quote me on that."

"You want Uncle Bo to give popo another piece of his mind?" Aunt Eunice asked.

I shook my head.

"Nah. We're good, Bo."

Samuels moved to the trunk of his patrol vehicle. I followed. He opened it and removed a camera.

Oh, right! Pictures!

I grabbed my phone and pointed it at Harve's psychedelic mailbox and took a couple shots. I moved back a few steps to get a fuller view of the entire mailbox and post.

Then I remembered.

The gnome. The lawn gnome I'd seen by Harve's mail post the night before when Townsend and I had driven by.

"Hey. Where's Harve's gnome?" I asked Samuels.

He frowned at me over the top of his trunk lid.

"What?"

"Harve's lawn gnome! Where is it?"

He slammed the trunk lid shut.

"I've got no idea what you're talking about. As usual."

"Harve had a lawn gnome sitting beside the mailbox post. I saw it last night. Did it get shellacked, too?"

Samuels shook his head.

"A shellacked gnome?"

"What's taking you so long, Doug? Ain't got all day."

I turned. Harve the Horse Whisperer, looking every bit the wrangler in a red plaid western shirt rolled up to his elbows, boot cut Levis with a big ol' horse shoe buckle, and a well-worn pair of boots, hoofed it down the gravel drive toward us.

"Oh. Hey. Hi." Harve put a hand up in my direction. "How goes it, Tressa? How's your folks? Family doing okay?"

"Good. They're good. How've you been?"

"Can't complain. No one would listen," Harve said. "How's the little herd? They're about due for a trim, aren't they?"

They were. But I was a little short this month. Who was I kidding? I was short every month.

"I was meaning to get hold of you," I said. "Things have been a little hectic."

Harve nodded. "I read about your big ol' bike ride," he said, a reference to my tandem trek across the state. "Reckon you've spent more time on a bike seat than a saddle this summer."

Sadly true.

"Can we get a move on, Doug?" Harve said. "I've got to get hold of the insurance guy."

"Did you have a lot of damage?" I asked.

He nodded. "Enough, the bastards."

"Bastar*d*s? Plural?" I shot a told-you-so look at Deputy Dawg. "Can I get some pictures for the paper?"

Harve's gaze shifted to Samuels.

"It's still a crime scene until we release it," he said.

I felt my lip curl. Crime scene my CSI arse. Samuels was being Deputy Dick.

I dug around in my bag for a business card and handed it to Harve. "I'd appreciate it if you would give me a call when the county has released the scene. Oh. And, Harve, about your gnome..."

"Good Lord. Not this again," Samuels muttered.

Harve scratched his chin. "Gnome? What gnome?"

"Trust me, Dawson," Samuels said. "And run!"

I ignored the deputy.

"Your lawn gnome is gone, Harve. The one by the mailbox."

He shook his head.

"Ain't never had me no gnome—lawn or otherwise. You sure it was my mailbox?"

"Yes, I'm sure. I saw it with my own eyes last night. It was sitting right there." I pointed to the mailbox post. "At the time I thought it was odd because I'd never seen it there before."

Harve did more scratching.

"What did this gnome look like?"

Now I was the one doing the chin scratching.

"Well, it was just getting dark, and I really didn't see it for all that long, but it had a white beard and had like a blue shirt with some kind of tan overall. Oh, and a pointy blue hat. I remember that."

"All gnomes have pointy hats," Samuels said with a smirk in my direction.

"Doesn't ring a bell," Harve said.

"Well it rings *my* bell!" I'd forgotten all about Aunt Eunice until she inserted herself in the middle of our little circle of inquiry. "That's Abigail Winegardner's gnome!" Aunt Eunice declared.

"Who are you?" Harve asked.

"Beauregard Blackford at your service," Aunt Eunice said. "And the gnome you're chewing the fat about belongs to Abigail Winegardner. I'd bet my life on it."

"Now hold on there! You accusin' me of stealing?" Harve said, puffing out his chest like an affronted rooster.

"Tressa Jayne saw that gnome right there," Aunt Eunice said and pointed at the mailbox. "Didn't you, Tressa?"

"Well, I saw a gnome—"

"And it had a blue shirt and pointy blue hat just like Abigail's."

"I told you before, I didn't have no gnome!" Harve said.

"We can't be sure it was Abigail's gnome, Au...er...Uncle Bo," I pointed out. "And if Harve said he didn't have one, he didn't have one. Harve's as honest as the day is long."

"The days are getting shorter, you know," she said and gave Harve the 'I'm watching you' look. "Abigail's gnome is a one-of-a-kind antique. Quite distinctive. If you saw a picture, do you think you could identify it, Tressa?"

Deputy Samuels snorted.

"Good grief. A photo layout of lawn gnomes?"

Great Aunt Eunice clapped the deputy on the back. "Great idea, Deputy! Now you're thinkin'. Thanks for putting that together. I'll get a photo of Abigail's gnome to you today," Aunt Eunice said.

Samuels' smirk wilted.

"Come on, Harve," he said. "Let's take a look around your place and get some pictures," the deputy said. "Maybe we'll find the culprit is a dwarf with a pointed hat and white beard."

I resisted the juvenile urge to flip the bird at the deputy's retreating back. Uncle Bo had no such qualms.

"Well, what do you know? We got us a rumble right here in River City," Uncle Bo said, sounding a lot more like my gammy than she probably suspected.

Beauregard Blackford was right.

That apple didn't fall far.

CHAPTER NINE

———

"Help yourself to another roll, Tressa," Abigail Winegardner called to me from another room.

I sat back in my chair and rubbed my tummy and stared at the plate of gooey perfection that was Abigail Winegardner's famous sticky buns.

Should I or shouldn't I?

"Oh, come on, Tressa. You know you want it."

I looked over at Aunt Eunice—or a version thereof—sitting at Abigail's dining room table next to me. She'd removed the mustache and wig but was still wearing the au couture line from the hobo haberdashery.

"I really shouldn't," I said, patting my waistline.

"Oh, come on. Live a little. No one makes pastries like Abby."

"Don't I know it," I said, having just consumed proof of that fact.

You'll cover for me with my gammy, won't you? Wink, wink.

I was about to select a particularly gooey third roll—but who's counting—when Abigail entered the dining room again.

"Here it is! I knew I had some pictures of Cedric."

I blinked. "Cedric?"

She nodded. "As long as I can remember, our little lawn gnome has been known as Cedric. And dear Cedric is no ordinary gnome."

I blinked.

"He isn't?"

"Oh, no. Cedric is quite old. He dates back to the 1920s."

Yikes! That *was* old.

"Here he is, our poor little missing lawn gnome." Abigail handed me several photographs.

I stared.

Holy *Leprechaun*, the movie! Three billy goats were missing their troll! Little Cedric here made *Chucky* look like *People's* Sexiest Doll Alive.

Dressed in a sky blue shirt and tights and matching pointy hat and paired with a short khaki-colored belted overall and pointed ankle high boots, it was the wee little bearded man's scrunched up, misshapen face, pointed ears, and maniacal eyes that had visions of killer ventriloquist dummies playing tricks in my head.

"Cedric has always watched over our yards," Abigail said, wistfully.

I frowned. Cedric here was as much of a benevolent guardian of the garden as a herd of rabid mutant jackrabbits.

And totally more terrifying.

"He's quite...unique," I said and winced, glad now I'd resisted the offer of the additional sticky roll.

"He's from the early twentieth century. Cast iron, too. He's really quite rare."

I forced myself to look at the picture closer. It certainly looked like the gnome I'd seen at Harve's mailbox the previous night.

"I knew I should've kept him in the backyard, but I thought it would be nice to put him in the flower bed out front for a change," Abigail said and shook her head. "I should've let him be."

"When did you move him?" I asked.

She shrugged. "Oh, late spring or around there. I had to have help moving him. He's quite a chunk."

"How big is, uh, er Cedric?" I asked.

Abigail put a hand out, palm down above her knee.

"He came to about here," she said. "I'd say he was somewhere around oh, thirty inches tall or so. Maybe half that across."

"You said you needed help moving him. He's fairly heavy then?" I asked.

"Oh, yes. I would imagine it would take two people to carry him any distance. But I expect one person could lift it and put it in a car and drive away."

Dang. Hellion Hannah wasn't off the hook yet.

"Could I borrow the photos?" I asked, getting to my feet.

"Of course. But what are you going to do with them?"

I shrugged, not about to tell Abigail that I was planning to lay down a short stack photo lineup of lawn gnome types for potential gnome witnesses.

"In my line of work I get out around the county a lot," I said. "I'll keep my eyes open for Cedric."

And pray I didn't turn to stone like Medusa's victims if I did find him.

I thanked Abigail for her hospitality, and Aunt Eunice led me to the back door. She'd made me park out of sight around the block and insisted we make our way to Abigail's back door separately. I wouldn't have been surprised if she'd required I use a password to gain admittance to the Winegardner domicile.

"It's the same gnome, isn't it?" Aunt Eunice said. "You saw a gnome by that Harvey the Horseman's mailbox, and it was Cedric wasn't it?"

"I'm not sure," I said, even though having laid peepers on Cedric one didn't tend to forget him.

"What are you going to do next?"

"I'm not sure."

"What kind of reporter are you?"

A reporter who had learned the hard way to look before she leaped headfirst into a story.

That kind.

"I'm going to do what I always do," I said.

Great Aunt Eunice blinked.

"You're gonna find a dead corpse?"

Was there any other kind?

"No, no," I put my hand up. "I'm going to ask questions. Nose around. See what I can find out. Do a little digging. You know. Investigate."

"You gonna keep us in the loop, right?"

I nodded.

"Oh sure. Of course. Absolutely."

"And mum's still the word regarding my little reunion surprise, right?"

"Oh, yes. Definitely. Mum is the mum." I made a little key locking gesture. "Believe me, I know nothing. Nothing at all." I gave her a quick peck on a wrinkled cheek. "I'll be in touch," I said and started to open the door.

"No! Wait!" Aunt Eunice grabbed her Uncle Bo hat and pulled the hood of her sweatshirt up over her head and pulled the strings so tight she looked like an American Bulldog. She cracked the door open and looked to the left and then to the right. "All's clear!" she said. "Go!"

I felt a hand in the small of my back, and the next thing I knew she'd shoved me out of the house and closed the door behind me.

Head down, I hurried to my car thinking how fortunate it was Aunt Eunice only visited infrequently.

I jumped in my car, started it, and drove away, reaching the stop sign at the end of the block when my cell phone rang. I pulled it out and looked at the screen.

My gammy.

"H'lo?"

"Tressa? That you?"

I frowned.

"Yes. Weren't you calling me?"

"'Course I was callin' you. Who else would I be calling?"

I shook my head.

"I'm kind of busy right now, Gram. What do you need?"

"I need for you to drive around the block and pull into the driveway and come in."

"What?"

"I can hear the chug-chug-chugging of your car."

"I don't know what you mean, Gram. I'm not—"

"I can see you, Tressa!"

I sighed. How does she do that?

I bowed to the inevitable and, as instructed, made a right and a few seconds later pulled into the house Gram shared with her new hubby. I saw the curtains move at the front window. I turned my car off and got out, catching the movement of curtains again—this time at Abigail Winegardner's front window. I shook my head.

Oh, brother.

Make that oh, sisters.

I jogged up to the front porch and opened the screen door. A long, bony, liver-spotted hand reached out and pulled me into house and slammed the door closed behind me.

"What were you doing at Abigail's?" Gram demanded, a set of binoculars hanging around her neck.

Evade! Evade! Evade!

"Why would I be at Abigail Winegardner's?"

"That's what we want to know."

"We?"

"Joe and me. Right, Joe?"

"Joe?"

"Did I hear someone mention my name?" Joe said, walking into the living room wearing a pink polo shirt and what appeared to be khaki capri pants.

"Nice, uh, outfit, Joe," I said with a pointed look at his ensemble. "You start buying off the modern miss racks?"

Joe's face blushed pinker than his shirt.

"I'll have you know these are the latest in men's European fashion," Joe said.

"Good to know," I said. "I thought maybe my gammy had some trouble with the laundry again and you had some, er, shrinkage."

"I'll just bet you did," Joe said. "Now, what were we talking about before you tried to distract us? Oh, yes. You were about to tell us what you were doing at our neighbor's house. Isn't that right, Hannah?"

"That's right. What's goin' on with you and ol' lady Winegardner?"

"Nothing! Really! Nothing's going on with the neighbor lady and me. I hardly know the woman!"

I felt a moment of déjà vu. If I wasn't mistaken, at a time in the not-so-distant past Joe Townsend had used these very words to reassure my gammy of his fidelity.

"What's that on your face?"

"What?"

"There. Around your mouth." Joe said. "You've got crumbs."

Before I could put a hand up to wipe the evidence away, my gammy was on me like a mouse on a trap baited with a *Rolo* caramel. She put her fingers up and literally snatched the crumbs from my lips and put them to her own.

"Abigail's sticky buns!" she hissed. "Patouey!"

"Okay, okay!" I put my arms in your basic 'I give up' pose. "So she offered me a bun. To be polite, I accepted. I assure you I didn't enjoy them."

"Them?" Joe said and lifted an eyebrow.

"Why're you visiting Abigail?" Gram asked.

I sighed.

"If you must know, it's about that gnome of hers."

"That butt ugly one? She still accusin' me of pilferin' the homely little halfling?" Gram asked.

"I was there to get a picture of the gnome in question," I said.

"Why?" Joe and Gram said in unison.

"I, uh, er, well, I thought I might have spotted it the other night, and I wanted to see if she had a photo so I'd know for sure."

I know. Lame. Really lame.

"Helloo! Lame and lamer," Gram said. "What about that man?"

"Man?"

"The man Abigail has living with her! The old duffer who looks like a homeless dude! That man!" Gram said.

I shook my head.

"I didn't see any man."

"The man you let out of your car, Tressa! The man who tried to sneak into ol' horse face's house without being seen!" Gram said.

"Oh. *That* man!" I said.

"Yes. That man," Joe said.

"Is he Abby's lover?" Gram asked.

Eww.

"I have no idea," I said. "And I don't want to know."

True and truer.

"He's a scruffy character," Joe observed. "All that cloak-and-dagger and duck-and-cover drama."

"And apparently quite unnecessary and ultimately unsuccessful." It was my turn to observe.

"Well, naturally," Joe said with a lift of his chin.

"Wait! You hear that? I think she's leaving!"

Gram grabbed her binoculars and raced to the back door.

"So, chickie. How does Abigail's homely gnome figure into your latest story?" Joe asked. "And no bull."

"I'm working a hunch," I said.

"Oh, God," Joe said. "I know I may regret this, but details please."

I shook my head.

"Your turn. Have you made any headway on our man of mystery project?"

"I have a few ideas," he said.

"And?"

"I'll show you mine if you show me yours," he said.

Double eww!

"Damn. It's just ol' Lady Winegardner leaving again," Gram said. "Looks like she left Lover Boy at home."

Or, maybe Uncle Bo was hiding in the backseat.

"I'm outta here," I said. "I've got a blockbuster story to write."

"Don't forget about the reunion this Sunday, Tressa!" Gram said. "And don't come empty-handed this year!" she added.

"Oh, I won't," I said. "I'm bringing something extra special this year."

"What's that?" Gram asked.

"Deviled eggs," I said and hoofed it to the door before my gammy could catch me.

And, yeah. You guessed it. The *devil* made me do it.

Get it? Deviled eggs. Devil.

Oh, fuggetaboutit.

CHAPTER TEN

"Let me get this straight. You want me to get a positive ID of a lawn gnome from the Colbys."

I nodded. "And show it to the Keefers while you're at it. It might jog a memory loose."

"I don't know if it will jog any memories loose, but it'll likely set off a gag reflex or two," Shelby said, grimacing at the scanned image I'd printed for her. "Why exactly are we doing this again?"

Great question. Now how to respond? Why was I pursuing this *line of inquiry* as the Brit crime shows put it?

"Well, you see, that little beaut disappeared from Abigail Winegardner's yard, and she seems to be operating under the misapprehension that her new neighbor—my dear, sweet gammy—purloined the little fellow."

"Oh. And did she?"

I shook my head.

"I doubt it. Too much effort. Cedric weighs a ton."

"Cedric?"

I nodded. "That's right. Apparently Cedric is very valuable."

We both did one-man's-trash-another-man's-treasure shrugs.

"I'd like to locate the gnome. You know—prove Gram didn't take it, and restore peace and civility to that neighborhood." I scratched my head. "What's weird is that I could've sworn I saw a similar figurine next to Harve Dawson's mailbox last night," I told Shelby. "But this morning when I was there, there was no sign of it, and Harvey swore he didn't know anything about it."

"Had you been drinking at the time?" Shelby asked. "I've heard of people seeing pink elephants but never lawn gnomes that only Stephen King could love."

"I was perfectly sober, thank you very much. Oh, and while you're out and about, drop by Dawson's and find out what kind of damage he had and get some pictures."

"*Oo*kay. So while I'm out soliciting gnome sightings and leading people to question my sanity, what are you going to be doing?" Shelby asked.

The door to the alley slammed shut. Our fearless leader had returned. Make that spineless leader.

"I'm going to have a little story development meeting with Mr. Rodgers," I told her. "And trust me. It's not gonna be a beautiful day in his neighborhood."

Stan had poured himself a cup of coffee and planted his rear in the chair when I pounded on his door.

"Who are you, and what have you done with my boss?" I yelled.

Stan jumped in his seat, coffee dribbling over the sides of the cup and onto the front of his shirt.

"Christ, Turner! What's the idea? Can't you see I'm busy?" He shuffled papers around on his desk.

"Busy taking a scalpel to perfectly good reporting?" I countered. "You did a Dexter on my article, man!"

Stan frowned.

"Dexter? Who's Dexter?"

"You eviscerated my article, Stan! Ripped it to pieces. Sliced and diced it!"

"Huh?"

"You cut out all the good stuff!"

Stan sighed.

"This is about the vandalism item then?"

"Ding, ding, ding! Give the alien life form a one-way trip to Ceres."

"Now listen, Turner, I know you're not happy with the editorial changes I made—"

"Editorial changes? Try extraction with maniacal precision! Snip! Snip! Snip!" I said, making a rock-paper-scissors scissors with my fingers.

Stan's Adam's apple bobbed up and down.

"Listen Turner, law enforcement requested we hold off on releasing certain information—"

"Don't you mean 'facts,' Stan? And have you forgotten the last time you took the county's advice on a story?" I asked. "Let's just say the term *bum steer* comes to mind."

"I don't see what the big deal is, Turner. They wanted us to give them some time, and I figure folks are smart enough to come to their own conclusions on whether the same people were responsible and to act accordingly."

"That's a cop-out, Stan. In more ways than one," I pointed out. "And weren't you the one who told me, we don't get to decide what's news and what isn't. We report and then let folks decide if we've done right by them. Isn't that what you said, Stan? Isn't that the newsman's mantra?"

Stan put his coffee cup down with a thud.

"Geez, Turner. I didn't know you were listening," Stan said, a surprised look on his face.

"Well, I was not only listening, Stan, I was taking notes. And I don't recall ever writing down that the *Gazette* permits law enforcement to censor our stories?"

"Law enforcement agencies ask the media to withhold certain details of an ongoing investigation all the time, Turner," Stan pointed out.

"Yes. If they're tracking a killer or a terrorist or there's something more nefarious afoot," I said. I stopped. "Wait. Is there something more nefarious afoot? Is that why you didn't run the original article?"

"Maybe I just did the cops a solid, Turner."

I shook my head. Something wasn't right here.

"You heard about Harve Dawson's place getting hit last night, right?" I asked. "Shelby Lynn's on her way to get some pictures. I suspect we'll have additional proof that the same vandals are responsible. What then? Do we sit on it some more?"

Stan shook his head. He looked tired.

"No. When we've got the proof, we'll run with it."

I frowned. "Stan, is everything okay?" I asked.

"Sure, Turner. Just peachy. You pick up the city and county arrest reports yet?" he asked.

"Just getting to that," I said.

"Don't forget we've got the Pioneer Days celebration at the County Park. You and Shelby got the donkey ball deal and the Wild West shindigs covered?"

"We're on it, boss."

The Historical Village celebration and fundraiser sounded like fun. The first night featured a donkey softball game pitting the city of New Holland against Grandville. And the next night, a Wild West masquerade party in the Knox County Historical Village that included a concert, dance, and silent auction. I smiled. I'd get to dress up in my best cowgirl regalia, enjoy cold beer and mouthwatering country cuisine, and boot-scoot the night away to toe-tapping music—oh, and get a paycheck for doing it.

Food, beer, shopping, and compensation. What's not to love, pilgrim?

I turned to leave.

"Oh and Turner?"

"Yeah?"

"You're right. We report. Readers decide," he said. "Thanks for the reminder."

Ahh. I felt a pitty-patter in my chest.

"Now, get your fanny out of my office and get to work!"

I sighed.

These boots were made for...gettin' the heck out of Dodge.

* * *

I listened to the hum of the dryer as I peered over the material I had spread out on a card table in the lower level family room at my folks'. I'd decided if I was going to have a houseguest, I better tidy up my place a bit. Which started with—laundry. Sigh.

Next to the card table, I'd set up a dry-erase board. Using fun dry-erase marker colors, I'd constructed a timeline of recent vandalism incidents with dates, times, and locations. By backtracking through various jurisdictions, Shelby Lynn and I had discovered additional incidents of property damage linked to the same group of vandals.

I stared at the whiteboard trying to make my own connections.

"I see we've taken doodling to the next level," I heard. "Soon you'll be ready for Sudoku."

I turned. Taylor stood grinning behind me.

"What are you doing down here?" I asked.

"Apparently not my laundry," she said and set her hamper on the floor. "What are you working on?"

"Just trying to put some pieces together on the vandalism story," I said. "See the big picture."

Taylor dropped onto the sectional beside me. She stared at the whiteboard and then thumbed through the photographs, examining each of them before going to the next. She turned her attention back to the whiteboard.

"I thought I heard voices in here." My mother, dressed in business casual even though she worked from home (I'd be in shorts and a tee) entered the family room. She looked at the mess I'd made. "What do we have here?"

"Tressa's getting the big picture," Taylor said.

"I see." My mom stared at the whiteboard. "Hmm," she said.

"Hmm? Hmm, what exactly?" I said.

"I was just looking at your timeline."

"Yes?"

"These incidents began several weeks before school started."

"Okay. Yeah. So."

"That could suggest a group getting back together. Reconnecting. Reestablishing relationships that might have lapsed over summer. You know. A reunion of sorts."

I winced at the mention of a reunion.

"Go on."

"Or, maybe you have the formation of a new dynamic going on," she added.

"Dynamic?"

"I see what you mean," Taylor said.

I wished I did.

"New relationships forming. A kind of bonding going on. A group identity being forged," Taylor added.

"It's certainly possible," my mother said, hovering behind us as Taylor flipped through the photographs again.

"Look at the vandalism," Taylor said, pointing at the spray-painted images. "It's organized yet there's an adolescent component to it. An immaturity. Pictures, but no words. I think you're looking at a group of teens here."

I blinked, impressed.

"Anything else?" I asked, thinking Taylor's undergrad psychology studies were paying off.

"Well, consider the spray-painting." She picked up one photograph. "The frenzied rainbow colors. The tornadoes. With pink so prominent. It makes we wonder if we're dealing with a group of girls. You know. Teen girls."

Oh, man. She was good.

"We need to narrow that down a bit. Teen could mean anyone from thirteen to eighteen," I said, looking at the timeline again.

My mother took a seat beside me on the arm of the sectional and shook her head. "Not necessarily," she said. "Not with the times and locations of the incidents you've noted."

"What do you mean?" I asked our very own in-house numbers gal.

"It seems likely that the individuals who did this had to have access to a motor vehicle. At least one of them had to be old enough to drive. And that means—"

"High school girls," I finished, triumphant and bilious at the same time.

Holy *Mean Girls* and *The Faculty*.

It was *Back to the Future* all over again.

CHAPTER ELEVEN

I sat in my car in the high school parking lot, chewed a fingernail, and looked on as high school students clowned around outside enjoying the last moments of freedom before the second bell moved them indoors. Not all that many years before, I'd been one of those reluctant scholars putting off the inevitable for as long as she could.

School and I had not been what you call simpatico. If it hadn't been for sports, and parents who kept my head in the game academically speaking, I'd likely have settled for a GED and a dual-track career in retail and fast food.

Not that there is anything wrong with those careers, but it made me feel good to know that despite being voted most likely to join the circus in my high school yearbook, my folks had enough faith in my abilities and intellect to require more of me than I'd wanted to give at the time.

I'd figured I'd let Shelby Lynn check out the Grandville High angle. After all, she'd only been out of school a matter of months, and it was a safe bet she'd be on better terms with the faculty than yours truly. But Shelby Lynn, claiming a prior dental appointment in New Holland, took dibs on checking out New Holland High, leaving me to deal with good ol' GHS and Principal Vernon.

Even the name still had the ability to make my sphincters pucker.

I took a long drink from my super gulp pop, wishing I had something that included a bit more liquid courage and sighed.

School days, oh, those school days.

I got out of my car and walked to the entrance, gaining curious looks from those waiting for the bell to signal lunchtime was over.

A warm summer day, shorts and skimpy tops, jeans (some baggy), and T-shirts were the outfits of the day. I entered the school and directly into the commons area where lunch was served and students hung out between classes and after school. I winced, wondering why it seemed so much louder now than it had when I was a student loitering in the commons.

The place was packed, most of the tables and chairs occupied by chattering and laughing students. I stood for a second, taking it all in, and waited for a wave of nostalgia to engulf me.

I tapped my foot.

Nope. Nothing.

No nostalgia. No warm fuzzies. No channeling Mr. Chips.

Nada.

I observed the student body for a few more seconds when my gaze hit on a student who sat alone at a table. Short-cropped dark hair, broad shoulders, and thick neck, much like many of his fellow students, the high-schooler's attention was on the cell phone he was holding.

I watched him for a second longer, noticing for the first time the resemblance to his larger than life cousin, Manny DeMarco. Last year Manny's cousin, Mick, had been of some assistance in whipping votes for unlikely homecoming king and queen candidates who'd been nominated for the honors by a group of malicious pranksters. Shelby Lynn had been a target for the mean girls who thought it was a hoot to put the girl they'd dubbed "Sasquatch" up for homecoming queen. It backfired on the meanies when, due in large part to Mick's uh, er, persuasiveness, Shelby Lynn Sawyer aka Sasquatch and Tom Murphy aka Tom Thumb were crowned Homecoming King and Queen.

You gotta love it when the good guys stick it to the jerk wads.

I hurried over to Mick's table, tiptoeing up behind him.

"I'm looking for Captain Underdog," I whispered in his ear. "I was told he could hook me up with a mean girl repellant."

Mick turned, a surprised look on his face when he recognized me.

"I thought maybe yous was in the market for more gerrymandering," he said.

"Jerry who?" I responded.

He shook his head and motioned to the seat across from him. I sat.

"Long time, no see," Mick said. "Since you split with the Man, Mick don't see Blondie much."

I winced. Sometimes when you let your heart rule your head, you don't think about unintended consequences. Apparently Mick had bought into my performance as Manny's fictional significant other and was feeling let down by the bogus breakup.

"Sorry 'bout that, Mick. You know how it is. It's been, well, you know, awkward," I hedged. "So how've you been?"

He shrugged. "You know. Busy."

"You're not a senior this year, are you?"

"I wish. Junior."

"You look younger."

"Mick gets that a lot."

I grinned. He'd picked up that weird habit of his cousin Manny's of referring to himself in the third person. It was kind of endearing—in a strange and off-putting way.

"Whatcha doing here?" Mick asked. "Too soon to cover homecoming."

"That's true, but I am here on a story," I said. "Hey. Maybe you can help."

Mick frowned.

"Oh? How so?"

"You've heard about the vandalism going on in the area, right?"

Mick frowned again.

"Guess so. Why?"

"It appears those responsible are likely high school students. I know how things get around in a school, and I thought maybe you might have heard something."

He shook his head.

"Nope. Can't say I have." He leaned forward in his seat. "What makes you think students are involved?"

I parroted what my mum and Taylor had said regarding the timeline of the events and the psychology of the possible perpetrators as demonstrated by the evidence left at the scenes that pointed to juvenile involvement.

"That don't mean GHS students," Mick pointed out. "Could be from any area high school."

"True. We've got Shelby Lynn checking out New Holland High," I said. "Are you aware of any gang activity here at Grandville High?" I asked.

Mick shrugged. "There's always posers."

"What about the girls? Any groups of girls that might be described as having a gang mentality?"

Mick shifted in his seat.

"Blondie thinks a gang of girls is doing this?"

"Like I said, some elements of the criminal activity suggest girls could be involved."

"What elements?"

"The artwork. The colors used."

Playing gnome games.

"You said somethin' 'bout pictures," he said.

"Of the spray paint."

"You have 'em with you?"

"Yes."

"Can I see 'em?"

I hesitated.

"You want Mick here to keep his eyes and ears open," he said. "Mick needs to know what he's looking and listening for. See?"

I considered his request. I was asking for his help. The photographs would be in the next morning's paper for the world to see, so where was the harm in giving him a sneak peek?

I pulled out the photographs and slid them across the table.

He thumbed through them and frowned.

"And you get to girls' gang from these how?"

"Mainly because hot pink tornadoes and rainbow colors hardly scream badass gangbanger," I pointed out.

"Uh hum. Well, well. Tressa Turner, what a surprise!"

I didn't need to look up to know that the guy who loomed over me was my ghost of school days past. My jiggling knees beneath the table confirmed it.

"Oh, hello, Principal Vernon. It's good to see you again." I lied.

"You're not wearing a badge, Miss Turner," he said.

I frowned.

"Badge?"

"A visitor's badge. It's part of the security policy we've implemented. Visitors are required to report to the office to sign in and pick up a visitor's badge."

"Oops," I said.

The principal got that look on his face I get when I've eaten too many free ice cream confections from my Uncle Frank's Dairee Freeze.

"To what do we owe the honor of your presence at GHS?" he asked. "Picking up transcripts again? Or have you located the textbooks you neglected to turn in when you graduated—six years ago?"

I squirmed in my seat.

"I, um, well, you see—"

"Tressa here is doing me a solid, Principal Vernon," Mick spoke up.

"A solid?"

Mick nodded. "T's gonna be my show-and-tell."

"Your...show-and-tell?"

"For career days in Life Skills," Mick elaborated. "We're supposed to bring someone representing a career in to talk to the class."

The principal's face became the color of a walker from zombie TV.

"Oh. I see. Won't that be...fun?" Principal Vernon turned to me. "You will avail yourself of a visitor badge when you visit in the future, won't you, Tressa?"

I nodded.

"Visitor badge. Career Day. Got it!" I babbled.

He sighed and walked away.

"Gee, thanks for covering for me, Mick," I said. "I owe you."

"Dang right you do," Mick said. "You're gonna be my show-and-tell for Career Day."

I winced.

Nice.

Mick turned his attention back to the pictures on the table. His phone vibrated. He picked it up, checked it, and keyed in a text. Out of the corner of my eye, I noticed a short, dark-haired girl making a beeline for our table. She stopped suddenly, looked down at her phone, looked up at us, pivoted, did a one-eighty, and headed in the opposite direction.

I frowned.

"Is something wrong?" I asked.

Mick finished texting and set his phone down, and I began to gather up the pictures.

"No. Why do you ask?"

I shrugged. "Never mind. So, do you think you can help me out by keeping an ear to the ground and letting me know if you hear anything?" I asked.

Mick nodded. "Sure. *If* I hear anything."

"Thanks!" I got to my feet. "I'd better split before I'm given detention."

Loud, feminine "look at me" giggles near one of the doors to the gymnasium got my attention. I looked up. Kari's Brian stood in the doorway, and the girl with the booming laugh smiled up at him.

I frowned.

"Hey Mick. Who's that?" I said, pointing to the gym doors.

"Who?" he asked.

"The hyena talking to Mr. Davenport."

"Hyena?"

"The laughing chippie."

"Oh. That's Miss Banfield, the new Life Skills teacher and cheerleading coach," Mick said.

I watched the interaction, my eyes narrowing to slits when Miss Martina Banfield reached out and touched Brian on the arm.

"Thanks, Mick," I said. "Oh, and don't forget to let me know when your Life Skills Career Day is." I gave Miss Mentee my most formidable evil eye. "I wouldn't miss it for the world."

CHAPTER TWELVE

I left the high school and drove to the courthouse to pick up the filings from the clerk's office and the call logs from the sheriff's office. Both offices are located in the ancient, if historic, courthouse. The clerk's office is on the second floor. The sheriff's office is on the first floor, and the jail in the basement. There is a campaign underway to get the taxpayers to sign on to a new jail facility that will also house the sheriff's office and dispatch. Until then, the three- story, aging edifice will have to do.

I started at the second floor. That's also where my sister-in-law, Kimmie, works in the treasurer's office. Whenever I was in the courthouse, I generally stopped by to say "hey" and raid her candy jar. I took the stairs, feeling less winded when I reached the second floor than I had before my million-mile bike ride across the state. Too bad since I'd vowed never, ever to grace the seat of a bicycle again for as long as I lived.

I hurried to the counter where folks could register or renew their vehicle registrations, transfer titles, take driver's exams, or obtain or renew driver's licenses or identification cards with photos you hope to God you never have to pull out and actually show to someone.

I peered over the counter. Kimmie wasn't at her desk.

"Where's Kimmie?" I asked her boss.

"She didn't come in today," Ruth Kramer, Knox County Treasurer, told me.

"Is she sick?"

"I assume so," Ruth said and walked over to the counter.

Assume?

"Oh. Okay. Guess I'll see you then."

"Tressa? Do you have a second?" Ruth looked at the other office mates and motioned me over to the side.

"What's up?"

"That's what I'd like to know," Ruth said. "I probably shouldn't be asking, but is something going on with your sister-in-law?"

"Going on?"

Ruth nodded. "I'm concerned. Kimmie has always been so upbeat, so...perky and together. But lately—" She stopped.

"Yes?"

"Lately she's been snippy and weepy and distracted. If I didn't know better, I'd say she was expecting."

"Expecting what?"

"A baby, of course."

"Oh. Right."

"Well, is she or isn't she?"

I bit my lip.

"I really couldn't say," I said, and it was the truth.

I knew Kimmie was totally committed to becoming a mother, but my brother told her he wasn't ready. (I, of course, was on the record as a yay vote in the baby battle. Unfortunately, as my brother pointed out numerous times, I didn't get a vote.)

I also knew Kimmie was fast losing patience with my stubborn, hardheaded arse of a brother. Last fall Kimmie told me she'd considered withholding sex from my brother until he, as she put it, "gave up his obsession with guns and games and grew up." But I didn't think for a minute, Kimmie would play the accidental pregnancy card on Craig.

Still, if she was as miserable as her boss suggested she was, it didn't bode well for the marital relationship—or my transition from Tressa Jayne Turner, good time girl, to Tressa Jayne Turner, doting aunt.

Rats.

I hit the clerk's office and picked up the filings, then made my way downstairs to the sheriff's office.

"Please! You need to send someone right away to check it out! Something is going on out there! Something...not of this world!"

It was that last part that got my attention. I stared at the diminutive man at the counter—and understood.

It was Dusty Cadwallader—also sadly referred to as "Major Tom," "George Jetson," "E.T.," "Marvin the Martian," "end-of-the-world-as-we-know-it" prognosticator, frequent reporter of strange lights in the woods and UFOs in the sky, and the only other person in Grandville with less credibility with local authorities than yours truly.

"Listen, Mr. Cadwallader," the clearly frustrated female deputy behind the counter said. "I already told you. The sheriff is asking that you fill out this form before he sends a deputy out."

"I see what this is. They've got to you, haven't they?" Dusty said.

"They?"

Dusty pointed at the ceiling.

The deputy shook her head and looked over at me.

"You here for the patrol logs?" she asked, the sour-milk expression not leaving her face.

I nodded.

"Be right back." She shoved a clipboard at Dusty. "And you! Write!" she ordered.

"I'm here to report a possible invasion, and they want paperwork! Fine! For all the good it'll do," Cadwallader grabbed the clipboard and stomped to a table in the corner and sat down. "Nobody believes me," he said to me. "They all think I'm crazy. Well, I'm not. I know what I heard, and I know what I saw!"

"I'm sure you're right," I tried to calm the distraught man.

"Yeah, right. You're just like all the others. Saying the things you think I want to hear. Humoring me. Thinking I'll give up and go away. But I won't. I know what I saw. And I know what I heard. And it was terrifying! Absolutely terrifying! Figures in black, chanting deep in the woods. Building fires and frolicking about."

Frolicking?

"I thought you saw UFOs and strange lights in the sky," I said, tapping my toe and looking at my watch. Where was that deputy?

"Oh, yes. I've had a number of close encounters of the third kind," Dusty said. "But this?" He shook his head. "This is something different. The dark worshippers dance 'round him. I can see him in the firelight."

"Him?"

He nodded his head. "A frightening specter of a woods nymph."

"Nymph?"

He nodded. "You know. Like a leprechaun."

I blinked.

"Leprechaun? You have leprechauns in your woods?"

He shook his head. "Not leprechaun*s*. Leprechaun. A grotesque, hideous one."

"What did this, er, leprechaun, um, look like?" I found myself asking.

"Oh, he's horrible. Just horrible. He has big, pointed ears and a white, grizzly beard, and both of his hands are scrunched up in angry, little fists like this." He made tight fists. "And those eyes of his? They're dark and sinister, and he has this sadistic leer." Dusty shivered.

An image of Cedric popped into my head.

"How close did you get to this, uh, leprechaun?" I asked.

"Oh, I didn't dare get all that close. I used my night vision goggles," Dusty explained.

Ah. A "believer" after my own Snoop Dogg Gammy's heart.

I scratched my head.

"The way you describe this, uh, specter, makes him sound like well, like one of those lawn gnomes you see in people's yards."

Dusty yelled and jumped out of his chair with so much force the chair tipped over backwards.

"That's it!" he yelled. "He looks just like a lawn gnome! A lawn gnome from hell!"

I blinked. Now where had I heard that before?

"I've got proof." Dusty said, lowering his voice and moving closer to me.

"Proof?"

His eyes shifted to the door the deputy would be coming back through any second now. "I've seen their mark."

"Their...mark?"

He nodded. "They put their sign on trees so the others will know how to find them."

"The...others?"

"Recruits. Followers. Disciples."

"Oh. I see."

And I did.

No wonder the guy was known around town as Mr. Spacely.

"You don't believe me either, do you?" he said. "I can see it in your face."

Damn my "tell-all" mug.

"You think I'm looney tunes," he said, making circles with a finger near his temple. "Lunar loco, cuckoo-for-Cocoa-Puffs crazy, howling at the moon hallucinatin'—"

"Now I didn't say—"

"Oh, I know what folks say about me. It's okay. Why should you be any different?" He went back to the table—his shoulders slumped and head down—and righted the chair.

"I'm sorry," I said, inching my way to the door thinking I'd loiter around the courthouse rotunda until Dusty took off. Ooh. Poor choice of words there all things considered.

"*You're* sorry," Dusty said, dropping back into the chair. "It's all in your head, Mr.

Cadwallader. You're being paranoid, Mr. Cadwallader. You're delusional, Dusty. You imagined it, Dusty. The figures in black. The chanting. The evil ogre. The pink tornadoes. They're all in your head."

Oomph!

I plowed into the door.

I turned.

"What did you say?"

"Huh?"

"Pink tornadoes! Did you say pink tornadoes?"

"Yeah. So?"

"What exactly did you mean?"

"Why do you care?"

"Please. Humor me."

He shrugged. "Those were the signs."

I must've had a "huh?" look on my face because Dusty shook his head and went on.

"The signs I was talking about before. The signs on the trees."

I frowned. "Wait a minute. There are pink tornadoes on trees in your woods?"

He nodded.

"You're damned right there are! They started showing up at the same time as the evil dwarf."

I rushed over to the table, grabbed hold of Dusty Cadwallader's hand, yanked him out of his chair, and dragged him across the floor.

"What's all the racket?" the deputy returned from the back room. She put the paperwork I'd requested on the counter, her gaze resting on my hand on Dusty's wrist.

"Mr. Cadwallader?" she said. "Is everything okay?"

Dusty looked at me.

"Is it?" he asked.

I nodded.

"I'm ready to believe you," I said, borrowing heavily from the *Ghostbusters*' tagline.

"They call me George Jetson, you know," he warned.

"Oh? I heard Mr. Spacely." I held out my hand. "Meet Calamity Jayne."

"Nice to finally meet you. I've heard of you, too," Dusty said.

"Mr. Cadwallader? That report?" the deputy reminded.

Dusty looked at me and back at the peace officer.

"You can disregard, Deputy," Dusty said. "Calamity Jayne is now officially on the case."

The deputy sheriff looked like she'd suddenly bitten into a chicken nugget filled with gristle.

"I feel *so* much better," she said. "And I'm sure Sheriff Samuels will get all warm and fuzzy when he hears about Miss Turner's involvement in your little *Galaxy Quest*."

I winced.

"You might still want to file a report with the sheriff," I told Dusty.

He shrugged. "I'll email it," he said and headed to the door.

I started to follow him.

"Hey, don't forget!" The deputy called out.

I stopped. Right. The call logs!

I hurried to the desk and grabbed the paperwork.

"Thanks," I said.

"I wasn't talking about the paperwork, I was reminding you not to forget tinfoil hats," she said. "Better safe than sorry, right?"

Mortals, I thought and shook my head, tailing Dusty outside to the courthouse lawn.

I grabbed my phone to call Shelby Lynn. No way was I planning to go on a hobgoblin hunt with George Jetson without backup.

I got Shelby's voice mail.

I texted her.

No response.

I called again.

Voice mail.

Shoot.

"Is something wrong?" Dusty asked.

If you considered tiptoeing through the woods in search of a demon dwarf accompanied by a guy whose truck plate read *Signs* wrong, then yeah. Something was definitely wrong.

"I'm waiting for a call from my associate," I stalled, texting Shelby again. I looked up. A familiar familial figure had just left the bank and was presently crossing the street and heading in our direction. "This way, Dusty!" I said, charting a direct path to intercept my quarry. "Frankie!" I yelled. "Yoo-hoo! Frank-kee!"

My cousin looked up. I couldn't tell whether or not he was happy to see me. Frankie's the only child of my Uncle Frank and Aunt Reggie. Aunt Reggie is my mom's sister. Uncle Frank and Aunt Reggie own the Dairee Freeze sandwich shop where I've worked off and on since I was sixteen. Uncle Frank is hoping to someday retire and hand the business over to Frankie.

Frankie is not so gung-ho about inheriting the family biz. Last year Frankie hoped to qualify for the Department of Public Safety peace officer academy. Unfortunately, Frankie just didn't have the right stuff—athletically, that is. Undaunted, he is now studying criminology and hopes to qualify for a job as a criminal analyst.

Unbelievably, Frankie's fiancé, Dixie Daggett, aka Dixie the Destructor, also heir to a restaurant dynasty, Daggett's Cone Connection, passed the same battery of tests Frankie epically failed. She is currently waiting to see if she receives a formal offer from DPS as a peace officer candidate. I'm skeptical. It's hard to picture someone whose shape and stature bring to mind the song, "Roll Out the Barrel," outfitted in a Smokey Bear trooper uniform.

Afraid Frankie would somehow guess I was up to no good and avoid me if he could get away with it, I stuck my fingers in the sides of my mouth and let out a long, shrill whistle.

"Frankie! Frankie Barlowe! Over here!" I yelled and moved in for the kill.

Frankie gave me a nervous look when I jogged up. He looked even more anxious when he saw the guy on my heels.

"Oh. Uh, hey, Tressa. How's it going?" Frankie said, sending not-so-furtive looks at Dusty Cadwallader. "Everything...okay?"

I nodded. "Great! Just great!" I responded. "You know Dusty here, don't you, Frankie?" I said, motioning to my not-so-confidential informant. "He eats at the Freeze fairly often, right Dusty?"

He nodded.

"I am partial to the rocket sandwich and Frank's out-of-this-world chili cheese fries."

I grinned. "Good one, Dusty," I said, before it became apparent to me from his puzzled look that he wasn't making a space joke. "So, Frankie," I said, quickly switching gears. "You're still studying criminology and basic criminal investigation techniques, right?"

"You know that I am." The whites of Frankie's eyes nearly blinded me. "Why?"

"I thought perhaps you might appreciate some, uh, practical experience," I said. "You know. Field work."

"Oh, criminy. What kind of drama are you trying to rope me into this time?" Frankie asked.

"A demonic-dwarf-from-hell kind of drama," Dusty interjected. "But I'm merely speculating here."

"Tressa?" Frankie said.

I grimaced.

"What he said," I told him and went on to give Frankie just enough of a teaser mystery to hook him. "And just think of the field experience you'll gain, Frankie! The opportunity to apply the scientific process! To participate in a forensic discovery mission that could lead to a bona fide criminal investigation! Think of how great this real-life forensic foray could look on a résumé or as the basis of a college paper! But I'm not going to pressure you into helping me out, Frankie. I'm not that kind of person."

Frankie looked at Dusty and back at me.

"I'm gonna regret this, aren't I?"

Did *Men in Black* long for a casual Friday?

Roger Dodger!

CHAPTER THIRTEEN

We ate Dusty's dust (literally) as we followed him to his little piece of the good life. Dusty lived in a modest house on fifty-odd acres. The homestead had belonged to Dusty's grandparents who Dusty lived with all his life. Well, up until they passed away, that is. No one ever mentioned Dusty's parents. I had the idea that they hadn't been around much.

"I thought—" *Hack, hack,* "you were working—" *hack, hack,* "the vandalism story," Frankie said.

I looked over at him and frowned. He had a bright red kerchief tied around his nose and mouth.

"What are you supposed to be? The Masked Marauder? The Barlowe Bandito? Frankie the Kid?"

He coughed again. "It's the dust! Roll your window up! My eyes are stinging, and my throat is scratchy!"

Have I mentioned my cousin is a bit of a hypochondriac?

"My air isn't working," I yelled over the roar of the wind noise. "And I am working on the vandalism story. At least I think I am."

"What do demon dwarves have to do with property damage by vandals?" Frankie screamed back, and I gave him a brief overview of my investigation thus far—along with the mystery of the missing lawn gnome subplot.

Now he was doing the staring.

"Really? Seriously? That's it? That's all you've got? I'm risking an asthma attack for a report of possible pink tornadoes and disappearing demon dwarves by a guy who once called to report strange creatures on his property and it turned out a farmer's cows got out?"

I winced.

"I'm playing a hunch, Frankie," I yelled back.

He reached out and put a hand on the dash.

"Oh, God. Now I know I'm going to be sick. How much farther to Oz?"

"We're looking for a gnome, not a munchkin, Frankie," I said. "And Dusty's place is another mile or two."

"He's kind of off the beaten path, isn't he?" Frankie yelled, putting a hand up to wipe the grime from the inside of his window.

"The better to tempt extraterrestrials and gang types, my dear."

And, also fewer opportunities for prying eyes and exposure. It didn't hurt that the property owner had a reputation countywide as a Grandville's answer to "Houston, we have a problem."

"We're here," I said, and pulled into the gravel driveway Dusty's pickup truck disappeared into.

I pulled into the grass near a line of tall pines that served as a windbreak for the property.

Dusty parked his truck and got out and walked around to the tailgate of his vehicle. He pulled the gate down and took a seat. A few seconds later a squatty-body of a dog with legs so short its belly nearly dragged on the ground, ambled down the driveway. Dusty bent over and scooped it up and set it in the back of the truck.

"What the heck is that?" Frankie said.

"A dog. Dixie Daggett variety."

"It looks almost like a pot-bellied pig."

"I rest my case. And remember, you said it, not me." I turned to Frankie, who was checking his backpack. "Do you have everything?" I asked.

He nodded. "Digital camera. Phone camera. Evidence bags. Swabs. Miscellaneous tools of the trade. First aid kit. Allergy meds. Nose spray. Eye drops. Yeah. I guess I'm good."

I winced. Have hypochondria. Will travel.

We got out and headed up the driveway. I saw Dusty's eyes narrow when they came to rest on the skinny dude outfitted with the red kerchief around his face, dark glasses, and tan straw hat with red strings, yet Dusty never said a word. I guess being marginalized for your own, er, eccentricities makes you less likely to question those of others.

"Nice...dog," I commented.

"Name's Roswell. Good watchdog in his prime. Now he can barely get around, poor feller. Need to put him on a diet."

"It's awful quiet out here, Dusty," I said. "Very peaceful."

"And isolated," Frankie added.

Dusty nodded. "Noticed that, did you? My land butts up against other folks, but it's timber or farmland. Nearest house is a good three miles."

"Now that's a comforting thought," Frankie snarked.

Dusty failed to pick up on the sarcasm.

"It sure is. I enjoy the solitude. I've never been all that good with people."

"Oh, I'm sure that isn't true," I said. "I just think everyone has their own comfort level with others. It's what makes each of us...unique."

I looked over at Frankie. He'd pulled duct tape out of his backpack and was winding it around the hem of each pant's leg.

"Ticks," he said and handed me the roll of tape before I could ask what he was doing.

"I'm good," I said. "But thanks!"

"I'll take some of that," Dusty said, and I watched him tape his ankles. "This will save me from changing into my camouflage," he said. "You know. You really need to get a set of camos," he told Frankie. "They have drawstrings. Very convenient and effective."

Frankie nodded. "Sounds like something I ought to check into," he said, pulling out his phone, his thumbs going like gangbusters on the keypad.

"Uh, if we could, uh, continue the camo conversation later, I'd like to see the site," I said, itching to see if Dusty was right about the pink tornadoes.

The gnome sighting? The jury was still out on that one, too.

"It's quite a hike. You okay with that?" Dusty asked.

I nodded.

"We're good. Aren't we, Frankie?"

"Exactly how far of a hike?" Frankie asked.

Dusty shrugged. "Couple miles."

Two miles? Two frigging miles!

"'Course I suppose we could take the four-wheelers," Dusty said, scratching his head. "I've never seen any activity out there during the day so we should be okay on that score."

"You've got four-wheelers?" I asked.

He nodded.

"Hondas," he said and slid off the gate. He scooped Roswell up and put the butterball inside the ramshackle house. "Got me a FourTrax Rancher and a FourTrax Foreman."

"I don't know," Frankie said. "They might kick up dust and pollen and—"

"Sweet! We'll take the four-wheelers," I said, not about to let an opportunity to ride a four-wheeler pass me by. Not to mention that the idea of hoofing it through the timber in ninety-degree heat and humidity didn't exactly get my motor runnin'.

"I've only got the two so we'll have to double up on one of them." He gave Frankie an up and down look. "You ever drive a four-wheeler?" he asked.

Frankie shook his head.

"You?" he said to me.

"No, but I've driven tractors since I was ten," I said.

"Piece of cake then," he said. "You better double up with me," he told Frankie.

"Double...*up*?" Frankie squeaked.

I could visualize his Adam's apple bobbing furiously up and down beneath his kerchief.

Dusty nodded. "Good then. It's decided. They're in the garage."

I lifted my shoulders and gave Frankie a "what can I do?" look and hurried after Dusty, grinning from ear to ear when I saw the Hondas—one green and black, one camo, both with black racks on back.

"You can use Ceres there," Dusty pointed to the four-wheeler closest to me. "We'll use Eris."

I raised an eyebrow.

"Dwarf planets," Frankie explained.

"Well, technically, Eris is a plutoid, not a dwarf," Dusty corrected before giving me an abbreviated tutorial on operating a four-wheeler. "We'll take it slow and easy," he said, backing the ATVs out of the garage one-by-one. "Just ease up on the throttle if you get to going too fast. Brake's here. Like I said, we'll take it slow."

"Shouldn't we be wearing helmets?" Frankie asked, and I shot him a dark look. A flattop on Frankie was no big deal. With my hair, it was a *'do* don't.

"Oh. Sure. Here." Dusty handed me a forest green helmet and a camo one to Frankie.

"Gee. Thanks." I said and gave Frankie the stink eye before checking the helmet to figure out the front from the back before I set it on my head. (I'd committed a bike ride faux pas when I couldn't tell the difference.) I cinched the chin strap tight and straddled the four-wheeler, revving the motor and listening to the purr turn into a roar.

Would you look at me now? Tressa Turner, four-wheelin' phenom!

"Take it easy, Calamity Jayne," Dusty warned from his seat on the four-wheeler ahead of me. "It's got horsepower, but it's no old, gray mare."

I idled down and nodded.

"Sorry. It's just a really sweet ride. Right, Frankie?"

I smiled as Frankie attempted to mount in back of Dusty, who, despite his short stature, wasn't exactly average weight.

When he finally did manage to get on the ATV, Frankie's knees were almost up to his armpits. I took advantage of the opportunity to snap a couple of pictures on my phone. You never knew when you might require blackmail material.

"You ready?" Dusty called back, and I gave him a thumbs-up. "Just follow me. And don't get too close!"

I gave him a second thumbs-up.

"Let's get this wagon rollin'!" I yelled and erupted into the theme song from *Rawhide* about heading 'em up and movin' 'em out.

Just as Frankie turned to give me what I was sure was his trademark 'I knew it' look, the ATV he was on surged ahead.

He reached out and grabbed Dusty around the waist to avoid being pitched off. I grinned.

This moment alone was worth a case of helmet head.

For the first mile or so, we stuck to a well-established trail. As we continued, the timber became more dense and the trail less of a trail and more of an obstacle course.

The ATV ahead of me slowed and stopped. I followed suit.

"I think we've gone as far as we can," Dusty said. "We'll have to go in on foot from here."

"Thank God," I heard Frankie mutter.

I shut my Honda off, pulled the helmet off, and rubbed the top of my damp head and winced. It was gonna be a hot oil conditioning night for sure.

"That way," Dusty said and pointed to the thick woods ahead of us. "We go in about a quarter of a mile, and that's where we'll find the signs."

"Lead on," I said, getting another chuckle watching Frankie perform strange and terrifying contortions as he struggled to get off the vehicle. "I give you a three," I teased.

"What are you talking about?"

"Your ATV dismount."

"You think it's so amusing, you can ride double with Dusty on the way back...little Miss

Helmet Head."

I was about to counter with a suggestion that perhaps Frankie might want to duct-tape himself to the ATV on the return trip, when Dusty called out.

"This way, Calamity! Frank!"

"Frank? Would that be Frank James? And how nice that you're on a first name basis already."

"Would you give it a rest?" Frankie said and adjusted his makeshift mask.

"Here! Over here!" Dusty motioned to us.

We tramped over high grass, fallen logs, weeds, and vines. I swiped at a buzzing near my left ear.

"Are we there yet?" I asked, sweat trickling down the valley between the girls.

"Just about," Dusty answered. "We're just about there."

For the first time it occurred to me that I really didn't know all that much about Dusty Cadwallader. For all I knew, we could be walking into an ambush.

I shook my head remembering that the Knox County deputy had seen me leave the courthouse with Dusty. He'd hardly try anything nefarious knowing he was the last person I'd been seen with—and by an officer of the law at that.

"Shhh! Quiet now!" Dusty stopped and put a finger to his lips. "We go in silent from here just in case there's someone—or some*thing* about."

I nodded, by now breathing heavily.

"He said silent," Frankie said. "If anyone's around, they'll hear that huffing and puffing of yours a mile away. Would you like a kerchief to muffle it? I brought extras."

"I'm good," I said, trying to get a handle on my ragged respiration.

"Shhh, now. Quiet. Here we go," Dusty said and motioned for us to follow.

I obliged, keeping close on his heels, attempting to breathe through my nose rather than my mouth.

Dusty stopped. "What was that? I thought I heard a whistle."

I winced. Damned nose whistle.

"I didn't hear anything," I said.

We continued through the timber, thick and dense, for another hundred yards or so until we came to a small clearing.

"This is it," Dusty said, stopping to look and listen before crawling over a row of fallen logs and into a circle devoid of trees. I followed, making my way over the downed trees and bending down to avoid a low-hanging branch before straightening to peer around me.

"Ouch!"

"Frankie?" I whispered. "You okay?"

"Thorns," he said.

I winced. *Indiana Jones* Frankie wasn't.

"There! There they are." Dusty pointed to four trees that formed a circle around the clearing. "Signs!"

I followed his finger and caught my breath.

Holy chocolate-coated candies. They do exist!

I motioned to Frankie who also stared at the graffiti. We walked from tree to tree, observing the artwork. He pulled his kerchief down to reveal a puzzled frown.

"Interesting," he said.

I nodded. "Yet somehow...kitschy. So. Do your stuff, oh mighty geek," I instructed.

He nodded and pulled his backpack off and put it on the ground, kneeling down to remove his equipment.

Dusty moved to a circle near the center of the clearing.

"Here's where they danced," he said. "And that's where the leprechaun or whatever you want to call it was." He pointed to a small circle of stones.

I could see where the ground had been disturbed by foot traffic, and it did appear to form a circle around the stones.

"Did you burn something out here?" I asked Dusty, and he shook his head.

"No. Why?"

I crouched down by the stones. "Someone started a small fire here," I pointed out. I took a stick and stirred the ashes around, uncovering a tiny scrap of what appeared to be a paper product of some kind. I squinted down at it. The edges appeared to be singed.

"Look at this, Frankie. What do you make of it?"

A second later, Frankie's hot breath hit my neck like a blowtorch, and a long pair of tweezers held in a latex-covered hand swooped by my ear and picked up the itty-bitty sliver of white.

"Looks like it could be the corner of a photograph," Frankie said. "It's stiff like a photo, but I can't be sure."

"Why would someone bring a picture out here just to burn it?" Dusty asked.

"I guess for the same reason they paint pink tornadoes on trees," I said.

"And why is that?"

"I have no idea," I said. "Frankie?"

He pulled a small plastic baggie from his pocket, deposited the charred scrap, and secured the top.

"It sounds like some sort of ritual," he said.

I swallowed. "Ritual? You mean as in the dude down *there* type of ritual?" I pointed to the ground.

Frankie shrugged.

"Could be anything really. A Satanic cult, pagan idol worship, druid worship, Wicca, or witchcraft."

"Witchcraft? You think we have a coven here? In Grandville?" My mouth suddenly felt dry as the cinnamon sticky rolls my gammy made for the county fair the year she tried to bounce the queen of yeast, Abigail Winegardner, from her blue ribbon throne.

"I didn't say that. I'm just throwing possibilities out there."

"I still say it's not of this world," Dusty said. "It's extraterrestrial. That's what it is. An alien life form bent on infiltration and annihilation."

"I don't know." I stood and brushed off my khaki pants. "I'm not sure hot pink is E.T.'s color." I conducted a visual search of the area, extending the search area to include a wide sweep extending beyond the clearing, stopping when the sunlight reflected off an item sitting back in the brush.

I picked up an empty bottle of vodka and handed it to Frankie to bag.

"You're serious?" he said.

"Vodka is the alcohol of choice for minors, dude," I said. I made my way through the underbrush to the object. I stooped to get a better look.

"Faith 'n' Begorrah, I think me found me *Lucky Charms*!" I said in my best Irish lilt.

"What? What did you find?" Dusty asked.

"A pot of gold, Danny boy," I said, with my lilt. "A pot o' gold."

"It's Dusty, not Danny," Dusty said, totally spoiling the moment and pulling the rug out from under my Irish jig. "And what exactly do you mean by 'pot of gold'?"

I sighed. Someday someone will recognize and appreciate the piquancy of my personality. I'm sure of it.

"I found a can of spray paint," I said, thinking that without my Irish brogue that sounded about as momentous as announcing you'd discovered lint in your belly button or a long hair where it shouldn't be.

"You did?" Frankie asked.

"Hot pink spray paint if my eyes don't deceive me," I said. "It's me lucky day. If you would be so kind as to fetch me an evidence bag, my good lad."

Frankie sighed, but hurried over. He carefully lifted the silver container into a bag and sealed it.

"Do you know what this means?" I asked.

"Fingerprints, DNA, forensic evidence," Frankie said.

"Well. Sure. There is that, of course."

"What else?"

I grinned. "It means Sheriff Sitsalot is about to have his lunch handed to him by Frankie the Kid, Marvin the Martian, and Miz Calamity Jayne. And crow is on the menu!"

Vindication, baby. It's magically delicious!

CHAPTER FOURTEEN

We completed a more thorough search, and Frankie drew a diagram of the area before we collected our gear and headed back to Dusty's. I'd galloped to my ATV and taken off ahead of my team, giving Frankie no choice but to ride double with Dusty.

He'd sulked (and hacked) and complained about not having time to shower before work all the way back to town. I'd dropped him off at the Dairee Freeze for his afternoon shift before heading back to the newspaper, our evidence secured in sealed evidence bags with labels filled out and initialed by crime scene tech Barlowe.

I hurried into the newspaper office, bags in tow. Shelby Lynn was just coming out of Stan's office when I walked by.

"I got your text. Sorry. I was…indisposed. What did you want?"

I waved her off.

"Oh, nothing really. Just a tiny, insignificant thing like breaking this case wide open." I put my hand out. "Fist bump!"

She stared at my hand and shook her head.

"What planet do you live on?" she asked.

"Planet Pulitzer," I said.

She shook her head.

"Ah. Fifty shades of delusional, I see," she said.

"That's what you think!" I explained what had occurred since we'd parted ways that morning and what we'd found in the woods near Dusty Cadwallader's farm.

"It looks like Dusty Cadwallader was right about visitors in his woods. And if those 'signs' Dusty showed us are any indication, it looks like those visitors of his are responsible for the recent vandalism around the county. Plus, with the evidence we collected, we might even be able to finger the culprits," I added trying not to sound like I was tooting my own horn.

"You need help patting yourself on the back there?"

I winced.

Guess I'd tooted after all.

"So how did you fare?" I asked.

"You mean with the have-you-seen-this-gnome identifications?" Shelby asked. "I think you'll be pleased."

"Oh? Did the Colbys recognize Cedric?"

Shelby nodded.

"Both of them?"

She nodded again.

"And there's no doubt?"

"Pretty sure. When Mrs. Colby said no one would forget a face like that and Mr. Colby mentioned something about gremlins, I figured the identifications were valid."

"What about the Keefers? Did they recall seeing Cedric anywhere near their residence?"

Shelby Lynn shook her head.

"No. Not near *their* residence."

I lifted an eyebrow.

"I sense a *but*."

"But…they're pretty sure they saw it at H&F, Home & Farm Hardware. It was out by the clearance lawn ornaments, gazing balls, and wind chimes."

"When? When did they see it? Him?" I asked.

"That's where it gets interesting. They say they saw it early this morning. They were bringing in a load of late sweet corn to sell at their stand by the vet clinic and pulled through the drive-through next door to get some coffee and took a short cut through H&F to avoid that ridiculously long traffic light."

"Well then, let's go!"

I jumped to my feet.

"Better pull back on the reins, Calamity," Shelby said. "I already drove by H&F. Your little friend has flown the coop."

I sank back into my chair only to pop back out of it.

"You can stay in the saddle there, cowgirl. I already checked. There's no video. The store uses dummy cameras."

I sighed. "What about nearby businesses?"

Shelby shook her head. "Nothing useful, sorry to say."

"Great," I said. "What did you find out at Harve's place?" I asked. "Stan says he'll run the entire piece if we have definitive proof. Do we?"

Shelby handed me a stack of photographs.

"Does an Appaloosa quarter crap on the steps of City Hall during the July 4th parade?" Shelby asked.

Nice.

I bet Woodward and Bernstein didn't start out like this.

Five minutes later we presented our case. We left out any references to antique lawn gnome sightings and focused on the evidence we'd discovered in the woods adjacent to Dusty Cadwallader's acreage that was directly related to the vandalism.

"Have you shared this with anyone else?" Stan looked up at us over the tops of his half glasses.

I shook my head.

"Strictly in house—well, except for Mr. Cadwallader and my technician," I told Stan.

"Technician?"

"My cousin, Frankie. But he can be discreet."

Stan chewed his cigar.

"Right. So, what's your next move?" he asked.

I shuffled my feet, not sure if I wanted to share my plan with the boss man.

"Turner?"

"Well, I, uh, thought—"

"Now you know me, Turner. I'm not one to micromanage, but I know what I'd do if this was my story."

"What?"

He sat back in his chair.

"It's not my story, Turner. It's yours and Shelby Lynn's."

"And the article?"

"What say we run with the pink tornado connection but leave out the Cadwallader angle for now?"

"Sounds reasonable," I said.

"I'll run it tomorrow. Which means you better turn your findings over to law enforcement before then."

I looked at Shelby.

"We kind of thought we'd let you have the honor," I said.

He shook his head.

"Not a chance. To the victors, go the spoils."

I turned to Shelby.

"You have a better standing with that department. Why don't you—?"

"Forget it Blondie. I'm part-time. This is a job for a full-time employee."

"Then it's settled," Stan said. "Good work, ladies. Keep it up!"

Dismissed, we left the office.

"I guess I'd better prepare myself for a meeting with our illustrious interim sheriff," I said.

Shelby nodded.

"And I guess I'd better prepare myself for a stakeout," Shelby said.

"Stakeout?"

"Well, you were planning to stake out Dusty Cadwallader's timber tonight to see if the vandals return to the scene of the crime?"

"How did you know?"

She smiled.

"You pick up a thing or two," she said.

"Oh," I said, taken aback. "Then you can pick up the munchies for our little stakeout. And remember, an assortment of sweets and salties, please. And no pop. I'll have to whiz like a race horse."

Shelby made a face.

"Anything else?" she asked.

I paused.

"A roll of tinfoil."

She raised an eyebrow. "Tinfoil. Seriously?"

I nodded.

It never hurts to err on the side of caution.

Since I'd be away that evening, I decided I'd better stop by my own homestead and feed the critters. The boys greeted me with hopeful tail wags.

"Sorry guys, but we have to cut back on the human food," I said, kneeling to give both Butch and Sundance some lovin' before filling their bowls and making sure they had ample water.

They tailed me through the gate and into the barn lot that housed a modest four-stall barn and tack area. I checked the automatic waterer, scooping the spitty scum off the top, whistled for our tiny herd, and headed to the barn to scoop grain into the feed boxes. By the time I filled the third box, I could hear pounding hooves.

True to form, three regal heads appeared over the top of the hill out in the pasture. Moments later, the Queen of Hearts led her cohorts, Blackjack and Joker, into the lot. Like the well-trained royals they were, they transitioned from a trot to a walk and, one by one entered the barn and right into their assigned stalls.

Beauty, brains, and barn etiquette. What more could you ask for?

I gave each of the horses a pat and a howdy-do before leaving them to enjoy their grub in peace. Horses aren't like people. They don't consider dinnertime a social event like we do. Bugging a horse when they're trying to chow down is a sure fire way to get on their bad side.

I washed up in the house, gathered the items I'd need for that night's surveillance in case I didn't have an opportunity to stop by home before heading out to Dusty's, and headed next door to raid the refrigerator.

I was getting ready to open the slider to the dining room when I heard voices coming from the folks' garage. I circled around the side of the house and saw both overhead garage doors open. The hood on my dad's pickup was up.

"Hello! Anybody home?" I moved to the front of the truck and spotted my dad's leg sticking out from beneath the truck. A second later he rolled out on his creeper and looked up at me.

"Having fun?" I asked.

He smiled.

"Does it look like it?"

I shrugged. "Maybe for you. You talking to yourself again?" I asked and held a hand out to help him up.

He shook his head and wiped his face with a towel. "Police scanner," he said and pointed to a gadget on the workbench that looked like a large walkie-talkie.

"You can listen to all the police calls, city and county?"

He nodded. "When weather and location permits," he said. "What are you doing home in the middle of the day?"

"I could ask you the same thing, Mr. Telecommunications," I said. My dad has worked at the local phone company for well over a quarter of a century. He started as a lineman. He still prefers fieldwork to pencil pushing.

"I'm burning vacation before I lose it," he said. "Your turn."

"I'm hungry," I said.

He nodded. "I think there's some pulled pork and baked beans in the fridge."

"Thanks, Pop," I said and started for the door to the house. I stopped.

"Dad?"

"Yes?" If you couldn't tell, my pop is a man of few words.

"I could use some advice," I told him.

He leaned on the truck fender and wiped his hands with a rag.

"Shoot."

"Well, you see, there's this friend who has this husband who has this coworker who is supposed to be mentored by the husband, but the friend is concerned at the amount of time the husband is spending with the coworker, and a friend of the friend saw the friend's husband and the husband's coworker together, and this friend thinks her friend with the husband might be right to be concerned about her husband and the coworker. Should the friend who saw the husband and the coworker together tell the friend what she saw or keep her well-intentioned mouth shut?"

My father frowned and continued to clean his hands with the rag.

"Does this friend of the friend with the husband think that the husband is doing something inappropriate with the coworker?" he asked.

I thought about it for a second.

"The friend doesn't think any funny business is going on. And she doesn't think the husband is the kind to, well you know, cheat, but she doesn't want to take any chances where her friend's happiness is concerned."

"I see. But the friend is worried she'll cause more problems for the couple if she tells her friend about the husband and the coworker."

"That's it exactly. What should the friend do?"

My dad moved away from the truck and put an arm around my waist.

"I think the friend should follow her instincts. I don't think they'll let her down."

I rested my head on his shoulder, and he gave me a squeeze.

"Thanks, Pop. I'll let my friend know what you said. I know your advice means a lot to her."

"I hope your friend knows how lucky she is to have such a good friend looking out for her," my dad said.

I felt the sting of tears. My dad may be a man of few words, but oh, what words!

The police scanner crackled again, and my dad moved to turn it down.

"Hey, Dad. Do you suppose I could borrow your scanner sometime?" I asked. "You know. To keep track of what's going on for the paper?"

He thought for a moment before picking up the scanner and handing it to me.

"Here. You can have it."

"I can't take your scanner," I told him.

He smiled.

"It's okay. It's not mine."

"It isn't?"

He shook his head.

"No. It's your grandmother's. She forgot it when she moved out."

We looked at each other and nodded.

"Thanks, Pop."

"Oh, and Tressa," he added. "Use it in good health."

I grinned.

"I hear you, Pop. I hear you. Now, about that pork."

My cell phone vibrated. I pulled it out of my holster and read the text message.

"Looks like I'm gonna have to take a rain check on the grub, Dad," I said. "Duty calls."

He nodded.

"Just remember what I said, Tressa."

"About the friend or about the scanner?" I asked.

"Both," he said.

I sped back to town, excited by Kari's text.

Remembered where I saw your pink tornadoes! :) Meet me at the football field after school!

I pulled into the gravel lot next to the field, and my phone vibrated again.

In the bleachers near the concession stand. Hurry!

I frowned and texted her back.

???

Now, Tressa!

I looked up at the bleachers and spotted Kari with both hands in the air waving at me. I waved back and jogged up the bleacher steps, dropping onto the seat in front of her.

"Okay, bestie. I'm here. Let's have it."

"How could he? How could he?"

I blinked.

"What are you talking about? He who?"

"My husband, of course. Mr. Mentor. How could he do it?"

"How could he do what?" I asked.

"*Her*!" she said and pointed a shaky finger at the football field.

"Her?"

"Martina the Mentee! Over there." She pointed again. "The horse face with all the teeth and hair making over my husband like he was God's gift to the mentoring program. What does she think she's doing here?"

"Since she's the cheerleading coach, she's probably working with the cheerleading squad," I said.

Kari turned to me.

"How do you know she's the cheerleading coach?" Kari asked.

I bit the inside of my lip.

"You didn't mention it?"

"How could I? I didn't know it."

"Oh."

"So, how did *you* learn she was cheerleading coach?" Kari asked.

"I think someone might've mentioned it when I was here earlier today."

She frowned.

"Wait. You were here today? Why?"

I squirmed in my seat—an oh-so-familiar blast from my own high school past.

"I was working the vandalism story," I said. "Which is why I'm here now, remember?"

"Cheerleading coach, indeed," Kari fumed.

"Kari? The tornadoes?"

"I've got a cheer or two of my own I'd like to—"

"Kari? Your text? The graffiti? *My* story?"

"Oh, yeah. Right. Well, I was going through some of the student work from prior years that Mrs. Griffin kept as examples of work on various projects before I got the Language Arts position."

"And?"

"And I came across bookmarks one student made." Her eyes kept darting from me to the field over my shoulder.

"Go on! Go on!"

"And there they were." Her gaze returned to the field again. "I'm giving him two minutes. Count 'em. Two minutes to walk away."

"What was there, Kari? What was there?"

Kari gave me an annoyed look.

"What?"

"The bookmark!" I reminded her. "What was on the bookmark?"

"Oh. Yeah. The bookmark." Her gaze wandered again. "Sis, boom, back off, biatch," she muttered.

"Kari! Please! What was on the bookmark?"

Kari shook her head.

"Tornadoes, of course. Fat little hot pink tornadoes, just like in the pictures you showed me the other night at dinner."

I stared at her.

"Tornadoes! Fat, Dixie Daggett squatty body tornadoes? You're sure they were the same?" I asked.

She nodded, her attention once again on the action down below.

"Positive," she said.

"You wouldn't happen to know the name of the student who made that bookmark?" I asked.

Kari's focus finally shifted to me. "Oh, wouldn't I?" She held a folded piece of paper out. "You're going to owe me, you know."

I nodded and took the paper and opened it up.

"Jada Marie Garcia?" I read. The name meant nothing to me.

Kari shrugged. "I don't know her either, but that's not surprising since I've only been teaching here for two years. This was done four years ago, I think, so that would put the artist in tenth or eleventh grade now, if she's even a student here anymore."

Which would be easy enough to find out.

I got to my feet.

"Thanks, Kari. And you're right. I owe you one. If this pans out, I'll owe you an über big one. Oh, hey. Here comes your hubba-hubba-hubby."

"Lucky me," Kari said.

"Hey babe. Hey T," Brian said, running up the bleachers in a fraction of the time it had taken me.

"I see Miss Banfield gave you permission to be excused," Kari said. "Or does your hall pass only permit you to be absent five minutes?"

"This again?" Brian said, and I started to inch my way down the bleachers.

"How come you didn't tell me she was the cheerleading coach?" I heard Kari ask.

"What difference does it make? I'm not a friggin' cheerleader!"

"And I'm not an idiot!" Kari countered.

They were still going at it when I got to field level.

I walked past the cheerleaders on my way to the parking lot and recognized the dark-headed girl from the cafeteria. The one who'd planned to join Mick until she saw a certain blonde sharing his lunch break.

"We're tough! We're awesome, and we can't be stopped! We're number one, and you are not!"

I winced.

Give me an *L*. Give me an *A*. Give me an *M*. Give me an *E*. What's that spell? *Lame.*

I felt eyes on my back all the way to the parking lot. I turned. Mick had joined his little friend. He had his arm around her shoulder but her gaze was on me.

I shook my head. Jealousy. That little green monster.

I sighed. Did one ever really get used to being a blonde bombshell?

Okay. Okay. You can stop laughing now.

CHAPTER FIFTEEN

I called the sheriff's office to make arrangements to see Doug Samuels and pass along the information we'd found at Dusty's but was informed that the acting sheriff was out of town and wouldn't be back in the office until the next morning.

I shrugged. Oh, well. I tried.

I pointed my Plymouth in the direction of home when my cell phone started playing the theme from *The Golden Girls*. You guessed it. My gammy's ringtone.

"Hello, Mrs. Townsend," I said.

"Who?"

I shook my head. Gram still had trouble remembering that since her marriage to Joe, she was now a Townsend. Funny. I kind of did, too.

"Hello, Gram. What's up?"

"I just wanted to find out what time you were picking us up."

"Picking you up?" I frowned.

"For our double date. Me and Joe are double-dating with you and Rick tonight. Dinner and a movie. Remember?"

Oh, crap.

"Gee, Gram, things are so crazy at work, it totally slipped my mind."

"Good thing I called to remind you, isn't it? So where we goin'?"

I sighed. I'd have to push back our stakeout time. Fortunately, my gammy had an early bedtime.

"How about Mexican?" I suggested.

"No can do. Had me a bad reaction to Frank's belly burner the other night. "

"Chinese?"
"Got carry out for lunch yesterday."
"Burgers?"
"I can get that half-price at the Freeze."
I sighed.
"Why don't you pick?" I said.
"I'm feeling...porky," she said.
"What?"
"Baked beans, coleslaw, ribs. You know. Porky."
"Best's Bar-B-Que. Got it."
"Pick us up at five thirty. That'll give us an hour and a half to chow down before the movie."
"What's playing anyway?" I asked.
"Some 'you mess with my family, you die!' movie Joe wants to see."

Merely conjecture mind you, but I'm guessing Liam Neeson here, and I got noo problem with that.

"You makin' any progress on my case?" she asked.
"Case?"
"Abigail's homely hobbit," Gram said. "You find him yet?"
"Gnome, Gram. Gnome. And I'm working on it," I told her. Oh, boy was I ever working on it. "So I guess we'll pick you up at 5:30 then."
"I don't want to smell like Rover, so unless you borrow the Buick from Taylor, leave the drivin' to your boyfriend," she ordered.

It might've occurred to me to be insulted had all my attention been focused on one word.

Boyfriend.

Ranger Rick Townsend was Tressa Jayne Turner's *boyfriend.*

Tressa Jayne Turner was Rick Townsend's *girlfriend.*

I swallowed around the lump that had settled in my throat.

Boyfriend and girlfriend.

It still didn't seem...real. Maybe that's why I was having trouble believing it. You know. The old "too good to be true" warning that makes you think twice before buying that heckuva deal gadget off Craigslist and has you conducting a background check on the "amazing" guy you met on an online dating site before setting up a meet-'n'-greet.

Ever since I'd let Townsend shiver-me-timbers on the honeymoon cruise, I'd felt like I hadn't quite got my land legs back. You know. A bit shaky. A little cautious. A tad unsure. A lot nervous. Always before when I made a momentous decision I didn't think twice, didn't second guess, didn't look back. It was full steam ahead come what may.

So why was committing to a relationship with Rick Townsend so different? Why was I so tentative and tense? Why so uneasy and edgy? What had my gut feeling like I'd consumed way too many green bananas and yams?

"Ugh." I rubbed my stomach.

"Tressa? You still there? What's all that moanin'? You all right?"

Was I? Time would tell.

"I'm here, Gram. And I heard you on the transport requirements," I said.

"And don't be late," she said. "I don't want to have to shovel the food in. I'll be belching barbeque like a steam engine all during the picture."

"I'll be on time, Gram," I said, reminding myself to put Gammy next to Townsend in the theater. "See you tonight."

I hit end and thought about Best's Bar-b-cue coming back up on Gram all night and rubbed my stomach again. Maybe it wouldn't hurt to have some antacid tablets on hand. Just in case.

I pulled into a parking space near the pharmacy on the square and hurried in. I'd pick up a few items, run home and clean up, and arrive at my gammy's house before she finished applying the second coat of perma-freeze hair spray.

I found myself in the aisle with the feminine products, and my gaze slid down the shelves to the section with the boxes that contained the little squares of er, contraception protection. If I purchased this product to have on hand, that would mean something, wouldn't it? In terms of the C-word. As in commitment. I bit my lip. Should I or shouldn't I?

I'd just picked up a box when a familiar voice reached me in the back of the store.

"You mean my heart pills aren't in again? A person could die waiting for her heart meds and you'd have a hell of a lawsuit on your hands."

I winced.

Marguerite Dishman—more commonly known as Manny DeMarco's "Aunt Mo"—and my former faux aunt-to-be. I'd done a good job of avoiding Aunt Mo since I'd ended my make-believe betrothal to her nephew, Manny. Aunt Mo was like a mother to Manny. She'd raised him from a pup—one of the few items Manny shared with me about his personal life—and the reason I'd agreed to masquerade as Manny's fiancée when it appeared Aunt Mo was on her deathbed.

But Marguerite Dishman had surprised us all by defying the odds, making what seemed like a miraculous recovery. I'd agreed to hold off on breaking up with Manny until Aunt Mo had regained her strength sufficiently to handle the disappointment. In the meantime I wasn't prepared for the full-court press Aunt Mo put on me to make wedding plans, even showing up on Gram's wedding cruise to pin me down on wedding plans.

If I hadn't developed a case of amnesia on the cruise, I'd probably be taste-testing cakes and picking out invitations by now.

Since the "breakup" I'd somehow managed to avoid Aunt Mo, and I intended to postpone that magic moment for as long as I could get away with.

"I'm sorry, Mrs. Dishman, but we're waiting for a call back from your physician. He has to authorize the refill."

"Authorize? Is he gonna authorize a million dollar court settlement against you when Marguerite Dishman collapses on the floor because of stress? Is he?"

"I'm sorry, Mrs. Dishman. If you'll just be patient, we'll put in a call to your doctor right away. If you'd like to have a seat—"

"Mo would like her meds," she said. "Good thing Mo don't like to drive or she'd take her business down the road to Save Smart Grocery."

"We could always deliver your medications, Mrs. Dishman," I heard the pharmacist respond.

"What? And do all Mo's bitchin' over the phone rather than in person?" Mo said. "Not on your life. Mo's nothing if she ain't real."

Oh, Lord. Aunt Mo was on a roll.

I'd just pick up my items at Bargain City, I decided, moving from one aisle to the next at the back of the store. I made it to the aisle nearest the door and inched my way to the front door.

"Tressa Turner, you can run but you can't hide! Aunt Mo sees you trying to slither out of here, missy," I heard. "You get on over here pronto!"

I made a sick face as sour stomach acid crept upwards on its way into my esophagus.

Reckoning Day.

Resolved, I headed to the pharmacy area of the store. Aunt Mo sat in one of the chairs reserved for customers waiting for their prescriptions or bored husbands waiting for the wives who insisted they accompany them.

"Oh, hey, there, uh…you," I said, unsure whether I ought to be calling her Aunt Mo any

longer.

"*You*. Hey, *you*? That's what Mo gets? Hey, you?"

I hung my head.

"I wasn't sure what to call you," I said. "You know. Given the circumstances and all."

"Mo told you to call her Aunt Mo and Mo meant it. She don't take back what she says even though other people don't operate the same. 'Sides, Mo here figures Tressa Turner will eventually come to her senses and figure out what a big mistake she made dumping my nephew."

I frowned.

"You do understand that I didn't really dump Manny—that we weren't really engaged. Your nephew simply wanted to give his beloved aunt something she wanted so very badly for him before she died, and he enlisted my help doing that. It's really very touching," I said and, for good measure, threw in a sniffle and a fingertip at the corner of my eye and dropped into the chair beside her.

"Good thing Mo's sitting down because that immense pile of bull you're shoveling is enough to bowl Mo over," she said. "Let me tell you something, Miss Tressa. Your acting? It sucks. Mo knows when someone is putting one past her. You think Mo here didn't know you were shinin' her on with all that engagement bull?"

I blinked.

"Wait. You knew it was all an act? All the time?"

She lifted her eyebrows and did a *hello* move with her head.

I frowned.

"If you knew it was a..."

"Scam?"

"If you knew all along that it was a...benevolent act performed for your benefit, why did you—?"

"Pester? Bug? Stalk?"

"...actively encourage me to plan a wedding you knew was only fiction?" I asked.

"Love," Mo said.

"Love?"

"Mo loves her nephew, Manny, like a son. Mo wants to see Manny happy. Manny deserves to be happy. Tressa Turner was the first woman to make Manny happy since—" She stopped suddenly, and I leaned forward in my chair.

"Since?"

"Never mind about that. All Mo's sayin' is Tressa Turner made Manny happy and if Tressa Turner made him happy, Mo was gonna do whatever she could to see that he got his gal. It's high time my Manny Boy was happy, that's all Mo's sayin', so don't be going all *Inside Edition* on me, hear?"

Mo's bluster and fluster intrigued the heck out of me, like she realized she'd been about to say too much and had reined herself in at the last minute.

"So you planned to steamroll me," I said.

She got a twinkle in her eye.

"Mo saw Tressa in the rubbers aisle," she said. "If a certain ranger hadn't been in the picture, Aunt Mo's pretty sure it wouldn't have taken a steam roller to get a certain cowgirl to the altar," she said and did another, "take that, missy" head and shoulders move.

I bit my lip. Could Mo be right? If Rick Townsend wasn't a factor, was it possible I would have ended up with Manny DeMarco, after all?

I shook my head. I couldn't think about that now. It was a moot point. Ranger Rick was not only a factor, he was my boyfriend, I reminded myself.

"I talked to your other nephew earlier," I said.

"Oh? You talked to Mick? How come?"

"I'm working on a story, and I asked him to keep his ear to the ground for anything he might pick up at the high school. He seems to do well with the ladies," I said, thinking about the pretty cheerleader I'd seen with Mick.

Mo smiled. "Mick's got game," she agreed.

"Chip off the ol' block, right?" I said.

She looked at me. "What do you mean?"

"His cousin certainly has game," I said.

"Oh. Yes. Manny's got plenty of that."

"So, how well do you know Mick's girlfriend?" I asked, thinking the way the girl had reacted both times she saw me was weird.

"Jada? Don't know her real well. Mick's only been seein' her for a few months."

I stared at her.

"Jada? That's her name? Jada?"

"Yeah."

"Jada who?"

"Jada something or other. Mo can't remember her last name. Something Hispanic, I think. Starts with a *G*. But the girls? They come, and they go. Like Mo said, Mick's got that Dishman lady-killer charm."

I frowned.

"And this Jada is Mick's girlfriend?"

"Yeah. She's Mick's girlfriend. Why you all het up and in Mo's face 'bout Mick's love life?"

"I'm interested is all," I said. "That's the kind of person I am. I'm interested in people. It's just my nature."

Mo shook her head. "I see you're still tryin' for a raspberry award," she said.

I blinked. "Huh?"

"The Razzies! For the worst acting performance," she clarified. "Miss Tressa Jayne Turner be a shoo-in, she would."

I grimaced.

"So Mick's only been dating this Jada since school started?" I tried again.

"What you mean by 'this Jada'? Tressa Turner know something Aunt Mo should know?" she asked, giving me the kind of look a prosecutor gives a hostile witness.

"Oh, no. No, I'm just curious, that's all. I saw them together at school today. So, how's Manny?"

"How do you think? If Mo didn't need her heart meds, she'd give 'em to Manny for his broken heart."

I frowned. "Manny has a broken heart? He didn't seem all that shaken up when I saw him last."

"Manny hides his feelings well, missy. Don't Tressa know that?"

I supposed Tressa did.

"Mrs. Dishman! We have your prescription!"

"'Bout time," Aunt Mo said, and I helped her to feet. "Mo wouldn't be happy if she missed her court shows. You wouldn't mind givin' Aunt Mo a ride home, would you, Tressa?"

"No. Of course not. Be happy too," I said, trying not to sound like I was still auditioning for a raspberry.

"No need, Barbie," I heard behind me. "Manny's got it covered."

I turned. He did indeed have it covered. In fact, he obliterated everything around him. A big, rock-hard wall of black, Manny stood with his arms crossed staring down at me. Every time I see Manny, he seems larger than the last time I saw him. Sometimes I find myself staring at all those chiseled muscles in wonder and amazement and it takes me a while to rediscover the ability to speak.

"Oh, hey Manny. I ran into your aunt Mo, and we were kind of catching up," I said.

His gaze went past me.

"'S'at right?" he asked. "How'd that go?"

"I'm still standing, aren't I?" I responded.

"Tressa and Mo had what you call a meeting of the minds, didn't we, Tressa? Aunt Mo thinks we understand each other pretty well, don't we, girlfriend?"

Oh, I understood Aunt Mo all right. She'd do anything to make sure her nephews were happy and apparently she still thought this cowgirl might still be the best candidate for the job when it came to the nephew towering over me.

Gulp.

"Tressa saw Mick at school. She wants his help on a story."

Manny's brows met in the middle.

"Help?" Oh He of Few Words said.

"Not help really. Just, you know, 'hey, give me a heads up if you hear anything' talk."

"Hear anything?" Manny frowned down at me.

"That's right! You never did tell Mo here what story you wanted Mick's help with."

"Oh I just thought maybe Mick might hear something about some of the stuff going on."

"Stuff?"

"The spray-painting. Vandalism. Thefts."

Manny's frown deepened.

"Thefts?"

"Oh, just some miscellaneous, er, lawn knickknacks," I said, not about to introduce Abigail Winegardner's gnome into the discussion. "We figure given the nature of the incidents, we're looking at a group of teens."

"We?"

I winced.

"My associates. My fellow reporter at the *Gazette*, my mom, my sister, me. You know. My posse."

One of Manny's lowered brows did a Mr. Spock move.

"Posse," he grunted.

"Tressa Jayne asked all kinds of questions about Jada Marie, too. Says she's interested in people. Just her nature, she says."

"Oh?"

Manny's brow went south again, forming a unibrow scowl.

"Well, would you look at the time?" I said, sensing Manny's displeasure like my pooches pick up the scent of the hated Hermione, my gammy's cat, after I've visited Gram. "I've got to run. Places to go. People to see. I'm so glad we had this little chat, Mo," I said. "You take care now, y'hear? Bye, bye, bye!" I made a beeline for the door.

"Yo. Barbie."

I stopped and turned.

"Barbie gonna pay for those?" Manny asked and pointed at my hands. I followed his look, mortified when I discovered the box of condoms clutched in my hand.

I shook my head.

"No. I don't believe I will," I said, placing the box on the checkout counter. "I sense the moment has passed."

Head down, I turned to the exit, avoiding eye contact with anyone and everyone.

"Shame." I heard Manny's voice soft and low as I walked out the door. "A damned shame."

His amused chuckle taunted me all the way out the door.

Cheeky devil!

CHAPTER SIXTEEN

"You got an extra napkin, Joe?" my gammy asked, grabbing the napkin from her new hubby's lap and sticking it in the collar of her peach blouse. "The coleslaw isn't as good as it used to be. Not enough mayo and sour cream. But the ribs are good, aren't they, Tressa?"

I nodded, securing my own paper towel bib.

"Very tasty," I said, gnawing on my final rib before putting it on my plate and sitting back. I sighed.

"I didn't think you were ever gonna come up for air there, Blondie," Joe said.

"Do you have a problem with women who enjoy their food, Joe?" I asked, sending a pointed look at his mate before settling on him.

"Do you, Joe?" Gammy asked. "You got a problem with that?"

Joe shook his head so ferociously I wouldn't have been surprised if he'd require a cervical adjustment.

"No, not at all! Not at all!" Politicians should have such convincing denials. "It's refreshing to see a woman enjoy her food with such gusto and relish."

Gram blinked.

"I'm not eating relish, Joe," she said. "Ribs with relish! Ugh."

I grinned.

My gammy is nothing if not literal.

"Isn't this nice?" she went on. "Double-dating with the grandkids."

"That's right. You're doing the dating scene," Joe said. "How many dates does this make?"

"Two," Rick said. "We had dinner with Brian and Kari the other night."

"They're newlyweds, too, aren't they?" Joe said. "Interesting. Very interesting."

I looked at my step-grandpappy.

"What do you mean, 'interesting'?"

He shrugged.

"Just that you've chosen to go out with newly married couples rather than singletons," he pointed out.

"And?"

"And that suggests an openness to that blissful state."

"What state?" Gram said. "Missouri? Minnesota? Arizona?"

"The state of matrimony," Joe said.

"That's a bit of a stretch," I said. "Kari happens to be my best friend, and Brian is a friend of your grandson. Your new wife is my grandmother, and you're Townsend's granddad. Naturally we socialize. The fact that both couples happen to be newlyweds is purely coincidental."

"I understand from Frankie that you have plans with Dixie and him tomorrow evening—an engaged couple if I'm not mistaken. Coincidence or something more?" Joe said, fixing me with an evil step-granddaddy look.

"Where do you get this stuff?" I said and looked over at Townsend. "Right?" I nudged his elbow. "I mean, seriously!"

"What exactly do you mean?" Rick said, wiping his mouth with a napkin.

"There's no big design or conspiracy behind our dating practices, right?"

"Dating practices?"

"We're just picking random couples to hang with, right? No grand plan. No specific intent. No secret agenda. Right?"

"What the devil are you talking about?"

"Well, would you look at that? If it ain't our snooty neighbor. I didn't know they let loose women in here."

"Gram!" I scolded. "People will hear you!"

"With that country music twanging away? No way! Look! Look! She's got her mustache with her."

My gut clenched, screaming out for the antacid tablets I'd gotten too flustered to buy, and then I remembered I'd already filled Ranger Rick in on the "mustache's" masculine masquerade.

"Abigail Winegardner carries a mustache?" Ranger Rick said, his expression similar to mine when I'd had a few too many cold ones and picked up a Sudoku to solve.

"Probably. But I'm talkin' about her mystery man," Gram said. "The mystery man who looks like he should be pushing a shopping cart."

"Gram!"

"Look, here they come. Act natural. Don't let 'em know we're watching."

I shook my head. The only way anyone could possibly be unaware of my gammy's scrutiny was if we were invisible and they were hearing-impaired.

I heard Townsend's quick intake of breath when Abigail and the gentleman who'd planted the kiss on his lips passed us on their way to a booth by the window, and the gentleman gave him an audacious wink.

"Big mistake," Gram said.

"What is?" I asked.

"Sitting by a window. Makes Abigail's wrinkles stand out like freckles on a redhead."

"Who do you suppose she's with?" Joe said, scratching his chin. "Maybe I should go over and—"

"Don't even think about it, Snoop Dogg," I warned, and three pairs of eyeballs zeroed in on me.

"What? Why shouldn't I go over and say hello?" Joe said.

"Yeah. Why shouldn't he?" Gram asked.

"That's right," Townsend said. "Why shouldn't he?"

Ah. So Ranger Rick was up to his old tricks.

"Why? Why? I would think that would be obvious," I blustered, giving Townsend a dirty look, trying to come up with a plausible reason why Joe should resist the temptation to approach the couple.

"Well?" Joe said.

I looked at Rick for assistance. He shrugged.

"Sorry. I got nothing," he said.

I shook my head.

"The reason you can't go over there, Joe, is because, well, you see, uh, Abigail could get the wrong idea. That's it! Abigail could get the idea that you're jealous—you know—of her admirer and, well, we already know she's carried a secret torch for you. Who can forget those sticky buns of hers, right, Gram?"

"Tressa Jayne's right, Joe," Gram said. "No use fanning the flame. What we need is to put out that ol' bag's torch, not light her fire."

Whew. Crisis averted.

"We'll follow 'em," Gram went on.

"Follow them?"

"Keep an eye on 'em. Where they go. What they do." She turned to give the Abigail's table another looky-see. "And that feller she's with? I know I've seen him somewhere. It'll come to me."

My stomach soured even more, and I winced.

"Something wrong, Blondie?" Joe asked, his eagle eye not missing a thing.

"Too much barbecue," I said.

Too much drama was more like it.

We finished our meals. When I declined dessert, Townsend looked over at me.

"You sure you're okay?" he asked. "We could beg off the movie and spend a nice, quiet evening at home, just the two of us. We could start a fire in the fire pit out back, open a couple of cold ones, toast some marshmallows, and you could tell me more about Abigail's mystery date who likes to kiss other men on the lips."

I blinked.

"Wait. You're inviting me to your place?" I asked. I'd only been to Townsend's place once. Well, by invitation that is. I'd been on his property a number of times since he purchased the fixer-upper in the middle of God's country. Why, you ask? I'd rather not get into it at this time, but the words *pranking, payback,* and *window peeking* may or may not apply.

I'll leave it to your imagination.

"Why not?" Rick asked.

"You've just never asked before," I said.

He shook his head.

"I asked. You just blew me off."

Probably because I never thought he was serious before.

"I suppose—"

"They're leavin'! Hurry up! We gotta go!" Gram said.

"Gram?"

"Come on! Abigail and her lover are leavin'! Shake a leg or we'll lose 'em!"

I gave Townsend a "they won't be around forever, you know" look, and he smiled and shook his head.

"You go on out to the truck, and I'll pay the tab and meet you out there."

I nodded and herded the seniors to the big red truck. I crawled into the back of the crew cab while Joe helped Gram into the front and then joined me.

"Here they come!" Gram said, watching the other seniors leave the restaurant and walk to a Subaru Outback.

"They're getting in Abigail's car!" Gram said. "Where's that boyfriend of yours? We're gonna lose 'em!"

"He's coming, Gram. He's coming."

Townsend opened the door and slid behind the wheel.

"What's the plan?" he asked, the look on his face saying he didn't really want to know the answer.

"We're waiting for Abigail and lover boy to leave. Then we follow 'em," Gram said.

"And why are we doing this again?" Rick asked.

"'Cause we can, of course," Gram said. "There they go. Step on it!"

Townsend sighed but complied.

"Don't lose 'em now!" Gram said.

"I got it, Hannah," he said. "I've followed more than my share of poachers, you know."

"Well, I don't figure on letting Abigail poach anything of mine," she said. "There they go! Well, whatdya know? They're seein' a flick, too!" Gram announced the obvious when the Subaru pulled into the Starbright Theater and parked. "You can let us out here and park," she told Townsend. "We'll go in and get our tickets and see where they sit."

"*Oo*kay," Townsend said, and he met my eyes in the rearview mirror. "I guess I'll see you inside."

"You better," I mouthed, and he smiled.

Once inside the theater, Joe purchased our tickets (I was a wee bit low on funds, I told him) while Gram kept an eye on her targets, and I stewed over what would happen if or when she discovered Abigail's mustached man was none other than her sister, Eunice.

"They're sitting down near the front. Huh. And I thought old bats could see in the dark."

"Gram! That's not nice."

"You takin' her side again?"

Joe joined us.

"They're down front," Gram said. "We'll sit up in the balcony. That way we can keep an eye on 'em and see if they fool around."

Oh, God. I was gonna hurl.

I texted Townsend our location.

"Welcome to the peanut gallery," I told him when he joined us.

"What? No popcorn?" was Joe's greeting.

"Welcome back," I said, when Rick returned with two jumbo buttered popcorns and sodas.

"What? No M&M'S?" I teased when Townsend took a seat beside me.

"Nice," he said. "Anything new on the mustache front?"

"Twenty hundred hours and all is well!" I droned.

Rick chuckled. "That's what you think. I'm still traumatized by that kiss. I think I'm ready for a good revenge movie."

I nodded. I could certainly do with a little payback right about now.

The previews ended, and the feature began.

Soft music filled the theater. I frowned. This was a novel opening to your traditional die-dirtbag-thug-kidnapper-criminal movie. Within the first two minutes, it was apparent this wasn't your traditional die-dirtbag-thug-kidnapper-criminal movie at all.

It was a die-you-poor-terminally-ill-young-man story.

"What's the big idea?" Joe asked. "What kind of movie is this?"

"It's based on a book about a young writer who has this serious illness and loves this girl who promises to finish his book when he dies," I said.

The man in front of us suddenly turned around.

"Gee, thanks," he said.

I frowned. "For what?"

"For the spoiler. I really was looking forward to finding out for myself, but you saved me all that time."

"Sorry," I said.

"Wait a minute," Joe said. "You're telling me that someone dies in this movie, but it's not due to head trauma or a gunshot wound or inflicted by knife, crow bar, or pitch fork? Not interested." He started to stand, but Gram grabbed hold of his arm.

"We can't leave until Abigail does!" she insisted.

I was about to concur with Joe and suggest we exchange our tickets when the phone in my pocket began to vibrate. I pulled it out.

"Hello?" I whispered into the phone, garnering nasty looks from moviegoers. "Yes. Yes. This is Tressa Turner. Dusty? Dusty is that you? You what? When? Where? Yes. Yes. I'll be right there."

I pocketed my phone.

"I'm not going to like what's coming next, am I?" Townsend whispered.

"Duty calls," I said.

"Can't it wait?"

"Can poachers wait?"

"Shhh! Quiet!"

"Maybe we should all leave," Townsend suggested.

"Shhh!" Gram said. "He's about to get his diagnosis."

"You go ahead and finish the movie," I said. "I'll call you later."

"Aren't you forgetting something, T?" Townsend asked.

"What?"

"Transportation. We drove my truck."

Crap. He was right.

"I'll call Shelby Lynn to pick me up."

"Tressa? This is getting to be a habit. A bad one," Townsend said.

"I know. I'm sorry. It's this story I'm working on. I got a tip. I'll stay if you want me to."

Even in the dark theater, I could tell Townsend was considering it. The seconds ticked off.

He finally sighed.

"Go on. Get out of here. I'll see the old folks home."

"What old folks? You talkin' about Abigail and her boy toy? You can't take them home. They'll know we've been tailing 'em," Gram said.

"Thanks, Mr. Ranger, Sir," I said. "I owe you."

"You have no idea. And one of these days, T, I'm calling in your marker."

I felt a shiver that had nothing to do with debt collecting or interest compounding and maneuvered past a line of legs, out into the aisle and out of the theater.

A minute later I had Shelby on the line. I told her about the call from Dusty.

"No can do," she said. "I'm on the other side of the county. Besides, I'm kind of jammed up right now."

I shook my head. "Jammed up?"

"I'm in the middle of something," she translated. "Can't you hitch a ride? I can meet you there."

I mentally ticked off the possible candidates in my head and sighed.

"Yeah. I can probably get a lift," I said.

I hit end and punched a couple numbers.

"Hello? Taylor? Are you familiar with *A Hitchhiker's Guide to the Galaxy*?"

CHAPTER SEVENTEEN

"This is great. Just great."

I looked over at my disgruntled passenger.

"What's the problem, sis?"

"You got me out here under false pretenses," Taylor accused.

I looked over at her.

"What do you mean, 'false pretenses'?"

"'Come pick me up, Taylor,' you said. 'Bring my car, Taylor, so you won't waste your gas,' you said."

"Yeah? So what?"

"At no time did you mention that you planned to drag me along on a trip to the outer limits—that's so what."

"Don't be a Grumble Gus, Taylor," I told her. "If my theory is right about the high school hooligans, this could be very instructive for a psych major."

Taylor crossed her arms. "Whose theory?"

"Okay, okay, *our* theory. And I didn't have time to take you all the way back home. But I did offer to give you my ticket to *Finishing Touches*, the tearful and poignant story of a dying young writer whose lover promises to finish his book until she realizes he's written it about another lover," I said.

"Hmm, let's see. I can crawl over irritated moviegoers to watch half a movie or accompany you to the boonies to investigate an eccentric's reports of lights in the woods. Wow. Stellar choices."

"Don't you mean *interstellar*?" I said with a snort. "I guess I could've called P.D. Dawkins to see if he was free." I looked over to gauge Taylor's reaction to my suggestion.

Patrick Dawkins is an officer with the State Patrol. I'd struck up a friendship with Patrick last summer at the state fair. I'd originally been drawn to Patrick because he liked me for who I was. That's extremely appealing to someone set in her ways—and refreshing for an individual who felt she didn't always come up to scratch.

Recently I'd discovered that Taylor wasn't exactly indifferent to the myriad charms of the handsome patrolman, and I'd been needling her ever since—in a big sisterly, all in good fun, sort of way.

"He's working tonight," Taylor said.

I blinked.

"How do you know?" I asked.

"From this." She held up the scanner my dad had given me.

"You were monitoring state radio frequencies?"

"Your radio doesn't work."

"Oh, right."

Taylor sniffed.

"I should've brought the Buick," she said. "When's the last time you cleaned your car out?"

"Everyone keeps telling me it's ready for the crusher so I figure why clean?" As if on cue, the Reliant coughed and sputtered.

"You could have a point," Taylor said.

I pulled into Dusty's driveway. Shelby Lynn was waiting with Dusty Cadwallader, dwarfing him by half a foot, easy.

"What took you so long?" she said. "Never mind. I see you brought the Plymouth."

I winced.

"So what's going on, Dusty. You mentioned something about weird noises and strange lights in the woods."

He nodded and took out a small writing pad.

"At 2030 hours I was out on the four-wheeler and saw lights in the distance."

"Over by the clearing?" I asked.

"Not initially. From the adjacent property."

"A farmer out in the field working, maybe?" Shelby Lynn said.

"At night and in August? There's not really that much to do in the field right now. Besides, most of my neighbor's property is timber like mine."

"And the noises?"

"Those came from the clearing."

"What did you hear?"

"Voices mainly," Dusty said. "I got off my four-wheeler and went in on foot, but I didn't want to get too close since there were three of them and only one of me."

"Them?"

"Three figures. They were dressed in black and had these hoods on. I really wanted to get closer, but I was afraid he'd hear me."

I looked at Dusty. "Wait a minute. He? One of them was a guy?"

"Definitely male. But what species?" He shrugged. "Who knows? It definitely had a deep, male-type voice."

"I thought you said we were looking at a group of girls," Shelby Lynn said.

I frowned. "I thought we were. Are they still back there, do you think, Dusty?" I asked.

He frowned. "Doubtful. It's been quiet since shortly after I called you. And I haven't seen any more lights."

"You said you saw them at eight thirty?"

He nodded. "I rarely get a cell signal out here, so I had to get in the truck and drive several miles to get out," Dusty said.

"So, what do you think? What's the plan?" Taylor asked.

"We go in," I said.

"Go in? The woods, you mean?"

I nodded.

"We check out the clearing, see if we find anything. And, if not, we wait."

"Wait? Wait for what?" Shelby asked.

"For *the return*, of course."

"Someone's still stuck in a Team Trekkie Time Warp, I see," Shelby Lynn remarked, a reference to my TribRide return experience that turned out to be one spaced-out space odyssey.

"I'm waiting for a plan," Taylor said. "Or maybe I better wait in the car. Your car, Shelby Lynn."

"Dusty?" I turned to the guy with the all-terrain transportation. "Can we risk using the four-wheelers?"

"Four-wheelers?" I wasn't sure who said it first, Taylor or Shelby.

"Dusty has two ATVs he kindly permitted us to use earlier. What do you think, Dusty? It's getting dark. We'll have to use headlights, and they might hear us coming. Is it too risky?"

He rubbed his chin. "I figure like last time we're safe enough for the first couple miles," he said. "We'll need flashlights to see anyway. I assume you gals didn't bring any night vision glasses."

"Couple of miles? Night vision glasses. What the hell?" Shelby said.

"The plan?" Taylor reminded.

"We go in on the ATVs as far as we can, observe the clearing in question and if it's clear we go in and see if there are any clues regarding the identity of the trespassers. Once we evaluate anything of evidentiary value, we stake out the clearing in case our hooded hoodlums return and catch 'em in the act."

"Uh. What exactly do we do if we, as you say, catch them in the act?" Taylor asked.

"We call 9-1-1 of course," I said. "The cops come. They clap handcuffs on the perps. We've solved a mini crime spree, and it's Miller Time!"

"You do know it's not going to work out that way, right?" Shelby Lynn said. "Not in a galaxy far, far away and not here in good ol' Knox County. You know that, right?"

"Shelby's right. What about the cell phone issue? If we need to call 9-1-1, one of us has to hoof it down the road."

"Good thing you're in great shape, Taylor," I said. "Besides. We're dealing with teenagers remember? What can happen?" I shrugged.

We gathered our items together.

"What about our munchies?" I asked Shelby.

"No time," she said.

I shrugged. I'd learned from past experience to keep a backpack with various tools of the trade. I had flashlights and batteries, a small first aid kit, bottled water, and some energy bars. I leaned into my car and saw the police scanner on the front seat. I grabbed it along with a set of ear buds. A good journalist always kept their finger on the pulse of the law enforcement community at all times.

By the time I got to the garage, Dusty had the four-wheelers ready to go.

"How are we going to do this exactly?" Taylor asked.

I loped to the nearest ATV and mounted.

"I've got operating experience," I pointed out.

Seeing the lay of the land, Shelby Lynn muscled her way past Taylor (not too difficult given her size and stature) and vaulted onto the seat behind me.

"Hey! Watch the shocks and suspension!" Dusty said. "Looks like you're with me, little lady," he told Taylor. "If I get goin' too fast, don't be afraid to reach out and hold on tight to my love handles."

The dark glare Taylor sent me before she stalked to Dusty's ATV warned of severe reprisals.

I sighed. Someday Taylor and I would have a close, trusting, loving relationship. I thought about the Blackford sisters, Hannah and Eunice.

Maybe I'd settle for mutually respectful and moderately understanding.

Two minutes into the ride, I found myself wishing Taylor was riding with me instead of Shelby Lynn. Every bump we hit, every time we came a skosh too close to the ATV ahead of us, Shelby put her mitt-sized hands around my waist and squeezed.

"Do you think you can manage to avoid at least one bump?" she grumbled in my ear. "This seat isn't big enough for you to channel Evel Knievel on an ATV."

"I'm sorry," I said. "I can't see that well. Besides, it's not every day I get the chance to four-wheel."

"I thought you said you drove one earlier."

"So I'm a bit of a daredevil. Who knew?"

"Most anyone who knows you, that's who."

"Exactly what do you expect to find out here anyway? *Teenagers from Outer Space?* Or a bunch of holes in the ground?" Shelby asked.

Funny girl.

"This is where the gang meets. We know that from the pink whirligigs. Maybe we'll get lucky—maybe we won't."

"And maybe we'll run into a tree, be thrown off, and break our necks."

"No worries, Shelby. With your center mass, you probably wouldn't get thrown far at all."

"Just be quiet and focus on your driving, would you?"

We retraced our earlier route, killing the lights when we got to the place we'd parked the first time around.

"What do we do now?" Shelby asked.

"You get off so I can," I told her.

I waited.

"So get off," I said.

"I can't."

"What do you mean, you can't?"

"It's my knees. They don't work so well. You'll have to get off first, so I can slide forward and roll off the side."

"How am I supposed to get off with you taking up all the room?"

"I don't know. Scoot forward over the front."

I attempted the maneuver but got trapped when my belt got hung up on a handlebar.

"Do you mind? Your butt is in my face."

"Sorry. I'm stuck."

"Stuck?"

"My belt buckle got hung up on the handlebar."

"You and your big, honking buckles," Shelby complained.

"Why don't you scoot backwards off the rear?" I suggested.

"I told you. My knees are wonky. They stiffen up sometimes."

"Stiffen up? Why didn't you tell me? I'd have brought along my oil can," I hissed.

"Like it's my fault I outgrew my joints. What about those thighs of yours?"

I stopped trying to extricate myself from the handlebars.

"What about my thighs?"

"They're taking up more than their share of room."

"Well, excuse me. You ride horses, you strengthen certain muscle groups."

"You should be able to open jars with those thighs."

"Why don't you brace yourself against me and push yourself up and back?"

"What do you propose I brace myself against? The only thing I can see is wall-to-wall Tressa Turner ass. And believe me, from where I sit, it's not a pretty sight."

"Is something wrong?" Dusty's whisper reached us about the same time as his flashlight beam did. "Oh, my God."

"What on earth?" Taylor said.

"We're just having a bit of difficulty dismounting," I explained. "We could use a hand over here. Taylor, a little assistance."

"What do you suggest?" she asked.

"A crane?"

"Oh, you're just a regular laugh riot," Shelby said. "Would you hurry up? There's a little pain involved."

Dusty hovered beyond the outer circle of light.

"I've never come across this problem before," he said.

"It's my belt. It's stuck on the handlebars."

"Did you try to take it off?" Taylor asked.

I blinked.

"Take it off?"

"Your belt. Did you try to unfasten it and slide it off?"

"Good grief," Shelby said.

I pushed my belt through the buckle, wiggled the buckle back and forth until the post slipped out.

"Pull it!" I told Taylor. "Pull on the end of the belt!"

She grabbed the buckle end of the belt and gave it a tug. The belt raced through the loops,

Taylor fell to the ground. I shot backwards, plowing into Shelby Lynn, sending her somersaulting over the back of the ATV. I landed on top of her, straddling her bass-ackwards.

"Great. Your butt's in my face again," she said.

"Look on the bright side," I said.

"Bright side?"

"We're off the ATV," I said.

CHAPTER EIGHTEEN

Once we managed to get untangled—and Dusty had recovered sufficiently from the shock of the spectacle on display before him to perform his duties as guide—we made our way into the woods.

"Lions, tigers, and bears. Oh, my!" I whispered.

"Grow up!" Shelby said.

"Shh! Quiet!" Dusty scolded. "Listen!"

We stopped.

"I forget. What are we supposed to be listening for again?" Taylor asked.

"The Mother Ship is my bet," Shelby said.

"So what are we doing again?" Taylor asked.

"We're going to stake out the clearing initially to see if anyone comes back."

"This ought to be fun," Shelby said. "Anyone bring a blanket?"

We spaced ourselves at various intervals around the clearing. I placed my backpack on the ground and sat on it, gasping when I sat down on something rock hard.

I pulled the bag aside. The police scanner. I'd forgotten all about it.

I pulled out a bottle of water and took a long drink, grabbing an energy bar, opening it, and taking a big bite.

I listened to the sounds of the nightlife and stared up at the night sky through the trees. A clear night, the air was still warm from the heat of the day. I slapped at a mosquito buzzing at my left ear and took another long drink of water, slapping at yet another skeeter.

Maybe this wasn't such a good idea, after all.

I finished the bar, drained the bottle of water, and checked my watch.

I felt my eyes start to become heavy. I yawned.

"I'm thirsty. I don't suppose anyone else had a chance to bring food or water," Shelby said.

"Sorry," I whispered, feeling ashamed that I hadn't offered to share. Still, I could hardly offer to share since I didn't have enough for everyone, right?

Half an hour later I was wishing I'd shared the bounty. I winced. My bladder felt like it was ready to explode.

My legs started doing the "gotta go, gotta go, gotta go, go, go" dance.

I can hold it. I can hold it.

I swayed back and forth, back and forth.

I can hold it.

I danced some more.

Not gonna happen.

Gotta go, gotta go, gotta go, go, go!

I shifted back and forth. Back and forth.

Gonna go, gonna go, gonna go, go, go.

I checked the area for a tree that provided ample…er, coverage finding one off to my left that served my purpose. I weighed the chances of discovery with the chances that I'd whiz myself and ultimately decided that the odds were one hundred percent that I'd embarrass myself if I didn't relieve myself. Bladder burning, I crept behind a tree doing a jig while I unzipped my pants, struggling to get my britches pulled down in time.

"Ooh. Ow. Ooh!"

"You hear that?" Dusty whispered.

"Sounds like it's coming from over by you, Tressa," Taylor said. "You see anything?"

"Me? No? No? Not a thing."

I took the opportunity to slide my pants down a bit. If I could inch them down a few more inches.

"Uw, ah!"

"There it is again. You sure you don't see anything, Tressa?"

"Yes!" I'd reached the crook of my knees. Good enough.

"Yes what? You see something?"

"Uh-huh," I said, squatting and letting it flow. "Ahhhh!"

"Tressa? Are you all right?"

"I'll check," Dusty said and before I could say "Don't look, Dusty!" he came crawling out of the bushes and hit me with his light.

"Holy crap!" he said, on the receiving end of an up close and personal view of my bum.

"No! No! There's no crap!" I assured him. "Just number one. No number two!"

"What's going on?" Taylor said. "Should I come over there?"

"No!" I said.

Dusty's head disappeared back into the bush, and I yanked my britches back up.

"Are you sure?"

"Pretty sure," I said.

"Looks good," Dusty said.

He couldn't mean...my derriere!

"The clearing," Dusty said. "I think we're good."

I let out a relieved breath.

"Good might be a bit of a stretch," Shelby muttered.

We circled the clearing's perimeter from different directions.

"Clear!" I called out.

"Clear? Are you for real?" Shelby said.

Our modest unit met in the middle.

I looked around. The clearing was deserted.

"Uh, what were we supposed to see again?" Taylor asked. "Evidence, you said, right, because I'm not seeing anything."

She was right. There was nothing here to see. Nothing at all.

"You're sure you saw people here tonight?" I asked Dusty.

"Affirmative," he responded.

I frowned, shining my flashlight around the area.

"Well, they sure didn't leave anything behind this time," I said. I bent down, taking a closer look at ground that looked like it'd been raked clean, like they did baseball mounds.

"Well, this has been instructional," Taylor said, throwing my earlier words back at me.

Shelby sighed. "So it's not a total loss, can we at least see those pink tornadoes you've gone on and on about?"

I nodded.

"You definitely have to see those! Pictures don't do them justice. May I direct your attention to Exhibit T for tornado, twister, or tree," I said. I pointed my flashlight at one of the trees that had been tagged. "And voilà!"

"Voilà what? I don't see anything," Shelby said.

"Me either," Taylor added.

I followed the path of my beam and my braggadocio deflated like a balloon with a hole.

Nothing. No tornado—pink, purple, polka-dotted, or otherwise.

"What mischief is this?" I muttered.

"Good grief," Shelby said.

"Are you sure you have the right tree?" Taylor asked.

I checked the others. No pink paint.

"I don't get it," I said. "They were here earlier right, Dusty?"

"They've made the signs disappear!" Dusty said.

"They? They who?" Taylor asked.

"I'm not sure you want to know," Shelby muttered.

"The Visitors! The Worshippers! The coven or sect or whatever you want to call them. They've obliterated the signs to cover their tracks. Oh, they're good. They're good," Dusty said.

I stepped up to a tree I was certain had been spray-painted and rubbed the palm of my hand over the bark on the front of the trunk. It felt damp, wet, and cool to the touch. I took a fingernail and scratched at the bark.

"Wait a minute! Look at this! Someone's spread something on this tree! It's still wet!"

Taylor and Shelby flanked me. Taylor shone her flashlight on the tree.

"You're right. It looks like mud."

"And look down here!" I squatted at the base of the trees. "Look at all these slivers of tree bark."

Taylor joined me, picking up some of the slivers and rubbing it between her thumb and her finger.

"It looks like someone shaved off the bark and covered it with some kind of mud mixture," she said.

"I'll take your word for it," Shelby said. "If I knelt down to see, I'd never get back up."

"Somebody's covering tracks," I said, vindicated.

"Why? We have photographs. Why erase them? Why now?"

All reasonable questions. I wish I had answers, reasonable or otherwise.

"They'll be looking for a new place to meet," Dusty said.

"That's it then," I said, disappointed our plans to expose the culprits had fizzled. "I guess we can head for the barn."

We made our way back to the ATVs.

"Oh, God. I forgot about the return trip," Shelby said.

"I'll take it easy," I promised, hopping onto the ATV. I turned the key and pushed the start button.

Err, err, errrr.

I put it in neutral and tried again.

Errr, rr, r.

"Hey, Dusty. It won't start," I said.

"Way to point out the obvious," Shelby said.

Errr, rr, rrr.

I frowned.

"Is something wrong, Dusty?"

"That's funny. Mine won't start either."

"You've got to be kidding," Shelby said.

Dusty got off the off-road vehicle and fiddled around at the back of the vehicle. He tried again.

No luck.

"You ever have anything like this happen before?" I asked Dusty.

He shook his head.

"Never," he said, tilting his head back to look up at the sky.

"I guess we're afoot then," I said, getting an uneasy feeling as well that sent my own gaze skyward.

"Miss Obvious strikes again," Shelby snarked as we began our trek back to Dusty's place.

"They like to mess with electrical systems," Dusty told me, taking the lead.

"I've heard that," I said.

"It's well documented. Radios go off and on. Headlights flicker. Cars stall for no reason."

I cast my own wary eye overhead.

It was well after midnight when we got back to our vehicles. I thanked Dusty for his help, offering to return the next day to help him retrieve the four-wheelers.

He shook his head. "I'm thinking they'll both fire off right as rain tomorrow morning," he said.

"Well, that was fun," Shelby Lynn said.

"Sorry," I said. "I really thought we'd get some answers tonight."

She shrugged. "No biggie. 'Night, ladies," she said and headed to her car.

I started the Plymouth and pulled out ahead of her.

We'd only gone a mile when the car radio suddenly came on.

"Ride Captain Ride" blared from the speakers.

I stared at the dashboard.

"What the hell? That radio hasn't worked in ages," I said.

Taylor reached out and turned it off. The interior light came on.

"What is the deal?" I said. "That light hasn't worked in forever either!"

"A fuse issue maybe?" Taylor suggested.

"Search me," I said. I didn't know where the fuses were even located.

"Where are your dash lights?" Taylor asked, and I looked down.

"Where did they go?" The dash was dark.

What was going on?

I pulled the car off on a wide shoulder. I looked in the rearview mirror and saw Shelby Lynn pull in behind.

"I don't suppose it would do any good to try the four-way flashers," Taylor said.

"You could try them," I said.

"You don't know where they are, do you?" she said, reaching over to point out a knob on the steering column.

I pulled it. Nothing.

"What's the problem?" Shelby Lynn appeared at Taylor's window.

"Looks like some kind of electrical problem," I said.

"You're kidding, right?"

"Would you be a dear and follow us into town?" I asked.

She sighed. "Fine," she said and returned to her car.

I turned the key to start the car.

Click click. Click click.

I frowned and tried again.

Click click. Click click.

"Are you freaking kidding me?" I smacked the dashboard with an open palm. The radio came back on.

David Bowie's "Space Oddity" filled the car's interior.

"What on earth?" Taylor said.

I looked at her.

"Or…maybe *not* of this earth," I said.

"What are you saying?"

"You don't suppose…"

"Suppose what?"

"Dusty said *they* like to mess with electrical systems," I reminded her.

We sat for a second listening to poor Major Tom float about far above the world.

Something smacked the driver's window, and I screamed like a little girl.

"What are you doing?" Shelby Lynn yelled over the music.

"Hitching a ride," I said. I stuck my thumb out the window. "Going our way?"

CHAPTER NINETEEN

I grabbed my goodies and jumped in the backseat of Shelby's vehicle, an older model Jeep Cherokee. Did everyone have a better ride than me?

"So, look at us! Three contemporary women fighting for truth, justice, and the American way! One kick-ass crime fighting team." I lifted a fist. "Girl power!"

"Oh, yeah. *Charlie's Angels* should be feeling really insecure right about now," Shelby said. "You do realize we just spent hours crawling around in the woods with a guy referred to locally as *My Favorite Martian*, exposing ourselves to ticks, mosquitoes, and any number of noxious weeds, and basically accomplished nothing?"

I frowned.

"I wouldn't say we accomplished nothing," I said. "We've established that the pink graffiti artists met in Dusty's woods and are now trying to cover their tracks. That's not nothing." I'd also established the possible identity of one of the artists but wanted to keep that information under my hat until I had more in the way of corroborating evidence.

"I suppose," Shelby Lynn said. "Where are we on the gnome angle?"

"Gnome angle?" Taylor turned in her seat to look at me. "What is she talking about? Not Abigail Winegardner's gnome."

I frowned.

"You know about the gnome?"

"Excuse me. We share the same grandmother. Of course, I know about the gnome. Abigail thinks Gram took it. She says she didn't. Are you actually investigating a gnome disappearance?"

"Well, actually we're investigating its appearance," Shelby Lynn said, and I wrinkled my face up in an "Oh, God, no! Don't tell Taylor!" face.

"I don't understand," Taylor said.

"That's okay, Taylor," I spoke up. "Sometimes the nuances of a complex journalistic investigation are difficult for lay people to grasp."

"Oh for crying out loud!" Taylor said. "It's obvious you believe Abigail's gnome was taken by the same people who have been committing the acts of vandalism. I'd just like to know how you came to that conclusion."

"Dogged determination and tried and true investigative techniques," I responded.

"Oh, brother. The gnome was spotted at a number of locations which were subsequently hit by the vandals," Shelby spilled the beans quicker than Gram spread dirt around she heard at the Kut 'n' Kurl, going on to tell Taylor the locations where Cedric had been spotted.

"So under your theory, the next place hit should be Home & Farm Hardware," Taylor concluded. "And you think what? That the vandals are incorporating an element of game play to their crimes?"

I blinked. When she put it that way...

"Exactly!" I proclaimed. "And a gaming angle fits perfectly with our working theory that the acts are being perpetrated by teens," I added.

"But why a lawn gnome?" Shelby Lynn asked.

"Well, it *is* a conversation piece," I pointed out.

If the topic happened to be demon gnomes from hell, that is.

"A fifty-pounds-of-cast iron conversation piece," Shelby Lynn said. "So what's going on with the Reliant?" Shelby looked at me via the rearview mirror.

"I don't know. It's never conked before without going through a series of sputters, coughs, belches, backfires, and spurts and stops," I said.

The description sounded a lot like my gammy after a trip to the all-you-can-eat taco bar.

"Tressa thinks this may be a case of alien automobile-interference," Taylor said.

"She does? You do?" Shelby eyeballed me from the mirror again.

I made a raspberry sound.

"I was just joking around. You know. Keeping it light. Keeping it loose. Finding the humor in any given situation as is my wont."

"Right," Shelby said. "Your *wont*."

We rode in silence for several minutes.

"Is anyone hungry?" I asked. "Because I could go for a burger and fries."

"I'm surprised you're still hungry after all those energy bars you stuffed in your face," Shelby remarked.

"What—"

"There's a wrapper stuck in your backpack zipper," Taylor responded.

I looked over at my backpack. Sure enough, the corner of a foil energy bar wrapper was sticking out from a zippered compartment.

I gave the backpack a punch and then remembered I still had a bag of candy-coated chocolate peanuts. I unzipped the bag, shoved the incriminating foil wrap down inside, and put my hand down into the bag. I pulled the scanner out.

I shrugged and turned it on, foraging around in my bag again until I found the ear bud. I stuck one end in the scanner and one in my ear and went back to the candy search.

I remembered that I'd eaten the candy the day before, so I put the bag aside, laid my head back on the headrest, propped my foot on the console between the front seats, and closed my eyes. It had been a long day. The motion of the car lulled me to sleep. In my dream state, I walked through a greenhouse of colorful flowers, stopping to bend over and admire the lovely petals. I was leaning down to admire the particularly brilliant blooms of daffodils, peach day lilies, and the whimsical blooms of purple coneflowers when I became aware I was being watched. I turned. On the path near my feet there he was.

Abigail's gnome.

His eyes glowed red and a guttural growl—one like you would associate with a movie about demons—came from the mouth of the gnome.

I ran to the corner and turned. There he was again. This time he snarled. I pivoted, moving back the way I'd come only to be cut off by the knee-high menace. I tried to scream but nothing came out. I changed tactics, sprinting cross-country through the plots of plants, punishing petals, grounding out greenery, and beating up blossoms.

Seeing the parking lot ahead, I kicked it up a notch, digging in for that final burst of energy when a hand reached out from the foliage at my feet and clamped onto my ankle.

"Aaaaahhh!" I screamed and sat bolt up.

"Do you mind?" Shelby Lynn's Shaq hand had hold of my ankle. "I'd rather my upholstery not look like a kennel on wheels," she said. "And stop trying to scare us with your alien antics."

I retrieved the ear bud that had popped out of ear and stuck it back in.

"Sixty-three twenty-five. Report of a possible 10-14 and 10-31 H&F, Home & Farm. Be advised sixty-three seventeen is in route from patrol."

I sat up in my seat.

"Did you hear that?" I yelled.

"For crying out loud, Tressa, give it a rest," Taylor said. "We're not going to buy into your space bogeyman drama."

"No! No!" I pulled the earphone plug out of the scanner. "The scanner! The county just dispatched a car to a possible 10-14 and 10-31!"

"What are you talking about?" Shelby asked.

I blinked. *What was I talking about? What* were *a 10-14 and a 10-31?*

I pawed through my bag for my phone.

"Forget it. I've got it." Taylor said, looking at her phone's display. "A 10-14 is a report of a prowler, and a 10-31 is crime in progress."

"I knew it!" I said, clenching my fist in an "I still got it!" move.

"Knew what?"

I leaned forward and stuck my head and shoulders in the space between the front seats.

"Would either of you skeptics care to take a wild guess as to the location the officers have been dispatched to?" I asked. "Go on! Take a guess. And your first two don't count."

Taylor and Shelby Lynn exchanged disbelieving looks.

"No way!" Shelby Lynn said.

"Is this another one of your attempts to freak us out?" Taylor said.

I shook my head. "I swear on our gammy's blue head," I said, making a jumbo *X* on my chest with a hand. "This is the real thing! So shift this Jeep into hyperdrive, my young apprentice, and make like *The Fast and the Furious*—only without the car crashes and near death experiences."

Shelby shook her head and put the pedal to the metal, slamming me back against the seat. I had to give her credit. She got us there fast and furiously.

Unfortunately, I felt like I was gonna hurl energy bars by the time we came to a stop.

Top lights pierced the night sky with both county and city officers on the scene. I pulled my backpack on, grabbed my phone and flashlight, and jumped out of the car, jogging up to the first officer I came to.

"Tressa Turner, *Grandville Gazette*. Can you tell me what's going on? Was there a break-in?

What was taken? Was anything spray-painted? Any pink tornadoes? Do you have anyone in custody?"

The officer turned.

"No comment," Deputy Dawg said, his standard greeting whenever our paths crossed.

"We predicted this, Sheriff," I told him.

He frowned.

"We?"

"My associates and myself."

"So you have associates now," he said.

"That's right." Shelby Lynn and Taylor flanked me. "The three of us predicted H&F would be hit next, didn't we, ladies?"

"She's right, officer," Shelby Lynn said. "That's exactly what we did."

"Oh? And how did you ladies do that? Look into a crystal ball? Use a psychic hotline? Consult your Ouija board?"

"We interviewed witnesses, examined crime scenes, detected certain patterns, and then made an informed prediction regarding where the next incident would take place. In other words, we did your job," I said.

Sheriff Sitsalot shook his head.

"You expect me to believe you knew this establishment would be hit next? What patterns are you talking about that led you to this conclusion?"

"Well, you see. There was this gnome—"

"Gnome?"

"You know. A lawn gnome."

"Again with the lawn gnome? And this lawn gnome told you that this store would be hit next?"

"Actually yes—in a manner of speaking," I told the deputy. "You see, Abigail Winegardner had this lawn gnome—a real ogre of a gnome, let me tell you. Anyway, someone nicked her gnome a month or so back. She thinks my gammy's the nicker, but she's not, but that's another story. Anyway, since that time, witnesses—including me—reported seeing Cedric at a number of locations that were the target of vandals prior to the incidents of vandalism."

"Cedric? Who is Cedric?"

"The gnome. That's his name."

"Cedric's the gnome."

"That's right."

"A gnome named Cedric is your informant."

"Well, in a manner of speaking. You see, as I indicated before, we—my associate and I— discovered—through exhaustive interviews and investigation—that a number of witnesses, including this reporter, identified Cedric, er, the gnome in question as being on or near each of the properties a day or two before that property was hit. The last reported sighting of Cedric was here at H&F. And, what do you know? H&F is the next target."

"It's the truth, Sheriff Samuels," Shelby Lynn said, stepping into the breach. "I know it sounds a bit strange and bizarre but—"

"Bizarre? A gnome snitch? What's so strange about that?" Samuels said. "And considering the source—no pun intended," he added with a why-am-I-not-surprised shrug, "it sounds perfectly consistent."

It was Taylor's turn to step up.

"Hello, Sheriff. Taylor Turner. I'm Tressa's sister. I know it sounds crazy. When Shelby and Tressa first told me about the gnome and its proximity to the vandalism incidents, I was skeptical, too. But when we heard you'd been tripped to H&F on this call, I was shocked because not more than an hour ago, Tressa and Shelby both said that if the pattern held H&F would be hit next, and they told me *before* this call went out. So I know they're on to something here."

Samuels looked like he'd just been told little green men had crash-landed on the courthouse lawn.

"It gets better," I said.

Now he looked green.

"There's more?"

"You remember Dusty Cadwallader. He was in your office earlier today to file a report regarding suspicious activity at his place."

"I know. More strange lights, odd noises, and unusual signs. I understand you and he left together."

The female deputy *had* blabbed.

"That's right. I felt Mr. Cadwallader had information relevant to our investigation," I said. "And he did. And those 'signs' he referred to?" I flipped my phone open, pulled up my gallery, and held out the display for him to see. "Tornadoes. Pink tornadoes to be exact."

Samuels blinked. I'd gotten his attention.

"You found these on Cadwallader's property?" he said, taking the phone and flipping through the pictures.

"Along with other evidence that your little gang of vandals hung out in his woods at various times," I said. "Then Dusty called me earlier tonight to report that *they* were back, and we headed out."

"I told Dusty that it's likely a bunch of teens partying and drinking," Samuels said.

"It appears we were too late to catch anyone in the act, Sheriff Samuels," Shelby told him. "However, we did discover that someone had, in fact, been there and had gone to certain lengths to cover up evidence that they had been there."

"Oh? How'd they do that?"

"We're thinking a wire brush and some kind of poultice made of mud and water," I said.

"What?'

"She's talking about the measures they used to cover up the pink tornadoes spray-painted on the trees that you see in the photos there," Taylor supplied.

"Sounds like teenaged drinking and partying," he said. Sheriff Samuels went through the photos again.

He stopped. Flinched.

"Oh, God. What the hell is this?"

I winced, hoping he wasn't referring to selfies taken during TribRide.

"This...thing."

He pointed the phone display in my direction.

I let out a sigh of relief.

"Oh, that's Cedric."

"Cedric the soothsayer gnome?"

I nodded. "I told you he was a real appetite killer," I said. "I'm thinking that's one 'have you seen this gnome' mug shot that the public can't help but recognize if they see it."

"What do you mean a mug shot the public will recognize?" Samuel asked, giving the image a final frown before handing the phone back to me.

"When you put this information out there so people will be on the lookout."

"On the lookout for a gnome. You want the Knox County Sheriff's Office to put out a BOLO on a lawn ornament?"

When he put it like that...

"Say, for the moment, I believe you about the gnome—which, by the way, I don't. If we put the information out to the public, wouldn't the perps also see it and figure out we were on to them? And wouldn't those individuals quit using the gnome as a landmark in their series of criminal acts, not only making the whole exercise pointless, but putting the perpetrators on notice that we're on to them?"

I hesitated, backtracking over the lawman's logic.

Holy disappearing dwarves!

He was right! If we outed Cedric, we'd tip off the vandals that we'd made the connection between them and him.

"Hey, Doug." A Grandville officer joined us. "Looks like they took off before we got the call," the officer told Samuels. "We've got property damage and the owner's on his way in to see what was taken, if anything."

"Any pink tornadoes, Officer?" I asked.

"How'd you know?"

"I knew it!" I said. "Fist bump, ladies!" I put out a fist. Once again, Taylor and Shelby stared at it.

"Thanks, Pete," Samuels said. "Give me a second to finish up."

"So, Deputy…Sheriff, have we convinced you that we're on to something here?" I asked. "What do you think?"

He shook his head and rubbed the back of his neck. "What I think, Miss Turner, is that you need to leave the crime investigation to the criminal investigators and stick to reporting the results of law enforcement's investigation. Now if you have information—witness statements, photos, physical evidence—anything you feel is pertinent to this case and helpful to law enforcement, we'd welcome that. But I have to caution you against striking out blindly on your own in a shortsighted attempt to nail that next big story," he said. "As I recall, it didn't work out too well for you the last time you flew solo."

"We came here to share information with you, Sheriff," Shelby pointed out. "But you clearly aren't taking us seriously."

"Excuse me if I'm finding the idea of a group of vandals utilizing a rogue elf—"

"Gnome," Taylor corrected.

"—gnome in their criminal activities a bit hard to swallow. It just doesn't make any sense to me. Now I appreciate you all coming out and sharing your theories, but it's time for you stick to doing your job and let us do ours."

"Sheriff!" Shelby started to object, but I put a hand on her arm.

"Don't bother confusing the sheriff with facts, Shelby," I said. "If he doesn't want to benefit from the fruits of our cutting edge investigative efforts, fine. We'll leave him to his work."

I walked away, dragging Shelby and Taylor with me.

Stan had requested I consult with the sheriff before the next day's article came out—the one that mentioned pink tornadoes and links between the incidents. So, I'd just consulted. Too bad for the sheriff that I had neglected to mention the article. I'd leave him to discover that little eye-opener over his morning cup of coffee.

I made a longhorn sign with my fingers.

You mess with a cowgirl—you get the spurs.

CHAPTER TWENTY

Despite my late night—or early morning, I suppose—I was ready to head out the door before eight. I grabbed my bag and keys and opened the door—and stopped in my tracks. I had no wheels. My vehicle was sitting on a gravel shoulder miles out of town with its hood up, a bright yellow, not-so-happy, ball ornament sporting a cowboy hat stuck to the top of the antenna. (After I'd driven off in a car that belonged to someone else last summer and found a stiff in the trunk, I figured having some clearly visible means of vehicular identification was probably a good idea, although the likelihood of that happening again is probably astronomical, right?)

I looked at the time, considering my options.

And there weren't many. Only one individual in my circle of peeps knew about cars and motors and things that go awry under the hood and also had access to a tow truck (if necessary) at a discount price. I pulled my phone out.

"What's wrong with the wreck on wheels now?" came my brother's surly greeting.

"What makes you think there's anything wrong?" I asked. "Can't I call my brother and wish him a good morning?"

"What did you break this time and where?" he asked.

I gave him the location and told him about the electrical glitch-out.

"It's never done that before," I added.

"Oh, please. The damned thing breaks down more often than the chubby guy on *Modern Family*."

"So can you pick me up?" I asked. "I really, really, really need to get my car going so I can get to work before Stan goes all, 'If you're late one more time, Turner, I'm going to blah, blah, blah, on me! And I'm right in the middle of this story—"

"I know, I know. Kimmie and I read about it this morning. Vandalism. Thefts. Pink tornadoes. A regular crime wave."

"So? Can you help me out, brother dearest?"

A long, loud sigh came through the speaker next to my ear.

"I started your way as soon as I saw your number," he said. "Be there in a few." He hung up.

I smiled. It was times like this that made putting up with my big brother's crapola over the years totally worth it.

I went out to the porch and sat down, spending some time with the pooches while I waited for Craig. He rolled up in his big black Ford tough truck that never seemed to be permitted to get dirty—another perk that comes with working at a car dealership—and I hurried to get in.

"Thank you sooo much!" I said, blowing him an ear kiss. "You are a lifesaver. You're like Iron Man or Superman or the Green Lantern or Thor or Captain America. You're like—"

"I get it, Tressa. I'm here. You can stop trying to butter me up."

I sat back in my seat.

"Well, excuse me for expressing my gratitude," I said, and looked over at him. "So, how's Kimmie?" I asked. "Is she feeling better?"

Craig looked over at me.

"What do you mean 'is she feeling better?'"

I frowned.

"I stopped by the treasurer's office yesterday when I was picking up the court stuff, and they told me she was home sick."

"What are you talking about? As far as I know she went to work yesterday. She didn't say anything about missing work or being sick."

I bit my lip. Oh, God. This was not good. Not good at all.

"Maybe I misunderstood," I said. "That's probably what happened. I get to talking, and sometimes I don't listen all that well. You know how I am. I just get carried away and go on and on and on, and sometimes I can get distracted, and I don't take time to hear what others are saying, and that's probably what happened here. I probably just misunderstood. I'm sure that's it. I just got to talking, and you know how I am when I get on a roll—"

"You're doing it now, Tressa," Craig pointed out.

"I am?"

He nodded. "Your motor mouth is at maximum rpms."

"It is?"

He nodded again. "And that's your tell."

I frowned. Busted.

"Tell?"

He shook his head.

"I've known you twenty-four years, lived with you for a score. I know what it means when your motor mouth is at maximum acceleration. It means you're nervous and agitated."

"Well, look who's going all BAU on us now," I said, trying to divert his focus from the reason for my runaway mouth. "And to think I thought your main gift was talking people into purchasing new vehicles when they come in for their 60,000 mile vehicle checks. You got a gift, my friend. You got a gift."

He turned to look at me, and for the first time I noticed the dark rings under his eyes and the crinkly lines in the corners that hadn't been there before. A pang of sisterly concern hit me.

"So Kimmie wasn't at work yesterday?" he asked.

I shook my head. I wasn't going to lie to him. Not about this.

I'm a horrible liar anyway. I never could get away with fudging the truth. I still can't.

"No."

I could tell from the sudden set of his jaw that he had clenched his teeth.

"You know, everyone needs a mental day now and then, Craig," I told him. "We can't be Wonder Woman or Superman all the time. Sometimes we need a day to just *be*."

"Bullshit! It's that baby!" Craig said suddenly, and I blinked.

"Baby? Kimmie's pregnant?" I asked.

He shook his head.

"No! That's the problem. She wants to be pregnant. She wants a baby. And she can't seem to think about anything else."

I winced. I'm not usually the person people go to when they have a life crisis or need advice. It's not that I don't want to be that person. I do. It's just historically I'm not the first individual others think to consult in times of emotional or personal crisis. I tend to be the one contributing to those highs and lows and peaks and valleys, if you get my drift. But I'd always wanted to be that go-to person.

I still wanted to be that person.

"Listen, Craig. I don't profess to know much about those complex and powerful maternal feelings women get when they want to start a family, because I'm not there yet. But I am a woman. And I think I understand what Kimmie is feeling."

When he didn't cut me off with some smart-assed remark, I went on.

"Kimmie is married to the man she loves. Now personally what she sees in the dunderhead, I really have no clue. But she loves him. And I know he loves her. It's like that nursery rhyme. First comes love. Then comes marriage. Then comes Craig with the baby carriage. It's only natural for Kimmie to want to move on to that next huge step. She's committed to the relationship—to that happily ever after. She's ready for that baby carriage."

"But what if I'm not?" he said. "Don't *my* feelings count in this relationship? Why is it that women think they're the only ones that matter, that how they feel trumps how the guy feels?"

Wow. Heavy-duty stuff. This cowgirl was definitely out of her league.

"Have you ever told Kimmie *why* you're not ready for fatherhood?" I asked.

He thought about it for a second.

"Well, sure. I mean. We've talked. I've told her I'm not ready."

I shook my head. Men could be so…clueless.

"I'm just guessing here, Craig, but I'm thinking that's what bothers Kimmie the most. What are your feelings about parenthood?"

He shook his head.

"I don't follow."

"Kimmie is ready for step three. Kimmie is ready for that baby carriage. And she doesn't understand why you don't feel the same way she feels. And I honestly think what worries her most is *why* you aren't ready to become a father. She looks at it like, *if* you love her, *if* you're committed to her, *if* you're going to be together forever and ever, then why aren't *you* ready? She is. How come *you're* not? Unless…"

He frowned.

"Unless what?"

"Unless you're not all those things after all. You're *not* totally and irrevocably in love with her. You *aren't* permanently committed to her. You *don't* think you'll be together forever and ever. Do you see what I'm saying, Craig? A woman looks at things way different from men. We take things personally—most everything personally when it comes to the guys in our lives. The basic fact that you don't want to have a baby right now might be sending Kimmie the wrong message."

"What do you mean 'the wrong message'?"

"She could be interpreting your feet-dragging as not being totally happy and secure in the relationship or happy with *her*. The fact that you've never once sat down and talked this out and told her why you're not ready for that baby buggy only adds to those doubts and fears. Does that make sense?"

I sure hoped it did, because I wasn't all that confident I hadn't muffed it, and I didn't think I had the wherewithal to be so eloquent the second time around.

"Well?"

"Well what?"

"Why don't you want a baby, Craig?" I asked.

"I do want a baby!" He yelled and put his hand through his blond hair, leaving it sticking up in places. "I'm just not—"

"You better not say the R-word!" I warned. "The real question is why aren't you the R-word? And don't tell me it's because you want to spend your time playing sports, or watching sports, or killing for sport, or fishing for sport, because I don't buy it. Not when I know how much you love Kimmie. So tell me something I will believe."

He seemed at a loss for words, which is rare for a salesman and given the fact we both carry Blackford genetic markers for oral activity. Well, you know what I mean.

"Would you believe that I don't know why the hell I'm not ready to be a father?" he said, but wouldn't look at me. "Honest to God, I have no idea why I'm not there yet. I'm just not there. And I'm beginning to wonder if I ever will be."

I heard the fear and uncertainty in his voice and my "aunticipation" level took a sudden nosedive.

I braved a look at him. He looked like I did when I discovered a murdering hitman had added me to his target list. I reached out and patted his hand.

"Then again, maybe it *is* about the sports and the games and the hunt," I told him, adding a little prayer that my brother had his epiphany before his wife had had enough.

"My car is just around the bend on the shoulder," I told Craig as we approached the section of road I'd left the Reliant. "It'll be on our left." I pointed out the front windshield.

We rounded the turn, and the vehicle came into view.

"Good God! Would you look at that?" Craig said.

I did. And saw what used to be my vehicle looking like a reject from a gay pride parade.

"Holy shit! Talk about trashed!" Craig said and drove onto the opposite shoulder, making a U-turn before pulling up a safe distance behind my poor Plymouth.

Oh. My. God.

I had a sudden déjà vu been-here-done-this moment. The last time it had been my Paw-Paw Will's Buick that had been desecrated. This time my Reliant had become the canvas for some modern day gang of psychedelic artists with an attitude and agenda.

"Why does this keep happening to me?" I whined to Craig. "Why me?"

He shook his head.

"I've got nothing for you, sis," he said, opening his door. "Ready for a closer look?"

I shook my head.

"Not really. I think I've seen enough already."

"You got the keys?" he asked. "I suppose we should see if it will start."

"Why?" I asked. "Obviously it can't be driven in that condition." The fact was, start or not, I wasn't about to drive a vehicle that made Joseph's coat of many colors look dowdy and would make Rainbow Brite feel inadequate.

"Just give me the key, Tressa!" Craig snapped.

I handed him the key. "No need to get snippy."

Craig looked in the rearview mirror before getting out and walking up to my vehicle. I put my sunglasses on and waited. I couldn't bear to look at my poor, pathetic, paid-for Plymouth.

The spray-painting, gnome-stealing, mischief-making thugs had obviously targeted me.

Why? Because my posse was on their tails, breathing down their necks, closing in for the kill.

"Oh, shit, shit, shit, shit, shit!" Craig's outburst reached me through the open driver's side window. "Son of a bitch! Jesus Christ! God damn it!"

I looked up in time to see Craig jump away from the car and head for the ditch. I frowned. It sounded like he was retching.

"Is there something...wrong?" I asked, reluctant to set foot outside the safe confines of the pickup truck.

"Ugh. God. Ugh. Dammit! Tressa Jayne Turner, get your ass out of that truck and get over here! Now!"

"Do I have to?"

"Tressa!"

"Coming!"

I opened the door and got out. I'd taken about three steps when it hit me. The smell. No, not a smell. An odor. No. Not an odor. Fumes. A putrid, noxious, not-of-this world stench that filled the nostrils and activated the gag reflex. I suddenly wished for Frankie's bandana.

"What is that smell?" I put a hand over my nose and mouth. "Is there a deer carcass in the ditch? It smells like death!" I asked Craig, who was still yacking in the grass.

"It *is* death!" he yelled. "It's roadkill on steroids!"

I took a few steps nearer the car—and my bro. The closer I got to both of them, the heavier the smell of rotting flesh became.

"What exactly do you mean by roadkill?" I asked, a tremor in my voice as the unmistakable smell of death almost choked me. Oh, God. It couldn't be. No way. The same person couldn't come across three dead bodies in a year's time unless they were Bones or Dexter, or a regular who hadn't been killed off on *The Walking Dead*. "Craig?"

"It's your car!" Craig said, wiping his mouth with the tail of his shirt. "It's your stinking, rotten, bloody, mangy car!"

"Now just a minute!" I started to defend my car's honor when Craig reached out and opened the passenger side door. A rancid bouquet, the likes of which I hope to never smell again, hit me with such force that my knees almost buckled. I clasped my other hand over the first, trying to keep the smell from getting into the olfactory passages.

"Look," he said. "Go ahead. Take a good look!"

I bent down and peeked in.

Roadkill on steroids had been an understatement. This was roadkill-palooza!

I found myself staring in fascinated horror at the strings and clumps and mounds of what had, at one time, been benign residents of the timbers and pastures innocently going about their business—now unidentifiable piles of guts and fur and bones and tendons that covered every inch of my car's interior, fouling the air for a country mile.

I felt vomit begin to fill my throat.

A second later, my stomach contents joined the already disgusting, decaying collection of carcasses and other dubious material soaking into the upholstery.

I stumbled to the ditch and ralphed up what was left of my breakfast, a tried and true cowgirl revenge saying running through my head.

Sometimes you've got to put on your big girl boots and prove that you can use the pointy end!

Somehow or another, it's almost always about the boots, pilgrim.

CHAPTER TWENTY-ONE

Color me one pissed off and put out cowgirl. (Just don't color me a perky shade of hot pink. The paint-happy scofflaws had done what I thought no one could ever do—ruin the color pink for this coral lovin' cowgirl forever.)

As a result, I also happened to be a cowgirl without transportation. I'd snapped photographs of the Reliant—inside and out—and said my final farewells to a car that, while it hadn't served me all that well, had kept me out of debt. Craig had called in a "huge" favor and persuaded a friend of his to come tow the Plymouth. The car would be kept at his friend's facility on the outskirts of town where the "Roadkill Reliant" as Craig's friend dubbed my unfortunate vehicle would be stored well away from the living, breathing populace until law enforcement could examine the vehicle and write a report. Once the cops took a look—and I hoped, a good long whiff—it would be hauled off to wherever it was they took worthless vehicles full of dead animal carcasses, guts, and gore to be disposed of.

There was no insurance claim to file. No one kept comprehensive on a vehicle that didn't even show up in the Kelley Blue Book and held no value as either antique or collectible.

I'd asked (okay, begged) Craig to make the call to the sheriff's office. I figured they had no ongoing hostilities with my brother and wouldn't be likely to start any since most local law enforcement liked to finagle free car washes from the dealership in exchange for making regular patrols through the car lot at night.

They'd said they would be in touch after they examined the vehicle. Craig dropped me by the house, before heading home to "take a long, hot shower and snort a bottle of saline."

But the most pressing item on my agenda wasn't hygiene—it was transportation so I could hunt down the hooligans who'd turned my Reliant into a rendering vehicle.

And what kind of reporter didn't have access to a vehicle?

An unemployed one, that's what kind.

I saw the Buick sitting in the driveway near the folks' garage. Taylor wasn't scheduled to work the Freeze until five. I'd be back in plenty of time. I hurried over to the car. If only she'd left the car unlocked and the keys inside. I tried the door handle. No luck. Darned Taylor's suspicious mind. I tried the back door. Locked, too. I started around to the passenger side to check and make sure all the doors were locked.

"What are you doing? Playing musical car doors? Or are you trying to pinch my car again?"

I looked up. Taylor, clad in yoga pants and a waist-length hoodie stared at me from the corner of the house.

"Well, it's actually Paw-Paw Will's car—"

"It's registered in my name, Tressa. I suspected you'd be over here this morning. I just thought it would be earlier."

"You did?"

She nodded. "I thought you might need a ride out to your vehicle to see if it'll start." She hit the remote entry button. The Buick's doors clicked. "Hop in."

"Sweet! Thanks, Taylor!" I said, not about to let a free ride pass me by, I complied, throwing my bag in the back before jumping in the front.

She got in and started the car and backed out.

"Can we just make a quick stop first?" I asked.

She gave me a guarded look.

"Not Area 51 again?"

"Oh, no. Nothing so exciting as that," I said. "I just need to make a stop at the high school and get some information."

"What kind of information?" was her wary response. "And from whom?"

"Ease up on the reins of doubt and distrust, sister mine," I said. "I merely need to visit the Media Center and look at a few yearbooks to confirm some information is all. Perfectly harmless research. Nothing to worry your pretty little head about."

"Oh, God. I'm going to regret this, aren't I?" Taylor said, pulling out of the drive and heading for town. "By the way, did you know you reek?"

I nodded.

"I figured."

After a quick stop at the Freeze for free vittles and sodas, we pulled into the school parking lot. I jumped out of the car.

"Aren't you coming in?" I asked Taylor who remained behind the wheel.

"I'd rather not."

"That's probably a good idea. You just stay here and keep the getaway car warmed up and ready," I said.

Taylor shook her head.

"You win. I'll come. If I can stay up wind of you. Besides, someone has to be a buffer between you and Principal Vernon."

I held out my hand.

"Hello, Buffer. Welcome aboard."

We entered the high school. The commons wasn't nearly as busy as it had been the previous day. The second lunch period had ended, and the third one wouldn't start for ten minutes or so.

I headed for the hallway to the Media Center when I felt a hand on my elbow.

"We have to sign in first," Taylor said, pulling me in the direction of the principal's office.

"But I don't want to," I said, getting the same feeling I had in high school whenever "Tressa Turner to the office" came over the intercom.

"You have to. It's a security issue," Taylor insisted. "All visitors have to sign in at the office and get a visitor's pass."

"Let's don't and say we did," I said, pulling in the opposite direction.

"We're getting a pass!"

Tug!

"I'll take a pass!"

Pull!

"Is there something wrong, ladies?"

Crapola. Did the guy ever use his office?

"Oh, hello again Principal Vernon," I said. "I was just explaining to my sister here the importance of us checking in at the office to sign in and receive our visitor passes. You remember Taylor, don't you?"

Both the principal and the sister-in-question gave me telling looks.

"Of course, I remember Taylor. What principal forgets a valedictorian? Hello, Taylor. How are you?"

Taylor shook his hand.

"I'm well, thank you."

"Last I heard you were studying psychology. I'm surprised to see you back so late in the year."

I looked at Taylor. Her face had turned a flattering shade of red. Of course, on jaundice yellow is flattering.

"Yes, well, I'm, uh, taking a bit of a break," she stammered.

"A break?" The principal's surprise was evident.

For the first time, I felt sorry for Taylor. I'd never had to worry about maintaining extraordinarily high expectations others placed on me. Whereas I'd always made sure to land somewhere in the middle of the curve, Taylor had always been the hated overachiever who wrecked the curve for everyone else.

"Taylor's helping out family while she weighs other more rewarding and highly lucrative opportunities," I said. "While psychology is a fascinating field of inquiry, Taylor isn't yet certain it provides the challenge and level of stimulation she is looking for in a chosen career. If you'll excuse us, principal, we'll just grab those visitor passes."

Take that and stick it in your detention slip pad, I thought and herded a silent Taylor into the office.

After several minutes of the office ladies making a fuss over Taylor and reminiscing about the time I got detention for shoving hard-boiled eggs up bully Chandler Radcliffe's tailpipe and speculating on "what that horrible smell could be," we were on our way, visitor passes in hand, to the Media Center.

"Happy now?" I said, grabbing Taylor's lanyard with the visitor pass dangling from it. "We're official."

"What are we looking for anyway?" she asked, and I explained what I'd learned from Kari about the middle school artist who liked to draw pink tornadoes.

"So you want to see what this Jada Garcia looks like?" Taylor said. "For identification purposes."

I nodded.

"I think I already know who she is, but I want to be sure." I told her about seeing the girl with Mick and Aunt Mo referring to Mick's girlfriend as "Jada."

"And you think the Jada Garcia who drew the pink tornadoes in middle school is the same

Jada who is dating Mick Dishman?"

"I think the chances are pretty good. After all, how many Jadas are there likely to be attending Grandville High?"

I grabbed a table in the corner furthest from the Media Center desk and let Taylor make the yearbook request. The librarian wasn't exactly a fan of a blonde physically incapable of keeping her voice at a whisper. Taylor joined me at the table, materials in hand.

It didn't take us long to find Jada.

"There," Taylor said, shoving the yearbook from the previous year in front of me. "Jada Marie Garcia."

"That's her!" I yelled, getting a hissed "Quiet please!" from the librarian. "That's her!" I said, lowering my voice to a whisper. "That's Mick Dishman's girlfriend! She's a cheerleader."

I sat and stared at the photograph.

Jada Marie Garcia. A pretty girl with long, dark hair and a big, white "rah, rah, team" smile.

I looked at the photo a second longer before, out of curiosity, I flipped over to Mick's picture. I found him easily. Or rather I found his name. Dishman. *Mickel* Dishman. I ran my finger across the line of photos to where his should be and frowned.

No photo available, the picture box read. I frowned.

No photo available? I shook my head. Poor guy. Usually the only people without photos were late enrollees or rebels like me who didn't photograph well and knew it.

I stared at the page of photos and sighed.

If only.

If only I'd been permitted the option of being "Tressa Jayne Turner, no photo available" my high school days might've been different. "Tressa Jayne Turner No Photo Available" would never have had to defend yearbook pictures that had teachers and classmates rolling in the hallways and photographers disavowing any knowledge of the photos in question.

I thought for a minute and flipped back to the sports section.

"What are you looking for?"

"Cheerleaders," I said. There they were. 'The Freshman Five," I read. There she was. Front and center, pom-poms at the ready. Jada Garcia. I looked at the other names. None of them rang any bells until I got to one—Keira Christine Radcliffe. I found her in the pom-pom photo and made a face. Last year when Shelby Lynn had been a homecoming queen candidate, Kylie Danae Radcliffe had also been in the running. I'd interviewed all the queen candidates, and Kylie had gotten my vote in the mean-girl competition. Judging from the name and the yearbook photo, I suspected Keira was likely Kylie's little sister.

I convinced Taylor to ask the librarian to make copies of the yearbook page with Jada's picture, the cheerleader page, and at the last minute, the page where "Mickel" Dishman's picture would have been.

"Why do you want that Dishman page?" Taylor asked after we'd turned in our visitor passes and left the high school.

"No reason, really," I said, wondering the same thing.

We'd crossed the parking lot when a short blast from a police siren got my attention. Oh,

Lord. What had I done now?

I looked up and spotted a trooper car in the lot.

"Look Taylor! It's Trooper Dawkins!" I said, grabbing Taylor's arm and jogging over to where the handsome young Smokey Bear had parked and exited his vehicle. "Hey, where's a trooper when a girl needs one?" I asked.

"Hey, Tressa. Hello, Taylor," the trooper smiled at us. "So when have you needed a trooper lately, Miss Turner?" P.D. asked. "Or do I want to know?"

A warning squeeze from Taylor with the pressure of a vice reminded me to keep a filter on my mouth.

"Tressa's car broke down out in the county last night," Taylor said. "We're actually on our way out there to see if we can get it going."

The trooper looked from Taylor, to me, and back to Taylor. He rubbed the back of his neck.

"That's strange," he said.

"Not if you know Tressa and her history with that Plymouth," Taylor said.

"What I mean is that I'm pretty sure the vehicle in question has already been towed in," Dawkins said.

"It has?" Taylor said.

"It has?" I parroted.

He nodded. "It's at Ray's Wreck and Salvage. I heard Dan's Towing wouldn't touch it."

"Wouldn't...touch it?" Taylor said.

He shook his head.

"All that roadkill and all. A heck of a mess."

"Road...*kill*?"

"You don't know?"

"Know...what?" Taylor said.

"The county's been out to Ray's," the trooper said, giving me a "the jig is up" look.

I sighed. I hear you loud and clear, Mr. Smokey Bear.

"What is he talking about, Tressa? What exactly happened to your car?"

I took a deep breath.

"Once upon a time in a galaxy far, far away there was this beautiful young girl who had this not so reliable Reliant and—"

Once I'd recounted the gruesome story of "The Roadkill and the Reliant," I reached out and pushed Taylor's chin up to close her gaping mouth.

"Oh, God. That is sick!" she said. "Really sick! And that happened after we left

Cadwallader's?"

I nodded.

"Wait a minute. Are you talking about Dusty Cadwallader?" P.D. asked.

We nodded.

"You were out at his place last night?"

We nodded again.

"That is weird."

"Weird why exactly?" Well, apart from the obvious.

"Because Dusty's aunt in southern Missouri got what she termed a 'disturbing call' from Dusty last night, and when she tried to reach him this morning, there was no answer."

I shrugged.

"He's probably out retrieving his four-wheelers," I said.

"Would those be the four-wheelers that are sitting out in the woods a couple miles from his house?" P.D. asked, and I started to get a bad feeling.

"Wait. How do you know about the four-wheelers?" I asked.

"Because I just came from there. We conducted a welfare check for the family and couldn't find hide or hair of Dusty Cadwallader. His vehicles were there, but no Dusty."

I frowned.

"What exactly was it about the call to Dusty's aunt that bothered her so much she felt it necessary for law enforcement to do a welfare check?" Taylor thought to ask.

P.D. adjusted the strap on the back of his trooper hat.

"The last time Dusty's aunt spoke to your four-wheeling friend, Dusty, he was convinced he was about to be abducted by 'black-hooded beings from another dimension.'"

I heard Taylor's quick intake of breath.

From Smokey Bear to *Starship Trooper* in a single bound!

Eat your heart out, Superman.

CHAPTER TWENTY-TWO

―――

"Where on earth do you suppose Dusty Cadwallader is?" Taylor asked once the handsome trooper had left us and gone into the high school.

"Where on earth?" I repeated and looked over at her to see if Taylor was making an *Otherworld* joke. She just nodded. I should have known better. Taylor is so…literal. "Maybe they just missed him. Dusty's got a lot of land. He could've been out walking the dog." I stopped. Roswell! "Dawkins didn't mention a dog, did he?" I asked Taylor.

She shook her head.

"So that could mean Roswell is with Dusty." For some reason that possibility made me feel better.

"Roswell?"

I nodded. "Dusty's dog."

She nodded. "So what's next then? You want me to drop you at the *Gazette*?"

I pulled the copies Taylor had made from my bag and flipped through them, eyeballing a group of girls who were making their way, rabbit food in hand, to one of the picnic tables on the high school lawn.

"You speak cheerleader, right?" I asked Taylor who'd been on the cheerleading squad until she'd decided the debate team was more her style.

"What?"

"You were a cheerleader once upon a time. You speak their language. How about we see what we can find out about little miss pink tornadoes from her homeys over there?"

Taylor's forehead crinkled.

"*Oo*kay. What's our angle?" she asked.

I thought for a second. Nothing.

"Most cheerleaders are attention seekers," Taylor said and gave me the eye. "Note I said 'most' cheerleaders, not all," she clarified. "Anyway, we might go in with the idea that you'd like to do a 'day in the life of' story about a cheerleader. That might provide enough of an 'in' for you to get the information you're after."

"That's good," I told Taylor. "That's very good. And if things work out, maybe I'll even pitch the idea to Stan."

"Aren't you forgetting something?" Taylor asked.

I shook my head.

"What am I forgetting?"

"Someone tagged your car—oh, and upended heaping helpings of roadkill inside it. If Jada Garcia is involved and you start asking questions, it could get messier."

"But we don't even know for sure that they knew that was my car. It could have been a crime of opportunity. You know. Oh, cool. An abandoned car! Let's trash it! That kind of thing."

"And they just happened to have buckets of rotting roadkill on hand to dump in some unfortunate soul's car at random?" Taylor said. "I don't know. I've never been a big believer in coincidence."

One familial trait we shared.

Was it simply coincidence that Jada Garcia was dating Mick Dishman?

Or...perhaps.

"You don't suppose Manny's cousin could be involved in these incidents, do you?" I asked Taylor.

She shrugged. "I have no idea. I don't know the kid. But you do. What do you think?"

I shook my head. It was hard to picture a kid who—by hook or by crook—had somehow managed to whip enough votes to elect a girl called "Sasquatch" and a guy with the nickname "Tiny Tim" as homecoming queen and king.

By hook or by *crook*?

I swallowed, recalling how I'd first met Mick's Uncle Manny and wondering just how much a chip off the ol' block Mick might really be.

"Are you all right?" Taylor asked.

I nodded and held out my hands.

"Take me to your cheerleaders," I said.

She shook her head.

"Did you see the capri pants Bethany Adams has on?"

"Oh, God. Who wouldn't? They make her ass look wider than a billboard!"

"She ought to rent space out on her butt. She'd make a fortune!"

"What about Sofia Bedford's haircut? It's so short! She looks totally gay!"

"Maybe she *is* gay!"

"I heard she could go either way."

The girls at the table—three blondes, one redhead, and a brunette—laughed.

I lifted my gaze skyward.

"Dear Lord, save us from judgmental twits," I whispered.

"Shhh!" Taylor elbowed me.

I cleared my throat.

"Er, excuse me ladies. I'm sorry if I'm interrupting your grazing—" another sharp jab from Taylor, "er your meals, but I wonder if you could help me out. You see, I work for the *Grandville Gazette*, and I'm planning to do a 'day in the life of a cheerleader' type story and—"

"I know who you are," Kiera Radcliffe interrupted. "You're the ditzy reporter who discovers dead bodies and gets into all kinds of trouble with the law."

I frowned.

"As far as the dead bodies go, it was only the two and any investigative reporter worth their salt will inevitably butt heads with law enforcement," I said, recognizing a teaching moment when I saw it.

"Lois Lane here is also the reason Kylie didn't get homecoming queen last year, and Bigfoot and one of the seven dwarfs were elected instead."

"Now just a minute—"

Taylor grabbed my elbow and hauled me away from the danger zone.

"Let it go, Tressa. Obviously, Kiera here prefers to remain hostage to her sister's disappointing achievement record and has no personal aspiration to rise above Kylie's so-so performance. I totally get it. I really do. Sisters have to stick together, don't they, even if it's at the expense of the younger sister who is forced to remain at a rather mediocre level of recognition and achievement to protect her big sister's ego?"

I wasn't sure exactly which of Kiera's buttons Taylor meant to push by her little 'she's keeping you down, sister' mind game, but it seemed to be working.

"You want to do a story on us?" Natalie Jorgensen asked.

I looked at Taylor and she nodded.

"Yes. Both individually and collectively," Taylor said. "You see when I was cheerleading I got the distinct idea that nobody really appreciated the fact that cheerleading is also a sport and it requires just as much time, hard work, and guts to be successful as organized athletics." I'd have to be blindfolded to miss the pointed look Taylor gave me.

Okay, okay, so maybe I hadn't fully understood the level of commitment cheerleading required. It seemed to me shaking one's pom-poms and bootie while yelling out lame cheers wasn't all that taxing.

"You were a cheerleader?" Dani Colridge asked.

Taylor nodded.

"And we would be in the paper?" Portia Patterson asked.

"Of course. Pictures and quotes. A full spread," I said, thinking no way would Stan Rodgers go for an exposé on cheerleaders unless they wore crop tops and knee high boots and cheered for professional athletes.

"You can think about it, if you like," I said, pulling out a stack of business cards and handing them out. "I suppose I should speak with your coach—you know—clear it with her first."

"We have a new coach this year. Miss Banfield," Portia said.

"Oh. I see." I put a finger out and acted like I was counting heads. "Is one of you missing?" I asked.

"Jada. Jada Garcia. She's sick today." Natalie said, earning a glare from Kiera.

"Oh. That's too bad. I hope it's nothing serious," I said.

Nobody at the table said a word.

"Does Jada have a best friend or boyfriend or someone I could give this card to?" I asked.

"We'll pass it along," Kiera said.

"Fine." I turned to the brunette who'd remained silent and impassive the entire time. "You're Cissy, right? Cissy McCoy, squad leader? Here." I put the card on the table in front of her.

She slid the card back in my direction.

"No thanks. Not interested."

I frowned.

"Oh. Okay. That's fine. But if you should change your mind—" I slid the card in front of her again.

"I won't," she said and pushed the card in my direction a bit more forcefully.

"Keep it anyway," I said, sliding it back over to her. "Just in case."

"No. Thank. You." Cissy picked the card up, ripped it into four separate pieces, laid them back on the table in a stack, and pushed the stack over to me.

A long, ass awkward silence followed before the remaining four cheerleaders picked up their cards and performed the same exercise, ripping their cards and sliding the scraps to the middle of the table.

I blinked.

Interesting.

Before I could respond, I watched the cheerleaders' gazes slide past me.

"Can I help you, ladies?"

I turned.

Martina the Mentee, wearing snug white capri pants and a black-and-white striped V-neck T-shirt with a white camisole underneath, crossed her arms and cocked her head at us in a 'state your business please' kind of way.

"Oh, hello," I said. "We were just introducing ourselves to the girls here. We're thinking of doing a feature on cheerleading." I handed her a card. "I'm Tressa Turner. This is my sister, Taylor. And you are?"

She smiled. One of those big, bleachy, successful orthodontic treatment ones.

"Martina Banfield."

"Oh yes. I've heard of you," I said. "You must be Brian's mentee!"

She frowned.

"You know Brian?"

"Know him? Why, I was in his wedding just last year," I exclaimed. "Fabulous affair. Very elegant and classy. His wife, Kari, is my BFF," I added, giving her my own not-so-perfect grin right back.

"I see," she said, frowning down at the card in her hand.

"And you want to do a story on my cheerleaders?" she said.

"If that wouldn't be a problem," I said.

"The administration and parents might have an issue—"

"Oh, please! What parent wouldn't like to see their daughter showcased in the newspaper? And the school admin?" I made a raspberry sound and waved my hand. "They eat this kind of thing up." I moved closer and put a hand near my mouth in a conspiratorial move. "Makes the head honchos look good."

"Oh, yes. I see."

"Here's an extra business card," I handed her a second card. "For Jada. I understand she's under the weather. Poor girl. I told your girls I hope it's nothing serious, but they didn't seem to know very much."

"Oh, yes, well, I'm sure it's nothing serious," she said. "I'll see that she gets your card." She turned to the girls at the table. "Ladies, if you have a few minutes before the bell rings, I've got some changes in a routine for the donkey softball benefit tonight I'd like for you to look over. I'll be in my classroom."

I looked at her.

"You're performing at the county park tonight?" I asked.

She nodded. "We're cheering for the city team and doing a couple of routines. Why?"

"That's awesome! I'm covering the festivities. Hey, just a thought. Kari will be there, too. Maybe you'll get a chance to meet her. She's just the sweetest, nicest, most wonderful person. Just an all-round peach of a girl. Well, I guess we'll see you there! Ta-ta for now!" I gave her a fluttery little wave, and she walked away.

One-by-one the cheerleaders got up from the table and followed after her—leaving Cissy alone at the table.

"You coming, Cissy?" Kiera paused and called back to her fellow squad member.

Cissy raised her chin and looked up at me, giving me a cold look before she took a deep breath and let it out in a big ol' *whoosh* sending the business card scraps on the table flying off the edge and onto to the ground. She got to her feet, sending me another scary look for the road and walked away.

"That wasn't very 'sis, boom, bah' of her," I said to Taylor.

"Well, maybe the 'boom' part," Taylor replied. "You know. As in lower it."

I winced.

See Tressa.
See Tressa run.
Run, Tressa, run!

CHAPTER TWENTY-THREE

Taylor dropped me at the newspaper office. I'd catch a ride home with my dad, clean up, and head out to the park with Taylor who would be helping with concessions. Uncle Frank would donate a portion of his sales to the Historical Village fund. I was looking forward to covering the event.

Who am I kidding? I was looking forward to *participating* in the event. I played softball. I rode horses.

Donkey baseball? Dude! I'm what you call a natural.

I hurried into the newspaper office and headed straight for Stan's office, eager to run the gnome theory by him. I put on the brakes when I noticed a sheet of paper tacked to the bulletin board in the hall.

"For sale," it read. "1987 Plymouth Roadkill Reliant. Unique paint job. Loaded with extras. One of a kind anti-theft security system. Perfect for that eccentric and hard-to-buy for family member. Previously owned by the notorious Calamity Jayne Turner. Vehicle can be seen at Ray's Wreck and Salvage. Gas mask and eye protection recommended when viewing the vehicle. All offers considered, reasonable or not."

I muttered a few choice words about men evolving from jackasses (or vice versa) and was about to expand on my theory when a bellow caught me in mid-hypothesis.

"Hey, Turner? You say something about a jackass?"

I flinched.

"As a matter of fact, yes, yes I did," I said, stepping into the doorway of his office.

"Oh, really? And what were you saying about jackasses, Turner?" my boss asked, sitting back and biting down on his cigar.

"I was saying that I, um, can't wait for 'Jackass, The Ballgame,' tonight," I improvised.

"That's what I thought I heard you say, Turner. Damned shame about your car," he said, shaking his head and switching gears. "I don't suppose it's salvageable," he said. "Tough break. I know how much you loved that old beater."

Who was he kidding? I'd cursed the beast backward, forward, and upside-down for years. Its only laudable qualities were that it was paid off, the insurance was how-low-can-you-go-low, you could park it anywhere without worrying about door dings, and the pups could go along for the ride without regard for toenail scratches or cloudy drool deposits.

"Thanks, Stan. I'm touched by your concern. Especially considering my vehicle was damaged in the line of duty."

"Line of duty?"

"That's right. I moved into Stan's office and leaned over his desk, bracing my fingertips against the desk's top. "I was working on a story at the time. Now that I think about it, the *Gazette* should really be responsible for my car damage. You have coverage, don't you, Stan? You see, if I hadn't been following a lead, this never would have happened."

"Following a lead—or following a cement lawn gnome?" Stan said.

All the huff and puff went out of me like a Halloween inflatable whose fan has been unplugged.

"Who blabbed?" I demanded to know.

"Shelby Lynn mentioned it. Now don't get all bent out of shape, Turner. She actually supports your divining dwarf theory. But me? I'm the guy the buck stops with. I'm supposed to be cynical. That's why I'm the boss. I need to be convinced, Turner. I deal in facts, Turner. Facts. You know. Like Joe Friday. Just the facts, ma'am. Just the facts."

I shook my head. The man was a total legend in his own mind.

"What else do you have besides a now-you-see-him-now-you-don't lawn ornament?" Stan asked. "What about suspects, Turner? You know. Live human ones."

I brought him up to speed on what we'd learned about Jada Garcia's affinity for pink tornadoes and the follow-up we'd conducted with the cheerleaders.

I placed the photocopy from the yearbook page on the desk in front of him.

"That's our artist," I said, pointing at Jada. "And those are her fellow cheerleaders from last year. Surprisingly, they're all on the squad together again this year."

Stan's brows lowered. He picked up the sheet of paper.

"And these girls are connected to the incidents how?" he asked.

I shook my head. "Well, so far they aren't. Not directly, that is. But Jada Garcia probably is. And you know the saying, 'birds of a feather.' I just think it's worth taking a look at her circle of friends more closely."

Stan continued studying the picture, tapping it with his index finger.

Tap, tap, tap, tap.

I frowned.

"Is something wrong, Stan?"

He shook his head.

"Headache," he said. "Remind me again, where Space Cadet Cadwallader comes in," he said and rubbed his forehead before opening his drawer to take out a bottle of extra strength pain medication.

I explained again about the pink tornado on the trees, the activity in the forest, the can of spray paint—

I stopped and slapped a palm to my cheek. The spray paint can! The vodka bottle! The evidence! I'd forgotten all about the items we'd collected at Dusty's. I'd meant to turn it all over to the sheriff for proper forensic examination, but in the chaos of the moment, I'd totally spaced it off.

I know. *Spaced* it off. Very punny, right?

Work with me, people! I simply don't have time for sophomoric space jokes.

"What's the matter with you, Turner?" Stan asked.

I shook my head.

"Just a million and one things to do and no way to get from point A to point B," I explained.

"You've got a way to get to the park, I hope," he said. "I want lots of donkey ball pictures. People love those. Cracks 'em up. And while you're at it, don't forget to get plenty of jackass pictures of Paul Van Vleet from *New Holland News* if the cocky bastard shows up. And I'm not talking about the donkey jackass."

I winced. Business rivalry could get…dicey.

"Shouldn't you be participating, as well?" I asked. "You know. To uphold the honor of the *Gazette*?"

"You're takin' his side, Turner?"

I shook my head back and forth until I felt my fillings start to loosen up.

"No, sir! Absolutely not, sir."

"Good. Besides, I figure my employees can handle Van Vleet et al. Your track record with junior, that twerp son of his, ain't half bad, Turner. Not bad at all."

I grinned.

"Atta girls" from Stan Rodgers?

OMG! They do exist!!!

* * *

I killed time in the newspaper office before hitching a ride to the ballpark with Taylor.

Baseball.

America's sport.

There's nothing better than sitting in the stands on a warm summer day with a cup of cold beer, a jumbo bag of buttered popcorn, a hot dog with the works, and nowhere else to be but taking in the game.

Okay. There might be one thing better.

Watching hapless and unsuspecting greenhorns run to a donkey and jump on and actually expect to get to first base.

Literally.

If you've never watched a donkey baseball game, let me give you a quick overview. First off, each team can have up to nine players, depending on the availability of donkeys. Outfielders and basemen each have an assigned ass…er donkey. The pitcher generally does not have a donkey and is only permitted to pitch—not field. The pitcher pitches the ball to the batter and when the batter hits the ball, the batter runs to his donkey standing nearby, grabs the lead rein, and gets on and starts to first base. Well, in theory.

Fielders must ride their donkeys to the balls, get off, and then get back on that donkey to toss the ball to the appropriate baseman to make the tag.

Again, *in theory*.

And...reality?

You've heard the phrase "stubborn as a jackass"? Yep. That 'rep' is righteously earned.

Nine times out of ten the hitter/runner never makes it to the base. Generally, the "runner" ends up either flying off the bucking burro-bronco or goes hurtling like a missile over the lowered head of donkey who likes to put on the brakes without warning.

Let me tell you, donkey baseball is not for the faint of heart. Or for the old or brittle. (Sorry, seniors. The truth may hurt, but not nearly as much as taking a flip or a nosedive from an ornery, cantankerous donkey.)

That's why each game is only three innings long. By the end of those innings, most competitors will say the games are still too long.

Generally you have four teams vie for the chance to advance to the finals. In this case, we'd dispense with the preliminary round and play one six-inning game featuring a team from New Holland against a team from Grandville. A long halftime break was scheduled to rest the players (both two- and four-legged) and substitute new players where needed for the second half.

Halftime was also when the big wigs would encourage people to reach deep into their pockets to support a worthy cause. Since this was a fundraising event, any monies left over after paying the donkey ball people would go to the Knox County Historical Society for improvements to the park and the historical village.

The break also featured halftime entertainment, including a mini-cheerleading challenge. No. The cheerleaders aren't mini, the competition is. Duh.

The "players" had all been unloaded from the trailers and were tied up along a makeshift hitching post. The diamond had been prepared with great big circles spray-painted around the bases, the enlarged "safe" zone a concession to the four-legged runners. I blinked when I noticed the color of the spray paint.

Pink. Fat tornado pink.

I got my equipment out. I'd checked out a good quality digital camera from the newspaper and had pinched my folks' digital recorder, so I could also get video of the event. I figured I could stick it up on the blog I'd started on TribRide and still contributed to now and then.

I was bent over, rear in the air, pulling something from my bag when I heard a click.

"Wait a minute! Hold that pose!" Another *click*. "I want to remember you just like this!"

I whipped around.

Dixie Daggett, camera phone pointed in my direction, looked at the phone and shook her head.

"I knew it! I should've used the panoramic view."

"That's weird. I'd have guessed you had panorama set as default mode for your selfies," I snarked back.

Dixie and I are still working through trust issues with one another. I think she's a *Weeble* masquerading as a human, and she thinks I'm the country and western version of a blonde Betty Boop.

"By the way, thanks for dragging my fiancé out to the boonies so he could come back with a first class collection of chigger bites," Dixie said.

"Frankie has chigger bites?"

"Only up the wazoo," Dixie said.

I frowned.

"When you say 'up the wazoo'…"

"He's got them everywhere, you lunatic!" Dixie said. "He's driving me crazy. I don't know what's worse, the incessant scratching or the accompanying sound effects."

"Sound effects?"

"The grunts, moans, and hisses he makes when he's not scratching and the "oohs" and "ahhs" when he is."

"That doesn't sound too terribly bad," I thought, thanking heaven that I didn't have to nurse the Frankfurter back to health.

"Oh. It doesn't sound so terribly bad? How would you like it if your boyfriend comes out with, "Oh, God that feels so good" and he's talking about using a plastic fork on his groin area?"

I winced. So not a mental image I wanted imprinted on my psyche.

Delete. Delete.

"How the heck did Frankie come in contact with chiggers?" I asked. "The guy wrapped himself up so much we could have stuck postage on him and sent him to Timbuktu. He got so liberal with the duct tape that we had to use a utility knife and pliers to get him loose."

"How did this happen? Because he was with you. That's how this happened," Dixie said.

"And you know Frankie and his sensitivities. He looks at a strawberry, and he turns into Fat Albert."

"Oh, geez, I'm sorry," I said and meant it. Anybody who spends any time out of doors eventually gets clobbered by a nasty case of the chiggers. So. Not. Fun. "Has he seen the doctor?"

"He's Frankie. What do you think?" Dixie said. "They gave him a shot and some ointment, but he's still doing his fleabag impression."

"Tough break," I said and shook my head. "Tough break."

"Speaking of 'tough breaks,' I hear you are no longer a member of the motoring public. Something about your car doing double-duty as a rendering vehicle. Rotten break."

I bit my tongue. News traveled at warp speed in a small town.

"There you are, Dixie," Frankie walked in, a finger inside his waistband. "Where did you put my ointment?"

"It's in my bag in the concession stand," Dixie said. "You need it again so soon?"

He nodded.

"I just want to apply some before the game starts. I'll probably get hot and sweaty, and that will aggravate the itching."

I blinked.

"Wait a minute. You're playing, Frankie?"

He shrugged. "The Chamber of Commerce asked Dad to provide a player."

"And he chose you?"

He shrugged again. "The Freeze employees who want to participate will take turns and rotate in and out. It's supposed to boost morale among the workers."

I grimaced.

Chances were good it would boost Uncle Frank's liability insurance if any of his employees took a hard spill.

"And you volunteered?"

Frankie nodded.

"A lot of the local cops, deputies, and firemen are playing," Dixie explained. "And you know Frankie when it comes to hanging out with the men in blue."

If you knew Frankie like I knew Frankie...

If you did know Frankie, you would be placing a heavy bet right about now that before the night was over Frank Barlowe, Junior would end up being a man in blue—black and blue—judging from prior athletic performances, that is.

"I hear Rick and Craig are playing," Frankie said. "Patrick Dawkins, too."

Sweet!

Studly men on immovable, mulish beasts providing primo blackmail material.

Good times!

"I know one person who won't be participating," Dixie said. "Your friend, Drew Van Vleet. He's over there hobbling around on crutches and giving you the stink eye. Sorry. That was awfully insensitive of me, considering your car situation and all."

"Wow. I didn't know a *Weeble* had a sense of humor," I said, turning to look behind me. Sure enough my former biking buddy, *New Holland News* reporter and all-round smarmy pseudo-journalist, Drew Van Vleet, shot me a dark look before turning away.

I sighed. Apparently he still blamed me for his little accident at the naked slide during TribRide.

"Come on, Frankie," Dixie took her intended's arm. "Let's get your ointment."

"Oh, and Frankie? Don't forget to lose the plastic fork if you do get a chance to go for a donkey ride. You don't want to puncture or deflate...er...anything."

Dixie shook her head at me, and they walked away.

I finished getting my equipment ready and wandered over to check out the donkeys. I'm a sucker for anything with four legs—especially ones you can ride. I petted each donkey player and learned his or her donkey names. There was Johnny, Toby, George, Garth, Waylon, Willie, Hank, Kenny, Dolly, Reba, Patsy, Loretta, Shania, and Outlaw.

Just a guess here, but I'm figuring Outlaw is a bit of rebel.

"Barbie makin' new friends?" I heard. Manny DeMarco, a mountain that blocked my view of the sun—and everything else—looked down at me from behind his dark glasses.

"It's always nice to make a new friend," I said. "What are you doing here?" Somehow I couldn't see Mr. Dark and Dangerous here jumping on a short-legged donkey and yelling "giddy up." "Oh, I bet I know. You're here to see Mick's girlfriend, Jada, perform, right?" I said, figuring I might as well try pumping Manny for info on the cheerleader girlfriend. "Aunt Mo's not here, is she?" I said, attempting to sneak a look around his bulk.

He nodded. "Mo's here."

"Oh, that's nice," I lied. "And Mick?" I peeked around Manny. "Is Mick here? You know I never did get to properly thank him for his help at getting the vote out at homecoming last year. I suppose he's hanging with his girlfriend, Jada. Well, if she's feeling better that is. She was under the weather earlier when I spoke to her fellow cheerleaders. Is she here? Jada, that is. I'd like to meet her. You see I'm doing a feature on cheerleaders—you know—showcase all the hard work that goes into cheerleading, and I'd really like to get the inside scoop—"

"Barbie's babbling."

I stopped.

Damn.

"Barbie asks a lot of questions," Manny said.

"It's my job to ask questions. Information is my stock in trade."

"Barbie's got Mick asking questions for her. Mick's a busy kid. Mick's got school and football. No time for Barbie's distractions," Manny said, and I felt a tiny stab of hurt and more than a little irritation.

"I'm sorry. I didn't realize I was imposing on Mick when I asked him to keep his ears open for anything he might hear about gang activity or incidents that have been occurring. Mick didn't seem to have a problem with it."

"Mick needs to focus on school. Period. And Manny and Mo gonna see he does."

Holy Tressa-passers will be shot on sight!

For the first time since I'd met Manny DeMarco I felt a frisson of real fear—a sense that I was treading on dangerous ground and had better retreat before it was too late.

"Oh, sure. Absolutely. Of course. I totally understand. Scholastics rule. No problem. I get it. Academics and athletics come first." I performed a nervous salute. "Roger that! Message received! Over and out!"

Manny gave me a last look before turning and walking away.

I patted Reba's neck.

"You heard me babbling like a fool, girlfriend. Why didn't you reach out and nip me in the hiney or something?"

"Am I interrupting a private moment?" Shelby Lynn's bulk almost replicated the same blackout pattern Manny's had.

"Reba and I were just venting about the vagaries of men. What's up?"

"Nothing much. I just received some very interesting information about the incident at H&F," she said.

"Oh? Enlighten me, my young apprentice."

Shelby did an eye roll number.

"It seems that the H&F job was not merely an act of vandalism. This time there was an actual break in and items were stolen."

I caught my breath.

"Oh, wow! What did they take?"

"That's where it gets interesting. They took ropes and knives and last but not least, a Kahr," Shelby said.

I frowned.

"A car? They broke in and took a car?"

Shelby nodded.

"Let me get this straight. They broke in and took knives and rope and a *car*? Was it a toy car?"

She shook her head.

"No. It was the real thing."

Something still did not compute.

"A real car. They took a real car."

"Yes! They took a real Kahr! A Kahr is a gun!"

"A car is a gun?" My cluelessness must've shown.

"A Kahr! *K-A-H-R!*" she yelled. "As in a nine-millimeter Kahr *revolver*!" Shelby Lynn said.

It took a second for that startling information to sink in.

"Oh. That kind of Kahr," I said. "Why didn't you say that in the first place?"

She just shook her head.

"You do know what this means, don't you?" Shelby said. "It looks like they've upped the ante."

I nodded.

Our merry little band of vandals had just turned rogue.

CHAPTER TWENTY-FOUR

By the end of the first two innings, my sides ached from laughing so much, and both cameras were chock-full of so-ready-for-YouTube footage and scrapbook quality photography. I watched as my "boyfriend" mounted a wily Waylon or Willie (I can't remember which) only to have the base runner stop suddenly, put his head down, and buck for all he was worth, shooting the DNR officer up and over the front of Waylon or Willie like shot from a slingshot.

Bah-zing!

By the fifth fall, even I wanted the proud ranger to raise the white flag and surrender to the superior athlete.

P.D. Dawkins showed his mettle, getting thrown twice before coaxing Johnny to first base. In the stands the Turner-Townsend contingent was well represented. The folks, Uncle Frank and Aunt Reggie, Gram and Joe, and Kimmie occupied the stands around me, along with best bud, Kari. Taylor was helping out in the concession stand.

"You see the way she keeps eyeballing Brian?" Kari nudged me in the side.

"Who? Loretta? Or is that Dolly?"

"No! That barracuda in yoga pants! She just can't take her eyes off my husband."

"Who can? From here it looks like he can't decide if he wants to ride the donkey or marry it," I said, observing his bear hug technique for staying on.

"At least your husband has the gumption to commit to something," Kimmie said. "My husband took one tumble, dusted off his pants, cursed, and gave up. No staying power. No staying power at all," she observed.

I winced, wondering if we were still talking about donkey rides or something of a more...intimate nature.

"Do we really have to put up with Martina McMentor at halftime?" Kari asked.

"I hear one of her girls is sick and she's going to stand in for her in the routine," Kimmie said. "I hear she's very good."

"At what?" Kari said. "Pretending to be a cheerleader or causing marital discord?"

"I meant I heard she was good with the girls. They really like her."

"She's not making moves on *their* husbands," Kari said.

"I don't think they have husbands," I pointed out and gave Kimmie a help-me-out-here nod of my head, which, judging by her next remark she apparently totally misinterpreted.

"Face it. Men are just plain stupid when it comes to women," Kimmie said. "And the longer they're married, the more clueless they become."

"At least your husband doesn't spend nights out with a phony wannabe cheerleader who claims she needs help with career goals of all things!"

"No. Mine spends his evenings on a computer researching his Fantasy Football player roster and watching ESPN or Sportsman's something or other."

"At least he's home."

"If you can call it that. I get more conversation from zombies on TV."

Serve, volley, smash. Serve, volley, smash!
Back and forth. Back and forth.
Back and forth the balls of marital dissension went.
Kimmie. Kari. Back to Kimmie. Back to Kari.
Bam! Bam! Bam!

I felt like I was center court at Wimbledon watching the Wives of Knox County Grand Husband Slam.

"Oh, look! They've got caramel apples!" I interrupted the latest smash and put a hand on each of the contestants' shoulders and pushed myself to my feet. "I've gotta get me one of those before they're out," I said, and scrambled off the bleachers.

I rubbed the crick in my neck I had from turning my head back and forth, back and forth, between the two clearly discontented wives.

I shook my head. Lord. If that was marriage I'd—

I stopped dead in my tracks.

If that was marriage I'd...what exactly?

"I'm surprised you're not out there. You know. You being such an accomplished rider and all."

I looked up.

County Deputy-slash-Sheriff Doug Samuels leaned against the hood of his patrol vehicle, a four-wheel drive Tahoe, arms folded across his ample chest, feet crossed at the ankles.

"I wouldn't want to make the other participants feel badly about themselves," I said. "I'll try my luck the last inning. But, gee thanks for acknowledging my riding skill. As you recall, it likely saved me from death by a crazed, lunatic murderer last summer."

Samuels grunted. He didn't like to be reminded of the events of last summer so, of course, I brought them up as often as I could.

"By the way," I went on, "I heard about H&F. The thefts. The Kahr theft. That's a gun, you know. Sounds like the crime wave is escalating. Stealing firearms is pretty serious, wouldn't you say? I'm thinking this development probably puts us beyond 'drunken high-schoolers being high-schoolers.' Right...Sheriff?"

A muscle pulsated in Samuel's cheek.

"I see I need to have another talk with my people about disseminating information," he said.

"Or I suppose, in this case, *not* disseminating information. I don't suppose it would do any good to ask you to sit on that information."

After the way he'd dissed me? He could sit on it.

I crossed my own arms. "What do you think?" I said.

He shrugged.

"Have it your way," he said. "It's just too bad we can't work together."

"Oh, really? You mean that, *Sheriff*? Because it so happens I have something of an evidentiary nature that might be of assistance in your investigation."

His irritable look became an "Oh, God, what now?" look.

"Okay. I'll bite. What might that be?"

I told him about the spray paint can and the vodka bottle and burnt paper in the woods at Dusty Cadwallader's.

"Okay, I know it's a long shot that there will be fingerprints on the spray paint can or the bottle. But I was thinking you could canvass the stores that sell the brand and color of paint and see if you can find out who purchased it. Or check the vodka bottle for the same. And you might be able to make out something from the paper we found. I think it might be a photograph that someone tried to burn."

"You have these items here?" he asked.

I nodded. "They're in the trunk of my Paw-Paw Will's Buick," I said. I'd bribed Taylor into taking me out to Ray's Wreck and Salvage and retrieving the evidence from Dusty's woods by telling her I'd behave where a certain trooper was concerned that night. "And don't worry. We've kept the chain of evidence. My cousin, Frankie, who's sort of studying to be a crime techie, processed, sealed, and initialed everything just like you see on those crime shows. Gil Grissom would be impressed. Well, he would be if he hadn't left CSI, that is."

Samuels did one of those head-clearing shake numbers.

"Yeah okay. I suppose I could take a look at what you have."

He walked with me to the Buick. I retrieved the key from the ashtray and opened the trunk.

"Whoo. That's ripe," Samuels observed.

I was handing over the evidence in question when I noticed the squad of Grandville cheerleaders—minus their graffiti artist, Jada, but plus Martina their handler—walk by us, six sets of suspicious eyeballs giving me and the county Mountie the once-over but good.

Once over might be understating. The truth was, I wouldn't have been surprised to see the cheerleaders make cutting motions across their throats—all carefully choreographed for perfect synchronization, of course.

"Something wrong?" Samuels inquired.

"Wrong?"

"You look like someone who walked into a darkened movie theater expecting to see *Frozen* only to have *Undead and Unfrozen* show up on the big screen."

Dang cops and their knack for reading body language.

"I'm fine, but thanks for asking," I said.

He grunted again.

"Anything else?"

"Yes, in fact. What's the latest on Dusty Cadwallader? Has he been located? Is he okay?"

The acting sheriff frowned.

"How'd you hear about Cadwallader?"

"I'm a reporter, remember? I have sources. So, they found him, right?"

Samuels shook his head.

"Our department has been unable to make contact with Mr. Cadwallader, but we're checking his home periodically."

"That's odd."

"Not if you know Cadwallader."

I frowned. "Where do you think he is?"

"Don't you know?"

I shook my head.

"No. Do you?"

"Of course. He's been abducted by an alien life form and taken to the mother ship where he is being poked and prodded and experimented on for scientific research purposes," Samuels said.

Great. Just what Knox County needs. A sheriff who thinks he's Letterman.

"I don't think Dusty's disappearance should be dismissed so lightly, Sheriff Samuels," I said. "One minute he's there and the next, *poof*, he's gone."

"Exactly," Samuels said. "And if you'd been called out to Dusty's place as often as our deputies have to listen to the latest cock-and-bull story about UFOs and creatures from another planet or galaxy, or solar system or whatever, you'd be less likely to call out the bloodhounds just yet. He hasn't even been missing a day. Usually we have to wait at least two days to open a missing person's investigation. Fortunately, ninety percent of these cases end up with the person showing up with a perfectly good reason for not being where other people think they should be."

"I don't know. I've got this feeling—"

The sheriff held out a hand.

"Spare me your feelings, Turner," he said. "I imagine they're about as credible as Dusty Cadwallader's E.T. sightings. Now, if you'll excuse me, I want a front-row seat for the second half so I don't miss your turn at bat. Or that of your cousin, that skinny Barlowe kid. That alone is bound to be worth the price of admission."

I resisted the urge to make an offensive hand gesture and settled for wishing a case of flaming hemorrhoids and a massive chiggers offensive on his person. Under my breath, of course.

I snared my caramel apple and made my way back to the bleachers, this time avoiding my sister-in-law and my best friend, plopping my fanny down next to my gammy and Joe.

Generally a mistake.

"So, what's the latest skinny on the crime wave?" Joe asked. "And don't tell me nothing because I saw you handing over those evidence bags to Knox County's head honcho. What was it anyway?"

"Like you said, 'evidence,'" I told him.

"That's it? That's all you're giving me? After all I've done to assist you—"

I looked at him.

"Assist me? Hmm. That must mean I have a list of can't fail 'gotcha' questions for Manny DeMarco. Let's see. Maybe they're in my bag here. Nope. No questions. Maybe someone emailed them. Nope. Nothing in my Inbox. Hmm. Perhaps said assistant is prepared to hand them over now." I put my hand out. "Oh, look. Nothing."

"I've been busy," Joe said, squirming in his seat. "I'll get to it."

"You're retired, dude. What could possibly take up so much of your time?"

"Joe tellin' you about our little project?" My gammy leaned across Joe and nudged me in the ribs. "We've been tailing Abigail Winegardner and her gigolo."

I blinked.

"Gigolo?"

"The mustachioed tramp—not Abigail. That other tramp."

I winced.

"Gram!"

"We're keepin' a logbook, aren't we, Joe?"

"A logbook?"

"Dates, times, locations," Joe supplied.

"*Oo*kay. Why are you keeping book on your neighbor lady and her…male friend?" I asked.

"'Cause I know that tramp!"

"Abigail?"

"No! The other one! There's something about that feller. I know that bum from some place. I just know it!" Gram said. "That's the main reason I'm sitting on this rock hard bench with my butt growin' numb. We're keeping an eye on our targets, aren't we, Joe?"

"Abigail and Au…her friend are here?"

Gram pursed her lips.

"They're down there near first base."

I followed her pointing finger. Sure enough, Abigail and Uncle Bo watched the festivities at ground level.

"They brought padded lawn chairs," she added. "How come you didn't think to bring lawn chairs, Joe?" she asked.

"We didn't know they were coming here when we started following them, Hannah," Joe said.

She thought about it for a second.

"That ol' Abigail. She's a sly one, she is," Gram said. "Luring us out here to sit on these god-awful hard seats."

"You do know there are penalties for stalking, don't you?" I asked Joe.

He winked.

"Only if you get caught."

"You clear my name yet, Tressa?" Gram asked.

"Say again."

"You find Quasimodo yet?" she clarified.

"No. Not yet. But I'm hot on his hand-painted, cast iron tail," I told her.

"Beats me who would want to take the ugly little Smurf in the first place," she said. "Must be some kind of mess-o-kist."

Thank goodness Ranger Rick picked that time to drop onto the bleacher beside me so I didn't have to respond. I got a whiff of outdoors, sweat, donkey, and the ranger's aftershave—a heady mix.

"Hail the conquering donkey soldier!" I said and gave a dippy salute. "Glad to see you're still in one piece, Mr. Ranger Sir. I must tell you, there were times I had doubts."

He took his baseball cap off and ran a finger through his sweat-soaked, dark brown hair.

"Damned stubborn asses," he said, and grinned. "I lost track of how many times I hit the ground."

"Eight, but who's counting?" I supplied.

"Nice," Townsend said. "But still flattering to know you couldn't take your eyes off me."

I smiled. "Who could? You looked like a bottle rocket being launched." I made a shrill, whistling sound followed by a dramatic crescendo. *"Pissh! Boom!"*

He rubbed his rear end.

"No wonder they make you sign a waiver of liability," he said. "My butt will probably be black and blue by morning." He put his arm around me. "Care to run me a nice, soothing bath and give me a massage and nurse me back to health tonight?"

I felt a shiver of excitement despite the heat of the evening.

Nurse Tressa Jayne reporting for duty!

"I might be persuaded," I said, my mouth as dry as the pitcher's mound.

"By the way, I see Brian and Kari are still at odds over Miss Pom-Poms over there. And what's up with Craig and Kimmie? Craig's been in a bad mood for months."

"Miss Pom-Poms? You noticed her pom-poms?"

Rick grinned.

"Pom-poms? What pom-poms?"

I shook my head. Men.

"I don't like all this…marital discord," I said, rubbing my stomach before handing my caramel apple to my gammy who'd been eyeballing it since I sat down. Last month my folks were having problems communicating and now Craig and Kimmie and Brian and Kari. All this matrimonial strife was putting me off my vittles.

"Relationships are complex. Couples have differences," Townsend said. "They work through them."

I shook my head. Why get married at all if it was so difficult and required so much work?

"Tressa? You're uncharacteristically quiet. That's not like you," Townsend said and put a hand to my forehead. "You're not coming down with something, are you?"

I swallowed the lump in my throat.

What I suspected I was coming down with was a raging case of commitment phobia precipitated and aggravated by the infectious nature of the disharmony prevalent in the relationships of those in close proximity to me.

But that's only a guess.

"I'm okay. Just lots of craziness going on right now. My job. My car. This story. My brother. My best friend."

My own feelings of crippling fear and impending panic at what was required of relationships these days.

Other than the aforementioned, I was peachy.

"Have you thought about what you're going to do regarding transportation?" Rick asked. "I know you probably don't have a lot of money saved. I could help you with a down payment on a vehicle."

I looked at him.

"You're offering to lend me money?"

He shrugged. "Call it a loan if you like. You need a car. I've got resources."

"Meaning I don't?"

He frowned.

"Do you?"

I didn't, but it irked me that he automatically assumed I didn't.

"I have a little put back." A jar of coins from beer can deposits put back on a shelf in the hall ready to be switched out for bills the next time I went to the bank qualifies as a little put back, right?

"Still, you might want to keep that as a nest egg."

Nest egg? Nest egg! When had I ever had the luxury of a nest egg? The only eggs I kept in my house were ones I fried with bacon or ones with crème filling I gorged on each Easter.

"Can we talk about this another time?" I asked, thinking when hell froze over might be too soon for me.

"Oh, look! It's time for the TSA portion of the show," Gram announced when the New Holland cheerleaders took their place on the field.

"TSA?" Townsend frowned.

"I think she means T *and* A," I interpreted. "Your pom-pom princesses on parade."

The New Holland cheerleaders did a decent job of performing to "Beat It," and the audience applauded enthusiastically.

"Hardly a showstopper," my gammy the entertainment critic said. "And that song?" She sighed. "It's been beatin' to death. What do you think, Joe? What do you give 'em?"

"Seven tops," Joe said.

"I give 'em a six," Gram said.

I shook my head. What was this? So you think you can dance with the cheerleaders?

"A six? That low?" Joe said.

Gram nodded. "Too much A and not enough T."

"Gram!"

She shrugged.

"It's lopsided," she said. "You think our team can beat the Dutch, Tressa?"

"I'm not sure I'm qualified to hazard an opinion," I said.

"Huh?"

"I have no idea, Gram. But I do like their costumes."

And I did. They were dressed like cowgirls with short tan vests that featured what looked like sheriff's stars, short denim short shorts, and suede boots.

I took my camera out and hit the zoom button.

"Panther Posse," I read on their stars. Points for theme. No points for originality.

My lens zeroed in on Martina Banfield who looked all Dallas Cowboy Cheerleader in her Grandville Heads West outfit. I blinked when I noticed the guy she was talking to—and laughing with Brian.

Kari's Brian.

Holy sis boom bummer! I could imagine how Kari was reacting to the little confab.

"Why are men so dismally and utterly clueless?" I asked no one in particular. "Why do their thought processes originate in a sexual organ rather than the brain?"

"Hold on! What are you lookin' at through that camera, Tressa Jayne? Give it to me!" Gram snatched the camera from me. "Let me take a look!"

I shook my head.

"I'm looking at men behaving like fools," I said, and Townsend lifted an eyebrow. "Present company excepted," I added, giving him a playful tweak on the cheek.

"I don't see nothing," Gram said. "Hang on. Wait a minute. I see it now."

"You do?" I said, wondering how my gammy could possibly know about Kari and Brian and Martina the Mentee.

She nodded.

"'Course I do. Frankie with his hand down the front of his pants? Who could miss it?"

I winced and took the camera back a millisecond after Gram pressed the button, memorializing the moment. I snapped off another one. You know. Just in case Gram's was blurry.

The Grandville squad moved into their places. Several seconds ticked by before their music selection exploded out of the loudspeakers.

Oh. God. They couldn't. They wouldn't. They didn't dare!

They couldn't be about to ruin "T-R-O-U-B-L-E" by Travis Tritt for me, could they?

I watched the routine with my own troubled mix, one-part admiration and one-part consternation.

The routine was flawless.

In fact, the last time I'd seen such high-kicking, knee-slapping, heel-grinding, honkey-tonkin' was at the Lucky Mule in Abilene, Texas on the occasion of my twenty-first birthday. Oh, what a night!

When the girls finished, the applause was thunderous. Even the New Holland contingent was clapping like there was no tomorrow leaving no doubt that the Panther Posse had just kicked the Dutchwomen's funny little britches.

My gaze wandered over to best bud, Kari. Even from this distance I could pick up the gnashing of her teeth. When the cheerleaders ventured into the stands to pass the buckets for a donation, I could almost swear I saw Kari hock a loogie into the bucket.

I winced.

Oh, buddy do I smell T-R-O-U-B-L-E.

CHAPTER TWENTY-FIVE

It was the bottom of the last inning. New Holland was up by one. My brother, apparently deciding to take another whack at taming the beast (no, not Kimmie if that's what you're thinking) had volunteered to hit again. Craig, like yours truly, was on the receiving end of more than a modest share of the Blackford "gumption" as my gammy likes to call it.

Our CPA mother has other, more analytically disturbing names for it.

I was on deck.

If Craig scored, his would be the tying run.

And me? The winning one. Naturally.

Craig stepped up to home plate and just like you've seen men of summer do since America's sport was invented—he lifted the bat and pointed it at the center field fence. As expected, the crowd's response was a combination of cheers and jeers.

I shook my head.

Cock-a-doodle Craig struttin' his stuff.

Craig drew the bat back, his gaze settling on the ball at the pitcher's mound. The pitcher made a big deal out of his windup and threw the pitch.

Whop!

The bat connected with the ball and sent it sailing over the head of the second baseman.

"Go, Craig, go!" I yelled.

Craig ran to Willie, his designated base runner and performed a spastic belly flop, landing on Willie's back like a desperate surfer trying to mount his surfboard before the great white shark that belonged to the circling fins selected a juicy limb and went to town.

He threw his arms around the donkey's neck like it was a lifesaver and hung on. Through a series of ugly fits and starts, through sheer dint of will, Craig managed to stay on Willie all the way to second base.

And the crowd went crazy.

Great. Craig the donkey jockey had shown his mettle, but unfortunately for me he'd also just raised the bar for his sister, the rodeo queen.

It was time to call upon my skills as a donkey whisperer.

Okay, okay. So I've never actually whispered to a donkey. I figure they're close enough to a horse to understand and respond to my communication style.

Reba would be the wind beneath my wings rounding the bases. Given I had two geldings at home, I decided I'd better go the one-girl-to-another route. Plus, it was Reba after all. How hard could it be?

"Hey there, Reba. How's it going? Everything good?" I asked, spatting her neck. "Listen, Reba, can we talk?" I said, moving closer to her ear. "You see Willie over there, don't you, acting like he's all that. Just like my bro. We can't have that now can we? We can't have the male of the species show us up. It's unacceptable. So we girls have to stick together. You know. Girl power!" I raised a fist. "Oh. Sorry. I mean, donkey power!" I lifted my fist again. "So what do you say we work together, Miss Reba? No bucking, braking, balking, or bedeviling this cowgirl—and let's show these jackass males how it's really done!"

Reba lifted her nose and snorted, blowing snot all over me.

"I'll take that as a yes," I said and wiped the crud off my chin.

I jogged over and picked up my bat, blinking when I realized the "honorary" umpire was none other than Doug Samuels.

I gave Samuels an "I've got my eyes on you" look before I stepped into the batter's box to receive the pitch.

The pitcher threw the ball, high and outside.

"Strike one!" Samuels barked.

I frowned at the "umpire."

"Seriously?"

He shrugged.

The next pitch to the plate almost qualified as a wild pitch.

"Strike two!"

I whirled around.

"Are you blind? That pitch didn't even come within a bat's length of the batter's box! I'd have to be a Marvel's superhero to reach it."

He shrugged again.

Okay. I saw where this was going.

I wouldn't play ball with him, so he wasn't going to play ball with me.

I tapped the dust off my shoes with the bat and stepped back into the box. I was going to hit this ball if I had to defy the laws of gravity to do it.

I leaned into the plate so far I almost toppled over. I tightened my grip on the bat and locked eyes on the pitcher.

Be the bat. Be the bat. I chanted in my head.

The pitcher wound up and released the ball.

Bam!

A loud *boom* reverberated through my cranium as the ball ricocheted off the batting helmet and bounced up over my head, smacking poor Reba between the ears causing the donkey to break free of its handler and take off across the infield in a tantrum worthy of the most dramatic donkey diva.

"Hey, wait for me, Reba! That's a walk! A walk!" I yelled. "That means I get to go to first!

On you! Remember our donkey power talk? Wait for me!" I ignored the laughter and the catcalls from the stands and took off in pursuit of my ride, figuring "what the hay?" They wanted a show. I'd give them one. "I'm coming, Reba! I'm coming!"

Where was a lasso when you need it?

A whistle so loud and shrill it almost made my eardrums pop, brought my base runner to a dead stop just like that. I walked up to the animal and grabbed hold of the lead rope.

"Good girl, Reba," I said and started to lead her back to home plate.

The donkey diva wouldn't budge.

I yanked on the rope. Still a no-go.

I dug in my heels and wrapped the rope around my palms and prepared to give it all I had when some wiseass owner let rip with another earsplitting whistle. Reba lifted her head and bolted full steam ahead at me, knocking me on my butt along the first base line.

I was about to get up and dust my britches off when another jackass thought it would be an opportune moment to blast "T-R-O-U-B-L-E" through the loudspeakers again. Before you could say, "Flash Mob" the occupants of the stands had joined Travis in a dancing-with-the-donkeys moment that would get a gazillion hits on YouTube. I propped myself up on an elbow and took in the surreal splendor, shaking my head when I spotted my gammy getting her groove thing on along with the rest of the spectators turned performers.

I shook my head. If you can't beat 'em...

I got to my feet, dusted myself off, grabbed Reba's lead, and led her back to home plate. I grabbed a hank of mane, vaulted into the saddle, and giddy-upped it to first base performing my best princess wave the entire length of the first base line.

What can I say? Travis Tritt and "T-R-O-U-B-L-E" trumps "Beat It" every day of the week for us good old girls. Right, Reba?

Once the game-stopper extravaganza had ended and the game resumed, I found myself, thankfully, on a now docile donkey. I gave Craig on second base a "we got this!" thumbs-up.

All we needed was a solid hit. Just one hit and we'd win.

I checked out the next batter and suddenly found myself with a case of the slumps.

The Frankfurter was the next batter up.

Forget "T-R-O-U-B-L-E." Cue "The Party's Over."

Honest to God, just watching Frankie and his batter's stance made me want to gouge my eyes out. And talk about prep work. The guy had more rituals than the Church and Wicca combined.

Adjust the batter's helmet. Scuff his toe in the dirt. Once, twice. Again. Spit on his hands. Choke up on the bat. Scratch his nose. Adjust his crotch area. Scratch his crotch area. Adjust again. Scratch his waistband. Then his nose.

Ewww! Where'd he just put that hand?"

"Sometime today, batter!" Someone yelled.

"We're turning gray here, dude!"

"Batter up!" Sheriff Samuels yelled, and Frankie jumped like a little girl. And that made him have to start his whole ritual ordeal again.

"Batter up!" Samuels screamed again.

I saw Frankie wince before he moved into the batter's box.

"No hitter! No hitter!" Someone from the stands jeered.

I turned. It was Drew Van Vleet, *New Holland News'* answer to the Family Feud question,

"Name something that leaves a bad taste in your mouth," standing near the fence between home and first. I'd call Van Vleet a horse's you-know-what, but that would only insult the horse.

"Give it a rest, Gimp," I yelled back. "At least *he's* brave enough to give it a shot."

"What is that supposed to mean?" Van Vleet yelled back. "I can hardly play given the injury you and that maniac inflicted on me."

"I think it's safe to say your injury was self-inflicted, dude. Get over it and move on."

"I'd love to move on. Only I can't do that very well, can I, because your dipshit cousin made me break my ankle!"

I shook my head. Some people just didn't get the concept of personal responsibility.

"No hitter! No hitter!"

This time the taunt came from behind home plate.

"What a minute!" I yelled at Sheriff Saggy Pants. "You're supposed to be impartial!"

"I am?" He shrugged. "Oops!"

I shook my head. The umpire strikes back.

The windup came, followed by the pitch.

Frankie held the bat up like a badminton racket, jumped into the air, and swatted at the ball like it was a plastic shuttlecock.

I winced.

"Strike one!"

Shocker.

A dejected Frankie went through his routine once again.

"Come on, Frankie! Don't let 'em get your goat!" I said. "Show us your stuff!"

"S*ttrr*ike two!" Sheriff Samuels bellowed before the ball reached the batter.

"Now hold on!" I yelled and looked at Frankie. He looked so forlorn I found myself wishing by some freakish miracle Oscar Mayer at the plate would step up and knock that ball clean out of the park—pun so intended.

Really. Is that too much to ask?

I watched Frankie perform his little ceremonial mumbo jumbo. He lifted his bat.

I held my breath.

"Come on, slugger! Let it rip!" I whispered.

The windup.

And...the pitch!

Tip-Tap!

It wasn't pretty, and it sure didn't go far, but Frankie's fly-swatting (not a pun) made contact with the ball—enough contact that the ball fell about twenty feet straight out from the batter's box.

"Whoo-hoo!" I yelled. Then, "Go, Frankie! Go!" when he seemed to be glued to home plate. "Move your ass!" I screamed at him. "Go! Go! Go!"

Frankie finally seemed to get that he'd actually hit the ball, and he ran to his donkey. Only then did I notice what donkey he'd drawn to run the bases with him.

Outlaw, the desperado donkey.

Frankie grabbed the lead reins and, to my amazement, pulled himself onto Outlaw's back and started in my direction.

"Second base, Tressa! Second base! Go! Go!" Craig yelled.

It finally dawned on me that Frankie wasn't the only one who needed to make donkey tracks around the bases, and I nudged Reba with my heels, praying she wasn't planning to make like congress when it came time to compromise and dig in hers.

By now, Craig had kicked his runner into gear and was making slow, yet steady progress towards third base. After several false starts, I finally had Reba facing the right direction and on the move to second base.

"Go Grandville go!" I heard as we made our way around the bases towards home plate and victory!

The base rounding was going well until a shrill whistle pierced the sounds of the cheering crowd.

"*Weeorreet!*"

Before you could say do-si-do, all three four-legged runners turned themselves around and headed in the wrong direction.

Holy hokey-pokey!

"What the hell?" I heard Craig yell.

Another, short whistle had the donkeys changing course again.

Whistle. Turn. Whistle. Turn. Whistle. Turn.

I felt like I was in donkey square dance hell. I could only imagine how Frankie's delicate stomach was handling the donkey-go-round.

"Go! Go! Before they switch gears again!" I yelled.

I breathed a sign of relieve when Craig finally trotted across home plate tying the score.

"Go, Tressa! Go!" I heard and rounded second, heading for third.

I snuck a peek behind me.

Roy Freaking Rogers!

Frankie and Outlaw, at a high lope, were gaining on us big time.

"Step it up, Reba!" I urged, pressing my heels into her sides to speed her up. "Yaw! Yaw!"

We hit third base, home plate in our sights. I squeezed Reba's midsection with my thighs—keeping my head down and center of gravity how-low-can-you go—offering encouragement and praise.

"Atta girl, Reba! We're going to make it, you donkey diva you! We're going to score!"

I hazarded one final look behind. Frankie and Outlaw had closed the gap. Mere inches separated us now

I looked at Frankie, his face frozen in stark terror as Outlaw opened his mouth and suddenly lunged at Reba.

"Oh, shit! Go, Reba, go!" I dug my heels into her sides. "Move your donkey diva ass!"

It played out in scary slow motion. I watched with a sick, horrified fascination as Outlaw's long ugly, yellowed, badly in need of a good brushing chompers formed an evil "gotcha girlfriend" grin just before he clamped onto Reba's hindquarters in an fierce, angry nip.

Raging hee-haws from Hades filled the dusty air around us.

Hee-haw! Hee-haw! Hee-haw!

Reba, like most females who'd just got bitten on the ass without even the courtesy of a howdy-do first would, retaliated. She kicked at Outlaw—*whap! whap! whap!*—and began to buck.

She bucked so hard I bit clean through my tongue. To this day I have no clue how I stayed on the enraged ass. Once the bucking ended, Reba set a frenzied course for home plate.

I pulled back on the reins to gain control, but there was no holding back the proud and pissed off, diva. I gave one long, hard *heave-ho* tug on the reins and felt them *snap!*

I shot backwards like a projectile fired from a slingshot and did a half-assed flip over Reba's backend. The last thing I saw before I hit the ground hard was the look of unbridled terror on the face of the Knox County Sheriff umpire before he was flattened by Reba the diva base runner.

"Help! *Hellp!*"

I recognized the voice, identifying the high-pitched girlie squeals of terror associated with my cousin.

"Help me!"

Suddenly the ball field took on the atmosphere of a battlefield, sounds of chaos and calamity combining with scared, angry donkey snorts and kicks and bucks that reminded me of an unsanctioned rodeo free-for-all.

"Oh, God! Help!"

Frankie and Outlaw—a blur of high-speed octane—crossed home plate, nearly trampling Sheriff Sam before running out of the ballpark. A mule-in-loco-motion, the duo passed the concession stand, flew by Uncle Frank's mini-freeze, kicked up dust crossing the road, and headed cross-country over fields of green and rolling hills.

"Oh, my God. Someone help! Hurry! They're headed down to the pond!"

"Oh, God! He's gone in the water! Get help! Get a rope! Get a life vest! Get an EMT!"

I covered my ears to block out the screams and stared at the sky from my prone position on the field, one thought consoling me as I sucked air into burning lungs.

At least we won the game.

How do you say "Donkey Kong"?

CHAPTER TWENTY-SIX

Frankie was fished out of the drink, wrapped in bubble wrap, and transported home by Dixie the Disgruntled. Johnny, Toby, George, Garth, Waylon, Willie, Hank, Kenny, Dolly, Reba, Patsy, Loretta, Shania, and Outlaw were rounded up, quieted with donkey treats, and coaxed into trailers. With a final, "I've never had a donkey do that," from Merle, the Donkey-Palooza owner, the donkey carnival pulled up its tents and moved on to its next palooza.

As you might imagine, the party broke up soon after that.

Since Taylor had the early shift the next morning, she'd headed home once the halftime show was over and missed the excitement. My folks, after checking to make sure I knew the date, the president, and could recite my Social Security number and the Pledge of Allegiance, left to help Uncle Frank and Aunt Reggie clean up and get the mini-freeze back to town.

I half expected Mr. and Mrs. Joe Townsend to join us, but they were still on surveillance duty so that left me and Townsend, Craig, Kimmie, Brian, and Kari to strap on the old feedbags and enjoy a cold one.

We decided to hit Skeeters, a place on the edge of town that was a cross between a sports bar and a neighborhood watering hole. We got a table, ordered drinks, jumbo onion rings, and two deep-dish Skeeter pies. Yum! I nursed my beer and, feeling someone's eyes on me, looked up and found Townsend studying me, a perplexed look on his face.

"What?" I said. "What?"

"You are way too quiet," he said. "You sure Reba didn't ring your bell, after all?"

I shook my head.

"I'm sure. I'm quiet because I don't have anything to say."

"Oh, boy. Now you've really got me worried," Townsend replied. "What's going on in that head of yours?"

"How long do you have?" I asked.

"As long as it takes, T," he said. "As long as it takes."

I sighed.

Nobody had that much time.

For the first time I realized how quiet our little group was. I looked around the table and frowned.

What a bunch of Gloomy Guses. We looked like we were at a funeral instead of a sports bar.

"A toast!" I said, lifting my glass of beer. "A toast to the come from behind winners of the first—and we all hope last—charity donkey ball tournament! To Grandville!" I held my glass out to clink, but my only fellow clinker was Ranger Rick. "And how about that Craig! Wasn't he outstanding in his field out there today?" I snorted. "Get it? Outstanding in his *field*? Baseball *field*."

"Nice try, T," Craig said, taking a long drink of his beer. "But getting a certain person to understand the effort required out there today is probably a lost cause."

"By 'a certain person,' I suppose you mean me?" Kimmie said, arching a perfectly shaped eyebrow.

"Among others," Brian muttered.

"What was that, Brian? What did you say?" Kari asked. "Come on! Speak up! I'm sure you didn't mumble when you chitchatted with Miss "T-R-O-U-B-L-E" out there tonight."

"What the hell is that supposed to mean?" Brian said. "She's a coworker. What am I supposed to do, just ignore her?"

"Why not? You ignored me."

"For crying out loud! I was busy playing the stupid donkey ball game! It's kind of hard to be at your beck and call when you're hanging on to the north end of a jackass going south and hoping to hell he doesn't decide to rub you off in the barbed wire fence."

"Oh, give us a break! You guys were all over that because it was a sport!" Kimmie said. "You got to bat and hit and throw and run and chew and spit and slide and swear. All those activities *boys* love to do. The only thing missing out there was camouflage and hunting gear."

"Oh, really? How would you know what it was like out there? You're watching on the sidelines from your comfy little cushioned seat in the bleachers, patting your hair and checking your makeup," Craig said, getting to his feet and patting the chair seat with a flourish before sitting back down and wiggling his bottom around in a prissy pantomime. "Ahh." He sighed. "Perfect."

"Oh, so just because I don't choose to spend my evening wrestling around with some dirty, smelly barnyard animals—and I'm not just talking about the four-legged ones—doesn't mean I don't know how to have a good time. I just don't happen to find fun in activities I outgrew ten years ago."

"You don't understand the nature of competitive sports," Craig told Kimmie. "You were a *cheerleader*." He made the word sound like "liberal" when a conservative says it and "conservative" when a liberal says it.

"How dare you! Cheerleading is just as physical as football or basketball or any sport," Kimmie hissed. "Isn't that right, Kari? Tressa?"

I shrugged.

"Yeah, I mean, I guess so."

"Oh, so you're defending that 'I want to be seventeen forever' Panther Posse piece of work now?" Kari snapped at me.

I blinked. What was happening? What was happening?

"What? Me? No way!"

"I think it would be best if we all took a deep breath, sipped our drinks, and just enjoyed spending time with friends and family tonight," Rick suggested.

"That's easy for you to say. Your significant other participates rather than criticizes. She cheers rather than sneers." Brian pointed out. "She's like one of the guys."

I made a face.

"I don't think—"

"Brian's right," Craig interrupted. "Tressa here isn't afraid to get all stinky and sweaty and grubby and dirty and have her hair get all tangled and mussed up—"

"I'm not sure—"

"Well, praise God for Elly May Clampett, and pass the vittles!" Kimmie said, her face flushed and angry.

"Now just a minute—" I put a hand to my hair.

"Shut up, Tressa!" Kimmie said and got to her feet.

"You want me to be one of the boys, Craig?" she asked. "Really? You want me to belch and fart whenever I feel like it? Drool all over my pillow and fall asleep on the couch in my underwear with a bottle of beer between my legs? You want me to quit watching my weight, quit working out, quit shaving my armpits and legs, quit having my hair and nails done? You want me to be one of the guys? Fine. I'm in. We'll see how long it takes for you to decide that being one of the guys ain't all fun and games, buster!"

Kimmie picked up Craig's glass and raised it to her lips, in a series of loud swallows, downed the sucker. She slammed the glass on the table, swiped a hand across her mouth and wiped the foam away, and let out a seriously loud belch.

She picked up Craig's keys from the table.

"You need a ride, Kari?" Kimmie asked.

Kari stood.

"You bet I do! Let's roll."

I watched as Kimmie and Kari "walked like a man" to the door and disappeared.

We sat in uncomfortable silence until our pizzas arrived.

One mega-meat lover and one veggie.

Nobody dug in.

"You heard me open my big mouth," Brian said. "Why didn't you stop me?"

"Stop you? How come you didn't give me a kick in the shin under the table before I basically gave my wife permission to adopt the lifestyle of a commune member?" Craig asked.

"Why didn't *you* stop us, Rick?" Brian asked.

"Sorry guys. It was like an impending train wreck. You know it's going to happen and there's nothing you can do, yet for the life of you, you can't look away. All you can do is sit back and watch it happen and help clean up the carnage left behind."

Two long, loud sighs from across the table acknowledged the immensity of the cleanup ahead.

"Shall we?" Townsend said, reaching out and selecting a piece of the mega-meat pie. I followed his cue.

"Aren't you guys going to eat?" Townsend asked when they made no move to fill their plates.

"I've lost my appetite," Brian said.

Craig only grunted in agreement.

"Give me a lift, Bri-Bri?" Craig asked.

Brian nodded. The donkey warriors got to their feet.

"Maybe we should stop and pick up a gift or something," he said.

"There's nothing open this time of night except bars and grocery stores," Craig said.

"We could pick up candy or a cake," Brian suggested.

Craig shook his head.

"You heard Kimmie. She's looking to make a point. She's one of the *boys* now," he said making quotes with his fingers.

They looked at each other for a second and grinned.

"*Grand Theft Auto,* baby!" They said in unison.

"Serves 'em right," Craig added.

I watched them leave and grabbed Rick's arm.

"Don't you think you ought to stop them before they make matters worse?" I asked.

Townsend shook his head and grinned.

"Trust me. Sometimes things have to get worse in order to get better. Those guys walk in with that video game for their wives—I guarantee you, it'll be a defining moment in both relationships. And maybe, just maybe, the catalyst for compromise." He picked up a big ol' slab of pizza and held it out for me to take a bite.

I grinned.

"Anybody ever tell you that you're smarter than the average ranger type?" I asked.

He gave me his Charlie Chaplin eyebrow number.

"There is no average ranger-type," he said.

I was about to dig into another slice of Skeeters' best when my phone began to ring. I looked down.

A. Winegardner, the display said.

I frowned and answered.

"Hello? Aunt Eu...er...I mean Uncle Bo? What's going on? How come you're calling so late? Is something wrong?"

I listened, shaking my head.

"Wait. I don't understand what you're talking about. I don't have that item."

I saw Townsend look up.

"No. I didn't find it. No. What? Wait a minute. Someone called you and said that *I* had it? That it was at *my* place? When? You're positive that's what they said? Okay. I'll check. Yes. Yes. I'll let you know."

I hit *end* and got to my feet.

"I've got to go!" I said, hunting for my car key.

Townsend frowned. "Aren't you forgetting something? You don't have a car. You rode with me."

Damn.

"We have to go then!" I said. "Now!"

Townsend must've heard the urgency in my voice. He got to his feet and threw bills on the table.

"Where to?" he asked.

"Home!"

I ran towards the counter.

"Where are you going? We're parked out this way," Townsend asked.

I grabbed a cardboard pizza box from the counter and ran back to the table, dumped the pizzas and onion rings inside and slammed the box shut.

"Waste not, want not!" I yelled, racing for the door.

Seconds later, barreling down the road in Townsend's big red truck well over the speed limit, Townsend finally looked over at me, waiting, I deduced for an explanation.

"Once upon a time..." he began.

I sighed.

"Call me Ishmael." I said. "You see, once upon a time there was this elusive lawn gnome—"

By the time we got to our little slice of the good life, I hadn't even made it to some of the juicier parts of this story. Nothing about Dusty Cadwallader's woods being Grandville's version of Stonehenge or Dusty's mysterious disappearance or the fact that all the marital turmoil unfolding around me was making me have serious doubts about the state of matrimony being a state I'd ever want to pitch my tent in. You know. *Those* juicy parts.

Townsend roared into my driveway and pulled up to the double-wide. Everything appeared quiet. Almost too quiet.

"Where are the pooches?" Townsend asked.

"I left them in the house. They've been...naughty. They keep wandering over to the folks' when I'm not here and doing their business. Mom said if one more client stepped in one more doggie dropping, she was going to start keeping track and fining me for each offense—then leave the evidence of each infraction on my doorstep."

Townsend winced.

"I know. Who knew, right?" I said.

I'd seen a different side of my mother during the terrible, horrible, no good, very bad bike ride a few weeks back and let me tell you, it was an eye opener. If I'd learned one thing, it was that Mrs. CPA would follow through. In a heartbeat.

Rick grabbed his flashlight, and we got out of the truck.

Everything appeared fine. Still...

I handed my house keys to Townsend. "You check the house. I'll just take a peek in the barn."

He handed me the flashlight.

"I better not step in any evidence of a pooch poop infraction," he teased.

Townsend headed to the house, and I headed to the fenced barn lot and the barn beyond. I climbed over the gate and dropped to my feet in the lot, shining the beam of the flashlight out in front of me, getting more nervous with each step.

You see, this was kind of another déjà vu moment for me. Last summer when I'd become embroiled in my first hometown whodunit, (quite by accident you understand) some sicko had targeted my critters and me. Well, actually in this case they targeted my gammy's critter—specifically her cat, Hermione. The cat had been strung up like a furry piñata. Fortunately I discovered her in time, and it ended well. At least for the cat.

I was getting that "something isn't right" vibe again.

I jogged to the heavy-duty, double-sided horse waterer first and directed the beam into both sides of the waterer. I sighed in relief. The water appeared clear and clean.

I took a step back. That's when the flashlight beam illuminated a flash of color on the dark green waterer. I took another step back and hit the front of the waterer with the full beam.

I gasped.

I'd been tagged! One hot pink tornado after another covered each side of the six-gallon capacity, fifty-pound waterer. I turned and bolted towards the barn, whistling for the horses as I ran. I got to the barn doors and stopped. A long pink tornado, a good seven feet tall and four wide, stood out in tacky contrast to the barn red of the structure.

Frantically, I whistled again.

"Please, let them be okay," I prayed. "Please. Please."

The reassuring sound of pounding hooves reached me, and I ran to greet my tiny herd.

The Queen, as usual, led the way, followed by Blackjack. For some reason, Joker always came last. They converged around me in a tight little circle, and I reached up to embrace them in a mama bear hug.

Thank God. Thank God they were okay.

I opened the barn door, deciding they deserved a midnight snack and flipped on the light.

The three amigos are very well trained. You open the door and they come in, single file, and walk sedately to their appointed stalls. Grade school teachers should have students this well behaved.

Once the Queen was in, her court followed. First Blackjack, then...

"Oh, my God!" I screamed. "Oh, my God! Oh, my God! Oh, my God! Oh, my God!"

I couldn't seem to quit screaming. Even when I heard the barks of approaching labs and Townsend calling my name, I couldn't stop.

"Oh, my God! Oh, my God!"

Townsend burst through the barn door, the labs on his heels.

"What's the matter? What the hell's going on?"

Now that I was all screamed out, I could only point and stare.

Townsend followed the direction of my trembling finger, and his mouth dropped open.

"What the hell?" he said. "What *is* that?"

"A horse of a different color," I said, my throat getting thick and my eyes starting to sting.

"What?"

"A horse of a different color!" I yelled. And that's exactly what he was. Some...*fiend* had taken to Joker's trademark Appaloosa spotted rump and his long, lovely black tail with oh-so-classy white tip and painted them pink! "How could they?" I said. "What kind of sickos are we dealing with?"

Townsend rubbed the back of his neck before entering the stall to take a closer look.

"The good news is it's not paint," he said, and I was at his side in a flash, reaching out to examine the strands of hair myself.

"Oh, my God! You're right." I ran a hand along his rump and rubbed the course strands of hair between my thumb and index finger. "It isn't paint. It's soft, not sticky."

"My guess is it's some kind of temporary hair color," Townsend suggested. "You know. Like kids use for Halloween or homecoming or just to be different."

My eyes narrowed.

Kids. Like high school kids.

"What about the other two? Did they get...colorized?" Rick asked.

I shook my head.

"Joker was the only one they could catch," I said. "He doesn't know he's a horse. He thinks he's human. He trusts people. At least he used to. But after last summer and now this..."

I felt myself tearing up again, and Townsend reached out and took me in his arms.

"Joker's fine, T. A couple of good, soaking rains, and he'll be good as new." He stroked my hair, reassuring me.

I rested my head against his shoulder. It felt right to be there. Safe. Uncomplicated. Easy.

All the things a committed relationship wasn't. Or didn't appear to be.

Car doors slamming brought me up. I frowned. The folks were late getting home.

It was too late to bother them with this tonight, I told myself, figuring morning was soon enough to be the bearer of bad news.

Then, "Philip! The garage doors! Taylor's car!"

"What the devil?"

Or, maybe it couldn't wait.

We secured the stall doors and hurried next door. Dad's truck was sitting outside the double garage, engine running, bright-beamed headlights fully illuminated and pointing at the overhead doors.

The beer in my stomach rebelled. I felt sick.

Please tell me those weren't hot pink tornadoes on my folks' custom made overhead doors and Paw-Paw Will's Buick?

"Wow. They got you guys, too, I see," Townsend said.

"Too? What do you mean?" my mom asked.

Townsend told them about the barn and Joker's tail.

"Oh my. How awful!" my mother said, coming over to put an arm around my shoulder. "Is Joker okay?"

I nodded.

"He's fine." Apart from the obvious trauma of a mighty Appaloosa having to bear the indignity of hot pink spots and a hot pink tail.

I braved another look at Paw-Paw Will's car. There would be hell to pay when Taylor found out. Not to mention my gammy.

"Where *is* Taylor?" I asked. "How come she didn't hear anything?"

My parents exchanged a frantic look and bolted into the house, coming out a few minutes later.

"It's okay. I got ahold of Taylor on her cell," my mother said. "She's fine. A friend picked her up after the game, and they're hanging out."

"Friend? What friend?" I asked.

"I didn't think to ask, Tressa," my mother said. "I had other things on my mind." She shook her head and looked at the garage doors again. "Who would do something like this?"

"Scumbags," my dad said. "Someone who doesn't have any respect for the property of others."

I had a pretty good inkling who was responsible.

I crossed my arms and looked at the long, tall tornadoes.

You want to play tag, scumbags?

Well, guess what? Now *I'm* it, *bitches*!

CHAPTER TWENTY-SEVEN

"Sorry, Taylor," I said again for the umpteenth time. "About the Buick." The Buick with the hot pink tornadoes that was our current mode of transportation—our options being limited as it were.

"It's not your fault...entirely," she responded. "But I do have to wonder how you keep making yourself a target for this kind of thing."

I shrugged.

"Bad luck? Misfortune? Negative karma?" I suggested.

She shook her head.

"Whatever you call, it zones in on you like a stray puppy looking for a forever home."

I nodded. I was a sucker for rescue pets, too. Okay. Most any pet. Well, except for fussy felines and anything that slithers.

"I gotta tell you. I thought you'd go ballistic when you found out about the car, but you're taking it surprisingly well." I looked over at her. "Why?"

"Why what?"

"How come you're so laissez-faire about this all of a sudden? The last time the car got trashed, you almost blew an internal organ."

"Laissez-faire? You sound like Joe Townsend. And as far as the car goes, I just choose not to let events I have no control over steal my joy."

I lifted an eyebrow.

"Steal your joy? Steal your joy? You've been reading self-help books again. *The Twelve Step Program to Inner Peace. Thirty-Day Anxiety Cleanse. Working out the Worry.*

And what do you mean by 'we have no control'? We have plenty of control!" I said. "We're on the offensive now. The ball's in our court, and I say we ram it down their throats. Figuratively, of course."

"I suppose you have a game plan that includes me," she said.

"Would I leave my little sis out?"

She shook her head.

"Care to share?"

"Certainly. If you'll share your whereabouts last night at approximately 2300 hours."

"What? You think I'm a suspect?"

"Heaven's no! I'm just nosy. Who was this mystery friend you were hanging out with? Emma? Heather? Jacinda? Toni? Felicia?" I named Taylor's high school friends. "Yvette? Pam? Faith?"

"Would you please stop? Tell me about this plan again."

Hold it. Miss Stick-in-the-Mud was actually asking for details of a plan *I* came up with? Never mind that I didn't actually have a plan. That she was diverting me from my line of inquiry had this reporter's "something's fishy" nose for news at bloodhound alert.

"Wait a minute!" I said. "Hold on. I know who you were with last night. P.D. Dawkins! Our very own studly state trooper, that's who!"

She kept her eyes on the road.

"It was nothing really. No big deal. Just a soda."

Just a soda? Just a soda!

Oh, my God! This was huge!

"Where did he take you? What did you say? What did he say? Did you exchange a good-night kiss?"

"Down, girl. We just hung out at the county park for awhile and talked. That's all. It wasn't a date or anything."

"You went back to the park?"

"He swung by home, and we got coffee and drank it at a table on the covered bridge."

"Oh."

"You sound disappointed," Taylor said.

"I'm not. I was just thinking how nice it would be if Craig and Kimmie and Kari and Brian would grab a cup of coffee and go somewhere nice and quiet away from everybody—somewhere like the park—and just talk to each other. You know. Put everything on the table and see what happens."

"That sounds simple enough in theory, Tressa. But it's not always as easy as sitting down over a cup of coffee and talking it out. Relationship issues are often time complicated and complex because people are complicated and complex. It usually takes more than a long talk to resolve those deep-seated issues. You're really worried aren't you?"

Yes, I was worried. Not only about my brother and his wife and my best friend and her new husband, but also about the implications for me. For *my* future. If they couldn't make it, what hope did I have?

"Do you think the deputy bought your version of events regarding last night?" Taylor asked, taking my mind off marriage crises and back where it belonged. On tracking down the culprits who thought it would be amusing to turn an Appaloosa Quarter into Rainbow Brite.

I winced when I recalled that conversation with law enforcement.

"Who called to report a possible prowler at your home?" the deputy asked.

"It was a source who asked to remain anonymous."

"And this anonymous source, what did they say exactly?"

"That they saw something at my residence."

"Something? Like what?"

"Just activity that I deemed suspicious," I evaded.

"What kind of suspicious activity exactly?"

"You know. Activity that didn't seem...kosher."

And so it went.

He zigged. I zagged. He served. I returned. He threw it out there. I tossed it back.

Ah, that heady dance of misdirection. I knew it so well I could perform it with my eyes closed.

Really? What did you think I was going to tell him? That I got a call from Uncle Bo, my cross-dressing, "homeless" aunt looking for a gnome?

Puhleaze.

"I doubt the deputy thought I was telling him everything. For sure his boss won't think so," I finally said.

"You do know this likely blows our theory about who is responsible," Taylor told me. "The cheerleaders have an alibi."

I winced. A spandex-tight one to be exact.

"Can you believe it? We're their alibis!" I said and shook my head.

"Along with video and hundreds of other people," Taylor pointed out.

"All except for one cheerleader," I said. "Jada Garcia wasn't there. She doesn't have an alibi. There's another thing that's bothering me about what happened last night." I said.

"Only one?"

"Well, apart from the obvious. How come they didn't tag *my* place?" I asked.

Taylor looked at me.

"They did. They got the barn. Your horse."

"The barn is adjacent to the folks' place. It was there before Gram's place went in."

"So?"

"So, if we go under the theory that this act of vandalism was to send a message to me, why didn't they trash my place? Why the folks'?"

"Because they thought you lived there, that's why."

I nodded.

"Exactly! And why would they think that?"

I could see Taylor trying to figure out what was going on in my mind—always a daunting task.

"Because they saw the Buick parked there," I finished. "Remember, you left much earlier than the rest of us. So that means…?" I waited for Taylor to make the connection—a rare experience indeed—so I savored it just a wee bit.

"That means they saw you at the park with the Buick and thought you were driving it," Taylor finally finished.

"Key-rect," I said. "In fact, I was standing at the trunk of the Buick when I handed the evidence over to Doug Samuels when the cheerleaders walked by and gave me their death glares."

"So, that could mean somebody or -bodies at the park relayed the vehicle information to their minions, and that's why they targeted Mom's and Dad's place and not yours!"

"Ding, ding, ding! We have winner!"

"Which means—" Taylor began.

"—It means our theory is still sound and the cheerleaders could still be involved. Especially when you consider that only one cheerleader—the one who just so happens to specialize in pink tornadoes—is the only one without a rock-solid alibi."

"So what's the plan again?" Taylor asked. "Divide and conquer? Or full-court press?"

I thought about it.

"A little bit of both," I said.

We walked into the school, and I frowned. It wasn't even seven thirty and already the courtyard and commons areas were filled with students.

"Why is everybody here so early?" I asked.

"Early? Classes start in forty minutes."

"Exactly."

"Oh, that's right. You preferred the 'I'm not officially tardy until the last bell rings' approach to attendance. Some students like to get here early and use the extra time to go over homework and get organized for the day."

I frowned. Maybe bringing Taylor along wasn't such a good idea.

"We better get our passes," Taylor said.

"Passes? Newsflash. We're not students!"

"I meant the visitor passes, Einstein," she said. "Remember?"

I grimaced. "Do we have to? We're not terrorists or criminals or anything. In fact, one could say we were here searching for lawbreakers. Besides, wouldn't a real bad guy up to no good simply wait outside until someone opens the door to go out and come in anyway? I don't think they'd bother going to the office for a visitor pass under those circumstances, do you?"

I could tell she was trying to find fault with my reasoning but was coming up empty.

"Still..."

"Honestly, Taylor. After last night, I'd rather say I'm sorry than ask permission."

"Where do we begin?"

"Do you see any of the cheerleaders?"

She shook her head.

"No. You?"

I shook my head. No cheerleaders. No Mick. No Principal Vernon. Thank heavens.

"What about the cheerleading coach?" Taylor asked.

"Martina Banfield?"

"Maybe they're hanging out in her room. I know I came early and hung out in the band room with Mr. Kunkel a lot of mornings."

I shook my head. Band geeks. I usually spent mornings before class in the office or making up work with the math teacher.

"It's worth a shot," I said and with the help of a student located Miss Banfield's classroom. The classroom door was closed.

"Should we knock?" Taylor asked.

"Knock? It's a public school. Why would we knock?"

"It's only polite."

I tapped my cheek.

"Let's see. My car was destroyed by roadkill. My horse has been turned into a merry-go-round horse. Our folks' custom garage doors look like child's play gone horribly wrong. Our poor Paw-Paw Will's prized LeSabre, which he entrusted to his beloved wife and who, in turn, entrusted it to her favorite grandchild, is now Shriner clown parade transportation. You still want to knock?"

"Let me at that door," she said, shouldering past me to grab the door handle and open the door.

"Excuse me? Can I help you?"

A few steps behind Taylor, I witnessed the exact moment Miss Banfield's helpful, welcoming smile, became one of outright annoyance.

Yep. It changed when she saw me. Imagine that.

"Hello again!" I breezed into the room with a bit of a swagger. Seven desks had been pulled into a circle, and all six cheerleaders, plus their coach filled the chairs. "I hope you're not all here serving morning detention." I said and noticed Jada Garcia was once again absent.

Miss Banfield got to her feet.

"Of course not. We're just evaluating last night's amazing performance."

"Oh, I wouldn't actually call it amazing," I said. "After all, I practically grew up on a horse."

"She's talking about *their* performance," Taylor pointed out.

"Of course she is," I said. "I was only joking."

I walked over to the circle of desks, about to observe that someone was missing again when the classroom door opened, and a powerful whiff of vanilla musk nose-smacked me in the olfactory. (I get it. Women like to smell good, but hello. For the sake of those who might be allergic, know when to say when.)

"Why hello. You're Jada, aren't you?" I said when I recognized the latecomer. "I'm Tressa Turner, with the *Gazette*. You were sick the last time I was here. I'm sorry you missed out on the halftime event last night. I'm sure you've heard by now, it was awesome! I hope you're feeling much better now."

She nodded and took a seat in one of the desks.

"Miss Banfield gave you my business card and filled you in about the little feature I'm planning. Right?"

Jada's eyes went to her coach.

"I heard something about it. But I'm really not interested in participating. I have so much going on right now."

"Oh, I know! I know! You've got schoolwork and cheerleading and, oh, that hunky boyfriend of yours. Mick Dishman, right? He's a hottie."

"What exactly were you wanting again?" Miss Banfield asked.

"What all reporters want," I said, leaning towards the coach. "A great story that causes lots of buzz and gets people talking."

"Well, I'm sorry, but we've talked it over and I don't think any of the girls are interested in being in your feature right now. They just don't need or want that kind of distraction right now. They have other things to focus on. Right ladies?"

Heads bobbed up and down.

"That's right. We aren't interested," Cissy said. "Are we?"

This time the heads shook.

"Count me out."

"No thanks."

"Too busy."

"Not a good time."

Lord. They sounded like me trying to get out of chaperoning one of Kari's middle school events.

"Honest," I pressed. "It wouldn't take much time at all. I'd just interview each of you separately and learn your stories, hear about your families, your strengths, weaknesses, successes, failures—"

"I believe my girls have indicated they don't care to participate, Miss Turner. If you would let us get back to analyzing our performance." She moved to the dry-erase board and picked up a cloth and quickly wiped it off. I was able to read the words, "self-object" and "need to belong" before they disappeared.

"Oh, wow! Maslow's hierarchy of needs," Taylor said.

I blinked.

Maslow's what?

Taylor moved to another section of dry-erase board and pointed at a large drawing of a pyramid comprised of five separate sections.

"Maslow's hierarchy of needs," she said. "Abraham Maslow was a researcher who came up with a theory relating to human motivation and development. You often see it in pyramid form like this with the most fundamental and basic needs like food and safety at the bottom while secondary needs that include things like love and acceptance and self-esteem appear higher on the pyramid."

"You know Maslow?" Miss Banfield approached Taylor.

"Of course. I was a psych major. His research of the forties and fifties was initially well received, but recent scholarship tends to indicate that such ranking of needs and the hierarchy itself is flawed and, therefore, to some extent invalid."

"Invalid? You mean it's wrong?" Jada asked.

"Not necessarily wrong but certainly not universally accepted," Taylor responded. "You see, needs can change from culture to culture and race to race and religion to religion based on those demographics and others. Needs tend to be highly individualized rather than a one size fits all application. If you see what I'm saying."

I gave the pyramid a closer look.

"Physiological needs like thirst and hunger were at the bottom. Above that came issues of safety like protection and security. Social needs like love and belonging were next up on the pyramid, with the warm, fuzzy, feel-good, esteem needs next. Self-actualization appeared at the tippy-top."

"I can't believe I'm hearing this!" Miss Banfield said, her voice sharp and shrill. "On the contrary! Maslow's work has been respected for decades as a leading template for developmental psychology."

Taylor shot me a "what the hell button did I push?" look and I shrugged.

I didn't even know what self-actualization referred to.

"I think we'd better agree to disagree," Taylor said. "There's certainly a broad body of work and research in this field, and it's growing all the time, that tends to indicate Maslow's research is at best incomplete and at worst, flawed—"

"You're wrong!" The cheerleading coach said. "Flat out wrong. And I think I'm going to have to ask you both to leave."

"Wait a minute. I'm sorry if I upset you," Taylor began, but the teacher put her hand up.

"You'd be upset too, if two strangers barged into your classroom and interrupted a private session with students."

"I'm sorry you feel that way," Taylor said.

"Why are you here anyway?" Martina asked. "She's the reporter. Why are *you* here?"

"She's my sister," I said. "And chauffeur, since my car was vandalized. But you wouldn't know anything about that, would you, Miss Banfield?"

"Of course not. It's the first I've heard about it!"

"How about your girls?" I turned to the cheerleaders. "You're popular, right? You're cheerleaders. Everybody wants to be you. Or wants to be your friend. Have you heard anything about all the vandalism going on? Because if school is anything like it was when I was here, if anything was going around the school, the cheerleaders knew about it. So? Do you? Know anything? I mean. Any guesses who might be pulling this crap? Any *hierarchical theories*?" I said, looking back at the teacher. "Any researched-based, educated guesses based on Mr. Maslow's theory of motivational needs, Miss Banfield?"

"That's it!" Martina said. She stomped to her desk and hit the button to the intercom.

"I need a principal in my classroom. I have parties in my classroom without visitor passes who refuse to leave."

"Don't get your spandex in a wedgie," I told the teacher. "We're going." I passed Jada on my way to the door. "You sure you're feeling better, Jada. You're awfully pale," I said and dropped a business card on the desk in front of her. "Just in case you change your mind."

I walked sedately to the door, opened it for Taylor, and gave a cheery little wave to the classroom occupants.

"See you next week!" I said.

"Next week?" Martina shook her head.

"Career Day! Mick Dishman is bringing me. I can't wait! Hmm. Maybe I'll even do a story on it. Toodles!"

I shoved Taylor into the hall. As soon as the classroom door closed, I grabbed her wrist and booked it for the nearest exit.

"What are you doing?" Taylor asked.

"Saving you from the humiliation of your first ever bawling out by a principal," I told her.

Am I my sister's keeper or what?

CHAPTER TWENTY-EIGHT

───

It was almost two hours later when I finally dropped Taylor off at the Dairee Freeze. She was a little late, and Uncle Frank was a little peeved. Okay. So she was a lot late, and Uncle Frank was a lot more than peeved.

I wasn't exactly thrilled to be driving a car that catered to a senior citizen clientele and sported hot pink swirlies resembling weird-shaped rotini pastas, but I had things to do, places to go, people to see.

I ignored most of the honks, catcalls, and heckling—that is, until a car pulled up behind me—"this" close to my back bumper (or Taylor's back bumper)—and laid on the horn. My gaze flew to the rearview mirror.

Another Buick.

Another senior citizen behind the wheel.

A close encounter of the gammy kind.

Gram and Stepper.

I gave them a "hey, hello, have a good day, see you later" wave and motioned for them to take the spot I'd been about to pull into.

Fat chance. When I pulled into a parking space around the corner from the newspaper office, they followed, parking right next to me.

Joe rolled down his window.

"Nice Pepto-mobile," he said. "Is that supposed to cure diarrhea or cause it?"

I shook my head.

"Tressa Jayne Turner! What have you done to Paw-Paw Will's car this time?" My gammy's bellow could be heard at the

Kut 'n' Kurl two doors down. "All those pink whirligigs. It makes me dizzy just looking at it."

"Sorry, Gram. But honest it's not my fault. You see, we've got this group of scofflaws—"

"Oh, wow, look who's going all thesaurus on us!" Joe said.

"What's dinosaurs have to do with Tressa trashing Paw-Paw Will's car again? She sayin' some T-Rex did it? 'Cause I'm not buying it."

"No. T-Rex didn't trash it, and neither did I, Gram. Some bad people trashed it. Very bad."

"Craig said the Plymouth got all filled up with dead animals. And now Pappy's Buick's crapped up. What about the gnome? You find it yet?"

"I'm getting closer," I evaded. "What are you two doing in town this fine morning?" I asked and watched Joe get out and walk around the car to assist his wife.

"It's hair day," Gram said once she was on the sidewalk. "I always get my hair done on Saturdays. Plus we got the Historical Village doin's tonight. That Blast from the Past Masquerade. Don't you remember?"

"That's Blast *to* the Past, and I haven't forgotten."

"You're dressin' up, right?"

I frowned. "Dressing up" had lost its appeal after I was traumatized at a tender age when I was the only one to show up at a youth group Halloween party in costume.

I went as a bum circa Freddie the Freeloader (for those of you who don't know who this character is, Google him and you'll totally get it) complete with burnt cork whiskers, white mouth, blackened teeth, hat, coat, scarf, and knapsack. Oh, and bright pink vest. (The traditional red not working for me.) To this day I remember how I felt when my best friend walked up to Craig, Taylor, and me and asked, "Isn't Tressa coming?"

The worst part is that I was never permitted to get over it. Photographic evidence of it follows me to this day via made-to-order novelty item "gifts" such as calendars, puzzles, wanted posters, playing cards, coasters, and T-shirts. And don't get me started about the social media implications. Every time I get "tagged," I'm terrified to look for fear I'll see Tressa the Humiliated Hobo staring out from the screen.

"We'll see," I finally responded.

"Hang around, Blondie, and I'll buy you a late breakfast," Joe instructed.

I shrugged.

"Okeydokey," I said, not one to pass up a free meal. And putting off quality time with Stan the Man for an hour or so did not pose the least, little hardship—that was for certain.

Joe was back from the Kut 'n' Kurl in record time. He opened the passenger door and got in.

"Hazel's ought to be cleared out by now," Joe said, "so you should be able to find a parking space up front."

"And you're buying again, right?"

He shook his head. "Broke again, huh?"

"Pretty much," I said and backed out. "Is Gram really upset about the car?"

"She'll get over it," Joe said, fastening his seat belt. "Besides, it kind of bugs me the way she regards this car as a shrine."

I looked over at the senior.

"Uh, er, Joe?" I made a motion towards my crotch and then nodded at his fly. "Your insecurity's showing."

I laughed when he gasped and moved to pull up his closed zipper.

"Ha, ha, ha. Very funny," he said. "And it's not insecurity on my part. I just think it's creepy as hell."

"Creepy? This was Paw-Paw Will's last car."

"So what? He'd only had it for a year. He bought a new one every three years like clockwork."

"Can we talk about something else less depressing?"

"How about last night's game?"

"I said 'less' depressing."

"Wasn't that brutal? Especially that last inning." He winced. "Entertaining as all get out in the beginning? You bet. Tough to watch at the end."

"But you forced yourself to watch, right?"

"Donkey train wreck! Hello! How is 'Mighty Frankie' by the way?" Joe asked.

"I was afraid to ask Uncle Frank when I dropped Taylor off," I admitted.

"Good call," Joe said.

We sat at the four-way stop waiting for my turn to go when my phone rang. I checked the number. It was Dusty Cadwallader's cell number!

"Hello? Dusty?"

I heard noises in the background but nothing else.

"Dusty, is that you? Hello?"

I picked up sounds like you hear when someone's butt dialed you.

"Dusty? Dusty!"

I lost the signal.

Dang!

I tried resend, but the phone kept ringing until it went to voice mail.

A horn behind me sounded.

"Move that POS!" I heard.

Nice.

I made a left turn, hitting the button to call Dusty's number again.

"Anything wrong?" Joe asked.

"Sorry, Joe. But I think duty just called. I'm going to have to take a rain check on breakfast, but I can drop you off at Hazel's."

"Hold your horses. I can tell when something's afoot," Joe said. "So what is it? I heard you say Dusty. Was that Dusty Cadwallader on the phone?"

I looked at Joe.

"You know him?"

"Know him? Mr. Spacely? George Jetson? Mork? Nanu nanu. Flash Gordon?"

"I see his reputation precedes him."

"Cowboy Bebop?"

"Oh, wow! That's a new one. I haven't heard that one."

"I know. Hilarious, right? Almost as hilarious as Calamity Jayne.

That sobered me up.

"So you *do* know him. How well do you know him?"

Joe shrugged. "We wrote the policy on his grandparents' home for years. They were a bit odd. Nice people, but they didn't get out much."

"And Dusty?"

"He was four years behind Rick's dad in high school. He could be a strange ranger, too. Dusty, not my son. As I recall he was heavy into science fiction. Quiet kid. Nice, but a little off, if you know what I mean. Why all the interest in Dusty Cadwallader, and what's he doing calling you?"

I hesitated. It was always a tough call on how much to tell Joe and how much to hold back. Either way, it generally backfired on me.

"He's been helping me out on this vandalism story. You know. As a source," I said. "And I guess he kind of went missing."

"How does someone 'kind of' go missing?"

"Well, his family thinks he's missing."

"But didn't you say that was him calling?"

"Yes."

"Then I guess he isn't 'kind of' missing any more. What did he say?"

"That's just it. He didn't say anything. All I could hear was a lot of background noise and wind noise."

"And you're concerned?"

I shrugged. "The family requested the county do a welfare check yesterday, and they couldn't make contact."

"Let me guess. You figure, given the call you just received, you ought to go check on him yourself, right?"

"Well, I, uh…"

"Sounds like a good idea," he said.

"It does?"

"Of course it does. His family says he's missing. The authorities couldn't locate him. The guy just called, but you couldn't make contact."

"Well, his cell service is spotty…"

"The guy could need help. We better go."

And there it was.

Bang!

The backfire.

"We? What *we*?"

"I've got time to kill," he said. "And I haven't done a ride-along in a while."

Apparently the *Green Hornet* here had chosen to hit the 'delete' button on his past ride alongs with me. Suffice to say our teaming up in the past hadn't worked out so well.

"Wait a minute? What about Gram?"

Joe waved her off.

"She's good for at least two hours," he said. "If we get hung up for time, I'll tell her to go ahead with that tattoo she's been considering. The tattoo place is just three doors down."

I looked at him.

"I don't even want to know."

After a quick stop at the drive-through joint for breakfast, (hey, a girl has to eat) we headed out of town.

"So how's the dating game with my grandson going?" Joe asked.

"Awesome! Swell! Amazing! Like totally…"

I pooped out at the end there.

"That bad?" he said.

"No! Of course not. We're still new to the dating scene, Joe. We've only had three or four dates. And you know how one of them turned out, thanks to you and Mrs. *Person of Interest*."

"You bailed before the night was over, anyway. Rick was none too happy about that, let me tell you."

"What? He told me to go. He said he'd be fine."

Joe shook his head.

"You really know nothing about men. What was he supposed to say? Ignore your job. Stay with me and Grandma and Grandpa?"

"You mean 'Stalker Grandma and Grandpa,'" I corrected. "We just haven't hit our stride yet," I told him. "Discovered our optimum speed and gait."

"Gait? Stride? You sound like you're talking about the Triple Crown." He shook his head. "How romantic. My grandson's a lucky, lucky fellow."

"Now wait just a minute," I said. "I think the terminology works."

"What do you mean, 'works'?"

"Well you see, Joe, the way I figure it, any long-term, committed relationship, like a marriage for example, covers a considerable span of time. It's like a marathon in many respects. You have to prepare, build up your strength and endurance. You have to pace yourself and find that comfortable stride, the easygoing pace that will permit you to have the best shot at finishing the race."

He looked at me.

"I get it now. It's all about staying power, isn't it?"

I straightened my spine and puffed out my chest.

"I'll have you know your grandson has plenty of staying power!" I huffed. "More than plenty!"

"Not that kind of staying power, and I wasn't referring to Rick. I was talking about you, missy."

"Me?"

"You've got no stomach for the long haul."

"No stomach? Hello. Do you know me at all? I can down two of Uncle Frank's belly burners with extra jalapeños and a side of chili cheese fries and still have room for ice cream."

He shook his head.

"Not that kind of stomach. I'm talking about intestinal fortitude."

"Like I said, I can put away—"

"Enough with the food! I'm talking about endurance! Resolve! Stamina! Tenacity! Guts!"

"Please, Joe. Don't use that word. Not after my car."

"Don't try to change the subject, Blondie. You ever hear the saying, 'I never promised you a rose garden'?"

"We're talking about gardening? Look who's changing the subject now."

"Funny," Joe said. "All I'm saying is that life doesn't come with a guarantee of anything. There's no guarantee that anything will last, because it doesn't. People die. People change. People leave. That's life. And getting through it requires determination, steadfastness, and pluck. And pluck is one thing you've got in spades, Blondie."

I frowned.

I knew what he was talking about. I knew the qualities it took to successfully maneuver your way through life and relationships. I knew the sacrifices and the hardships. And I also knew, deep down, despite all my fluster and bluster and denials, and despite Joe's assertion that I had pluck "in spades," I wasn't sure I had whatever it was it took to go the distance. I wasn't sure at all.

And I wasn't the only one who would get hurt if I couldn't keep up, if I couldn't stick-to-it, if I couldn't go all the way.

Rick would be hurt, too. And I wasn't sure that was a possibility I could risk.

"Here's Dusty's place," I said, pulling up the incline of his gravel driveway. "That's weird."

"What? What's weird?

"His vehicle. It's still parked in the same spot it was two nights ago."

"You've been out here before?"

"Yes. I told you. Dusty was helping me."

"Yes, you did. But you didn't specify the nature of that help. Would you care to elaborate now?"

Would I?

"I'm covering the vandalism and thefts in the area. You know that. Right? Well, I ran across Dusty at the courthouse, and we got to talking and…"

"And?"

I told him about the report Dusty had been there to file, the pink tornadoes, our subsequent examination of the woods, and the discovery of the pink tornadoes and the spray-paint can, along with the stakeout that had called me away from date night.

"So you see, the last time we saw Dusty, he was fine and planned to go retrieve the four-wheelers the next morning."

"You're telling me both ATVs stopped? They just stopped?" Joe asked.

I nodded.

"Oh, and my car, too."

"Your car?"

I nodded. "But that was down the road a piece."

"And you don't find that…coincidental?"

"What do you mean? You think someone tampered with them?"

"Someone or some*thing*." He started to sing the *Ghostbusters* song.

"Knock it off, Egon" I said. "So not funny."

"Neither is the fact that you decide to wait until we arrive at Area 51 before you bother to tell me that not only have you tracked hoodlums in the woods, but there are cases of strange electrical problems, reports of lights in the sky, and—noteworthy here—a freaking dead zone when it comes to cell phone service."

"You're forgetting the guy who reported alien activity on his property numerous times is also missing, but do go on."

"Here I am, thinking this is at most a heroic rescue operation, and all of a sudden we're Scully and Mulder."

"Oh, really. So you came with me because you might get some recognition and glory? Joe, Joe, Joe. Where's your altruistic side?" I shook my head and tsk-tsked. "Your fellow Rotary Club members would be so disappointed."

"I just don't like being roped into something under false pretenses."

"*Roped* into something? I offered to drop you off, but oh, no, you had time to kill, remember?"

"If I knew I was going to have to listen to your lame comparison between dating my grandson to a never-ending footrace, I wouldn't have come."

"Glory seeker!"

"Commitment-phobe!"

We sat there for a minute while I tried Dusty's phone again. No luck.

I sighed.

"You're right, Joe. You better stay put. It's not an easy walk. Lots of holes and ruts and roots to trip over. And it's pretty warm out there. So, yeah, you're right. You shouldn't risk it. I'll go."

I grabbed my backpack. After our earlier hike in the woods, I'd replenished the energy bars, tossed in a couple bottles of water, and added some basic first aid supplies. I got out of the car, leaned inside the open window, and handed him the car keys.

"If I'm not back in an hour, save yourself and go for help," I said. "If the car starts, that is."

I started to walk in the direction Dusty had taken us two nights earlier.

I heard a car door slam and permitted myself a "nicely played, Tressa" grin before I turned.

"Just stretching my legs," Joe said, from the fender of the car.

"Oh."

I took a few more steps.

"You know, Blondie, you've got a habit of thinking that if a person asks for help, it shows weakness. I figure the opposite. It takes a big person to ask for help."

I thought about it. He was right. It had never been easy for me to ask for help. It still didn't come easy.

"I guess you're right, Joe. Would you come with me? I'd appreciate the company," I said.

Joe nodded and waved his hand.

"I'm good here, but thanks for asking," he said.

I blinked.

"Wait a minute! What? What did you just say—?"

He grinned.

"Simmer down, Scully. I couldn't resist messing with you. I'm coming."

He pulled his Chan Man hat down and adjusted his fanny pack before joining me.

"I suppose I have to call you Mulder then," I told him.

He shook his head.

"I prefer 'Fox.'"

"Of course you do," I said and grabbed his arm. "This way, *Fox*. And watch your step. I wasn't kidding about the rough terrain."

We'd walked about three-quarters of a mile or so when I heard it.

"Hold up. Did you hear that?" I asked.

Joe gave me an "oh, brother" look.

"You trying to get back at me for making you ask for my help and me turning you down?" he asked. "Because that's just sad."

"No! Listen! Do you hear barking?"

We both held our breaths.

"Yep. It's a dog," Joe said. "So what?"

"So, Dusty has a dog, and the police didn't see him when they came looking either. Maybe that's Roswell!"

Joe made a face.

"Roswell? He couldn't come up with a real space dog name like Astro?"

I shrugged.

It was no Butch or Sundance, but it had a certain charm.

"If that's Roswell, maybe he can lead us to Dusty."

We continued along the path we'd taken two nights earlier until we came to the four-wheelers.

"Ooh. Sweet!" Joe jumped on the nearest ATV. "You said they wouldn't start?"

He monkeyed around with the controls for a second before the vehicle roared to life. He revved the motor. "Houston, we have ignition!" he announced. "I say we take these the rest of the way. It will save time if we are on a rescue mission."

He had a point.

"Do you even know how to drive an ATV?" I asked.

"Know how? I was in the military. I drove all kinds of vehicles."

Not exactly the answer I was looking for.

"Try the other one," Joe went on. "See if it starts."

I did. It fired right off, too.

What the heck?

I got a bad feeling then. If both ATVs were operating, why were they still here? Why hadn't Dusty moved them?

Unless...

He couldn't move them.

The helmets were still with the four-wheelers. I put one on and turned to instruct Joe to do the same. I should've known. He already had the camo helmet strapped to his head, the bill of his baseball cap sticking out the front.

He raised a hand.

"Ready for takeoff, Scully!" he yelled.

I sighed.

"Just don't get too close to my tail section, there Mr. Fox," I warned.

"Just Fox. Not Mr. Fox," Joe corrected.

I bit my tongue and edged the ATV ahead, driving over some of the same ground we'd covered by foot the last time. The barking was louder now. I put a hand up before slowing the four-wheeler and coming to a stop and turned to put a finger to my mouth to let Joe know to be quiet.

There it was again. Another faint bark.

"We need to go in by foot from here," I told Joe. "Why don't you stay and keep an eye on things."

"I see. Trying to hog all the glory for yourself," he said. "No way, sister. I'm in!"

"Frankie got chiggers when he was out here," I warned Joe.

"Oh, please. The kid's an insect and allergen magnet."

"Well, don't say I didn't warn you. I don't want to hear you whining later that I didn't provide full disclosure."

"I think the role of Scully is going to someone's head," Joe muttered.

We headed across the timber.

"Roswell! Roswell! Here boy!" I put my fingers in my mouth and let out a long whistle. "Roswell! Here boy!"

"Do you know how lame that sounds?" Joe shook his head. "What kind of dog got stuck with that lame name?"

I put my hand up and pointed.

"That kind of dog," I said, rushing up to the pup.

Joe stared.

"That's a dog? It looks like the dog version of Garfield."

"Dusty did say Roswell had a bit of a weight issue."

I knelt down and petted the overheated dog, reaching in my bag to get a bottle of water before taking my helmet off and pouring some of the water into it.

I held the helmet out to the thirsty animal.

"That a boy, Roswell. Drink up, and then you have to take us to Dusty."

Once the dog finished, I got to my feet.

"Come on, Roswell. Take us to Dusty. Come on, boy!"

We followed the dog into a thickly wooded area of timber. I stumbled over a downed tree and almost fell.

"Careful, Joe. It's tricky footing here."

Up ahead about twenty-five feet, Roswell stopped and began to bark.

"Good boy, Roswell! Good boy! I think we found him! Dusty! Dusty!"

I worked my way around another large, downed tree and over to Roswell. When I got on the other side of the tree, I could see Roswell was licking Dusty's face.

"Good boy!" I said. "Good boy!"

"You find him? Is he alive?" Joe asked.

I winced.

Oh, God. I hadn't even thought about that.

I hurried to Dusty, the pungent odor of alcohol more noticeable the closer I got.

"Dusty!"

Dusty lay with his back against the tree trunk, curled up in the fetal position. I dropped to the ground beside him and put a shaking hand to his forehead.

Warm. Very warm.

I put my bag down and grabbed the water bottle and pulled a pair of short white crew socks from the bag. I poured water over one sock and dribbled water over Dusty's face.

"Dusty! It's Tressa. Tressa Turner. Can you hear me? Open your eyes if you can hear me."

I saw his eyelids flicker, and he let out a long, loud, "thank you, God" sigh of relief.

"Dusty, open your mouth and try to swallow," I instructed.

His eyelids flickered again, and his lips parted. I squeezed water into his mouth and on his lips and took the damp sock and wiped his face.

"Woo wee!" Joe said, leaning over me. "Smells like the morning after a binger out here. Is he okay?" Joe said, leaning over my shoulder.

"I can't really tell, but at least he's alive."

"Dusty? Can you hear me? It's Tressa Turner?"

I could see he was trying to focus. He looked like I imagine I do the morning after you've been on the bathroom floor all night hurling in the john.

"Yes. I can hear. You found me. Thank heavens, you found me!" he said, and I knew he was going to be all right.

"Actually Roswell here found you," I said, wiping his face. "He stayed with his master." My chest suddenly felt tight. "Man's best friend."

"Best friend?" Joe whispered in my ear. "He'd have been a better friend to his master if he'd gone for help."

"Joe!"

"The truth hurts, Blondie."

"Help me get him up!"

With Joe's assistance, we helped Dusty to a sitting position.

"Oo! Ow! My foot!" Dusty said. "I think I broke it."

He accepted the water bottle and emptied the contents. I handed him another one, and he drained it.

"What happened, Dusty?" I said. "The police were out here looking for you."

His eyes became wide and scared, his gaze moving like a crazed, cornered animal.

"They came for me," he said.

I frowned. "The police?"

"No. Them!"

"Who them?"

"Them! The Ones."

"The...ones?"

He leaned in my direction.

"The invaders," he whispered. "That night. After you left. They came back. They came back for me."

I felt Joe's hand descend on my shoulder like a vice.

"Did he say invaders?"

"They came for me, and I ran. But I fell. Why didn't they take me?" he asked. "Why?"

"Maybe this is why," Joe said. I looked up at him. He held an empty bottle of vodka.

I frowned. That explained the bar stench. And, perhaps more.

"How much have you had to drink, Dusty?" I asked. "The EMTs are going to need to know."

He looked up at me.

"Just what you gave me. That's all I've had to drink since I fell."

I shook my head.

"No, Dusty. I mean, alcohol." I picked the bottle up. "How much alcohol have you had to drink?"

He stared at the bottle.

"Where'd that come from?"

"Here. Joe found it."

"Joe? Joe who?"

"Joe Townsend. He sold insurance to your grandparents."

"He did?"

I nodded.

"That's strange. I'm pretty sure they're dead."

"No. I meant he sold insurance to them before, when they were alive."

Dusty frowned and looked at Joe.

"Do I need insurance?" Dusty asked.

"Never mind. Don't worry about that, Dusty. What the medics will need to know is how much alcohol you consumed."

"None."

"None?"

He tried to shake his head.

"I don't drink."

"What about the bottle, Dusty? And you smell kind of like you're...fermenting."

"I told you. I don't drink. Never have. It dulls the senses. Makes you vulnerable...you know. To *them*."

I looked up at Joe. This time he did the cuckoo sign with his finger at his temple.

"Okay, Dusty. We're going to get you help. Just sit tight, take sips of the water, and rest. We're getting help."

I pulled my cell phone out and hit 9-1-1. The call wouldn't go through. I checked the bars. No signal.

"I'll try mine," Joe said, getting the same results.

"Dead zone," Dusty said, his voice hoarse and raspy.

"You got through to me," I told him, and he frowned, a puzzled look on his face. "Where's your phone?"

"It's here somewhere, but it's useless. I told you. It's a dead zone."

"You can quit saying that any time," Joe said.

I looked around and found his phone near where he'd been lying.

"Here it is!"

"I told you, it's no use. I tried to call until the battery ran down."

"Hold on. What? That can't be," I said. "You just called me."

He tried to shake his head, but apparently it took too much effort.

"I've been out cold for hours," he said.

I hit the power button on Dusty's phone. The phone lit up. The battery showed it five percent charged.

"It was dead!" Dusty said. "It was dead!"

I hit buttons until I found the outgoing call log.

There it was—a twenty-second call to my number at 1035 hours.

"It's here, Dusty. In your call log. You must've made the call."

"I didn't. I couldn't," he said.

I patted his hand.

"Never mind. It doesn't matter. What matters now is getting you medical attention."

I tried 9-1-1 on his phone.

No bars. No signal.

What the heck?

"Told you," Dusty said.

I got to my feet and tried again.

No signal.

We tried each of the phones again.

No luck.

I took Joe to the side.

"We can't carry this guy. Not as weak as he is."

"Or as big as he is," Joe added. "Or as drunk."

"One of us is going to have to take an ATV and ride until we get a signal and call 9-1-1."

"One of us?"

"Okay. You," I said. "I'll stay with Dusty."

Joe nodded.

"Roger. I'll be back with help ASAP! Should we synchronize our watches?"

"I think we're good. Just go!"

"Ten-four!" he said and clicked his heels and saluted. "I'm on it!"

I shook my head. Looked like Joe was going to get his glory after all. I said a little prayer until I heard the sound of the ATV starting up and getting fainter and fainter.

I dug in my bag and grabbed an energy bar and handed it to Dusty.

"Go easy there," I warned, and pulled out the first aid kit and started cleaning and applying antiseptic to his cuts and scratches. I'd leave the ankle to the professionals.

I watched as color returned to his face, and his eyes appeared brighter. Periodically, I tried to get out on our phones with no success. I remembered the police scanner I'd borrowed from my dad and grabbed it and turned it on. I'd know exactly when Fox had accomplished his mission.

Ten minutes or so went by before Dusty spoke.

"You know. I thought I was gonna die," he said. "Just lie there and decompose."

I winced. Not a good mental picture.

"I was getting weaker and weaker, and I thought, you're toast, Dusty. And you know what?"

I shook my head.

"I was lying here, going in and out, in and out, feeling so alone and scared and, all of a sudden I knew she was here, with me."

"She?"

"My mom."

I felt my heartstrings tighten.

"She died when I was ten."

"I'm so sorry, Dusty. That must've been hard."

"I felt better when I knew she was with me," he said. "I knew when I smelled the vanilla, that she was here with me, and I felt less afraid."

I sat back.

"Vanilla?"

He nodded.

"My mom always wore this musky vanilla perfume. Drove my grandma crazy. I could always tell when Mom had been in a room because she left the scent of vanilla behind wherever she went."

"Vanilla perfume," I repeated. "You smelled vanilla musk perfume out here. In the woods?"

He nodded.

"It's the last thing I remember."

I bit my lip and thought about his story.

"I know what you're thinking. It's like the phone and the alcohol. You think I'm hallucinating," he said. "Just admit it. You think I'm crazy. Like everyone else."

I shook my head.

"No, Dusty. You're wrong," I said. "As a matter of fact, I think I may have just become a *believer*."

He stared at me.

"Really?"

I nodded.

"Really."

Cheerleaders from the Seventh Circle of Hell anyone?

CHAPTER TWENTY-NINE

The *dead zone*.

It all came down to the dead zone.

And vanilla musk.

And the fact that Dusty really didn't drink.

But mostly, the *dead zone*.

"Explain your convoluted dead zone hypothesis again, Turner," Stan said.

"And this time without the glowing tributes to your courage and genius and pluck, or whatever the heck you're going for there," Shelby Lynn added. "I just ate."

I shrugged. Einstein was unappreciated in his time.

I laid my cards on the table. Well, actually cell phones, but you get the idea.

I picked up my phone.

"Here we have—"

"Ease up on the legalese there, Turner. You're not thinking about channeling Perry Mason again, are you?" Stan said. "'Cause I'll tell you right now Exhibit C is for 'cut the counselor crap' and get me the *CliffsNotes* version that explains why I'm looking at two phones unless they contain embarrassing photos of a jackass riding a jackass."

How do you say, professional rivalry run amok?

"Have it your way," I said.

"I'm the boss. That's how it works."

"Okay, boss. Here's the deal. I received a phone call from Dusty Cadwallader's cell phone number at 1035 hours. It only lasted twenty seconds or so and all I heard was noise. Return calls made to Dusty went to voice mail. It's all here on the phones. Do you follow so far, or should I bring out the dry-erase board and markers?"

"Tick-tock, Turner."

"Anyway, given Dusty's family members were concerned enough about him to request a welfare check and hadn't, to my knowledge, made contact with Dusty, I, like any caring, upstanding, and plucky—"

"Turner!"

"—headed out to his place."

"Where does Joe Townsend come in?"

"Oh, he was just along for the ride, really."

"Oh? I understood he said it was his idea to go check on Dusty, and if you hadn't agreed, he'd have gone on his own," Stan said.

"What! Why that wrinkled little—"

"Turner…"

"Anyway, we get to Dusty's place and, with Roswell's help, we located him."

"Roswell?"

"Dusty's dog. Joe thought it was lame, too, but you know Astro isn't all that clever either—"

"Oh, Lord. Kill me now," Shelby moaned.

"As I was saying, we find Dusty, and he tells us about being chased in the woods and falling and hurting his ankle and being knocked out, and I mention about him calling me, and he swears he didn't call, that he'd tried but didn't have a signal, and that eventually his phone died. Well, I'm sitting there holding my phone that showed his call and his phone that also showed the call to me in his history but also still had a charge. I'm thinking the guy is a little confused and disoriented and might not be thinking too clearly. Remember, at the time I thought he might have been, er, alcohol impaired."

"But he wasn't, right?"

I shook my head.

"Zero blood alcohol content. Dusty asked the doctors to share the results with me. And it jibes with what he told me about not drinking."

"Even though there was an empty liquor bottle and he smelled like a wino?" Stan asked.

"How do you say planted evidence?" I said.

"Wait a minute. So you suspect subterfuge," Shelby said.

"All I'm saying is that someone went to a lot of trouble to make it appear Dusty had been drinking. Obviously it was someone who didn't know Dusty was a non-drinker. And, ladies and gentlemen of the jury, that same someone made the phone call to me from Dusty's phone."

"Wait a minute. Now you're losin' me," Shelby said. "How do you know someone else made the call from Dusty's phone? Why couldn't he just have forgotten he did it?"

I let her queries hang.

One thousand one. One thousand two.

"Oh. Wait. Now I get it. Now I understand. Dusty couldn't have made the call because of the—"

"*Dead zone!*" we yelled in unison.

"Good God," Stan said. "It's contagious."

"That's right. The dead zone. You see there was no cell signal where Dusty was. I tried. Joe tried. In fact, Joe had to get in the Buick and drive down the road before he got a signal. Given the injury to Dusty's ankle and his overall physical condition, there's no way he could have hoofed it the distance required to make that call and get back to where he was found before Joe and I got there. No way, pilgrims. *Plus* the person or persons had to take time to charge Dusty's cell phone before they made the call."

"No biggie there. Lots of cell phone chargers are universal and can be plugged into a car's cigarette lighter," Shelby pointed out.

"So, Perry, I suppose you've figured out a motive for this ruse," Stan said.

"Guilt," I said.

"Guilt?"

"Guilt. Whoever made that call knew what happened to Dusty and where he was. How? Because Dusty was also telling the truth when he said someone was chasing him."

"He said aliens were chasing him, Turner," Stan reminded me.

"Okay so they wore hoods. The point is the caller had to have been there when Dusty fell and knew he was missing. That person felt guilty. Guilty and afraid. Afraid Dusty could die out there. So they went back and took his phone, charged it long enough to make the call to me, put the phone back, and staged the scene so it looked like Dusty had tied one on. Then when he told his story about an alien abduction attempt, no one would believe him because he was hammered and because he was, well, Dusty Dodger from the twenty-fourth-and-a-half century."

"So one of our band of hell-raisers has a conscience," Stan said.

"And I'm pretty sure I know which one it is." I tapped my nose. "Thanks to these—the olfactory nerves of a bloodhound."

"Not to mention the proboscis of one," Shelby said.

"You mentioned something about a 'smell test' before," Stan said. "What's up with that?"

"Vanilla," I said. "Vanilla musk to be exact."

"Come again?"

"Vanilla musk perfume." I explained Dusty's heartrending, tearjerker, mother moment in the woods. "He remembered smelling vanilla musk! He recognized it because his mother wore it,
God rest her soul."

"So the ghost of his mother who reeked of vanilla musk visited him in the woods to comfort him?" Shelby asked.

"No! But one of our perps did!"

"Which perp?" Stan asked"

"The one with the conscience, of course. And also, by the way, the one who—just this morning—was a bit too heavy-handed with the vanilla musk. Miss Jada Garcia."

"Oh, my gosh! So it *is* the cheerleaders after all!" Shelby Lynn said.

"Put the champagne cork back in the bottle, you're getting ahead of yourselves," Stan said. "What about last night? The damage at your folks' place? Your pink pony? The cheerleaders have alibis, remember?"

"All but Miss Vanilla Musk," I said.

Stan frowned.

"I looked at the pictures you took, Turner. I don't see how one girl could have done that all by herself."

"How tall is Jada Garcia anyway?" Shelby asked. "All of five feet?" She grabbed my phone and opened the gallery. "It's hard to tell for sure, but from the location of some of the tornadoes, it looks like she wouldn't have been able to reach that high."

"A ladder maybe?"

"Who takes time to drag a ladder out to spray-paint graffiti?"

"And what about Joker?" Shelby asked. "Think about it. It would have taken at least two people to do the number on him. One to hang on to his halter at one end and one to do their stuff at the other."

I winced.

They were right. Jada must've had help when she hit our place to set up an alibi for her "sisters in spandex." And judging from the location of the paint, that…helper had to be much taller than Jada.

I got a sick, sinking feeling in the pit of my stomach. I may have moaned.

"What the hell's wrong with you, Turner?" Stan asked.

All right. I *did* moan.

"The reality of saving a man's life is starting to sink in I guess," I said. "It's exhausting. But I'm holding up well, thank you."

"Oh jeesh," Stan said. "Here we go again."

I let Stan go on about drama divas and deadlines while I focused on the daunting prospect ahead.

Not only did I have to confront Mick Dishman with evidence that implicated him in criminal activity of the most heinous kind (horse defacement in the first degree), I'd likely have to go through a mountain of a cousin who'd already warned me off and a pit bull of a gatekeeper known as "Ahnt Mo" to get to my quarry.

Skinflint Stan notwithstanding, this ace cub reporter would be putting in for hazardous duty pay and calling on the inherent ferociousness of a mama bear avenging the colorization of her likely-to-be-gender-confused, not-so-pretty-in-pink Appaloosa to win the day.

I decided to go bearing gifts. Food gifts. Aunt Mo was partial to her grub, like someone we know and love. After seeing her at the pharmacy, I figured she could do with a bit of sweetening up, so I stopped by Town Square Bake Shoppe and picked up a cake. Not just any cake. A fudge cake. Not just any fudge cake. Town Square's Best Ever Chocolate Lovers' Chocolate Fudge Layer Cake.

Famous throughout Knox County.

Okay. So it was a bribe. And, as bribes went, it wasn't cheap. But it was also an investment.

The more I could coax from Aunt Mo over cake and a cold glass of milk, the less ugly it would get.

For me.

Luck was with me, and I managed to score the last cake, doing a quick end run around a chubby little grade school kid, rolling around on the floor and pointing at the chocolate confection in question, screaming, "My cake! My cake! My cake!"

Ha! Fat lot you know! That's my cake now, brat.

The cake was out of the display, into a box, and into my hot, little hands, and I was out the door before Damian knew what happened.

I figured I was doing both mother and son a favor. Mom could blame me, and I'd get the love handles instead of the boy.

In record time (and to record horn toots, hoots, and heckling) I pulled up in front of Aunt Mo's. Aunt Mo lived in a two-story stucco house that had been added onto. It had a big old front porch and a new two plus attached garage. I didn't see a car in the drive but figured they could be parked in the garage.

I hurried up the porch and rang the bell. I noticed the curtains at the big picture window move. Someone was home. I rang again.

"I know you're in there," I said. "I saw the curtains move. It's hot out here, and I have fudge cake. Not a good combo."

The front door opened.

"Whatchu doin' here, girl?" Aunt Mo eyed me with suspicion.

"I came to visit. I thought, you know, after seeing you at the pharmacy and all that we never really got a chance for closure after all that engagement drama."

"And you thought cake would give Mo closure?"

"Well no. Not just any cake," I said. "But Town Square's Best Ever Fudge Cake might be a tasty beginning." I lifted the box up so Aunt Mo could get a whiff of fudge heaven. "But if you're not ready, I do understand." I sighed and turned to leave.

"Now don't get your big girl pants in a bunch," Mo said and leaned away from the door to look to her left and her right before reaching out to grab me and pull me into the house. She shut the door behind us, before getting up on her tippy-toes to peak out the tiny window on the front door.

"Are you expecting someone?" I asked.

"What makes you think that?" Mo asked and took the cake from me and moved from the living room into the formal dining room. She set the cake on the dining room table and continued into a large and modern kitchen.

"This is nice," I said, looking around.

She nodded. "That's right. It's one of them add-ons. Kitchen, bath, laundry, master bedroom, and garage. Mo's got everything she needs on one level now. Mo don't do stairs," she added.

"That's handy. I love the design. Did you do it?"

"Mo? Hell no. Mo's no contractor. Now Manny—"

"Manny?"

"Manny nothing!" she said. "You lost any rights to any info on that fine man when you dumped him for that slick Rick," she said, going to the cupboard to get plates. "Glasses are up there. Milk's in the fridge. Use the tray," she added.

"I didn't actually dump Manny for Rick Townsend you know. That implies Manny and I were a couple," I pointed out, opening cupboards until I located glasses and had poured each of us a glass of cold milk. "And we weren't. We were more like…coconspirators."

"Bring that," she nodded at the tray with our milk, forks, napkins, and elegant cake serving set with matching handles.

I picked the tray up and followed her back into the dining room and set the tray down.

"Rick's a really nice guy," I said.

"And Manny isn't?" Mo asked, dropping into a chair and opening the lid on the cake box.

I thought about it for a second then shook my head.

No. Nice wasn't a word I'd ever use to describe Manny DeMarco.

Mo cut two generous slices of cake and put them on plates. She gave herself the more generous of the two.

I picked up my fork.

"So what really brings Tressa Jayne Turner to see Aunt Mo?" Marguerite Dishman said before I could take a bite of my cake.

"I told you. Mending fences."

"Mo ain't got no fence that needs mending, and if she did, she wouldn't ask Manny's heartbreaker to mend 'em."

"I didn't break Manny's heart, Aunt Mo."

"How do you know? You can't see inside a person."

I supposed that was true.

"So, is Mick around?" I asked.

"Why do you want to know?"

"I just thought maybe he'd like a piece of cake," I said.

"Well, he ain't here."

"Oh, that's too bad."

"Why? You think you're taking the cake?"

I shook my head.

"No. The cake's yours. My little gooey fudge peace offering." I took a bite of cake and shut my eyes, savoring the moist fudgy flavor. I followed with a milk chaser. "You know I was looking at the yearbooks at the school the other day and came across Mick's name and thought it was funny."

"Whatcha mean, you thought it was funny?"

I looked at Mo.

"Oh, no. I don't mean that like it sounded. I'm not photogenic either. What I meant was I saw his pictures and thought, wow! Brilliant! I wished I'd thought of that."

"Wished you'd thought of what?"

"Of the picture thing," I said.

"What picture thing?" Mo asked.

I looked up from my plate.

"The no picture thing," I said.

"No picture thing?"

"All the spaces for Mick's photographs have *photo not available* across the boxes. He even opted out of the team pictures. I wish my folks had let me get away with that."

It would have saved me countless hours of detention due to schoolyard fisticuffs.

Mo pushed her plate away.

"What makes you think anybody's getting away with anything? What makes you think that? Nobody's gettin' away with anything. Why'd you say that?"

"I don't. I didn't. I was just making chit-chat."

I frowned. I hit a nerve but danged if I knew which one. Since Mo was already upset and I didn't have a clue why, I figured I might as well get it over with and bring up the subject of Mick and Jada and the suspicions that had actually brought me here.

"Aunt Mo. We need to talk about Mick," I said. "You see. I know."

Mo's fork hit her plate.

"You know?"

I nodded.

"I wish I didn't. But I do."

"How'd you know?"

"I'm a reporter. It's what I do. I'll admit it was a shock. How long have you known?"

Mo frowned.

"Since the beginning," she admitted.

"The beginning? Why didn't you say anything?"

"I couldn't. I have to protect Mick."

I nodded. "I understand. But you must know this can't just be swept under the rug."

"Mo and Manny plan to deal with it eventually—when the time is right."

I got up and moved around the table and crouched next to Mo. I took her hand.

"Mo, don't you see? The time is now. You can't keep your head in the sand and hope this goes away. It won't. Damage has been done. Your neighbors' hard work trampled on and reduced to nothing more than sophomoric scribblings. People injured—while proud, noble steeds face the indignity of being turned an unflattering shade of pink. Oh, Aunt Mo! You can't imagine what it was like. Seeing those hot pink spots. That putrid pink tail!" I squeezed her hand. "The madness has to end! Help me, Aunt Mo! Help me stop this madness!"

Aunt Mo's looked down at me, her mouth open, eyes bug-eyed wide.

"You've gone and done it. You've snapped your twig, Tressa Jayne Turner. Or did you slip something extra in that cake? All this going on about putrid spots and hot tails!"

I winced. "That would be hot *pink* tails," I clarified and then frowned. "Wait a second. Hold on. You said you knew all about it—" I stammered.

"Barbie proposing to Aunt Mo?" I turned my head. Manny stood in the doorway of a room just beyond the dining room. "'Cause from here that's what it looks like."

I shook my head and got to my feet.

"How long have you been there?" I asked, but guessing it was pretty much the entire time.

I turned to Mo. "How come you didn't tell me Manny was here?"

"'Barbie' didn't ask," Aunt Mo said.

"I came to talk to Aunt Mo about Mick," I said.

"Manny heard."

"I figured. And?"

"Thanks for the cake, Barbie."

My mouth flew open this time.

"What? That's it! That's all you've got to say? 'Thanks for the cake, Barbie?' You're not going to deal with this?"

Manny came over and grabbed my arms and lifted me up and off my feet. Yes, I said off.

"Frontier night's tonight. Aunt Mo needs her rest. Barbie needs to split."

"B…but—"

Before I could react, he literally (no exaggeration) carried me to the door and set me on the porch.

"Manny'll see you tonight. Save a dance."

I stood on the porch and fumed.

What just happened?

I shook my head.

Well, hell hath no fury like a woman who's been handled like dry cleaning picked up at Fresh Start Cleaners.

Or one deprived of cake. And not just any cake.

Town Square's Best Ever Chocolate Lovers' Chocolate Fudge Layer Cake.

Save a dance, my ass.

He'd be too busy watching his back to dance.

I'm a cowgirl. I haul fifty-pound sacks of feed. I use pitchforks regularly. I move twelve hundred pound animals out of my way with a single shove.

Be afraid, Manny DeMarco.

Be very afraid.

CHAPTER THIRTY

I stood by myself, now and then scratching, taking in the sounds and colors of a true down-home, good time gala. Vendors lined the lane that ran along the buildings that comprised the historical village.

There was the stagecoach inn, the old-time depot, the general store, the old country church, the little red schoolhouse, and the historical museum. As a family—between ball games, picnics, camping, and fishing—we'd spent countless hours at the county park. It felt like an old friend.

Well, except for the occasional gaggle of rabid geese that, from time to time, laid claim to the park as home turf. Waves of bittersweet nostalgia took me back to a simpler time and place when life was carefree and uncomplicated.

"Well, howdy there, little lady? Don't I know you from somewhere? If I don't, I'd sure like to. Hehehe. Know what I'm sayin'?"

My own blast from the past and back into present day came in the form of Uncle Bo, who looked even more like Freddie the Freeloader, than I had in my hobo day. Or Red Skelton had, for that matter.

"Aun—"

"Ah, ah, ah." Aunt Eunice rapped my arm with the knapsack she carried. "Don't blow my cover, Calamity. One more day until the big reveal."

"You're not planning to dress like that tomorrow, are you, uh, er, Uncle Bo?" I asked, thinking that would be one *Extreme Homely Makeover*, and one that shouldn't be attempted in a place where food was being served.

"I haven't decided yet. I want to go for the biggest wow factor. By the way, you'd be doing me a big favor by running interference between that sister of mine and her Seeing Eye guide dog of a husband. Everywhere I go those two are on my tail, including the crappers. Why, I went in the men's bathroom the other day and your grandma almost followed me in. I can't take it anymore! She's going to spoil the surprise! Oh, criminy. Here they come again! I'm out of here!"

And *pfft*! She was gone. I took a second to appreciate her flight. For an old guy, Uncle Bo moved like greased lightning.

I felt an itch inside my waistband at the back and started to scratch again.

"Tressa! Tressa Jayne! That you?"

Okay. Yes. I'd gone ahead and dressed up. Let's face it. I was never going to turn down an opportunity to dress up like my notorious namesake, Calamity Jane. Get real.

It hadn't taken much in the way of 'costuming' to make me fit the part. Blue jeans, cowboy boots and hat, western shirt, and big ol' belt were fashion essentials already in my closet. I'd had to scare up a vest, settling for the colorfully flamboyant hot pink vest made famous in my ill-fated hobo performance. With a hot pink kerchief to match tied around my neck, a toy gun and holster set strapped to my hips, and a short, braided whip known as a quirt for effect, I was the quintessential lady outlaw.

In other words, I didn't look all that different from normal.

"It's me, Gram." I turned. "Holy hell...*o*, Martha Jane Cannary!" I said, taking a giant step back.

"Surprise!" Gram yelled.

I blinked. Surprise didn't come close. Shock and awe? You're getting warmer.

I blinked again. It was like looking in a mirror—if the mirror was older than Methuselah and made everyone who looked into it appear the same.

"Who's Martha Jane?" Gram asked.

"Martha Jane Cannary—Calamity Jane's real name," I said, still put off by the spectacle before me. Gram was almost a carbon copy of me, down to the jeans stuck into the boots, pink vest, (although hers was fringed) and toy gun belt. The only thing missing was her quirt.

"Isn't that the hobo vest?" Gram asked, eyeing the area of my boobs.

I nodded and scratched one of the girls.

"It don't have no fringe. Calamity Jane had fringe, didn't she, Joe?"

I finally thought to look at Joe—and wished I hadn't.

"Who are you?" I asked, taking in the long black wig and handlebar mustache, black bolo tie, fringed suede shirt, and hat with a brim the shape of a pizza pan. "Mario meets Fabio?"

"Funny stuff, Miss Ants in Your Pants," he said. "I'm Wild Bill Hickok, of course, with the lovely Miss Martha Jane. What's with the quirt in the pants?" he asked.

I pulled the quirt out and tapped it against my palm.

"I have no idea what you're talking about," I said, feeling an almost unbearable compulsion to stick the quirt down my right boot and scratch.

"Did you finish writing up the Cadwallader story?" Joe asked. "I trust I'm given the recognition I deserve. After all, if I hadn't traveled cross-county to seek out help—"

"Cross country? You drove an ATV to a car and a car down the road and made a phone call. You did a good deed, Joe. Be content in that knowledge, and don't seek society's stamp of approval. You'll be happier for it."

"I see. That means you've cast yourself in the starring role, and I'm a supporting character," Joe said.

"It's better than a walk-on, Bill," I said.

"What'd that bum want with you, Tressa?" Gram asked. "He didn't prop-position you, did he? Looks like a dirty old man to me."

I shook my head.

"No. He was just looking for the bathrooms."

"That feller goes to the toilet more than anyone I know, don't he, Joe?" Gram said. "Every time I turn around, that bum is goin' into another bathroom. Whatcha think he does in there?"

I raised an eyebrow.

"There you are! Sorry I'm late. Work was a bear today."

I felt a hand at my waist and turned, relieved to discover it belonged to Ranger Rick.

"Not a literal bear," Townsend qualified, looking at my gammy. "Just a very long day."

"Who you supposed to be?" Gram asked, taking in Rick's black jeans, western shirt, and boots.

"I'm a simple working man who was too tired to dress up," he said.

"Lot of men wearing your costume," Gram said. "Come on, Wild Bill. Let's get over to the restrooms so we can trail that hobo hombre when he comes out. Later!"

I watched the *Apple Dumpling Gang* walk off, letting out an, "Oh, Lord, that feels good!" sigh when Townsend started to rub the center of my back.

"Lower! Lower! Put a little fingernail into it. Yes. There! There! Oh, yes! Yes!"

"Are we interrupting something…creepy?"

"Another country heard from," I said. "Transylvania. Hey, you two. Don't you look…interesting?"

Five feet three inches of *Roll Out the Barrel* Dixie and her malady-magnet fiancé, Frankfurter Barlowe were dressed as… Okay I had no idea who or what they were dressed as. Frankie had on an old-looking black suit with a white shirt and narrow black tie. He had a toy stethoscope around his neck and one of those weird headbands with a big ol' reflector thingie around his head. Dixie wore…nothing. Well, not nothing as in naked (thank goodness), but nothing as in no costume.

"Dr. Who the heck are you, I presume?" I said to Frankie.

"Dr. Janus Pritchaerd, one of the first medical doctors in the county, at your service," Frankie took a bow and the metal doohickey on his head slid off onto the ground. "Watch your feet! Don't step on my head mirror!" he warned.

"And who might this be?" I waved a hand at Dixie. "Dr. Janus's first medical patient who, sadly, succumbed to some rare and exotic illness like party-pooperitis?"

"We can't all be illiterate, alcoholic circus performers with a storytelling résumé that includes among other things, embellishment, prevarication, and profanity," Dixie said. "I eschew such banalities. I'm merely here in a support role."

"Oh. I get it. You're his undertaker," I said.

She shook her head.

"Still itching, I see, Frankie," I said, watching him take a tongue depressor and put it down the side of his waistband. "Tough break."

"What about you?" Dixie asked. "

"Me? What do you mean?"

"You got Rick going at your back like it was a cat scratch pad and, while I'm not an expert on equine tack, I'd swear sticking a quirt down your boot isn't the appropriate usage for said item."

I pulled the quirt out.

"I don't know what you're talking about. I'm fine. Just getting a back rub from my boyfriend," I said. "Keep it up. A little lower. Lower. There."

Dixie shook her head.

"We heard about Joker and the paint damage and all," Frankie said. "Do the police have any leads? What about that evidence we collected at Dusty Cadwallader's? Has that helped the investigation at all?"

I lifted my shoulder several times. Up and down. Up and down. Ah. That felt good.

"I don't have a clue what the county is doing, if anything."

"Look. There's Kimmie and Craig! Over here!" Frankie called. "Here! Oh, no. Looks like they're having another argument."

I craned my neck to see.

Sure enough. From here I could spot Craig's pissed-off-but-trying-not-to-show-it tell, his left hand on his hip and the fingers of his right hand repeatedly massaging the top of his head as they ran through his hair. Kimmie's tell was no less apparent. At barely five feet tall, she had a beer in her right hand and was doing her "let me tell you something" finger pointing with the left.

"This still the baby battle?" Dixie said.

I nodded. "Round ninety-seven."

"Too bad. That kind of thing should be discussed and agreed on before the wedding, not after."

I looked at her.

"It should?"

"Absolutely. It's the only way to approach a marriage since both parties bring their own expectations—some of which are totally unrealistic by the way." She shot her fiancé a quick look.

Jab.

"Dixie's right. Couples should sit down and clearly articulate what they want from a marriage and from their partners, not expect them to read their minds, isn't that right, Dix?"

Feign and jab.

"You would agree, wouldn't you, Frankie dear, that a person wouldn't need to be a mind reader if their partner shared what was going on in that oh, so, precious but occasionally *Magoo* head of his from time to time."

One to the chin.

"How could I disagree, *sweetie,* when you're always right?"

Sucker punch.

Townsend gave my shoulders a final squeeze.

"I'd better go see if I can ratchet Craig down a notch," he said.

I nodded. If Craig didn't stop running his hand through his hair, he'd be bald by morning. Townsend gave me a kiss on the neck, and I watched the view as he walked away. It never ceased to get my heart rate going *thumpity-thump.*

"There you are!" I was jerked out of my arse appreciation by a hard yank on my arm that pulled me across the grass.

"You're coming with me!"

I stared at my bestie. She was wearing an old-fashioned and somewhat severe dress with a high lace collar. Her hair was pulled back in a hairnet with wire-rimmed glasses perched halfway down her nose. She had a book in her hand.

"Kari! You look fabulous. Let me guess. A spinster librarian."

"I'm a schoolmarm, but the spinster? It could definitely happen. Come on!"

She yanked on my arm again.

"What are you doing? Where are we going?"

"We're spying on my husband," she said. "This way!" She grabbed my hand now, leading me away from the village and down the path towards the recreational areas and the water beyond.

"Spying? On Brian? Why?"

"I saw him leave with that Dallas Cow of a Cheerleading Coach," she said.

"Martina Banfield? Are you sure?"

She nodded. "I followed them. I saw them go into the covered bridge. And they never came out." For a moment the fury in her voice gave way to hurt.

"That doesn't sound like Brian," I said. "Besides, she's too flash—" I stopped.

"Go on! You were going to say she was too flashy for him, weren't you? So she's like this big ol' blinding billboard with her breasts and her bling, and I'm what? A black-and-white snapshot of some nobody you find in a billfold you buy? Is that what you're saying?"

I shook my head. "I think that's what you're saying. I'm saying she's not his type. She's all hair and boobs and teeth and show. You're real and genuine and funny and smart and beautiful and sensitive."

"Okay. You've talked me down. You can stop."

I smiled. "Besides, Taylor and I spoke to her, and that girl is all about her career." I said. "She's like obsessed with this dude named Marlowe."

"Is he a teacher?"

I shrugged. "He might've been. But I'm pretty sure he's dead."

She looked at me.

"So what do you think they're doing in there?"

"Now that, young lady, is a perfectly reasonable question. Why don't you go find out?"

"You mean just walk right on in and say, 'Oh, hello there. What the hell are you doing with my husband?' Like that?"

"Just like that."

"You could do that. I can't do that."

"And you're sure they're in the covered bridge?"

She nodded.

"I have an idea. You ever play *The Three Billy Goats Gruff*?" I looked at her and shook my head. "You had such a sheltered childhood. Permit me to explain."

A few minutes later we were beneath the bridge, directly under the mentor and his mentee.

We'd already silenced our cell phones, and I was already regretting my impulsive action when the voices above us filtered downward. I put my fingers to my lips in a *shh, quiet!* number.

"I need to get back to Kari," Brian said. "She'll be wondering where I'm at."

"You said you cared!" Martina said, and I reached over and clasped a hand over Kari's mouth a millisecond before she exploded.

"I do care. But you're crossing lines. Getting too close."

"How can you say that? It's just that I'm passionate. I feel deeply about this. About what this could mean. Why don't you understand?"

"I do understand, Martina. And I do care. But this is getting out of hand."

"Forget it! Forget I even asked. Go back to your boring little life and your boring little wife!"

I almost lost Kari on that one. Thank goodness her roar of outrage was muffled by the sounds of running feet on the floorboards of the bridge.

"I will end him!" Kari said, once I got off of her.

Who's tromp, tromp, tromping over my bridge?

A schoolmarm with three *R*s on her mind.

Revenge, retaliation, and ringing someone's bell—that was so not a recess one.

That's who.

CHAPTER THIRTY-ONE

By the time Kari and I had rejoined the Historical Village's answer to *Back to the Future*, I was itching worse than my pooches did after they've taken a midnight run through the thicket.

Kari and I parted ways. I wasn't comfortable with this, but as soon as I got to the area cordoned off for dancing, I noticed Gram standing outside the restrooms.

"Would you believe he's in there again?" Gram exclaimed.

"Joe?"

"No. Joe's getting a beer. Him. Abigail's bum. The guy has a problem. S'pose it's his prostrate?"

"I doubt it, Gram," not bothering to correct her. "Why don't we get something to eat and wait for Joe over there?" I steered her over to the bratwursts. "Aren't these just lovely? Oh, look! Sauerkraut!"

I got Gram a heaping helping and got her settled at a table.

And then I saw them.

Mick Dishman and Jada Garcia.

The demeaning duo who'd made a joke out of Joker.

The terrible twosome who pink tornadoed our property.

The football star and cheerleader who didn't have a clue who the f-bomb they were dealing with.

These boots were made for kicking cheerleader booty.

I set a course for the oblivious couple, Mick dressed in all black (naturally) and Jada in a Panther Posse outfit, this time worn over tight black leggings. Uber tacky.

I struck out across the area roped off for dancing, zigging and zagging between the dancers until I cleared the revelers.

My name is Tressa Jayne Turner. You colorized my horse. Prepare to dye.

(Love *The Princess Bride*, don't you?)

I knew the second they saw me and accurately divined my intent. The next second I found myself yanked off my feet and into a group of two-step swing dancers.

I looked up into the face of Manny DeMarco.

"Who the hell do you think you are?" I said, for some reason moving right into the dance steps like I'd received a proper "shall we dance?"

Feet together. Walk. Walk.

Quick. Quick. Slow. Slow.

Turn.

"The man who's going to save Barbie."

"Save me? From what?"

Walk. Walk.

Quick. Quick.

Slow. Slow.

Turn.

"From herself."

"Ha! Fat chance! It's that horse-hating, homey cousin of yours who is going to need saving. From me!"

Quick. Quick.

Slow. Slow.

Turn.

"Barbie needs to chill."

Slow. Slow.

Stop!

I planted my feet, pointed my finger, and jabbed Manny DeMarco in the chest.

"The name is…Tressa!" *Poke. Poke. Poke.* "And don't you forget it!"

I whirled on my heel, prepared to resume my initial course when I heard someone yell my name, and Taylor rushed up looking like Linda Evans' character, Audra, on *The Big Valley* but without the cleavage. I could see her eyes go all "what is he doing here?" huge when they spotted Manny behind me.

"Are you...busy?" she asked.

"Kind of. Why?"

"It's Kimmie. She's...well, you'll see. That is, if you can break away."

I looked over to where Mick and Jada had been, and they were gone.

"Dang!"

"Tressa? Can you come?"

I nodded.

"Thanks for nothing, DeMarco," I said, giving him my finest Martha Jane Cannary up yours look before following Taylor.

"What's the big deal about Kimmie? So she's enjoying a beer or two. I don't see the harm in—hot time in the ol' town tonight!" I stared at my sister-in-law. At least I thought it was my sister-in-law. It was hard to tell with all the war paint. Streetwalker variety. "What happened to Kimmie's pioneer outfit? The one with the cute yellow and white checked apron and matching bonnet?" The demure one.

"Apparently a saloon girl was hiding beneath, ready to spring forth."

A saloon girl with a hankering for burgundy and black corsets, sheer frilly black bloomers, black fishnet hose, black lace gloves, and a black velvet choker.

"Where's Craig?" I asked.

"I saw him with Rick and Frankie earlier. I called Frankie and told him what was going on and told them to keep Craig away. Oh, God, Tressa. He can't see Kimmie this way! He'll go bat shat crazy!"

I couldn't take my eyes off Kimmie. She stood by the light pole, one hand on the pole, her body swaying seductively like she was gearing up for her first set.

Slack-jawed frontiersmen and their pursed-mouthed wives couldn't seem to take their eyes off the show either.

"Do something!" Taylor urged.

I thought a second.

"How good are you on-the-fly?"

"You know I suck at improvisation or impromptu."

Leave it to Taylor to throw big words around at a time like this.

"Just follow my lead. You're the prudish shopkeeper's wife and I must say, perfect for the role, and I'll be the law around these here parts. Ready?"

"No, but I'll do it anyway. For Kimmie and Craig."

"Good. You get that motivation workin' for you, Miss Prude. And…action!"

"What's this here goin' on in my town?" I hollered, and took off in the direction of the pole dancer, sounding like an Iowan with a head cold rather than Marshall Dillon. "Is someone disturbin' my peace?"

"Oh! Thank God, it's you Miz Calamity! We've got soiled doves right here in our beloved Historical Village. Please, Miz Calamity. Help us!"

I had to give her credit. As a prude, Taylor wasn't half bad.

"Never fear, Miss Prude. Calamity Jayne is here," I said. "Now, young lady," I said, reaching my hand out to Kimmie, "you're comin' with me!"

"No, thank you," Kimmie said.

I blinked.

"Maybe y'all didn't hear me right, Miss Soiled Dove, but you are comin' with me."

"I heard."

"And?"

Kimmie shook her head.

"I don't think so."

"No?"

She shook her head.

"No."

I grabbed hold of her and leaned in with my lips to her ear.

"Kimmie. You may be drunk, but you're not too drunk to understand that you've got one shot here. One shot to keep your reputation intact. One shot to bow out of this gracefully. One shot to get out without losing something you may never get back. One shot. Don't blow it."

Kimmie hiccoughed then sighed.

"I thought we were friends, Tressa. Sisters!" she hiccoughed again.

"We are. Both of those. That's why I'm here instead of your husband. So," I said, raising my voice to performance level again. "What's it gonna be, Miss Dove?"

She sighed loudly and put the back of her hand to her forehead. "Oh, Miz Calamity! I've been a baad girl. Take me to the hoosegow." She held her hands out as if to be cuffed, and I led her away—straight into the hands of my waiting parents who whisked her off the stage.

"Oh, Calamity! You're our hero!" Taylor said and ran up and put her arm through mine, and we walked off.

Tepid clapping sounded—it was improv after all—and I may have heard a comment or two about lesbian lovers, but it was loud, and I could have been mistaken.

What mattered is that we'd saved the day for Craig and Kimmie so they could fight another one. Less publicly, one hoped.

I gave Rick a call and filled him in on what was going on with Kimmie and how we'd had to sort of talk her down off the ledge—or, in this case, the pole.

"You missed the Turner trio's one-act play," I said. "It got mixed reviews. How's my bro?"

"Let's just say he's feeling no pain."

"Oh, God. We can't put the two of them together until they sober up," I said.

"No worries. We're heading over to my place for coffee and more coffee," he said. "How about Kimmie?"

"The folks are looking after her. She's more indignant than intoxicated."

"What about Martha Jane Cannary? How is she?"

"Heading for the bunkhouse shortly. Is Frankie still with you?"

"Affirmative. He has a fondness for boys' night out."

"I don't think Frankie's had too many bromances," I said.

"Brian called a little bit ago," Townsend reported. "He's on his way over, too. Kari told him to get bent. Don't know what that means exactly."

Nothing fun for Brian—or Townsend, that's for sure.

"Well, you boys enjoy your night. I'll hitch a ride with Taylor. Call me later?"

"You better call me. I might require a welfare check."

I grinned at his jest and purchased a beer (you'd think just one person who saw my performance would offer to buy) and walked over to a nearby table and sat down, listening to Garth Brooks sing about friends in low places.

"Sing it to me, Garth," I mumbled, thinking about Kari and what we'd heard under the covered bridge and what that meant for her and Brian and what the future held for Kimmie and Craig and Rick and me.

Soon, Taylor joined me. And Kari. Then Dixie.

An alcoholic cross-dressing sharpshooter. A pioneer prude. A schoolmarm. And a party pooper.

Glum and glummers.

"What a day," Taylor said.

"What a week," Kari said.

"What a month," I said.

"What a pathetic bunch of whiny babies," Dixie observed. "So today sucked. Get over yourselves. Our men are occupied. We're on our own. We've got beer. Music. Cowboys—or reasonable facsimiles."

I smiled.

"Dixie's right. I mean the whole episode with Kimmie was bound to make Dixie nostalgic for last summer."

"Last summer?" Kari asked.

"At the state fair. Bottoms Up."

"Oh, God. You're not going to bring that up again," Dixie said.

I put my hand out.

"Picture this. A hot, stuffy, smoky beer tent. Sawdust on the floor. A makeshift stage. The lights dim, and our star steps to the mike. And the caterwaulin' begins. Enter Dixie Daggett, Queen of the Karaoke with her rendition of *Should've Been a Cowboy,* but I can't mount a horse."

"Oh, for God's sake. Get some new material! And all I'm saying is, what's to stop us from enjoying ourselves for a few hours?"

"That, maybe," I said, pointing at the county sheriff's car that pulled up, lights flashing.

A second patrol vehicle followed it.

"Now that can't be good," Dixie said.

"You don't suppose someone complained about Kimmie's and our performance, do you?" Taylor asked.

I made a raspberry sound.

"If that's all that agency has to do—and I know for a fact it isn't—then this county is in need of Miz Calamity more than I thought."

I watched Doug Samuels get out of the lead patrol car, followed by the deputy in the second vehicle. They disappeared around the side of the two-story stagecoach inn next door."

"I wonder what's going on?" Taylor asked.

"Probably some obnoxious drunk," I said.

"I thought you said Kimmie went home," Kari said, and I winced.

"I wish I'd thought to bring my scanner with me," I said. "I left it in the Buick."

"You know. A reporter worth her salt would be over there with her nose stuck in the middle of all that," Dixie said. "I bet Drew Van Vleet is over there right now with his nose so far up Sheriff Samuel's—"

I jumped to my feet.

"I'm going! I'm going!"

"No need. Here they come," Taylor said.

"Looks like they have a couple of people in custody," Dixie said.

I watched the procession and, for a second, the crowd parted, and I got a glimpse of the individuals in handcuffs who were being led to the patrol cars by the officers.

I stared. My jaw dropped like a trapdoor.

"Oh, my God! Is that Robbie Rodgers?" Kari asked. "Isn't he your boss's kid?"

I nodded.

"It is!"

"Who's that other kid?" Taylor asked. "I don't think I know him."

I did.

It was Manny's cousin, Mick.

"I wonder what's up with that," Kari said.

"I'm going to find out," I said, watching the patrol cars pull out of the park. "Taylor, the keys to the Buick, if you'd be so kind."

"I wouldn't. I'll drive."

"I need a lift, too," Kari said.

"Me, too," Dixie said.

"We piled into the car, Dixie and Kari in back. Taylor behind the wheel and yours truly riding shotgun. Taylor was about to back out when a sharp rap on my window scared the living bejeebers out of me.

"What the hell was that?" Dixie asked.

"I can't see anything with this blasted tornado on the window!" I said, hitting the power window button to roll it down.

"Aaagh!" I screamed when a face peered back at me.

"Who is it?" Kari asked.

"It's me. Jada. Jada Garcia. Please! I need your help!"

I stared at the girl.

"Why should I help you?" I asked. "You maimed my horse."

She shook her head.

"No. No. I didn't. I didn't do that."

"Well then, your boyfriend did," I said.

"Mick? Oh no. It wasn't Mick. Please! They can't see me talking to you. Let me in!"

I looked at Taylor, and she nodded.

"Get in back and hunch down, and tell us what this is all about."

"It's Mick. He's been arrested."

"I know that. He, no doubt, deserves it."

"Oh no! He doesn't. He doesn't deserve it at all. But he will be in big trouble if the police go search his car."

"What kind of trouble exactly?" Dixie asked. "What will they find?"

"A gun," Jada said. "A stolen gun."

Four gasps filled the Buick's interior.

One from a schoolmarm. One from a pioneer prude. One from a party pooper.

And one from an ace cub reporter who totally didn't see that coming.

CHAPTER THIRTY-TWO

"Can we just drive?" Jada said, cowering in the backseat. "Please! I can't be seen with you!"

"Like none of us have heard that before," Dixie muttered.

Taylor pulled out of the park, and we headed in the direction of town.

"Oh, God this is terrible. Poor Mick! He doesn't deserve this!"

"Neither did my horse," I said.

"I told you. We didn't have anything to do with that! I swear!"

"Where to?" Taylor asked.

"The *Gazette*. There shouldn't be anybody else around at this hour. We'll park in back and use the alley door."

We parked, and I herded everyone into the breakroom/conference room, taking a moment to call Shelby Lynn and give her a head's up.

"What a dump!" Dixie said.

"You're free to leave at any time, party pooper," I pointed out.

By the time I got Jada a soda out of the machine and handed it to her, and I'd grabbed some munchies from Vendo Land (hey, I think better when I'm chewing), Shelby Lynn had arrived. I performed intros all round before we got down to business.

"I'm not sure this is a good idea," Jada said, fidgeting with her pop-top. "I don't know if I can trust you. But Mick seems to think you're okay, even if you did dump his cousin."

"Dump his—"

"For another time, Tressa," Taylor said.

"And when you brought that delicious cake—"

"Good Lord! Did everybody get cake except me?"

"Tressa!"

"Start from the beginning," Dixie said, "for those of us at the table who've been kept in the dark so long we are now sensitive to the light."

"Need to know basis, Dix," I said, joining everyone at the table. "Need to know."

She shook her head.

I reached over and popped the top on Jada's soda and set it back in front of her.

"Calm down, take a drink, and, as Miss Grumblepuss just suggested, take it from the top."

Jada took a long sip of her drink, made a loud swallow, and set the can down.

"It's so confusing. I don't really know where to begin."

"Let's start with the gun. That seems to be the most pressing thing right now. Tell us about the gun," I instructed.

"It was *me*, not Mick. *I* stole the gun. But I didn't want to. Cissy made me!"

"Cissy? Cissy McCoy?" Shelby said.

She nodded.

"How does a fellow cheerleader make you steal a gun?" Taylor asked.

Jada shook her head.

"You won't understand. I know you won't. It started so innocently. We'd all been on the squad last year. Me, Kylie, Natalie, Dani, Kiera, Portia, and Cissy. When Martina was hired at the end of last year, we were so excited to have someone like her be our coach."

"When you say someone like her—"

"You remember Mrs. Tomatich, the PE teacher and cheerleading coach," Shelby said.

Enough said.

"Martina Banfield is different," Jada said. "She's uber cool! Before the end of the school year, she made a point to get together with us. We hung out all the time. She took us places, bought us lunches, pedicures, manicures, clothes. She got us alcohol and once in a while, even weed."

"Okay. That's way beyond the pale," Taylor observed.

"I was going to say 'creepy as hell,'" Kari said.

"Oh, it was nothing like that. She just really, really wanted us to bond. She's really into team building and establishing trust and things like that. She's super smart about psychology and group dynamics and relationships and stuff."

"I'll just bet she is," Kari said and cracked her knuckles.

"Martina told us all the work we put in on the exercises as a group would help us in our competitions. And it did! It worked. We were totally in sync. We had such a level of trust."

"You keep saying using past tense. We *were* in sync. We *had* a level of trust. Did something happen to cause that to change?" I asked.

She took another drink of soda.

"This is where it gets hard and where you won't understand."

"Try us," I said.

She took a deep breath.

"Those exercises I mentioned? They were trust exercises."

"Trust exercises? What do you mean?" Taylor asked.

"Martina said in cheerleading and dance, trust is the most important thing. We had to trust that our sisters would be where they were supposed to be when they were supposed to be there and do what they were supposed to do when they were supposed to do it. She said that in order to establish that level of physical trust we needed to establish psychological trust. She put it like we *literally* have each other's backs."

I looked at Taylor.

"Does that sound kosher?"

"It depends on what those 'trust' exercises were."

"At first they were harmless," Jada said. "We'd tell each other things no one else knew."

"Like secrets?" Shelby asked.

Jada nodded. "First we'd tell our own secrets, things we'd done or thought, and then we started to share secrets about other people. Things we knew about other people that the others didn't know."

"You mean gossip," Dixie said.

"Sort of. But it was shared with the understanding that it wouldn't go any further than the group. And it worked. None of us broke that trust."

"So you had a big love fest and dished dirt on other people. Where does breaking and entering and stealing a firearm come in?" I asked.

"Martina said we needed to 'up the ante,' she called it. We needed to put ourselves at actual risk of harm to build upon the trust we'd established. Without inherent risk, trust is irrelevant, Martina said."

"Martina says a lot of things," Kari muttered.

"Upping the ante? So, that's what they're calling criminal activity now?" Dixie said. "Nice."

"It wasn't a big deal at first. We'd go into a store and help the other sister shoplift and cover for her. Then that wasn't enough so we started stealing weird items from people's homes. Stupid things like solar lights and pin wheels and outdoor thermometers and bird baths—"

"And garden gnomes from Planet X!" I said.

Jada's forehead crinkled and then cleared.

"Oh. You mean *Fides*."

"Fides?"

"It's Latin for *trust*. Cissy showed up with him one day and proclaimed he was a symbol of our trust. Cissy decided *Fides* would 'mark' our territory."

I grimaced. Eww.

"What I meant is that we would place Fides somewhere on the property we planned to hit next, take a picture, and have this ceremony in the woods where we'd drink and dance around Fides and burn the photo of the place we'd just hit. I thought it was lame, but you don't say no to Cissy."

"So that's what you were doing in Dusty Cadwallader's woods," Shelby said. "Drinking and dancing around a garden gnome?"

"Portia's grandparents live on the other side of the clearing. Their property backs up to Dusty's. We'd sneak through her grandparents' woods to get to the clearing. It's not that far. We'd park our cars at Portia's grandparents and take one car for our exercises."

"Those aren't exercises, Jada. They're crimes," I said.

"So you went from stealing lawn gnomes and black and gold flamingos to spray-painting? Why?" Taylor asked.

"It just got out of control. We started with a few pink tornadoes on a few buildings, and it just snowballed."

"Those chubby tornadoes from your middle school booklet!" Kari said. "I knew it!"

Jada looked up.

"That's it? That's how you knew it was me? From a middle school assignment?"

I nodded.

"Mrs. Davenport is a language arts teacher. Your former teacher kept your work, and Kari here came across it when she took over. She remembered seeing the drawings and mentioned it to me when they found their way into the works of the vandals."

"I thought you were suspicious of me from the beginning, but I never knew why."

"I'm still waiting to hear about the gun," I said.

"I wanted out. I wasn't comfortable. I'd been talking to Mick, and he said we should go to the police, but by that time I was in too deep. And I was scared. Cissy is scary. It's like she needs this in her life. It's the most important thing to her. The Sisterhood, she calls it. She started bullying and threatening. She threatened my little sister if I didn't stay with the group. I'm sure she threatened most of the others, too. When she saw I was ready to quit cheerleading, get out of the whole thing, that's when she told me if I proved my loyalty to the group by doing one more exercise, she'd let me quit. If I didn't, something terrible could happen to Jules."

"Your sister."

She nodded.

"I know I should have gone to the police, but I believed her. There's something not right about Cissy—something that this bond of trust brought out in her. Something ruthless. So I went along. I helped with the break in, and I took the gun."

"And you gave it to Mick."

She nodded.

"I sure wasn't going to give it to Cissy. She's psycho! So, yes, I gave it to Mick. He promised to get rid of it, and that was it. I was out."

"Only it didn't work out that way, did it? Because Cissy wouldn't let you leave after all," Taylor said.

Jada nodded.

"She told me we had an 'unbreakable bond' and no one left The Sisterhood."

"That's seriously medieval," Dixie said.

"Let's go back to Dusty Cadwallader for a minute," I said. "I know you're the one who made the call to me from his phone that may have saved his life."

Her eyes got big again.

"How?"

"I have a gift, my friend," I said, figuring I could let her in on the dead zone and vanilla musk clues later.

"Oh. God. Hand me something salty. Quick! I need to settle my stomach," Dixie moaned.

"What happened to Dusty in the first place?" I finished.

"Cissy. Cissy happened. She was pissed that we were losing our Sacred Sisterhood Ground. We'd not only picked that location to meet because it was close to Portia's grandparents, but because of that Dusty guy."

"What do you mean because of Dusty?" Taylor asked.

"Everyone knows he's got issues. Everybody laughs at him and calls him names and says he's crazy. You know. For believing in all that UFO stuff. Cissy said it would be the perfect place to meet. Even if the guy did report strange activity in the woods, no one would believe him. And they didn't. Until you did," she told me. "When we lost the meeting place, Cissy was so angry. She said that we needed to get back at him and teach him a lesson for interfering with The Sisterhood. So she bought these ridiculous alien masks that glow in the dark, and we put them on and went back out and found the guy working on these four-wheelers. He ran. We chased him, and he fell."

"And you left," I said. "All of you just left him there."

"I didn't know he was hurt! I thought he just tripped and he'd just make his way back home. When I found out he was missing, I got worried."

"How did you find out Dusty hadn't been seen?" I asked.

"Some kid at school has a relative who dispatches. He said something about the guy being missing, and he must've been abducted by aliens. You know. Being a smart ass."

"So you drove out there, found him, took his phone and charged it, got a signal, called me, and took the phone back to Dusty. And the vodka?"

"I shouldn't have done that. I wanted to make it appear the guy was drunk and fell. I figured if he said he was being chased by a pack of aliens everyone would think he was hallucinating or whacko or both. Especially if it appeared he'd been drinking."

"But it backfired because Dusty doesn't drink," I said.

"It also backfired because that's what got Mick arrested," Jada said.

"What do you mean?"

"The vodka bottle. The cops found one in the woods and traced the sale back to Mick. I took both bottles from Aunt Mo's."

"So, the bottles link Mick to the vandalism *and* the attack on Dusty Cadwallader," I said.

"And lead them right to the gun! You've got to do something! Mick didn't do anything. No vandalism. No trespassing. No thefts. The only thing he did was clean the paint off the trees in the clearing to help me. That's all."

"Wait a minute. What about my place? What about my horse? If you and Mick didn't do that, who did?"

"It wasn't us! I swear!"

"Wait a minute. She could be telling the truth," Taylor said. "Look at the photos of the tornadoes at your place and all the previous ones. Notice any differences?"

"These are tall and skinny and rather crudely done," Kari said, pointing to the ones on the folks' garage door and the barn.

"The other ones are short and plump," Shelby said.

"Don't say it," Dixie said, giving me 'don't-go-there' look.

"They could have been drawn by someone else."

"I am telling the truth! I am! I swear it wasn't Mick or me!" Jada said.

"Then who was responsible then?"

"Wait a minute. Didn't you say Robbie Rodgers was arrested, too?" Shelby Lynn said.

Jada nodded.

"He's Natalie Jorgensen's boyfriend."

"He is?" I asked, thinking Jada might really be telling the truth about the hit out home. All of a sudden it started to make a sick kind of sense.

"Robbie's big buddies with Dani's boyfriend, Caleb Tucker," Jada said.

"And he could have found out about Abigail's gnome from his girlfriend or even Stan and made that call to Abigail," Taylor pointed out.

"You think Stan's kid caused the damage at your place to provide an alibi for his girlfriend?" Dixie asked.

I shrugged. "You've heard the saying, 'the things we do for love.'"

Including, it seemed, finger-painting an Appaloosa.

"Please! You've got to help Mick before they find the gun!" Jada said.

I considered my options for a moment. "I'll see what I can do," I finally said and left the room to make the call. One advantage you have when you call Manny is that it never takes up much of your time. The conversation went something like this."

Ring, ring!
"H'lo."
"Manny?"
"Yo."
"Tressa"
"Yo?"
"What's that called again where police can search an arrested person's vehicle and look in a trunk?"
"On it."
End.

I returned to the break room. Jada jumped to her feet and ran to me.

"What happened? What did you do?" she asked.

"Manny's on it," I said, and I could see her visibly relax.

"Thank God!" she said. "I told Mick he should get Manny involved, but he wouldn't do it."

"Speaking of involving adults," Taylor said, "What about Miss Banfield? Did she know the extent of what was going on?"

"I don't think so. I think she lost control but didn't want to admit it, so she looked the other way. It's not her fault that Cissy flipped out and got totally obsessed—"

"Not her fault?" Kari jumped to her feet. "She's a teaching *professional*. She not only crossed boundaries, she obliterated them. And talk about trust. Students should be able to trust that their teachers are going to act in a manner consistent with the standards and ethics of their profession. She failed you. She failed all of you. And the saddest part? You still don't realize it."

"Well, I think we know what the next step has to be," I told Jada. "You have to come clean with the police."

It was like I'd told her Justin Bieber was dead.

"No! God no! I can't do that. I can't betray The Sisterhood. Cissy will make good on her threats. I know she will."

"Not if she's held accountable, too."

"She'll lie and say it was all me. I was the one who planned it all. I stole the gun. I hurt that UFO guy. You already said all the evidence points to me. I'm not going to take that chance. I'm out and staying out."

"Well, I can tell the police. They'll believe me."

Dixie's snort spoke volumes.

"If only we could catch your 'sister' in the act," she said.

Jada gasped. "Oh, my God! Maybe you can!"

Five heads turned to look at her.

"What do you mean? Are they planning another girls' night out?" I asked.

Jada nodded.

"'Paint the past pink' Cissy called it. Like destroying the past was something majorly cool. I told you she was screwed up."

"Wait a minute? Are you saying what I think you're saying?"

"Earlier tonight Cissy took Fides to the Historical Village. Tonight," Jada said. "After the *Blast to the Past*. They're hitting the museum."

Marty Freakin' McFly!

First pink Appaloosas. Now pink museums.

It was time to pull the plug on the sister act and take back the night.

CHAPTER THIRTY-THREE

Jada gave us a quick overview of the "trust exercise." It was Harry and Marv in *Home Alone 2* all over again.

Before the museum was locked up for the night—two of the girls (Portia and Kiera) would hide inside the building among the exhibits. The other four "sisters"—a generous supply of hot pink spray paint cans in their arsenal—would come to the back door of the museum at 2 a.m. to be let in. And in the time it takes to say "Kodachrome" what had been displays of the rich culture, heritage, and history of the county would be reduced to sticky, worthless, pink junk.

Oh, hell no! Not on Martha Jane Cannary's watch!

"So what do we do with this information, exactly?" Shelby Lynn asked.

"I say we let the police handle it," the Pioneer Prude said.

"I say we contact the parents," Schoolmarm Kari said.

"I say we go out there, sneak in the museum, and go a little *Revenge of the Nerds* on some cheerleaders," Party Pooper surprised me by saying.

I looked at her.

She shrugged.

"I like history. And I hate cheerleaders."

"How about we split the difference?" I said. "Shelby Lynn, you've got a contact with the sheriff's office you're keeping from me, right? Can you trust him?"

"Her," Shelby Lynn said.

"*Oo*kay. Her. Is she on the up and up?"

Shelby Lynn nodded.

"Get ahold of her, and tell her we're working on a case that requires...discretion. Explain we have reason to believe a crime may be about to be committed, but the information comes from a confidential source. Don't give her specifics until you're sure she won't do an end run around us."

"I hear you," Shelby said.

"Kari. Sorry, sweetie. Parents at this point would only complicate matters, but thanks for the input. Miss Destructor," I told Dixie. "I like the way you think. I feel confident that with some insightful tweaking we can work with your suggestion."

"Tweaking?"

"We'll have to lose the cheerleader whooping," I told her. "They're minors."

"So what are we doing, exactly?" Shelby asked.

"Here's how I see it. Like our crafty cheerleaders, we too hide in the museum before it's locked up. We wait for the cheerleaders to reveal themselves—and by revealing themselves, I of course mean come out in the open. We surprise them. Shelby rides in to the rescue with the county. The juveniles are detained. Parents are called. The museum is saved. And order is restored to Knox County."

"Just one minor detail. Won't we also be guilty of breaking and entering if we hide in the museum before they lock up?" Taylor asked.

"Our intentions will be pure, honorable, and upstanding ones. Remember, I'd rather—"

"—ask for forgiveness than permission," Taylor finished. "I remember."

"I suppose you'll want us to dress in black," Dixie said.

I shook my head.

"We're supposed to blend in, right? With these frontier getups, we could almost pass as mannequins."

"Note she didn't say 'dummies,'" Dixie said. "I don't know if you've forgotten or what, but I'm not wearing a costume."

I looked at her.

"You're not? Don't worry. There's bound to be a barrel or old time wash tub you can hide behind," I said. I put my hand on

Jada's shoulder. "I'm not comfortable with you being involved, Jada."

"But I have to be! Don't you see? If I don't show up, they won't go through with it! Cissy will realize I narked them out, and there's no telling what she'll do then. I'll be fine. All I have to do is be at the meeting place and ride to the county park. That's it. We get there, and go in. Busted! It's over. Don't you see? The best protection for me is to pretend to participate. Please! What would you do if it were you?"

I squeezed her shoulder.

"The same thing you want to do," I told her.

"That's what I thought," she said. "Is there a restroom? I really need to use it."

I took her into the hall and pointed at the door across the hall.

"It's going to be okay, Jada." I said. "Really. It is."

She hurried into the bathroom, and I went back to the break room.

"Are we really going to let her do that?" Taylor asked.

I shook my head.

"Thank God!" Kari said.

"You know, I've been thinking about Martina Banfield," Taylor said.

"What about her besides she's totally unprofessional, dangerously immature, and has a seriously messed up moral compass?" Kari asked.

"It's all this stuff about psychological trust and those bizarre exercises and her telling the girls that in order to trust, they had to put themselves at risk. It's just out there," Taylor said.

"And then there was her freak-out when you challenged that dude's pyramid," I said. "Beyond bizarre."

"Another thing," Kari said. "As an educator, it's hard for me to believe she didn't have a clue what was going on, how her social experiment was going horribly wrong."

Taylor nodded.

"If I didn't know better I'd almost think she was manipulating those girls. Programming them. And watching how they reacted under certain circumstances like a cognitive behaviorist."

I frowned. "I'm not sure what that last part means, but do you mean like those mazes with rodents?"

"The Tolman research," Taylor supplied. "Very new and revolutionary."

"So research, huh?"

She nodded.

"Very avant-garde at the time."

"I'll take your word on that," I said. "Hmm. So, would that kind of research be anything like the research one might conduct if they were working on say, a thesis for a master's degree in the field of psychology?"

Taylor's eyebrows lifted.

"Yes. I suppose."

I thought about it for a second.

"You need to call Brian, Kari," I said.

"We're not on speaking terms at the moment," she said.

I shook my head.

"Kari, just call the man and find out what Martina Banfield's master's thesis is about!"

"Okay! But what should I say when he wants to know why I'm asking?"

"Tell him it's a quiz to see if he really is just helping her with her thesis. He'll probably think you're tipsy anyway."

"Okay. I'll make the call, but I won't grovel!"

She shinnied to the other end of the room.

"What are you thinking?" Shelby asked.

"I'm thinking if my theory is right, Miss Banfield is looking at more than a trip to the principal's office."

Kari was back in record time.

"You're not going to believe this!" she said.

"Try me," I said.

"Martina the Mentee's thesis analyzes," she stopped and read from a scrap of paper in her hand, "female gang dynamics within a rural, upper middle class population and its culture and identifies the hierarchy of needs relevant to that demographic."

And there it was!

The missing link!

"Oh, my God!" Taylor gasped. "Oh, my God! She's been using those poor girls! Using them as lab rats for her research!"

"It sure does look that way," I said. "It looks like she got them to trust her, treated them as equals and friends, spent time with them, lavished them with gifts and affection, and solely for the purpose of using them as research subjects."

"She pulled their strings and observed their reactions like some psycho puppet master," Dixie said. "That's what she did."

"Brian confided that the principal is worried about how close she's getting to her students and had asked Brian, as her mentor, to see what he could find out before they brought her in. I knew she was trouble the first time I laid eyes on her," Kari said.

"I can't believe she would do that to her students," Shelby Lynn said.

I shook my head.

"Those poor girls. When they find out how she used them, they'll be devastated," Taylor said.

"That's why we keep it to ourselves. Don't say anything to Jada. Not yet. She has enough on her plate right now. She still thinks Miss Banfield is Mary Poppins," I said. "Let her believe for a few more hours."

"Speaking of Jada, she's taking a long time in the bathroom," Shelby said, and I hurried out into the hall.

I rapped on the bathroom door.

"Jada? It's Tressa? Are you okay?"

No answer.

"Jada?" I knocked again before turning the knob and opening the door. The bathroom was empty. "Jada!" I checked the other offices before I returned to the break room.

"She's flown the coop," I said.

"Where do you suppose she went?"

"My keys!" Taylor said. "I left them here on the table. They're gone!"

We ran out back. The Buick was also gone.

"Great. What do we do now?"

I thought a second. Chances were Jada was on her way to meet up with the others—which meant she would be expecting us to be at the museum. I wasn't about to disappoint her.

"We stick to the plan," I said.

And then show little Miss Master's Degree how females within a rural, middle class population look out for their own.

It'll be a lesson worth learning.

Trust me.

CHAPTER THIRTY-FOUR

We were in.
And playing the waiting game.
Waiting for all hell to break loose, that is.
Since Jada had absconded with the Buick, we'd all piled into Shelby's Jeep and headed back to the county park and, to our surprise, discovered the Buick parked on the way end of the parking lot near a line of trees.
We went over our plan.
Our objective, we finally agreed, was to prevent damage to the museum and its contents—to wrest relics from the grip of thugs and safeguard history for its posterity.
If the culprits got away, we'd let law enforcement deal with that later.
Our mission was to protect and preserve the past.
Sniff. Sniffle.
I get all teary-eyed just thinking about it.
We'd searched the dwindling crowd for The Sisterhood, without luck, concluding that the two sisters assigned to hide in the museum were already in place. We'd mingled a bit more before making our way, one-by-one, into the museum.
I'd tried to dissuade Kari from participating in the 'intervention,' but the possibility Miss Banfield might show up was like telling me George Strait was saddling up again for just one more farewell concert two doors down and giving my ticket to someone else.
Not. Gonna. Happen.
Getting by the county historical society members took a bit of doing. They're serious about their historic treasures. We used the old divert-and-conquer routine. It didn't hurt that most

of the committee members were of my gammy's generation and their reflexes a bit...rusty.

With a little maneuvering (okay, I got hung up on a nail and ripped my hobo vest) I'd managed to conceal myself in the back of an old farm wagon in the agriculture section of the museum. I had no clue where the others were—friend or foe.

Shelby's "contact" had agreed to our conditions, and the county would be in the area to assist when the time came. We'd silenced our phones and planned to communicate via text if necessary.

The museum, a fixture at the historical village, had seen various forms until they finally decided on a steel building similar to those you find in farm operations. Rectangular in shape, it could accommodate many more exhibits than its previous structure.

The museum had no high-tech security, no video cameras, no faux video cameras. Just keys and locks and what some people might deem an old-fashioned and naïve trust in the better natures of their fellow citizens.

As far as I knew nobody had ever messed with the museum before.

Until now.

I checked my cell.

Two o'clock and all was definitely not well!

The damnable itching! It was driving me nuts!

Boots crossed at the ankles, I tried to keep from scratching.

I thought about the museum, how many times I'd visited, the exhibits—and occupants—that I enjoyed most. Like the old-time doctor's office with the mannequin doctor and nurse and the old-time instruments. Or the dentist with his vintage chair and mannequin patient with his mouth wide open. Or the parlor exhibit with the old-time settee and antique rocker that featured a mannequin family wearing the latest in pioneer fashion, (Lord, did they have dinky feet back then!) The old-time switchboard with the redheaded mannequin operator that always reminded me of Lucille Ball in her *I Love Lucy* days.

There was an early aircraft exhibit, a barbershop with a barber poised to give that first whisker cut, and a music exhibit with old time organ and phonographs.

The post office, located in the general store a few buildings down, was another favorite. I always remember being caught off guard by the bespectacled postmaster peering at me from behind the window. They had a checkerboard set up on a barrel table with two old men mannequins squaring off. Quaint, but in a creepy kind way.

The exhibit I didn't care for was the wildlife one with the stuffed red fox and coyote and other taxidermied creatures of the prairie. The one that really bothered me was the mother wolf with her pups. It always made me sad to see them rolling about their sawdust stuffed mother, knowing they never got a chance to run and jump and play.

I hissed through my teeth.

I couldn't ignore the infernal itching any longer. I had to scratch, or I'd jeopardize the mission. Okay. I'd abandon the mission if I didn't scratch.

Then I remembered it. The quirt. I still had it. Throughout the evening I'd used it to scratch. I'd hung the quirt loop from the grip of my fake gun in my fake holster on my fake gun belt.

Ever so carefully, I rolled to my side and attempted to pull the quirt loop up and off the faux firearm. I managed to maneuver the quirt free of the gun and slowly eased it down my pant leg and into my right boot.

"Ahh!" I couldn't prevent the moan of ecstasy when the tip of the quirt found its way to the itch.

"Shh!" I heard from below me and frowned.

I stiffened, feeling like an old-time corpse being transported to an old-time undertaker.

Nothing fancy, Jedidiah. A simple pine box'll do.
Who was that?
Sister or…*sister*?
I texted Taylor.
Is that you?
She texted a question mark back.
I tried again.

Farm exhibit?
Yes.
I'm in the wagon.
I know. Everyone else probably does too.
Nice.

We'd figured just prior to the two a.m. rendezvous time, we'd leave our hiding places and arrange to have one pair of us near the front door and the other pair, at the rear. That way, no matter what door The Sisterhood tried to break and enter, we'd have it covered.

Literally.

Once they stepped inside, we planned to throw a blanket over their heads, surprising the burglars and limiting their movements. Then one of us would run to the light switch and turn on the lights, our signal alerting the authorities outside to move in.

Give me a *B!* Give me a *U!* Give me an *S-T-E-D*. (No, I didn't say, "give me an STD." You people.)

What's that spell?
Busted!

I decided it was time to "come out, come out, wherever you are!" so I pulled myself to a sitting position, wincing at every creak and groan the wagon made.

"Shh!" I heard again.

I lifted my leg to climb off the end of the wagon (not a simple task in the dark) when I felt a sudden sharp tug at my waist, my belt catching onto something and leaving me hanging, harnessed to the side of the wagon by my gun belt.

I managed to pull my cell phone out.

Got hung up. Literally. Dangling from wagon. Help appreciated.

A few seconds later I felt hands on my legs.
My hero! I texted.

Taylor's grunt telegraphed that there would be no text in response.

"What have you managed to do now?" she whispered.
"Can we discuss my foibles later?" I whispered back. "Just give me a boost up and off the corner," I said.
"Seriously?"

"Just do it!" I hissed.

"Where do I grab?"

"My butt! Push it upwards."

"That's easier said than done!"

"I'll remember you said that. Put your shoulder into it! Now push!"

Taylor managed to give me just enough of a heave-ho that coupled with my own efforts to lift myself up and off the corner of the wagon, I managed to slip off and drop to the ground like the scarecrow in Oz.

I got to my feet and grabbed Taylor's hand.

"This way to the back door!" I whispered.

"Now she whispers," Taylor hissed.

We passed Lucy, the phone operator, her lips dark against her pale face, the effect terrifying in the limited light. I let out a gasp, willies running down my spine, when the doctor in his white coat and his anorexic nurse appeared next.

Holy house of wax! The historical museum may be kicks and giggles during daylight hours but at nighttime it was a total freak show of horrors.

"What's wrong?" Taylor asked.

I shook my head.

"Nothing."

But no way in hell was I planning to walk by the dentist's office with his howling patient. Or those poor, stuffed wolf cubs.

No flippin' way.

A sound to our left stopped me in my tracks.

"Did you hear that?" I asked.

"It sounded like a groan."

Or a growl, maybe, I wondered, thinking of the mama wolf.

"This way," Taylor said.

"No, this way!" I said, wanting to avoid the wild kingdom. You know. Just to be safe.

Another strange grunt-groan and I grabbed Taylor.

"That wasn't human," I whispered.

"Get ahold of yourself!" Taylor said.

My butt vibrated, and I pulled my phone from my back pocket and displayed the text so Taylor could read it.

It was from Kari.

Need help!

Help with what? I texted back.

Dixie. She's stuck!

Where?

Under the bed in the boudoir exhibit.

I looked at Taylor.

"The pioneer bedroom."

Dixie's wedged. Need help lifting bed and pulling/pushing. Can't do both.

Okay. I admit it. I giggled. Chalk it up to nerves.

We made our way as quietly as we could to the boudoir. I looked at the tiny bed, still amazed by how little pioneer people used to be. Kari was kneeling on the floor and peering under the bed.

I leaned down and looked myself and winced.

So not a pretty sight.

"How—?"

"Never mind with hows or whys!" Taylor hissed. "Let's just get her out!"

Kari and Taylor took opposite ends of the bed prepared to lift on command. I got the ugly job. Pulling Dixie the overstuffed under-the-bed-box out from under the bed.

"Don't. Say. A. Word." She warned when I got in position. "Not. One. Word."

I shrugged.

It could wait.

I grabbed hold of Dixie's belt with one hand and propped one foot against a nearby chest of drawers to provide support.

On the agreed "three," Taylor and Kari lifted, and I tugged.

"Three!"

Again.

"Three!"

And once more.

"Three!"

Thwap!

Dixie the human dust bunny was freed from her dusty prison.

I helped her to her feet. She dusted herself off, flexing and stretching and rotating various body parts.

I shook my head and took my phone out.

Did you eyeball those dimensions at all?

A second later she was texting back.

I got under it didn't I?

Fluke.

It was after two now. Anyone still in the museum was either deaf or we'd lost any element of surprise we had.

And then I heard it. A strange creaking sound.

"Stations!" I whispered, grabbing the blanket off the bed and motioning to Taylor to follow.

Kari and Dixie peeled off in the direction of the front door. Taylor and I continued to the rear and in the direction of the sound.

Squeak. Squeak. Squeak. Squeak.

I motioned for Taylor to get ready.

We approached the last exhibit before the back door. The parlor exhibit.

Creak. Creak. Creak. Creak.

We crept closer.

Creak! Creak!

Closer.

I squinted at the parlor scene.

Father. Mother. Sister. Brother.

I stopped.

Recounted.

One. Two. Three. Four. *Five. Six.*

My gaze slid to a figure on the settee and another one in the rocker whom, I was pretty sure, hadn't been there before.

Creak. Creak. Creak.

The rocking chair began to rock.

A flashlight beam hit me square in the face, and I stumbled forward.

"They're here!" I yelled. "In Merchant McCall's parlor!"

I lifted the bedspread and felt Taylor grab one end.

"Get 'em!" I yelled as we charged forward, blanket aloft. We descended on the parlor, a drunken sharpshooter and a prude of a pioneer. We lifted the blanket high and gave it a toss, casting it down over the heads of the trespassing gangstas like a big ol' dragnet.

"We got 'em!" I yelled! I ran to one of the villains in this little dime store western—the one who had been rocking out—and plopped down on her lap. I heard a loud grunt. Taylor twisted the other end of the bedspread around suspect number two and held on.

"We got 'em!" I yelled. "Hurry! The parlor! The parlor!"

Kari and Dixie ran up.

"What happened? Oh, my gosh! You caught them!" Kari exclaimed. "You really caught them!"

"*We* caught them," I corrected. "This ought to teach you not to try to rewrite history," I scolded the desperadoes. "What's that? I can't hear you," I said when the perp I was sitting on tried to talk beneath the heavy bedspread. "Yell a little louder!" I cheered.

"Uh, Tressa. I'm not so sure we aren't celebrating a big prematurely," Taylor said.

"Huh?"

"Look at their shoes."

The culprit's flashlight had dropped to the floor, light still on, beam pointing at the shoes of the rocker.

Orthopedic shoes.

Senior citizen orthopedic shoes.

I shook my head.

Since when did cheerleader gangs wear best balance shoes with comfort arch supports?

I'd just gotten to my feet and was about to pull the blanket away and expose the miscreants when all hell broke loose outside the museum.

Sirens sounded. Red lights flashed. The roar of an engine accelerating.

And we hadn't even turned the lights on to signal for help yet.

I ran to the back door, flipped the dead bolt back, and opened the door.

I was about to advise that the situation was under control when I noticed the two black-hooded figures with their hands up illuminated in the squad car headlights.

"You got 'em! Whoo-hoo!" I was about to let out a victory cry until I got a good look at the faces in those hoodies. Then I just wanted to cry.

"Joe? Gram!" I flipped the light switches on. The LED lights lit up the back lot like daylight.

"Gram? Joe?" I couldn't believe what I was seeing.

"Hold it there. Keep your hands where I can see them." The female deputy that always seemed to have office duty had her flashlight on the seniors, her other hand hovering near the grip of her holstered gun. "Nice and steady now."

"It's all right," I said, not sure it was at all. "That's Joe and Hannah Townsend. They're my, uh, grandparents."

The deputy approached them and did a pat down. I was hoping against hope that this time Joe wasn't packing an unregistered Colt Python.

"What are you doing here?" I asked the couple once they had been officially cleared.

"We're after that bum," Gram said.

"Bum? What bum?"

"Abigail's bum. The homeless hobo! Her gigolo!"

"Why are you looking for him here?" I said.

"'Cause that's where he's at."

"What bum are you talking about, ma'am?" the deputy asked.

"The one that Joe and I saw go into the museum and never come out."

I felt the beginnings of an eye twitch, and my sphincters started to do their clench number.

No. It couldn't be!

I turned and ran back into the museum. I ran up to the Mr. Merchant's parlor in time to see the blankets being pulled from the heads of our suspects.

I closed my eyes. I didn't want to see it. And ran over an object directly in my path.

I fell.

Hard.

I opened my eyes and shoved the hair away from my eyes.
Grinning maniacally down at me was Cedric, the Homely Lawn Gnome from Hobgoblin Hell.
I shook my head.
How do you say *Night in the Museum?*

CHAPTER THIRTY-FIVE

I kind of felt sorry for Deputy Carruthers, the female deputy who had set up the surveillance. I knew how it felt not to be taken seriously. It niggled at you like an itch you couldn't scratch.

Once a thorough search of the museum turned up no one else playing hide-and-seek, the law enforcement officer found herself in the middle of a real life rumble, senior citizen style.

"I told you I didn't steal that butt-ugly troll," Gram said. "And there's your proof!" She pointed at the now-you-see-him-now-you-don't gnome.

"Well, you can't say there wasn't reason for me to suspect you, Hannah," Abigail said. "Every time you walked by Cedric, you spat on him."

"Cedric? Who's Cedric again?"

"The gnome," I reminded her.

"'Oh. Well, scuze me for having to 'specterate. Ever hear of sinus drainage?"

"Explain again what you two are doing here?" the deputy asked Uncle Bo and Abigail.

"I spotted old Cedric here when Abigail was gettin' ready to lock up," Aunt Eunice said in her best good ol' boy speak. "See, Abigail's on the historical society. When I saw the gnome in question, I remembered what Tressa here told that snooty sheriff of yours about the gnome showing up at Harve somebody or other's place just like another place that got trashed. I figured she might be on to something, so Abby and I conducted our own surveillance. Know what I'm sayin'?"

"I see. And what did you plan to do when and if the vandals showed up?" Carruthers asked.

"Scream like bloody hell, and call the cops on the cell," Uncle Bo said. "I may be brave, but I ain't stupid. Know what I'm sayin'?"

I shook my head. I couldn't believe Uncle Bo was still trying to perpetuate the charade.

Me? I just wanted to get out of the past and back to a place and time that didn't include creepy gnomes from *Journey to Planet X* and *Teenagers from Outer Space*.

"Will you be needing anything further from these witnesses?" I asked the deputy. "Since Mrs. Winegardner has a key to the museum and permission to come and go, it seems she and her, uh, er, friend, here are in the clear."

"What 'bout us? We free to go, too?" Gram asked.

The deputy seemed to hesitate. "I suppose so. Unless Mrs. Winegardner and Mr. Beauregard here want to press charges for stalking."

"Stalking!" Joe's Adam's apple went up and down and up and down like the temperature in Iowa in late winter. "Now I don't think—"

"Of course, we won't be filing charges," Abigail said. "After all, we're neighbors."

I saw Gram give Abigail a funny look.

"Come on, Hannah," Joe said. "Let's go home."

We watched the odd couples leave while Carruthers and the reserve officer did one final search of the premises.

"So where do we stand?" Shelby asked the officer.

"In a holding pattern," Carruthers said. "I'm already in hot water. I'm way past my authorized shift. I was only supposed to work the gala and go out of service," she explained. "It would be different if we'd actually caught someone in the act, but all I caught were four harmless old folks."

Obviously she didn't know Uncle Bo, and my gammy and her hubby like I did.

"Sorry, Beth. I didn't want to get you in trouble," Shelby said.

"No problem. The good ol' boys always seem to find reasons to keep me off patrol. But I promise I'll present it all to Samuels tomorrow and see what he suggests. We'll likely start with rounding up suspects, especially Jada Garcia and her circle of cheerleaders, bring them in and have a nice long talk and get this sorted out. Meanwhile, I'll have patrol do extra checks out here overnight." Deputy Carruthers shook Shelby's hand. "Thanks for the tip anyway," she said, and left with the reserve officer.

"So that's your source," I said to Shelby.

She nodded.

"She's a good cop, and she's getting a bum deal from the good ol' boys club. I thought a bust like this might get someone's attention and get her out of the office."

"I'm sorry it didn't work out, Shelby," I said and meant it.

"At least the museum is safe," Taylor said. "That's what counts."

"And with the gnome safely locked in the museum, he won't be the foreteller of any more mischief tonight," I added.

"I can't wait to tell Brian about that piece of work mentee," Kari said, as we walked back to the cars. "He'll be blown away."

"Just don't do go overboard on the I-told-you-sos," I warned. "Being magnanimous when you're right and you both know it goes a long way towards making your partner feel like more of a worm than he already does. You don't have to rub his nose in it."

"Oo. 'Magnanimous!' Someone's been using the online dictionary again, I see," Dixie snarled, apparently still smarting over her brief stint as a super-duper sized bed slat.

Tired and glum, we took our time walking to the parking lot where Jada had left the Buick. As I walked, I scratched.

"What's wrong with you?" Taylor asked. "You've been scratching all night."

"My guess? Fleas," Dixie said.

I shook my head and tried not to scratch.

"What?" Dixie said. "I could've suggested something more crude as the source of your itching, you know."

"From personal experience?" I responded, feeling irritable and depressed.

"Ladies, please. We're tired and disappointed, but we can't turn on each other," Peacemaker Taylor said. "We have to stick together."

"Dixie's sure got the sticking part down," I noted.

"Yeah? Well, nobody can say you don't come up to scratch, Miss 'Is That a Quirt in Your Pants?' Turner," Dixie countered.

"Oh, for heaven's sake. Dixie got wedged under a bed and Tressa got hung up on a farm wagon by her holster. Can we agree we were lucky tonight? No one got hurt, and no damage was done," Taylor exclaimed.

"Hung up on a wagon?" Shelby said.

"I think they heard it the first time, Miss Town Crier," I said. "Way to out me, *sister*," I snapped at Taylor. "Maybe I should air some of your dirty little secrets?"

Taylor gave me a 'don't you dare' look.

"Can we just go home now?" Kari said. "I honestly can't wait to see Brian's face when I break the news about Miss Martina Banfield."

"You'll have to wait. He's at Townsend's," I reminded her, thinking it was probably better for both of them to have a cooling-off period.

"So what do you suppose happened tonight?" Taylor asked. "Why the change of plans?"

I shook my head.

"Honestly? I have no idea," I said. "But I'm worried. I'm very worried about Jada."

I pulled out my phone and tried the number she gave me, walking in the direction of the only car left in the parking lot, the only car anywhere I reckoned that had fat, pink tornadoes all over it.

"Stop!" Dixie put a hand out. "You hear that?"

"What? The last dying gasps of dust bunnies under a certain pioneer bed?" I asked.

"No, Miss Bed Bugs. The phone!"

We stopped and listened.

"I don't hear anything," Kari said.

Dixie shook her head.

"I'm sure I heard a phone."

I tried Jada's phone again. This time it went to voice mail.

We headed to the car. By now, it was after three, and I was one tired Martha Jane. I got in the front, and Taylor got in behind the wheel. Kari and Dixie crawled into the back.

"Aaah!"

Screams erupted from the backseat of the car, and I watched two passengers bail from either side of the vehicle.

"What the hell?" Dixie said.

I turned around in time to see a head pop up from the backseat.

"Aaaah!" I followed Dixie's example, jumping out of the car and landing in a heap on the gravel.

"Oh, my God! Jada?" I heard Taylor say.

I shook my head. Same tune. Different day.

The dome light in the Buick came on, and I stared. (Okay. So I've been without a working dome light so long I'd forgotten cars came equipped with them.) "My God! Jada! What happened to you?"

I got up and got a look at our unexpected passenger.

Jada Garcia looked like she'd been a few rounds in the ring—and lost the count epically.

"Crissy happened," Jada said, wiping tears. "She's lost it! She's completely lost it!"

"She hit you? Why?" Taylor asked. "Did she find out you spoke to us?"

She shook her head. "No! No! I went along like we agreed. But then Cissy started talking about making a big statement this time and how cool it would be to burn the museum down. She was so scary. I didn't know what to do. I was too afraid to tell her that I'd already told you about the plan. I was afraid of what she'd do. To me. To everybody in the museum. She was so bent on torching the place. So I told her about Martina's study instead. I heard you all talking about it at the newspaper office. I told her what I thought she was doing. She got so angry with me, she started punching me and hitting me. She called me a liar and said Martina wouldn't do that to us. She even put a knife to my throat. I thought I was going to die. When I told her about the thesis, she got this look in her eyes. Real cold. I realized then she had feelings for Martina—deep feelings that went beyond coach or friendship or sisterhood."

"Where is Cissy now?" I asked.

"That's just it. She went to find Martina! I'm afraid of what she might do if she finds her! I tried to call Martina, but she's not answering her phone. Please! Don't you understand? Martina's in danger! We have to find her or something terrible is going to happen! I know it!"

We piled into the Buick.

"We need to call the police," Taylor said. "Get them involved in the search for Cissy. Jada needs to file a police report so they can pick Cissy up."

"I'll call Carruthers," Shelby said. "She ought to get the credit."

"If Cissy has Martina, where would she take her?" Dixie asked.

"I think I know!" Jada exclaimed.

Taylor, Shelby, and I looked at each other.

"The clearing!" we said.

Taylor peeled out of the gravel driveway and hit the county road that would take us to Dusty's place.

"Maybe I should drive," I suggested.

"Maybe you shouldn't," Taylor said, kicking it up a notch.

I stared at her.

"You're going over the speed limit, you know. A lot over."

"I know. Maybe I'll luck out and get stopped, and we can alert the authorities."

"If she's there, she'll hear us coming," I pointed out.

"We can go through Portia's grandparent's timber! It's much closer!" Jada pointed out. "If Cissy hears us, she'll think it's the other sisters."

Jada directed us to the area.

"Oh, my God! It's Cissy's car!" Jada pointed at a black Taurus. "She's here!"

"Any luck with Carruthers?" I asked Shelby.

She shook her head.

"It went right to voice mail."

"Shouldn't we call 9-1-1?" Kari asked.

"I'm trying," Shelby Lynn said. "But I can't get any bars now."

"We don't even know for sure if she has Martina," I said. "But we might still have the element of surprise."

"Tressa's right. If Cissy hears sirens, she could panic and do something drastic," Taylor said.

"So, what do we do?" Kari asked.

I thought about it.

"Didn't you say that you wore black-hooded outfits when you met out here?" I asked Jada.

She nodded.

"Cissy kept them in the trunk of her car. Why?"

"Wait a minute!" I ran to Cissy's car. I opened the driver's door and located the trunk latch and pulled. The trunk mechanism clicked. I ran to the trunk and lifted the lid and shined my cell phone light into the back.

"Son of a Mother Ship! What *not* on earth!"

Several glow-in-the-dark alien masks stared up at me from the dark trunk.

"Those are the masks we wore when we chased that Dusty guy," Jada said.

I felt the corners of my mouth turn up.

It came to me then. A *Grinch* of an idea.

You know. A "wonderful, awful idea."

I picked up a mask and put it on.

"Wait a minute! You can't mean—!" Taylor started.

"Are you serious?" Kari exclaimed.

"Do they have an extra short robe?" Dixie asked.

"Do they have extra long?" Shelby asked.

I grinned and held out a robe.

"How do you say, 'Take me to your Leader'?" I said.

Robes donned, alien masks on our heads ready to pull down over our faces when the time was right, we walked by the light of a cell phone, sisters from other mothers, silent travelers from another dimension.

Jada led the way. I was next, followed by Taylor and Kari. Our mini and maxi aliens rounded out the six-pack.

Our plan was simple. Surround the clearing, observe, and when and if we saw an opportunity, launch our alien attack.

While the walking distance from this direction was less, the terrain was just as rugged with dense woods and thorny bushes and overturned trees making the trek tricky. As planned, we began to space ourselves apart. I stayed with Jada. No way did I want to face Aunt Mo if anything happened to Mick's girl.

It didn't take long for us to pick up the sound of raised voices.

I put a hand on Jada's arm and moved around her, putting a hand to my lips.

"It wasn't that way at all, Cissy! Don't you understand? You're part of something monumental! Groundbreaking! You should be flattered I chose you!"

Holy criminy! Talk about Martina the demented mentee.

"Flattered? Flattered! Flattered that you lied to me and used me? I thought you cared about us! Cared about *me*!"

I hazarded a step closer and reached out and pushed tree limbs apart so I could get a view of the clearing. A lantern sat in the center of the clearing. Martina sat on the ground near the circle of stones, her hands bound in front. Cissy paced back and forth. I gasped when I saw the flash of a blade in her hand.

"I do care about you, Cissy!" Martina said. "I do! But you have to understand that this research is important!"

"More important than us? More important than the trust we had in you? More important than The Sisterhood?"

"Don't you get it? I created The Sisterhood, Cissy! Me! All those get-togethers, all those gifts, all those girls' nights out? I was the one who brought you together to make an unbreakable bond."

"So Jada was right? The alcohol? The shopping? The partying? It was all so you could use us to collect data?"

I could hear the hysteria building in Cissy's voice.

"Don't you see, Cissy? If we better understand the motivations that encourage girls from rural, middle class families to form gang affiliations and engage in gang activity we can use those incentives to guide them into positive, beneficial activities."

"We trusted you! Don't you get it? We trusted you!"

"You can still trust me. Now that you know about my research—"

"Research? That's all you care about! Research! All the time we thought you cared about us when all you wanted was to create your own girl gang so we could be your guinea pigs! I hate you! I hate you! I hate you!"

I felt Jada's fingers squeeze my arm.

"Do something!" she whispered.

She was right. With Cissy's rage skyrocketing, a violent blastoff couldn't be far off.

I pulled my mask down and signaled for Jada to do the same, hoping the others had picked up on Cissy's escalation and had donned their "space suits."

I was just about to step out of the woods when a sudden flash of light halted my steps. Cissy stopped yelling, standing motionless in the center of the clearing staring up at the dark sky instead.

Another short, quick burst of light came and Cissy continued to look skyward. Out of the corner of the mask's eyehole, I saw Martina take advantage of Cissy's lapse. She got to her feet and charged into Cissy from behind. Cissy's knees buckled, and she went down. The knife flew from her hand and landed on the ground next to Martina's hand.

"I'm sorry you don't understand, Cissy," Martina said. "But you're right. It wasn't about you. It was never about you. It was all about the research. It still is."

Martina's bound hands went for the knife, and I stuck my fingers in my mouth, sounding a panicked charge.

Reeoreet!

I let loose with the loudest, most eardrum-piercing horse whistle I'd ever produced, and it echoed through the clearing like the battle cry it was.

I yelled and made like the Light Brigade, running full bore ahead, and screeching like a banshee from the Death Star. Or what I figure a banshee would screech like since I've never heard one and don't care to.

"Aaaaaa!"

I had Martina in my sights. I was just about to pounce when a blur of black to my right whooshed past me and plowed into Martina from the side with such ferocity that the mentee flew into the air like a rag doll before landing in a heap in the dirt.

I hurried to Cissy and sat on top of her.

"We're not going to have any trouble are we?" I said, keeping my mask on. "Because you won't like me when I'm angry."

Before Cissy could respond, a high-powered flashlight beam hit me straight on, nearly blinding me.

"Knox County Sheriff!" I heard Deputy Carruthers bark. "Keep your hands up where we can see them!"

I raised my hands above my head.

"Don't shoot! We come in peace!"

CHAPTER THIRTY-SIX

Dusty Cadwallader was right. His clearing in the woods was officially ground zero in terms of alien activity.

I had to wonder how close Deputy Carruthers and her reserve officer were to shooting first and asking questions later when they ventured into the clearing to find a six-pack of black-robed alien life forms wrestling around in the dirt with two humans.

I gotta tell you. I'm super happy both officers showed restraint.

Shelby Lynn had removed her mask first, giving the shaken deputy and reserve her assurances that behind the other five masks were living, breathing women of the human species. One by one, we'd unmasked. I blinked when I realized my best bud, Kari, had been the one to broadside Martina with such force an offensive lineman trying to pick off a blitzing defender would be impressed.

"How did you know to come here?" Shelby asked Carruthers. "We tried, but couldn't get a signal."

"Dusty Cadwallader called to report lights and noises in the woods," she said.

"And you came?" I asked, finally getting off of Cissy.

"Cadwallader was pretty insistent. He'd limped to his truck and driven down the road to call. Plus I figured with what happened to him, I'd better check it out."

"You are officially my second favorite police officer!" I said.

She gave me a funny look.

"She wanted to kill me!" Cissy said, sobbing and pointing at her crumpled cheerleading coach. "She wanted me dead!"

"Fortunately for you, your friend, Jada, led us here or she might've been successful."

"It was that light. I saw that light," Cissy said.

"Light?" Carruthers asked.

"The light in the sky. I looked up to see what it was and that's when Martina attacked me."

Deputy Carruthers looked at the women in black.

"Any of you see this strange light?"

I looked at the others.

"I might've caught a flash of something," I said.

"Could it have been a spotlight?" Carruthers asked.

I shook my head.

"Yes."

"Huh?"

I nodded this time.

"No."

The deputy gave me a wary look, ordered the reserve to see to Cissy and went over to check out the schoolteacher who'd hopefully just learned her lesson—albeit the hard way.

"Wow, Kari! I didn't know you had it in you," I said. "Remind me not to get on your bad side."

"You mess with your students. You're going down," she said, dusting gravel and dirt off her sleeve.

Amen.

We ended up at the county courthouse where we gave our statements to Deputy Carruthers and Acting Sheriff Doug Samuels.

"We dragged all the cheerleaders in, and they've admitted to the vandalism and thefts and the break-ins," Samuels said.

"How come they didn't follow through with the museum job?" I asked.

"They basically chickened out. It was overkill. Several of the girls have grandparents who are members of the historical society, and the girls decided to bail. They still can't seem to wrap their heads around the fact that their beloved teacher orchestrated it all, setting the wheels in motion just to write a paper."

"Set those girls up is more like it," Taylor said. "They didn't know what hit them. And all for academic credit."

I shook my head. "I always knew too much studying could be harmful to one's psyche."

Taylor gave me a disgusted look.

"There's obviously some deeper issue going on with Martina that contributed to her obsession with her thesis research to the point that she would use her students like laboratory specimens. When she lost control of her creation, she couldn't risk anyone finding out she was behind it all, so she kept silent. And kept collating."

"She'll have plenty of time to collate where she's going," I said.

"Which will probably be some sort of mental facility," Deputy Carruthers said. "She's still back in the holding cell babbling about inherent risks and unbreakable bonds, and some guy named Maslow."

"I hope you have her on suicide watch," Taylor said.

Samuels nodded.

"So Mick Dishman really didn't have anything to do with any of this other than purchasing alcohol underage and doing a little cleanup for his girlfriend, and he's copped to all that."

"What I'm not totally clear on is why you arrested Robbie Rodgers? What did he do?"

"He tie-dyed your horse, that's what, Turner."

I looked up. Stan Rodgers, looking like I felt, stood in the doorway.

"What?"

"Einstein and his buddy knew that their girlfriends were involved in the vandalism to some extent, and they decided to help them out by giving them alibis rather than giving them up to the cops. They did the number on your folks' house and your animal."

I blinked. I sure didn't see that one coming.

"We'll pay for the cleanup, of course," Stan said.

"And my car?" I asked, seeing an opportunity and taking it.

"We'll talk," he said.

I nodded.

Right.

As we got ready to leave, I stopped in front of the acting sheriff.

"You know. Things might have ended a whole lot worse had Deputy Carruthers not taken Dusty Cadwallader seriously," I told him. "She's the first person from your department to do so. And thanks to her, everything turned out. I hope you realize that, *Sheriff*."

It was the first time I'd called him sheriff and really meant it. Because the title, "sheriff," meant something. It meant trust—something I'd learned a lot about these past few days—and a commitment to service no matter if the ones you're serving might be a little bit 'out there.'

There's a new Sister Act in town, pilgrim.

We looked at each other for a long moment before he nodded.

It was a start.

It was close to daylight when we finally left the courthouse, discovering husband, fiancé, and boyfriend of two months waiting outside.

Kari, I was cheered to see, was too exhausted to do much gloating, her observation that her husband should have picked up on his mentee's sick laboratory research met with a "Hey, what can I tell you? I'm a jock, not a shrink," defense along with Brian's assurance he had meant to report his concerns to the principal the very next day.

Sadly, it works.

"Look. There's Manny DeMarco," Taylor said, as we stopped by her car. "That's his cousin, Mick, right? Wow! Talk about family resemblance."

Ranger Rick Townsend's jaw clenched visibly. It's a Manny reaction.

"That's Mick," I confirmed and watched the two talk, thinking about what Taylor had said.

"We'll follow you home, and to make sure you don't fall asleep we'll keep our bright lights on the whole time," I told Taylor.

She shook her head.

"Thanks."

Townsend practically lifted me into the truck's cab.

I itched all the way home.

He got me in the house and ran a bath for me and helped me undress.

"You know you've got poison ivy, right?" he asked.

I winced.

My fears were confirmed.

Townsend smiled.

"Care for some company tonight?" he asked. "Tomorrow's Sunday. We can sleep in."

Simple and uncomplicated and easy.

And that's when it hit me. That's when I had my light bulb moment. Maybe one key to having a long and lasting relationship was not to overthink it.

Maybe simplicity was the key. Maybe it was *my* key.

I took his hand and led him to the bathroom.

"I may require oatmeal in my bath," I said.

"Martha Jane, is this your way of saying, 'If you scratch my back, I'll scratch yours'?" he asked.

I giggled and scratched and giggled some more.

Am I a sucker for a great-looking guy with a sense of humor and oh-so-clever tongue?

What can I say?

I'm a believer.

CHAPTER THIRTY-SEVEN

I stood at one of the food-laden tables and set down a big ol' platter of deviled eggs and scratched. Townsend's diagnosis was halfway correct. I did have a bad case of poison ivy. I also had chigger bites up the wazoo. Well, not really up it. Just in the groinal area. And around the waistband. And ankles.

I did the chigger cha-cha while I made my food game plan.

Potlucks.

What's not to love?

A hand reached around me and snitched a ham rollup.

"Eyeballing the goodies, I see," Joe Townsend remarked.

I nodded. The Turner-Blackford bunch always did put on a heck of a spread.

"I was hoping I'd run into you, Joe," I said. "A little matter of unfinished business. I held up my part of the bargain. I solved the gnome mystery. What about you? Those 'Mystery Manny' questions."

"Technically, you tripped over it. Hardly Holmes worthy. Besides, we would have found it the same night," Joe pointed out.

"But I found it first. Look, Joe, if it's too much for you—"

"I've got a few in the queue. You'll get your questions!" he barked and grabbed another rollup and stomped off.

"What's he all het up about?" I turned. My gammy, resplendent in a peach and white striped blouse, white capri pants, and a straw hat stood beside me.

"They got something for that, you know."

"For what?"

"That feminine itching. It's one of them over-the-counter jobs. You don't have to embarrass yourself by going to a doctor."

I shook my head.

"It's not—"

"It's too bad Eunice couldn't make it this year. It's not a reunion without Eunice."

I frowned. "The last time she came you told her if she showed up again, you'd take after her with a lawn dart."

"She knew I was jokin'. That's what sisters do," she said. "Like when you took after Craig with that Wiffle ball bat. And when you razz Taylor about being the queen of where fun goes to die."

"I was never more serious—"

She suddenly reached out and grabbed my arm.

"Look! Over there! Abigail's peri-more. What's Abigail's gigolo doing here?" she asked. "Did you invite him?"

"Me? No!"

I watched Uncle Bo, in his regular bum attire, smile and nod as he made his way in our direction.

"He's comin' over here!" Gram said, the hand on my arm latching on like eagle talons to prey.

"Well, what do you want me to do about it?" I asked, looking around for an escape route. "Trip him?"

"Would you?"

"No!"

Uncle Bo walked past us and made his way to the little stage in the corner of the shelter house where someone had set up a CD player that was playing oldies. Weird, I know, but it's kind of a tradition. We'd heard such sixties classics as *Build Me Up Buttercup, Suspicious Minds,* and *I Heard it Through the Grapevine.* Uncle Bo reached out and turned off the music—a mix of songs from the sixties.

"What's he think he's doin'?" Gram asked. "That was James Brown."

I made a face. After this, I suspected *Papa's Got a Brand New Bag* was going to take on a whole new meaning.

"Ladies and Gentlemen, family and friends," Uncle Bo took center stage. "I want to take this moment to say, I'm baack!"

With that, Uncle Bo ripped off his disguise—hat, wig, coat, shirt, pants, and last, but not least, mustache, and out stepped a smartly clad Aunt Eunice.

"Let's get this party started!" she yelled to the dumfounded onlookers.

She switched the music back on, and James Brown came back on singing about Papa's brand new bag.

Aunt Eunice, high-fiving and fist bumping, boogied her way over to where we stood, a regular *Mrs. Doubtfire*. Well, maybe not regular.

"I knew it was you all the time, Eunice," Gram said, her lips pursed.

"You did not!"

"I did, too!"

"Did not!"

"Did, too!"

I backed away, but not before sliding my food contribution closer to the feuding females.

"Did not!"

"Did, too"

I backed off.

An egg flew past.

And another one.

I pulled my phone out and hit the video button as James Brown ended and the sisters of soul, The Supremes, took over.

I looked over at Townsend deep in conversation with my brother and the chorus began.

Nope.

You can't hurry love.

But then again, maybe you can give it a good ol' girl's kick in the pants now and then.

Hmm. Wonder what Martha Jane would do?

* * *

"And that, leaders of tomorrow, concludes my Career Day presentation on what it's like to be an investigative journalist. Are there any questions?"

A girl in the front raised her hand.

"Is that your real hair or do you do something to it to make it do that?"

"Did you really fall asleep during your own graduation?"

"Does your horse really have pink spots?"

I looked at my watch.

The end of class bell saved me. I exited the school as fast as my slouch boots could carry me.

"Thanks for coming, Tressa," Mick said. "Jada appreciates it." He gave his girlfriend a hug.

"No problem, Mick. No problem at all. I loved being Jada's show-and-tell. But who are you going to have come speak as your career day show-and-teller?" I asked.

"Manny."

I frowned.

"How'd you do that? You can throw your voice and sound just like Manny," I said. "Oh wait. Manny's right behind me, isn't he?" I asked and turned.

"Barbie."

"Manny," I stared him down. Or rather up. "I hear you're going to give a career day chat."

He nodded.

"Interesting," I said.

"Hey, Manny. Mick's gonna walk Jada to her next class. Be right back."

The couple went back inside.

"So, this talk. What are you speaking as? What jack-of-all-trades are you going to be today?"

"Barbie's in a rare mood," he said, his eyes never leaving my face.

"Hmm. Let me guess. Are you a bus driver? A chauffeur? Bodyguard? Consultant? What was that other term? Oh, yes. Facilitator! Or, perhaps you're speaking as a father?"

Manny's gaze sharpened.

"Barbie spending too much time with Dusty dudes who see little green men," he said.

"I'm ready to ask you question number one, Mr. DeMarco. Prepared to be amazed."

Was it my imagination or did Manny seem a little nervous?

He folded his arms across his chest.

"Fire away," he said.

I reached into my bag and pulled out the vintage Darth Vader mask Craig had worn for trick-or-treat the year I went as Chewie and Taylor, Leia.

I put the mask up to my face.

"Manny," I said, sounding like a severe asthmatic. "Are you Mick's fathah?"

Manny blinked.

That's right.

He blinked.

For just an infinitesimal moment, I caught Manny DeMarco with his poise down.

And that, ladies and gentlemen, is what you call a cliffhanger.

ABOUT THE AUTHOR

Award-winning author, Kathleen Bacus is a former state trooper and consumer fraud investigator. A Write-Touch Readers Award winner, Golden Heart® Finalist, and Kiss of Death Award of Excellence Daphne® Finalist, Kathleen is hard at work on her next book.

To learn more about Kathleen, visit her online at
www.kathybacus.com

Enjoyed this book? Check out these other fun reads available in print now from Gemma Halliday Publishing:

www.GemmaHallidayPublishing.com